THE ORGAN
BUILDER

THE ORGAN BUILDER

Robert Cohen

1817

Harper & Row, Publishers, New York

Cambridge, Philadelphia, San Francisco, Washington
London, Mexico City, São Paulo, Singapore, Sydney

A portion of this novel originally appeared in *Ploughshares*.

FIRST EDITION

Copyeditor: Marjorie Horvitz
Designer: Erich Hobbing

Library of Congress Cataloging-in-Publication Data

Cohen, Robert, 1957–
  The organ builder.

  I. Title.
PS3553.04273074   1988   813′.54   87-46131
ISBN 0-06-015909-X

---

88 89 90 91 92 HC 10 9 8 7 6 5 4 3 2 1

*For my mother and father
and for Nat Godiner, in memory*

I would like to thank the Corporation of Yaddo, the MacDowell Colony, and the Virginia Center for the Creative Arts, for their generous support. I would also like to acknowledge my debt, in researching this book, to the staff of the C.B. Fisk Company, and to the following writers on physics: Lansing Lamont, Richard Rhodes, John McPhee, Freeman Dyson, and Robert Jungk.

It is the vacancy that is a thing by itself, a thing that makes us endlessly wonder.

—HENRY JAMES
The American Scene

PROLOGUE

15 July 1977
Mendocino, California

Dear Abby—

I see things when I close my eyes.

I realize how that sounds. Like I've gone mad. Especially when I go on to say that these things I see aren't really there. But of course they are *really there. I see them. They're very close, right inside my lids, in fact—tiny geometric forms that dart around like phantoms. Instinctively I try to follow them, to plot their rogue patterns, but they glide and veer and stray, eluding the hard translucent spots that I only gradually recognize to be the shadows of my pupils. It's not long before these spots—my spots—soften, and blend right into the jocular frenzy of shapes, until there is no distinction, no separation; until they are inextricably a part of what they see. And so the night passes.*

I suppose that's why I'm addressing these words to you, Abby. If I don't assign them a function, there's the risk that they might dissolve, too. It happens, you know, especially on a night like this, with that anemic moon and the sky like smoke over the ocean. I can just spy it—the ocean, that is—through the cypresses outside the window. I can hear it, too: percussive and circular and relentless as time itself. Not a very encouraging sound.

But I am out to make an attempt. I've been drifting backward through the chamber of my self for as long as you've known me, and now I am going to put some work into changing direction. That's why I am still here in Mendocino, my back to the continent. That's why I am alone in my dark, congested room. That's why I am working on this document.

So why all this explanation, you're wondering.

Well, it's obvious, isn't it. To avoid beginning. Where, when, what, who . . . endless possibilities. Memory is a powerful tool, but it does not always serve. No, not by itself. It's too messy, too digressive. Too full. It needs a collaborator.

All right, then. Tonight is an anniversary for me, Abby, and on such occasions the need wells up to begin again. There might just be a rhythm to these shapes I see, a melody of some sort, and it's time I try to dance to it, to jump into the mess and see where it takes me. I might even make a little music of my own. Improvise. Conjure. Invent. Abby, do you think it's possible to invent what has already happened? If so, then perhaps in time I'll be able to do something of the same with the future. And then, who knows, I might even find a place out there again.

Thirty-two years since the sun rose twice—that's as good a place to start as any. Here goes, then.

Or better yet, bombs away. . . .

Countdown

Naturally we begin in darkness.

I am in bed, lying between stiff white sheets, the thin mesa air cool and sleek on my face. I cannot sleep.

Five o'clock.

In the other room my mother groans, stirs, clicks on the bed-table lamp for the second time in as many hours. I hear a rustle as she pulls on her robe and slips into the kitchen to light the stove. At the sink she mutters to herself, something about the water, a familiar complaint. She switches on the radio but keeps the volume low.

Five-twenty.

The news announcer says clearing skies. Then his voice fades into static, into music, into static again. A sigh from my mother. A small woman, she sighs heavily, enormously; they shake the apartment, her sighs. The wind outside licks at the windows.

Five-twenty-five.

I close my eyes as the counting begins. At first it sounds sluggish, clumsy. But soon it acquires momentum, and when it does it grows, evolves, gathers grace, turns into a march, a roll call, a stately, somnolent parade.

. . . fifty-five . . . fifty . . . forty-five . . .

Behind the numbers there's music. A slow, dreamy waltz. It sounds exotic, vaguely eastern. I've heard it before, this music, there's no doubt about it.

. . . thirty . . . twenty-five . . .

In the kitchen my mother draws her breath, rises, comes to stand by the half-open door to my room. I watch her through narrowed lids as she looks me over, me and the room together, as though it, the room itself, has a presence of its own, a character she has nurtured.

. . . fourteen . . . thirteen . . . twelve . . .

Outside, the desert sky has just begun to lift. The numbers and the music keep coming, and the wind keeps whimpering, and my mother lets out one of her pregnant sighs, and we are all, mysteriously, awake and alone together when the numbers finally cease their backward tumbling, when it has grown so very quiet, save for the toads trilling outside the window, so quiet and so impossibly still. . . .

And then, from the south, as if in answer to an unvoiced question, the eruption of light.

Part I

THE UNCERTAINTY PRINCIPLE

Chapter 1

It was May Day and the streets were mad with sunlight. The winter had been long, long and sodden and gray, and now that the good weather had sprung it hit you with the force of conspiracy. It woke you up, toasted your bread, sent you off to work with a breathy kiss. There was the illusion of things being in their rightful place, of safety and benevolence. Strangers smiled at you guilelessly on the sidewalks. Newspaper vendors encouraged you to enjoy your day. Even the taxis floated unhurriedly along the narrow streets, fenders gleaming yellow, cross-pollinating the enormous, shadowy garden of lower Manhattan. An obese Jamaican man stood at the corner of Nassau and Pine, teasing the surface of a wide steel drum. The notes that escaped were sly, ethereal; each seemed to carry with it a shadow, a promise of a sweetness just beyond itself which was almost palpable. I stopped for a moment before entering the tall building behind him, and listened. At the time I knew, or thought I knew, only two of the laws of physics, and the drum music recalled one of them: that everything, all matter, down to the atom itself, is for the most part empty space.

I found use for this thought when I emerged from the elevator on the thirty-ninth floor and promptly crossed paths with Bill Webber, senior partner. Webber was tall and high-hipped, with a sagging jaw and mottled pink scalp, and he conducted his affairs with a backslapping demeanor that suggested he was a good deal friendlier a person than he was. His gaze, as he approached, was dryly specific, but impersonal. He did not, for one thing, know my name, though I had been with Pinsker & Lem for eight years and had been his principal associate on at least half a dozen cases. This made running into him in the corridor a tiresome exercise, and I reminded myself, as he ambled in my direction, clucking his tongue and nodding his pink head at some private obsession, that he was, after all, mostly empty space, and whatever there is that's in a name was not worth the discomfort that Bill Webber's peculiar salutation was about to cause me.

"Hey there, Skipper," he singsonged, stopping just long enough to pat my shoulder. "Really on the move these days, aren't you?"

I had no idea what he was talking about, so I offered him a preoccupied corridor smile and continued on toward my office. The sun, slanting in through the blinds, made narrow islands of light on the carpet, a horizontal ladder into the depths of the maze. Before I'd gone very far, however, I heard Webber stop and clear his throat. I knew what that meant: that he had work for me, or for any associate he could enlist, which was what had sent him out roaming the corridors in the first place. Immediately I coughed twice, loudly. This was meant to cover what I was doing with my feet, which was, essentially, running. In this fashion, I was able to turn the corner into my secretary's cubicle before he could summon me back.

"Well, well. Why so hot and bothered? Who's out there this time?"

"Webber."

"Get away clean?"

"He called me Skipper. It was horrible."

"Poor Hesh. Always on the run. Life, it must be such a trial." She snickered happily. "Me and my puns, huh?"

Shelley Lubin leaned back from her typewriter and looked me over briskly. She was a petite, round-faced girl of twenty-four, pretty but with a certain stoical irony about her that wasn't always sympathetic. We got along fine, though. She had gone to a good school and done well, but since then had encountered setbacks that had hardened her and given her wit. She did not care for her work, but she did it competently and without complaint, which was more than I could say for myself.

"Did you hear the gossip?"

"I don't want to hear the gossip."

"It's about Charlie Goldwyn," she said.

"I don't want to hear the gossip about Charlie Goldwyn. I have work to do. Have you seen Jerome?"

"He's already in your office. He's been there," she said, lowering her voice and leaning forward, "since eight o'clock. He's kind of a creep, don't you think?"

"He's just ambitious."

"That's what I meant. Now, you want to hear about Charlie?"

"No."

4

"First of all, you're playing racquetball at twelve-thirty. Secondly, word has it he has stomach cancer. Advanced. Try to get him to order something bland at lunch."

"Last month he had Hodgkin's, according to the word. Before that it was leukemia. Who spreads this word, anyway?"

"I just call 'em as I hear 'em, boss. Ours not to reason why. But I've got a suspicion."

"Yes?"

"I think he spreads it himself," she said. Then she turned back to her typewriter, which clicked on with a compelling hum, and busied herself transcribing words I'd spoken into my Dictaphone the previous afternoon. I went into my office.

Upon coming to the firm I had been assured by old man Lem himself that there was no logic at all to the location of one's office. I was younger then and generally took people at their word when they spoke to me with quiet authority and, as Lem did on that—and no subsequent—day, laid their arm over my shoulder. For all I know it was indeed true at the time, but it was not true any longer. Now Lem was retired in Maui and I had a western exposure. This was a handy thing when it came to sunsets and predicting the weather, but in the baroque hierarchy of the firm it was a kind of purgatory—a window on the sulfurous, roiling marshlands of New Jersey, its smoky flat face pockmarked with automobile corpses and refinery tanks, the turnpike a diagonal scar down one cheek. There was also the Statue of Liberty, for consolation, but the lady appeared feckless and self-absorbed on her tiny crumbling island. I spent a lot of time looking her over, nonetheless. My marriage had ended and I was feeling somewhat desperate for female company.

It was my habit to stand at the window and let time float past for as much of the morning as I could before settling down to work. It helped matters that I arrived late and invariably left early. The year before, I had, according to Shelley's figures, logged fewer billable hours than any senior associate at the firm. I had also logged fewer billables than any of the junior associates, with the exception of a narcoleptic named Feinberg, who had been fired in April. Once I found him in one of the briefing rooms, slumped over his legal pad in the middle of the morning, and I had thought, how nice, how enviable, to just click off that way, to step off the train between stations without so much as a suitcase. When I shook him awake he had none of the panic you'd expect in a junior associate—he merely blinked sleepily, like a cat, told me in a level voice what he had been dreaming, and went back to his statute. Later, when I heard he was

5

fired, I tried to recall the dream he had described and found I couldn't. This didn't surprise me. I'd never been very good at remembering my own.

Jerome had established himself at my wide oak desk; his elbows were twitching from the furious progress of his pen. He wore one of his pressed blue Arrow shirts and the scales-of-justice tie I'd given him at Christmas. "Good morning," I said, throwing my jacket over a chair.

"Morning." He kept scribbling. The sound was frantic, full of implication. I paused by the desk, waiting for him to finish. Jerome looked pale and happy, his small, delicate features contorted with thought. He was a law student at Yale, on leave for a year to, as he put it, "scout the territory." His eyes were clear and blue, undimmed by self-doubt; he was twenty-one years old and planning a big life for himself. I was more than a little afraid of him. But I was also afraid of what would happen when he left.

Finally, he put down his pen, plucked an apple from his briefcase, and leaned back in my desk chair with an air of accomplishment. "This should do it," he said.

"You're a marvel. You really are. It's very humbling."

He smiled modestly. "Get a chance to look at that Walker file?"

"No. Problem?"

"We can handle it. I believe we'll be able to establish public domain." He was nibbling a straight line across the apple's equator. "You might take a look, though, if you get the chance. It's a tricky one."

"I'll do that," I said. "I'll take it home with me."

"Suit yourself," he said with a shrug. A good part of Jerome's mastery seemed to derive from the unwavering indifference he brought to all the untidy minutiae of the day: food, world events, other people. His enthusiasms were private, inscrutable. I could not even say for sure that he liked me, though he seemed more than comfortable in my office.

We settled down and worked through the morning on a fairly uninteresting copyright case. It was our job in such cases to defend our clients' right to appropriate the ideas and idioms of their betters, in order that they might serve the culture's seemingly limitless taste for the second-hand. Our clients produced remakes and sequels that made more money than the originals, published best-sellers that paraphrased scholarly works, pressed albums that contained riffs and lyrics purloined from obscure recording artists. The crucial point was that our clients were very rich, and it was up to us to use the laws of copyright to allow them to remain so. That was our job, our vocation, our calling. Most of the time we won dismissals, which was, in its way, somewhat nicer than losing. But it was Jerome's work that did it.

It is always shocking to look at someone you admire and recognize nothing of yourself in that person. At Jerome's age, I was only midway through the protracted vagrancy of my undergraduate studies. Even later, when I entered law school, it was a kind of holding action, a way of keeping things—the war, principally—at bay. Everybody was young then, and being young, if one remained alive, seemed enough. The trick was exemption, to find a pocket of it and stay and be young there. I found mine in Cambridge. Holed up in the library with my yellow pads and thick legal tomes, I was able to filter out the sputter and roar of the bullhorns outside and apply myself, in fitful bursts, to the study of that Constitution which was being so routinely abused all around us. Slow work for a fast time. I wasn't alone, either. Many of us had come there in search of a place apart; we were trying to pull a dodge, to step out without stepping in, and it almost worked. Only one day school was out and the men in the immaculate suits came for us, waving money and telling us what it was we wanted, and we could not tell them they were wrong. Because we were no longer sure.

I had been with the firm eight years. For two of them, my first and last, I had been a very capable lawyer. In between, I had drifted. Somehow my energies had atrophied and gone sour. Perhaps they had been worn down by the pressure, or dulled by the relentless triviality and avarice of corporate litigation. I didn't know. All I knew was that I had come to embody a certain waste that leaked from the firm like a toxin. I couldn't trace its source—it seemed to pervade the building and all its inhabitants; it seemed, in some way, essential to the operation. To fight it was to lose. That much I did know. I had come to the law with the standard fantasy of learning the business of power, and I had learned it, possibly, all too well.

The moment I met Jerome, however—I did the interview for the firm— I knew he was a different breed. He was bright and eager, not so much eager to please as eager to *be* pleased. When he walked into my office there was an inevitability suggested, a geometric equation that had been factored to this result: This was the point at which his arc and the world's plane must intersect. "You should know, Mr. Freeman, that I'm well prepared for this," he told me. "In high school I read Plato, Aristotle, Machiavelli, Hobbes. When I got to Yale I studied economics, data analysis, and international law. I went through the humanities early, you see, but then I moved on. All that content gets confusing, wouldn't you say? I have a deep regard for form, organization, underlying principles. All my recommendations say so."

"You're not supposed to see your recommendations," I said, in part to cover the fact that *I* hadn't as yet seen them. Also I hated doing interviews, had something of a hangover, and had already made up my mind to hire him—I needed an assistant badly—before he walked in the door. "They're supposed to go directly to us."

He nodded as though I'd praised him somehow, then leaned forward in his pressed blue suit and smiled lazily. "I'm determined, Mr. Freeman. Sometimes excessively so. It overrides my judgment at times. I'm sorry."

"No you're not."

He blushed. "What I meant was, I apologize."

I had, then, a moment of pure insight. I understood that this pale vision across the desk had been sent to redeem me as a lawyer. He would lend me form and organization from his surplus, toughen me for the long haul. He'd help me recover some of my skills, so that I could better suffer boredom, fight off cynicism. Eight years. If I didn't make partner within the next ten months, it would pretty much finish me off at the firm, and I was not yet ready to be finished off. With Jerome's help, my prospects, I sensed, could improve.

And they had. We were busy, we were winning cases, we were in demand. Only, just how far from redemption I remained, as his tenure wound to a close, was anybody's guess.

Still, there was Bill Webber, who had told me that very morning I was on the move, and there were Charlie Goldwyn and Walter Todd, each of whom had had me to dinner in the past month and invited me to join their respective poker games. Of the two, I preferred Charlie, a wise and corpulent man in his late fifties, with thinning black hair which he disdained to comb and great baggy Lyndon Johnson ears that lent gravity and humor to an otherwise overbearingly petulant face. He was a commotion of forces. Together we played racquetball a couple of times a month, after which he'd habitually blow himself to a lunch so grossly excessive as to sicken us both. At the end, berating himself for overeating, he'd order saccharine for his coffee and sip at it like a penitent. It was hard for me to resist such a man.

Today we lunched at Palo's, a new Tribeca saloon filled with money artists and their consorts. We took our time, ordering appetizers, entrées, desserts, coffee. As usual, we said little to each other until the check was on the table. Then, as though warding off a demon, Charlie began talking in earnest, talking and waving his hands, getting the circulation going. "Understand, Hesh, I don't like racquetball. I play it but I don't enjoy it. Neither do I enjoy the law, *qua* law, though I enjoy being good at it. There are a great number of things I don't like, and yet I do them anyway. I go to parties and openings and philanthropic events with Lorraine, when I'd rather be home in front of the tube with my pants off. Why? you're wondering."

"Right," I said. "Why?"

"Because there's one thing in this world I do like. I like food. Fast food, canned food, even bad food. Take health food, for instance. I like it. I like wheat germ. I like sprouts. I like tofu. Do you know anybody that actually *likes* tofu?"

"As a matter of fact," I said, "my ex-wife—"

He waved his big hand at me. "Let me finish. I'm talking about motivation. I'm talking about what makes a person go on, persevere. I'm a very simple man, and I have very simple motivations. I work so I can eat, I exercise so I can eat more, and I'm nice to my wife so she'll cook me things. I give her orgasms, understand, only in part because I love her and want to give her pleasure. The rest is culinary, strictly." He paused, dabbing a cloth napkin to his wet brow. "Look at you, nodding your head. Are you nodding because you understand or because you don't understand?"

"I didn't even know I was nodding my head."

"You don't know your own reactions. That's your problem. How do you expect to make partner when you're so unconscious?"

"I don't know," I said, letting my eyes rest on the table. "I suppose somebody high up who knows my work will have to pull for me."

Charlie laughed shortly and leaned forward, pushing the check aside with his elbow. "Frankly, Heshie, your work hasn't been much, until these past months."

"Walter Todd doesn't think so."

"Todd? Don't be comical. He can't do you any good. He's a goy, for one thing. For another, he may be on his way out. There are things in the works that I can't go into here and now. But don't worry. I've got a soft spot for you, *bubi*. You've got a helluva backhand. Maybe you'll squeeze through yet."

"Squeeze through what?"

But Charlie was already struggling to his feet with a theatrical moan and signaling for the waiter to take his credit card. It occurred to me that I had forgotten to ask him about the stomach cancer. He did look pretty bad: flushed, sweaty, on edge. I knew he had recently taken on a big, seamy case for Eastern Oil, and I wondered if he was merely showing signs of stress. I wondered, too, if he would try to enlist me, à la Bill Webber. And exactly how I'd say no.

We walked out into the ambient sunshine. On our way back to the office, Charlie stopped off to buy yellow roses from a street-corner florist.

9

"She's making chicken Kiev," he explained, gingerly feeling the stems. "I figure what the hell."

"You're quite the romantic, Charlie."

"Ah," he said, pleased with himself. "Remember, next week you come to poker at my place. My friends are all easy marks. We'll drink beer, pass gas, be male for a change. Whattaya say?"

"That sounds nice."

"Nice," he muttered.

"No, I mean it. I'll be there, Charlie."

"Maybe it makes you uncomfortable. Mixing work, social life. Maybe it's a hard thing for you, getting to know someone, senior partner and all. . . ."

"Charlie, give me a break. I said I wanted to come." We stopped in front of the great elevator banks in the lobby, waiting for that whoosh of chrome, that melancholy chime-stroke which snapped you awake from the transient dream of lunchtime. "We're about done with that brief on Sallie v. Weinstock. You want to have a look?"

"Sorry," he said. "Got an appointment." He glanced at his watch and frowned rhetorically. "This is my life, Heshie. A series of appointments, with only a few paltry meals to offset the boredom. Time to reshuffle the deck, eh?"

I suppose the reason I favored Charlie Goldwyn over the other senior partners was his predilection for this sort of earthy, bedraggled philoso-phizing. That, and the fact that my making partner seemed to depend on his good favor, made me hope that the rumors about his health were just silly office gossip, spread by some malicious clerk in the copy room who had once been snubbed or abused. Dear god, I thought—watching Charlie waddle toward the pay phones, the tails of his brown suit jacket crumpled over his buttocks like a cheap, soiled tablecloth after a debauch—don't let him die on me now. Then the chrome doors wheezed shut, and the suits and the leather briefcases came toward me, and I smelled that familiar vodka-and-coffee smell that told me lunch was over.

Waiting for me in the corridor again was Bill Webber. "How's the old girl, Skipper?" he asked, before I was past him.

"Fine, Bill," I said. "Yours?"

"Oh, fine." He nodded happily, looking for all the world as though he were engaged in a conversation.

"Gotta go, Bill," I said, swinging my gym bag past my knee. "Big securities case for Charlie, you know. Major pressure."

10

"Oh, well . . ." He frowned, his hands open before him. "Listen, if you get some time later . . ."

But there was Shelley, working the crossword, and there were my messages, and the familiar name on the familiar oak door of my office, and Bill Webber and his forbidding caseload were only specters in the quiet, static-charged corridor outside. Shelley tried to tell me something, but I closed the door behind me and immediately went to the window to check on the Oriental fellow on the thirty-ninth floor across the street.

Were I in search of a doppelgänger, I could not have found a less likely prospect. He was short and smooth-faced, forever hunched over a computer terminal on his desk, ticking out what must have been stock recommendations, and even when he spoke on the phone he maintained an air of self-containment as pure as a dolphin's. Not once, in the two and a half years of my western exposure, had he looked up from his desk to catch me staring at him from across the street. Occasionally I tried to time my lunch break to his, hoping I'd run into him down on Nassau. I imagined us sharing lunch at the nearest diner, finding traces of kinship, making wry jokes—two artists, two professors of paper, advice brokers to the impatient rich, playing in our glass houses. But I knew this would never happen. He would have nothing to say to me, nor I to him. He might even think me dangerous.

Now, though, he wasn't in his office, which I found unsettling. It made me want to flee mine—which was, I might add, the way I often felt when he *was* in his office. But I remembered Bill Webber, lurking in the shadowed corridor, and resolved to stay put and attend to the work for which I was handsomely paid.

I checked a brief. I dictated a memo. I jotted some notes for a deposition I was going to take in a couple of days. The clock ticked its tidy rhythm; the papers on my desk rearranged themselves. My fingers played connect-the-dots with the coffee stains on the blotter. At one point, from somewhere atop my head, a black hair detached itself and fell onto the white border of a memo. When I saw it, I picked it up and spun it by the root. The frayed ends whirled in precise arcs, a tiny inverted maypole of decaying proteins. Something plunged inside me. What signal, I wondered, had prompted it to jump ship? And how long before all the others followed suit? It was a mutiny, a subversion. I was beginning to turn the corner, to see what lay ahead. For a short while you gain, of course. You accumulate teeth and sinew, grow bulky with expectations. But just when you think you're about ready to put it all to use, some internal gear shifts, some Henry Ford of the cosmos pushes the planned-obsolescence button, and after that it's all loss and loss and loss, going and going until gone. You huff and flail away at the gym but you're only sprouting holes. The junk heap is ringing its warped bell, and we all know the tune.

Sometimes in the shower, when I looked down at my palms to find a few threads of hair wrapped around my knuckles, I picked up the washcloth and rubbed my skin viciously, as though that would come off too. And to my immediate horror, some of it would. It made soggy balled-up flakes and washed right away, hurried along by the warm, insistent water. I'd watch it go, feeling airy and strange, and—in a small way I had no wish to investigate—almost happy.

I was at the window again when Shelley buzzed me. "It's Joanne," she said. "I already told her you're here."

"Okay, fine. How are things out there, by the way? Any sign of Webber?"

"All clear. But bad news on those tickets you wanted. The man says the Yankees are in Cleveland tonight."

"Dammit," I said. I must have said it more than once, because when Joanne came on the line, her first words were, "Now, don't be hostile. I don't want anything from you."

"I wasn't swearing at you," I said. "In fact, I was just telling one of the partners how you were a couple hours ago."

"How was I?"

"A wreck. Barely able to function. If I remember correctly, you were, in your confusion and loneliness, beginning to look into Catholicism."

When she was finished laughing, she had the generosity to sound thoughtful. "That's funny. I always tell people you're happier without me. Who was the partner, by the way?"

"The honorable William Webber."

"Is that the white mouse who tried to make me at the Fitzgeralds'?"

"You never told me that."

"He called me Ladybug," she said. "A real charmer."

Jerome came to stand in the doorway, waving a file. "I'm a little busy right now, Jo. Let me call you back."

"Righto," she said, and hung up first.

Here's a confession: I married Joanne because, somewhere inside me, I suspected she would one day resemble my mother. Not physically, but in the way she would respond to my transgressions, to the world's vagaries, to her own melancholy. But I had been wrong. She had turned out a good deal flintier than my mother ever was, and driven by a sturdier engine. When we married, she had been a happy, pliant, and not very sophisticated girl, a darling of her father's, the kind of girl who favored ceramic bowls and imported coffee, who liked to think of herself as bohemian though never doubted she would one day co-own a house with a polished wood floor, near—but not in—Boston, or San Francisco, or New York. In her early twenties, her certainty and optimism made her gay, a little wild, even, and it was at this point that I met her. She was a junior at Tufts and coming off her first major romance; willow slender, with long black hair which she brandished like a cape and a thirsty intensity about the eyes which was part spiritual and part, I was to find out later, nearsightedness. She was smoking hash when I first saw her. We were at one of those Cambridge parties where you half-expected Marx himself to put in an appearance, so imminent seemed we to the zeitgeist, and when I saw Joanne Kaufmann squinting at me from across the room, her little hash pipe glowing through a blue haze, I felt a tug in my chest I had not felt in a long, long time. I made my way over, spilling some wine on my shirt, and came to a stop some three feet away. She looked at me hard, with a puzzling, stoned impatience. "Well?" she demanded. "Is this it?" She said it so plainly, with so little awareness of how strange it sounded, that I nodded my head, if only to make it true. "All right," she said, "I'll get my coat." It turned out later that she had mistaken me for her date, of course—she'd left her glasses home, out of vanity—and though we went on to have what seemed to me, even then, a few too many quarrels for two people so attracted to each other, we started sleeping together that week. I found her a little too given to sociological cant; she found me too imperious and lacking in spontaneity. Still, our very failings lent a strength to our affair, a tension, a challenge, as though romance was a form of philosophy forged through dialectical struggle. In fact we had some wonderful months together. There were afternoon movies, ambitious dinners, experiments in sex, and loud, protracted sidewalk arguments over novels and plays and politics that were sometimes so virulent we wouldn't speak to each other for days afterward. Then we had some not so wonderful months. Typically, we thought we could set things right between us by getting married, though in fact it only doubled the burden of our mutual expectation. We couldn't get the timing straight. We had to become each other's parents just when we thought we had broken free, and then Solly came along and we really *were* parents. A certain seriousness of purpose was required of us, and it wasn't present. Fundamentally, we lost respect for each other, and made our retreats. Joanne began to dabble in museum education, spending long afternoons in Manhattan, from which she'd return strangely irritated. I made use of the firm's generosities: the gym, the season tickets to sporting events, the occasional flirtations. I'm fairly sure neither of us had affairs, though I'm not at all sure why not.

Now, in the nearly two years since I'd moved out, Joanne had undergone what seemed to be an accelerated toughening of spirit. She had finished her master's and begun working part-time as a social worker in a Bergen hospital. She went out with a lot of men. Dealing with her now, I found myself in a state of perpetual imbalance. In my absence she had either discovered a reserve of genuine power in herself or else developed a facade so flawless and complete that it didn't matter where it came from. I didn't know any longer why I thought she would resemble my mother one day. I didn't even try to know. At a certain point, unless you're extremely clever or stupid, you stop trying to know such things.

I finished quickly with the file, initialed it, and brought it out to Shelley. "You going to call her back?" she asked, arching an eyebrow.

"Of course I'm going to call her back."

"Don't get mad at me. I'm one of the good guys, remember?"

"Sure. We're all good guys." I said. I shut my door behind me and called Joanne back. "Where were we?"

"I was calling for Solly, as it happens. He wants to know when he's being picked up, and where the seats are, and something else. Oh yes. He wants to know if you'll be staying to the end. There's something he wants to watch on TV at ten-thirty."

"That shouldn't be any problem," I said. "The Yankees are in Cleveland."

"Oh, Hesh." She inhaled and then blew out her breath deeply, leisurely, as though exhaling smoke from a cigarette. "You've really got a flair for disappointment, you know that?"

"I'll pick him up at seven," I said. "We'll get a pizza or something. I'll make it up to him."

"There's one other thing. A man called for you this morning. From Los Angeles."

"Who?" I knew very few people in Los Angeles. I know very few people, I thought, period. "Didn't you get his name?"

"It was early," she said. "He got me at a bad time. Sorry."

"Why would he call me there?" Jerome, frowning, turned to go. I let him.

"How would I know? Probably because it's still your listed address. That sometimes suggests to people you live somewhere." She paused and sighed with some irritation. "Anyway, I may have been a little rude.

14

There was something pushy about him that put me off. I didn't give him your number, either. Partly because I figured you'd rather I didn't, and partly—"

"I know. He called at a bad time. Isn't that how you put it?"

There was a silence on the line. "I shouldn't think you'd be jealous, Hesh," she said finally. "It doesn't seem appropriate. Or even in character, for that matter."

"Nice to hear I still have one," I said.

"One what?" But before I could answer, she broke in: "I've got a class. Try to give Solly a good time tonight. I have a feeling he needs one."

So do I, I was going to say, when the line went dead. It would have been a brief, trenchant confession, a little pamphlet on the subject of estrangement. With luck, it might have touched Joanne in her hidden places, perhaps even led to a session of unbending in some dark midtown bar. But there are times for confession and there are times for hanging up, and Joanne—off to do aerobics, or learn Greek, or practice carpentry, or any of the hundred-odd activities that made of her hours a roundelay of stimuli—had already moved on to something new.

My son Solly, when I picked him up in front of the house that evening, was wearing his usual outfit: jeans, a ripped T-shirt, and, pulled down low over his forehead, a blue baseball cap, one size too large, its visor creased in the middle from its residence in his back pocket. At first glance, his face wore an expression I thought somewhat more complex than the average seven-year-old's—a blend of casual expectancy and vague indifference, as though he harbored an oblique confidence that life would treat him well, but would not be too shocked should things continue pretty much as they were. He was small for his age and, despite a squinty nearsightedness inherited from his mother, very handsome. He had large walnut eyes, olive skin, and a plump, expressive mouth, which was pursed into a grimace at the sight of my old Toyota.

For a moment, when I pulled up, he seemed to hesitate. He looked over his shoulder, his feet splayed on the perfect Jersey sidewalk, where some boys a few years older were playing catch in the middle of the road. He wasn't ready for them yet, and he knew it—he was given to fits of awkwardness and shyness that inhibited him. He seemed to realize, though, that he would have to change, to find his place among them, and that neither his mother nor I could be of much use. All this was in his face when he turned to me, his mouth opened in a tentative greeting. He was a precocious kid—sharp, moody, and occasionally arrogant about weakness, though he had not as yet detected most of mine.

"I know," he said, climbing into the car. "They're in Cleveland."

"Did your mother tell you how sorry I was?"

"Okay," he said, an offhanded response that meant no. He fingered his cap and looked out the side window, at the boys playing catch. "I wanted to see the movie on Channel Eleven anyway. Alan says it's the best."

"Who's Alan? And what movie? And buckle your seat belt, okay? I don't want to lose you."

He pulled on the belt with reluctance, his fine dark-brown hair falling over his eyes when he dipped his head. I reached out and touched the nape of his neck, just once, lightly.

"*Duck Soup,*" he said, pulling away, and I nosed the car out into the evening traffic.

We drove east into a gathering dusk, headed for the George Washington Bridge. Because I now lived in Brooklyn Heights in order to be closer to work, on the occasions when I saw my son we seemed to spend most of our time mired in traffic on one bridge or another. This often set up a slow, congested mood between us which we seemed powerless to dispel. Tonight, to make the best of it, Solly turned the ride into sport, pretending to hold his breath until we hit the off ramp and began our descent into the hazy spatter of the city.

Along the way we listened to a radio call-in show about baseball we both enjoyed. The host was short-tempered and cantankerous, most of his callers were oafs, and the radio in my car was a temperamental thing that received the station only indistinctly, so that there was a certain perversity to our pleasure in listening, an indulgent mindlessness. Mostly what we caught was a bewildered static, punctuated by loud jingles, odes to beer and automobile dealers. American noise. And yet the undulating waves of transmission were relaxing, rhythmical, almost cleansing. When I first began working as a lawyer, I used to smoke marijuana on the way home, exhaling out of cab windows. After twelve hours in the office, wrangling with fine distinctions and byzantine protocols, it helped to muddy the waters a bit. This was common practice; the stress required accommodations. Feinberg took his naps. Bill Webber blew thousands of dollars a month on wild hunches at Belmont. Walter Todd raised oversized vegetables in his garden, which he regularly left to rot in the pantry of the partners' dining room. Charlie Goldwyn ate, drank, and did most other things excessively, a sort of walking promotion for the seven deadly sins. Of the lawyers I knew, only Jerome seemed immune, and perhaps that was because he was not yet a lawyer. At night he'd play chess with his roommate, then work on his note for the *Law Review*. Some people simply did not have the imagination for call-in shows.

"Alan is Mommy's friend," Solly announced when we'd traveled half the length of the FDR Drive. "From the hospital."

"Do you like him? Is he a nice person?"

Shaking his head no, he said yes. It was the kind of ambiguity that seemed to come naturally to him. "He says funny things."

"Funny ha-ha or funny strange?"

He thought this over for a moment, puffing out his cheeks. "Funny," he decided.

That shut us both up for a while. "Can you give me an example?" I asked.

"He says I have another name."

"Sure you do. Solomon. You know that. Like the king in the Bible story."

"That's not what he meant."

"Then what did he mean?"

"I don't *know*," he whined. "That's why it was funny."

Now it was my turn to think, and to draw a slow breath, as the car zoomed past the South Street exit. We circled around and made our way onto the Brooklyn Bridge as the night completed its descent. When we were out over the water, Solly clutched his cap and I turned up the radio. The two of us drove the rest of the way in silence, as the commissioner of baseball was assailed by a series of shut-ins, jocks, and trivia freaks, each implicitly certain that this—their passionate, clamorous interest— would carry them through the summer and beyond. Each spoke comfortably, as though among friends. There is no medium quite like the human voice, in my opinion, for conveying desperation.

Chapter 2

August 1943: Compensations of Ignorance

I have looked into Nothingness, and found it friendly.

He remembers thinking that, now. He is standing before the figure of his infant son—writhing, red, and sweaty, behind the maternity room glass in Santa Fe's small, cheerless hospital—but he is remembering that other time, in the basement of Pupin Hall. It was late on a winter night, and none of the other grad students were around. He'd turned off the cyclotron, the way Anderson had instructed him, and then he'd put his eye up against the vacuum seal before the air rushed in, and he'd seen it. For a long, incredible instant, he'd been witness to an absolute emptiness, the most pure anti-thing that man can engineer. He remembers the force of the suction on his eyeball. He remembers how it felt. Friendly.

Here, watching his tiny son squirm behind the glass, Eli Friedmann experiences an inner tightening. Why fix on the cyclotron's vacuum now? He senses a commonality between the two phenomena. Or an antipathy, a polarization. He's not sure. He's got to think about it. One force seems benevolent, the other somehow malicious. There will be a time—a long time—when he will be certain which is which, but that certainty will only coincide with what he will later recall, with no great fondness, to be his youth.

And he *is* young, only twenty-three, during the long night of his son's birth. It's lonely with no other people in the maternity ward. An intoxicated Pueblo Indian is sleeping it off on the reception sofa, down the hall, crying and thrashing about in his nightmares. Ruthie and the baby, exhausted from the struggles of labor, are sleeping too. Which leaves Eli pacing the airless corridor, trying to get his thoughts together

18

for the next day's symposium on the Mesa. And failing. Already, it seems, the pressure is getting to him, and there's such a long way to go. It's not a good sign. He must try to hold things together. In a few hours Ruthie will wake, and he won't be there, just as he was not there when she went into labor the previous afternoon. He was, instead, seated among some seventy-five men in a Quonset hut eighteen miles to the northwest, discussing how best to go about imploding plutonium in order to yield an explosion that will win the war. At the end of the colloquium, California champagne was passed around in paper cups, his son's impending birth was toasted under a cloud of pipe smoke and chalk dust, and the company adjourned, tramping off to their respective labs along duck-board pathways.

He didn't say much, of course. In fact, he said nothing at all, aside from an occasional vague murmur of agreement. Who is he to contribute? A graduate student of theoretical physics does not take liberties with the likes of Oppenheimer and Fermi, no matter how promising he may think himself to be. Eli Friedmann knows he is not such a hot property as all that. Tall, gangly, long-necked and slouch-shouldered, with flaming red cheeks and coarse brown hair that resists his wife's brush, he knows he appears foolish, boyish, not yet a master of himself. When he speaks it comes out a stammer. He is not articulate, cannot voice the designs in his head, cannot so much as sustain a conversation with his own wife. What, then, he occasionally wonders to himself, *can* he do?

There's music. He has trained himself, and worked hard, and now he can do things on his instruments—sonatas and concertos, swing and blues, ballads and boogie-woogie. He can blow a sax with real fury, tinkle a keyboard with a reflective magic. It is his one genuine pleasure, his major accomplishment. Still, even so, he lacks polish. His music—his original compositions—do not suggest ease but depth, depth and strug-gle, and there is something dark and bass-haunted in them too. Even his Bach has portents of Wagner. He is not a natural, he supposes, and it shows. He works too hard. Ruthie says that's part of his problem.

In truth, *she* is part of his problem. Ruthie Orlinsky was a strange, inward girl when he met her: dark, anemic, and given to rebellion. This was fine when she directed it at her parents, closed-minded Orthodox Jews on Pelham Road; or at the Fascists in Spain, whom she tried to defeat by sewing hundreds of scarves for the Republicans. But now she is beginning to train those black deep-set eyes on him, him and his career, which are taking her places she does not wish to go, and Eli can feel things starting to slide under his feet. She is wearing him out. She is stubborn and reckless and easily offended, a swirl of unfocused desires.

19

When they make love she clenches him so tightly his shoulders bleed, and her low-pitched shuddering groans can be heard, he is certain, all over Los Alamos. She is exciting. She is embarrassing. She is small, but with a grandness and stature of emotion that frighten him. She is half lost and knows it. She is hard on herself, but she is harder still on him. What will come of all this, he doesn't know. He hopes, of course, that this baby will be the answer, only his instincts are already telling him that it will only make things worse.

At dawn he leaves the hospital and begins the hour-long drive up the Mesa. The landscape is calming; its vast scale seems to dwarf and envelop him, fold him and his concerns within history, geology. Already he feels the place growing into him: The dry heat, the stillness, the red earth and the pumice underfoot, the smell of the cottonwoods after a thunder shower—all seem to be making inroads, working on him with their cyclical force. Ahead to the west lie the Jemez Mountains, sweeping down to the Valle Grande and Jaramillo; around them the Parajito Plateau fans out like a scallop. In his rearview mirror, the peaks of the Sangre de Cristos blink whitely across the desert floor. The names are like exotic Latin verses of some unfathomably melodic song. On Eli's tongue they sound wistful, foreign, as though learned in a dream.

This America, he thinks. Such a strange, unsettling country, this America that includes a New York and a New Mexico, a culture that's a scatter of fragments. What is the glue?

Well, he thinks, maybe I am. There is a rightness to it, something at work beneath the surface, bringing Jews to the desert in a kind of reverse-Biblical journey, an Exodus to yield a Genesis. What greater threat—and inspiration—to a landless people than to set them adrift in this wilderness? No wonder Ruthie complains. At least he has his work, and the good fortune to have duty and ambition mingle this way. He is getting the chance to do science, real science, while over in Europe tens of thousands of young men his own age are being killed in battle every month. So he shouldn't complain, he tells himself, about the other things.

At the main gate he shows his ID to the sentry, smiling an unrequited smile. He's waved past the barbed-wire fence. Some of the Europeans are troubled by being fenced in; it brings up terrible thoughts of home. For him, too, the precautions are bothersome. The G-2 security men who follow him on his trip to town, peeking from under straw hat brims; the sentries; the code names. Even his son's birth certificate has been altered to read *P.O. Box 1663*. They can't even allow him a proper home, he muses, not so much as an address. An uneasy beginning. It's absurd. Any scientist knows you can't protect a law of nature from discovery. The

20

secret itself is already out, the genie's bottle uncorked: Atomic fission *exists*. There's no way to stop the process now. All that is left is to see it through.

He shouldn't complain, but it bothers him, these concentric circles of secrecy. Urban, introverted, he is made self-conscious by the sense of being accountable to men in uniform. Often the most simple equations seem beyond him. His fingers go stiff, the chalk crumbles in his hand. Stop this nonsense, he has to admonish himself. You're a boy wonder, a force in the world. Stop trembling every time a stranger looks at you the wrong way.

"Yo there. Herr Friedmann."

Stepping out of the car, he turns. There's Max Baker tromping out of the PX, mournfully gnawing a Hershey bar. It's hot, and the sun is already strong, and yet Eli notices that Baker's fair skin is dry as powder. There's something unnatural about this man, he thinks. He doesn't care for his long, shrewd face, his Brooklyn insolence, his silly jokes—calling the mesa Lost Almost, for instance—or the way he addresses his colleagues in German, and yet he can't dismiss the man, either. Though they are approximately the same age, Eli feels younger—and at the same time older, more stodgy, conservative, settled—than the bachelor, for whom the chocolate bar is breakfast.

They have exchanged at least five minutes of small talk before it occurs to Eli to mention the birth of his son.

" 'Some are born to sweet delight, some are born to endless night,' " recites Baker, scuffing the dirt with his shoe. "Or I might have that backward."

"Yes, well, let's hope it's the former."

"Sure. Absolutely. How's the little wife bearing up, by the way?"

Eli wipes his brow and shields his eyes. "She was sleeping when I left. Labor went on for a long time."

"Frau Ruthie. She's a firecracker, that one."

"Yes," says Eli uncomfortably. "Yes, she is."

"I should be so lucky. It's hell over in the dorms, you know, everyone playing Johnny Five Fingers over Rita. Whatever happened to Veronica Lake? That's what I want to know."

Eli listens to the cadence of the names, waiting for Baker to finish. Halfheartedly, he attempts to read the cover of the weathered foreign-language journal Baker carries under his arm. *Zeitschr. f. Physik.* "We'd better head over," he says abruptly.

Baker waves him off. "Forget it. Colloquium's canceled."

"Why canceled?"

"How should I know? Who tells me anything? Herr O. has the runs or something. Who cares?"

"But I . . ." Eli, flustered, finds his weight tipping unsteadily. He's exhausted, and the sun is hot, and he feels vaguely unbalanced. "I only came back so soon because of what we were discussing yesterday, when we left off. Otherwise . . ."

"Please," says Baker. "It's no great loss, one day, to the world of science."

"You're irresponsible, Baker. You consistently undervalue us. You make it sound as though we're wasting our time—"

"Oh Lord," calls Baker, addressing his appeal to the heavens, "deliver me, willya please, from all this reckless innocence?"

"Enough, Baker."

"No, it's not enough. It's nowhere near enough," he says, crumpling the candy wrapper and flinging it carelessly over his shoulder. "I'm going to do you a very large favor, Herr F. Seeing as how we're going to be working together and all. I'm going to set you straight."

"On what, exactly, do I need setting straight?"

"Well, frankly, you've got an attitude problem."

Eli is moved to laugh out loud. "*I* have an attitude problem?"

Baker, however, isn't smiling. "You seem to be laboring under the impression that you're a scientist. But you're not. None of us are, really. See, the science part, as you should know, is over. It's already been done. In Berlin, in New York, in Chicago—all over the place—but not here. This is something else entirely, what we're doing. There's no place here for your little Tom Swift visions and tinkerings, no place at all. Because what we've got going here, Herr F.—and by here I'm including Hanford and Clinton—what this is, see, is a very well-endowed factory. You got your top administrators, like Herr O., your R and D men, like us, and your low-level functionaries who don't know what the hell's going on, like those SEDs over there banging on that fence. You got managers. You got security. You got a lot of mumbo-jumbo code words to make us think we're something new and special. But it's a joke. We're no different, really, from those slobs who built the pyramids, or the Chinks that built the railroads. We're just your run-of-the-mill engineers, working on a bigger scale. Clerks and coolies in white coats."

"You don't really believe that."

"You don't really know what I believe, do you?"

"No, but I've observed you at work. You're an excellent physicist, Baker. You work long hours, you—"

"Observation of a phenomenon drives up the entropy cost of more precise observation," intones Baker coldly. He taps the journal with his finger. "It's all in here. Variation on Heisenberg. Any increase in knowledge at the molecular level is exactly compensated by increased ignorance about the surrounding environment. I think we can agree this is true—*ya*, Herr F.? Ignorance is here to stay. The best we can do is shift it around some. Don't go shifting yours onto mine, okay?"

Eli stops at the door to the lab. He resists the urge to take hold of Baker's sleeve, certain already that he cannot win an argument with this man, certain that it is somehow wrong even to try, especially just now, with his wife blanched and weary on a hospital bed in town, and a new person to consider, a new responsibility to shoulder, a new set of—what else to call them but fluctuations?—to accommodate. Baker's logic, he knows, is flawed, anyway. If what he's saying were true, there would be no particular reason to do, or learn, anything. But one can make the distinction between knowledge and *useful* knowledge, between information that obscures and information that wipes clean the window of the world. And one thing, at any rate, is clear. "You're forgetting the *cause*, Baker. Hitler's investing in cyclotrons, heavy water. That's new and special. Shouldn't that prospect be enough?"

Spitting noisily, Baker then wipes his mouth on his sleeve, and shrugs. "You want to know the truth? It's not Hitler that bothers me. What bothers me are places like this. . . . Who's to say our sleepaway camps are any better than his sleepaway camps?"

"Yes, but if not for theirs, we wouldn't be here."

"Think so?" Baker looks off, over his long nose, into the distance, where a crew of dark young men—Zuñis or Pueblos—drive back from the mines in a flat-top truck, faces streaked with dust. Neither speaks for a moment. Eli has the feeling, as he often does with Baker, that the man finds him amusing but dense. He doubts they will ever be close, which saddens him. But maybe it's best that way. Once, in the middle of a meeting in their sector, Baker leaned across and handed him a note, written in a hasty scrawl on a crumpled government-issue napkin. It read simply, *We're only a phase.* The words seem, for Baker, a kind of credo. At the meeting, with the note in his hand, watching Ernst Lemann complete an involved equation on autocatalysis, Eli felt his brain cloud with oppositions—the neat black-and-white of his work and the stark scrawl of his fears. Consciousness as an aberration, a joke-gift from the universe. But Baker, he sees, is the worst kind of nihilist. Men, after all, are capable of tremendous, lasting achievement. Think of Chartres. Of Michelangelo. What was Alvarez calling it? *A drama greater than the birth of Jesus.* Well, yes, that's right. . . .

Baker has turned back toward him now, has asked a question Eli, engaged with inner wrestling, hasn't caught. Because of the early sun's glare, he temporarily finds himself reflected in the other man's glasses—sees his own face split in two, the inquisitive eyes fractured from the lean, determined jaw. A new thought troubles him. Suppose Baker is right, and we cannot add to our small reserves of knowledge. Suppose that all intellectual pursuit is only that, a shell game of the mind. Then what chance is there, ultimately, to find anything but what his parents found in socialism, what Ruthie's parents found in Orthodoxy, what he himself is finding, at this very moment, looking into the face of his colleague—what else but a distorted reflection of his own features?

". . . to tell someone sometime, you know. The world has its conventions."

"I'm sorry," Eli stammers. "What did you ask before?"

"The boy."

"Boy?"

"Your son, Herr F. What'd you name him? Albert? Enrico? Jules?"

"Oh," he says, and takes a breath before answering. It will be the first time he has spoken the name himself, and he would like to have its object squarely in mind when it happens. "Herschel," he says. "For my late father."

"That's nice. Kind of old-fashioned. I like it." Baker, delighted with this new verbal toy, repeats the name a number of times as they pull open the door and enter the silent lab. The echo of his voice slides over the bare walls, lingers for a moment, and then fades. The next sound Eli hears, as he pulls on his white lab coat, is the abrasive warble chalk makes when it is pushed too forcefully across a blackboard.

Chapter 3

Charlie Goldwyn lived in a wide, low-ceilinged apartment on Central Park West which had been decorated by his wife, Lorraine, after a semester of interior design courses at the New School. It had, as they say, a distinctive look. The dark wood floors had been buffed so expertly as to reflect the soles of your shoes. The furniture was angular, spare, and spaced far apart, as though to discourage loitering. On the walls, framed reproductions of Mondrians and De Koonings made neat rectangular interludes in a symphony of off white. My first impression was that I had entered a kind of igloo, but I kept this comment, as I kept most comments, to myself.

Charlie himself—as I'd noticed at his dinner party the previous month—moved about the place with something of the tentativeness of a short-term subletter. Upon my arrival, I had been instructed to take off my shoes. "That's the ticket," he'd observed approvingly, thrusting my coat in the vicinity of the closet. "Japanese style. Here, I'll join you." It was frightening, really, to watch him that night—this massive, ruddy-faced, anxiety-plagued fellow, tiptoeing softly down the hallway, leaning forward daintily on the fragile chair seat, holding his breath as he eyed his guests' movements, wondering who would forget the coaster for his drink, or slam the bathroom door, or leave thumbprints on the glass coffee table. In the end, predictably, it was Charlie himself who committed these infractions, as though impelled forward by the sheer momentum of his good intentions. But that was later, after a few drinks and much talk of books he hadn't read and shows he hadn't seen. For the bulk of the evening, barefoot Charlie had kept a low profile, content to allow Lorraine—an attractive, diminutive woman of fifty, worn thin from dieting—to choreograph the party, while he sat benignly at the head of the table, working his way through the better half of a leg of lamb and

25

winking at me periodically, as though the two of us were conspirators in some gleefully subversive plot.

And I suppose we were. It was a plot, I thought, against inertia, against the slow, inexorable drift of our energies down the hole of Pinsker & Lem. Each of us, in his own way, was pretty far gone, it seemed to me, but Charlie had something firmer at his motivational core, something greater even than food that he turned to in moments of stress, and it was this secret that he had undertaken to share with me. Hence my invitation to dinner. To break bread with Charlie was to enlist in a moral crusade. Every calorie was an assertion of something vital, a jab at the ribs of some anorectic *Them* who wished us ill. As we ate, that evening, he'd wink and direct platters of food my way, as though to fatten me up for an impending struggle. Occasionally he made jokes at the expense of the other guests, most of whom—in fact, all of whom—were Lorraine's friends. The jokes weren't funny, but the effort spent on them seemed to justify second portions of mousse and Linzer torte. Later we'd played Ping-Pong on bloated stomachs, swinging erratically. All in all, it had been a pleasant evening, colored by the sort of mild naughtiness I associated with Charlie in mixed (that is, nonlawyer) company.

On the night of the poker game, however, Lorraine and her downtown friends were not in evidence, Sinatra was booming flatulently through the speakers, and four oversized, affluent men were sitting around a bridge table behind glasses of bourbon and tall stacks of chips, sweating through their shirts (their ties and suit coats made a messy pile on the loveseat) and grumbling crankily at their cards. I didn't recognize any of the players and I didn't see Charlie. For a moment I stood in the doorway awkwardly, clutching my windbreaker in one hand, waiting to be noticed. None of the men glanced up. A soft buzzing kicked on in my left ear—an annoyance that besets me occasionally, when I am out of my element. I'd been hearing it a lot of late.

"So you're here."

Behind me, Charlie emerged from the kitchen, shouldering a platter of cold cuts with his left arm and cradling a basket of sliced rye in the crook of his right. He dumped the load on the sideboard and turned to glower at me. "Have a sandwich and sit down, and maybe I'll forgive that you're late. Guys your age don't appreciate punctuality. Isn't that right, Sid?"

Sid—a pale, round-shouldered man in a colorless sweater—nodded vaguely and proceeded to deal out the last hole card in a game of seven-card stud. He looked tired, defeated; the corners of his eyes formed deltas of worry lines.

"Psst. Hesh." Charlie beckoned me over to the sideboard. There, he

26

draped a beefy arm across my shoulders and, in an exaggerated whisper, began to introduce the players. "Sid's been playing with us eleven years. Options analyst. This kind of thing's his life, understand, but he's moody, a whiner. Next to him is Stan, with the glasses and baby fat. Also goes back to the beginning. He's an actuary, and it shows—plays the averages, never bluffs. Plus he's vegetarian now, so I have to find him an avocado or he gets sore. Herb, the tall guy with the fancy watch, he came in '75. Owns a chain of dry cleaners. Very, very dumb. Look: He's still not sure if a flush beats a full house." As his exposition continued, Charlie's voice grew louder. Everyone in the room heard every word he said, and no one seemed to take notice. "That guy at the end of the table is Al, the Grim Reaper. Two years he's been with us and he hasn't cracked a smile. Big-shot editor at some paperback house, no one's sure which. He's read all the books, though. Chat with him; maybe you can loosen him up. Talk about Kafka or whoever. The guy needs to be distracted—he's up eighty, ninety bucks from last week, most of it mine. I don't like the man, personally."

It was easy to see why. Having drawn out the betting with small raises, teasing chips into the pot, Al now turned over a full house, tens over sevens. This was followed by a moment of incredulity, then a chorus of extravagant moaning and some rubbing of brows, as each player pored over the wreckage of his strategy for clues to what had gone wrong.

Unsmiling as a judge, Al scooped the pot to his side of the table. With long, steady fingers, he stacked the chips into neat piles of five. He was a cool customer. He sat forward in his chair, spine straight as a typist's, his powder-blue silk shirt buttoned to the top. The hair at the back of his neck, which I could see in profile, was thick and white and freshly clipped, in the manner of someone who received a haircut once a week. Though he was winning steadily, he did not appear to be enjoying himself. But then nobody else there seemed to be, either.

Except, I supposed, Charlie. He seemed to be in superb form. The way that Charlie Goldwyn went at poker was the way he went at racquetball, at food, at litigation—recklessly. He nursed along weak pairs, went out on a limb for unlikely straights. He was overeager, unmindful, sloppy. If he had the good fortune to win one hand, he promptly bet too much on the first cards of the next, embracing an illusion of momentum. It was difficult, at times, to watch him. I found myself literally looking away. Twice he interrupted his own *shpiel* to hawk violently into a handkerchief. This was the man, I reminded myself, who was going to help me make partner.

It struck me as mysterious, the way his friends put up with him. He seemed to bring out in every person at the table—the way, for instance, a small child will—the extent of each man's resignation or resentment in the face of needy desire. There was the indulgent Sid, cooing and purring. There was the judgmental Stan, shooting his disapproving looks. There was the reform-minded Herb, cautioning Charlie not to show the other players his cards. And there was Al the imperial, majestic in his detachment. I was unsure where among them I properly fit; for the most part, I held my ground and kept quiet.

"You can't take four cards," said Stan. "I said jacks or better to open, and you opened. Now you want four cards?"

"I know what I'm doing," Charlie said.

"Charlie," said Herb, "it's the principle. If the game's jacks or better, you *need* jacks or better."

"And how do you know I didn't have it? Maybe I just wanted different cards. Is that such a horrible thing?"

"Play the hand," said Al.

They played the hand. Al took it with three nines. Charlie had ace high. Seeing the results, he stood abruptly and marched off to the sideboard to make another sandwich.

He was losing big, and as the evening wore on, his mood turned sour, abusive. Soon I began to recognize the other Charlie, the Charlie who provided the source of malicious gossip at the office, the Charlie who terrified his subordinates and bullied his peers, the Charlie who, in the face of adversity, succumbed to capriciousness and cruelty as inevitably as some men—Sid, for instance—succumbed to melancholy and silence.

"Sid, you're a faggot with those jacks. Bet already. You like it up the ass, don't you Sid? I've heard plenty."

Sid, down forty dollars, seemed to have passed the point in the evening where he gave much of a damn about getting even. Impassively, he looked at me, shrugged, and folded his cards. Just a game.

"There he goes, El Foldo," crowed Charlie. "Al, here's your ten, and I bump you ten."

"It's not your turn," Herb said. "Hesh bids next."

Charlie, piqued, gave a short laugh. "Sure. Sure he does. Only he'll pack it in. This much is obvious." He leaned over in my direction, as though to peek at my hole cards. I drew back, bringing my hand up close to my shirt. I didn't need to check—I knew I had two queens there, which, with a pair of sevens showing, put me well ahead of what was on the table. Charlie, I thought, was bluffing, and bluffing badly. Also he was acting obnoxious, and alienating everyone present, for no apparent reason. The part of me that still—after eight years as a lawyer—believed in justice, decided to teach him a lesson.

"Raise you ten," I said, throwing a twenty-dollar chip boldly into the pot.

Despite himself, Herb grinned. "That's twenty to call, Charlie."

"What is this, kindergarten? I can count, thank you." Charlie dipped his head, examined his cards through narrowed eyes, attempting to look shrewd. After a moment, an overripe smile pushed out his cheeks and he let off a snigger, directing a stack of blue chips the size of a shot glass toward the pot. "Gentlemen," he announced, "Mrs. Goldwyn raised a fighter."

Herb mumbled something under his breath and turned over his hand.

Whistling softly through his teeth, Stan counted the stack of chips in the pot with his pinkie. "Seventy big ones. Big loss to take on a bluff."

"Who's bluffing? These stiffs are the bluffers. Me, I'm sitting pretty."

"Big talker." Behind his horn-rims, Stan's eyes searched his hand for potential. Sure, sure, it was just a game; but it was no fun on the sidelines. And Stan was a competitor: You could see it in the way his fingers jumped around his cards, the way his nostrils flared arrhythmically. But Charlie had him figured right—direct, disdainful of the fineries, obedient to the numbers. He, too, folded his cards.

It was Al's turn. The Grim Reaper had three fifths of a flush showing, which was nothing to go on, and his luck had not held over the past hour or so. A few times I'd glanced up to find him staring at me curiously, as though trying to place me, or to figure out exactly in what way I was responsible, not only for his reversal in fortune, but for the entire evening—the dank, clingy late-spring air, the staccato aimlessness of our collective dialogue, and, of course, Charlie. Al had the look, I thought, of an aesthete suffering a melodrama, and he was not going to make it through Act Two.

"Let's go already," urged Charlie. "At some point tonight I've got to move my bowels."

That seemed to do it. Without a word, Al put down his cards, pushed back his chair, and went off to the other room, his gaze all the while fixed at some point above our heads. For a literary man, he was awfully quiet.

"Ha! I knew he didn't have it. That guy's been getting away with murder, but no longer—right, boys? That's fifty to you, slugger."

The silence that followed was thick and opaque as mud. The players sat there with their skeptical concentration, quietly sipping drinks, not looking at me, not looking at Charlie—looking, instead, at some irregular fold in the tablecloth, or the pattern of ridges on the border of a chip. It was as if Al had taken with him all semblance of the sport with which we had begun. What was left was merely *us:* five disparate, expectant personalities hovering around an unfocused center. Perhaps this was Charlie's true intention, I thought—to take us in all our softness and make us hard. Perhaps this was why we all seemed to be tolerating him; we had struck a sort of bargain, and each of us had to see it through.

"Fifty bucks, Heshie. Let's see what you've got in that skinny little stomach of yours, yes?"

Chewing mournfully on a sandwich, Sid reminded him that it was what I had in my *hand* that counted; but we all knew that wasn't strictly true, and besides, he was as much a loser that night as any of us.

I had, with one hole card remaining to be dealt, two pair, queens and sevens, the sevens showing. Charlie, if one looked at his cards charitably, could have the ghost of a chance for a ten-high straight; or, should he have a pair in the hole, a possible three of a kind. I was an amateur at reading into bets, but I knew there was nothing in what had transpired so far to suggest that Charlie had begun with a pair. Therefore, I concluded, I need only stay in the game to win. A pot that size would take care of child support for a month. More to the point, I would show Charlie what I was made of. I might even show myself what I was made of. I leaned forward. "I'm out of cash," I said.

Charlie snorted. "Heshie, your credit's good with us. Not to worry. It's a friendly game."

"In that case," I heard myself say, "I see the bet."

From the stereo, a neat click of the tone arm. Sinatra was gone.

Collectively, we had found our focus: a diagonal axis had been drawn across the table, from Charlie to me, and as Sid dealt out the final hole card with short snaps of the wrist that sent the cards skimming across the green cloth, the tension along that axis began to rotate, to move in waves, forward and back; it became an almost palpable thing. My ear, clouded with noise all evening, suddenly felt light and clear. The new card was a six, which gave me a useless third pair but kicked off a thrumming certainty inside me. All those twins; the game was mine.

After a brief pause, Charlie pushed another fifty into the pot. His face was bright red, but then his face was often bright red. Still, he seemed pleased about something, smiling at us all with genuine warmth, his lunchtime self. "Well?"

Al returned from the other room, his tie loosened a severe half inch. He sat down and scratched his sideburn thoughtfully, sizing up the play. Either he had lost some of his assurance, or else I had gained more of my own—in any case, Al did not seem so special to me right then. Indeed, it struck me that Charlie had more character than his friends. A gift for something larger than behavior. He could afford to be excessive because he had in him great reservoirs of, well, excess. *Twenty-eight years at Pinsker & Lem*, he seemed to be telling us, *and I am not dead. I am growing at the waist, getting larger by the day. Soon I will be a house, a cathedral, a mountain. I am Mrs. Goldwyn's big boy!*

"I'll see that," I said, "and bump you fifty." And that, I figured, would be that.

But I had more, much more, to learn. There he was, rising up out of his chair, eyes bulging, stomach heaving gigantically over his belt, a force of nature, aspiring to tragedy, reaching into the back pocket of his ballooning slacks for that stubby sword, his checkbook. "What's the limit?" he called out wildly, a cranky, feverish tremolo. "What's the limit?"

Sad Sid shook his head, reluctantly complicit. "Charlie," he began, "maybe we should—"

"The limit, Sidney!"

"We said a hundred, coupla months back," he said, eyeing the front door longingly. "But . . ."

Herb, a little less gently than he'd spoken before, said, "I thought this was a friendly game, Charlie."

"You want friendly?" Charlie scribbled his signature, then took the check and shoved it in Herb's face like a summons. "How's this for friendly? You ever see anything this friendly in your whole life?"

Another pause. Stan, his brow deeply creased, let out a muffled belch of displeasure. "Sit down and play the hand already," he muttered. Al nodded, almost invisibly, and ran a quick finger around the circumference of his chips. Nobody seemed terribly surprised, all in all, with the way things were going down.

"Back to you, Heshie."

I sat there considering. The key to gambling, as I understood it, was to forget that what you're playing with is representational of money, or goods. A fifty-dollar chip is not fifty dollars but a colored chip: a plaything, a piece of plastic; light, insubstantial, self-referential. A bet is merely a promise of faith, a trick of language, a conspiracy of guile and courage. So is a check, for that matter. I picked up a pen and wrote one for a hundred and fifty dollars, then threw it, fluttering like a sparrow, onto the pot. Just a game.

"Bump you fifty," I remembered to say, after a moment.

By the rules of the house, Sid reminded us, Charlie could raise me one last time. But from the look of things, I was sure he'd fold. His features, in the time it took for my check to alight on the pile of chips, had gone

31

slack. His shoulders drooped, his arms rested limply across the folds of his midsection; he seemed to have shot his wad. Relieved, Herb leaned back for the first time and cracked open a pistachio nut with his teeth. The other men, too, visibly relaxed. Only Al remained in his former posture, watchful and unsmiling as ever, while, just outside the window, Central Park unfolded in all its darkness and concealment, indifferent to our little drama.

"Your move, Charlie," Herb said finally. "Ready to try a new game?"

"Yeah," echoed Stan. "How about letting the rest of us back in? It's getting late. I got work tomorrow."

As though something in these words answered a question for him, Charlie—without moving forward in his chair, without so much as squaring his shoulders or lifting his gaze from his cards—began to talk. His tone was low and conversational: He might have been giving an order to a well-intentioned but slightly obtuse cocktail waitress. As it turned out, it would be a long speech, and something of a classic, and we all gave it, despite the late hour and the bourbon, the attention it seemed to deserve:

"I am going to call you, Hesh," he said. "That and, since this is table stakes, raise you what's on the table. But just to make things more interesting, I'm going to throw in a few extras. I feel that since this is my house and all, I should be allowed to bend the rules a little. Here's what I'd like to include, Hesh. I'd like to include in my bet the table itself, this fine piece of oak at which we're sitting so comfortably. In fact, I'll throw in the whole apartment. This isn't all, however. I am also betting my IRA at Chase Manhattan. Here is the name of my broker; I'm writing it down. There are several stocks in my portfolio, Hesh, fat ones. All included in the bet. Plus the place in Wellfleet, which to tell you the truth could use a coat of paint. But never mind, never mind. Frankly, I think this is an attractive offer I'm making. This place, that place, the stocks—a lot to consider. Of course, I intend to win. I'm a winner. *In re* poker, I'll admit I haven't been so impressive tonight. Hardly a role model. But I intend to recoup, you see. Now, you're a clever young man, obviously. The truth is I envy you those sevens you've got showing. They put you in a good position, strategically. As for me, maybe I'll make my straight, maybe I won't. The truth is, if you really want to know, I haven't even looked at the third hole card. But there you go. That's my bid. The rest is up to you."

There was a long, embarrassed pause. Finally, Al said, in a low, even voice, "Cut the crap, Charlie."

"Fine," our host said immediately, as though he'd been waiting for it. "Al has a valid point. Maybe the extras are a little irregular. I won't dispute that. In fact, you know what? Forget the extras. Rules are rules—right guys? What's on the table?"

Herb counted. "Five sixty-five."

"Fine. Here's the check. Now you decide, Heshie. In or out."

It was a little late, but at last it was clear to me, and, from the weary, knowing looks going around the table, to us all, what exactly I was doing there. I had not been invited out of friendship, or collegiality. I had not been invited because I was such a good poker player. I had not been invited, even, on a whim. I had been invited because Charlie Goldwyn's appetite for self-destruction and public humiliation had grown so ravenous that it threatened to subsume him entirely, and he knew it. I had been invited because his friends, as he called them, were clearly full-up with him, and he them, but because of the complex interdependencies and rituals of their arrangement they had not yet let each other go, and he knew it. And finally, I had been invited, as had just been demonstrated clearly—for I'd already, before he'd even finished talking, folded my cards—because Charlie had found in me a dangling, unheroic young man with neither the courage nor the inclination to resist him. And now we both knew it.

"If you're going to make partner, you arrogant schmuck, then you're going to have to learn to eat shit. You must be able to handle waste, litter, messiness, garbage. This is what the raw material of litigation feels like. Our *terra firma,* if you like."

For some reason, this remark—delivered at the front door, on my way out a few minutes later—elicited from me a smile. "Why should I, Charlie?"

"Because I'm the only one who can help you, that's why. Todd is a tidy man. Neat. He looks good but he'll get sick and die. I'm going to last."

"No," I said. "I mean, why should I want to make partner? It doesn't seem to have done much for you, has it?"

Charlie looked me over soberly. He seemed to be considering just how much he wanted to say to me right then. Finally, his decision made, he went on in a new, more paternal, tone. "Hesh, you need structure. We all do. You don't have what it takes to go your own way; that much you do know. That's why you've hung on so long with us already. You don't like what you do, but you're along for the ride. So get off the high horse already, yes?"

The terrible thing, of course, was that he was absolutely right. Every time in my life I'd abandoned a structure, I'd promptly joined up with another one. There was some energy, I suspected, missing in me. "I'll see you tomorrow," I said, "at the office."

"At the office," he repeated gruffly, and closed the door.

When I got to the elevator I found Sid buttoning his rain slicker before the large hallway mirror. Neither of us said anything at first. Sid, I noticed, was a good-looking man—graying at the temples, an open face, strong, capable hands. Now that he was standing up, he looked as if he could erect a house, fly a plane. At home, he'd told me earlier, he had a lovely son, home on vacation from Cornell.

When the elevator arrived, he looked up and smiled crookedly. "Charlie was difficult tonight. I've never seen him so bad, so troubled. I don't understand what's wrong with him, but whatever it is, I want to apologize."

"Don't be silly," I said. "You're not responsible."

He nodded, willing to be convinced. "You're a nice young man. Compassionate. Frankly, for a second there I thought you were going to call him. At least, I wanted you to. So did he, I think."

"Thanks. But it wasn't compassion, you see."

By this point we had arrived in the lobby. Together we exited onto the wide sidewalk. The night was damp, starless; the taxis hissed by with their solitary freight. "Drop you somewhere?" asked Sid, his arm raised to the sky. "I'm headed uptown."

I thanked him again and explained I was going downtown. I realized that it was unlikely I would ever see this man again, and the thought— as such thoughts will—disturbed me enough to set me chattering. I told him about my neighborhood in Brooklyn, about the size, rent, and light exposure of my apartment. If a taxi hadn't stopped, I might well still be there, swapping confessions with Sid Rosenman, but as it was, I was left with his last statement, said just before he ducked his head and closed the cab door behind him. "Every morning I wake up at six," he said, "and paint a watercolor. Then I take a shower and go to work." He shrugged his broad shoulders under the raincoat. "My boy tells me I'm starting to get better."

I watched the cab disappear into the web of traffic lights, conscious of the weight of my wallet in my back pants pocket. Then I turned south, toward midtown. I had gone most of the way back toward the subway station before I discovered I was running.

Chapter 4

The night my marriage ended I went into the backyard and set the hedges on fire. There was, that evening, a brisk March wind and a slate-gray sky, which successfully smothered what would otherwise have been a fine full moon. I had seen it the evening before over New Orleans, where I had taken an impromptu six-day weekend. Except for my host, a lawyer named Siskin, whom I'd roomed with one semester in Cambridge, nobody, including my family, had known where I was—which, looking back, I suppose was the point. It was not a very rewarding trip, as I did little but walk the streets and idle in Siskin's apartment, but it set the tone for what followed my return, which was this: Joanne came home from the market to find me lying on the living room sofa, leafing through a magazine, and said that she was sorry that I had felt the need to do something so childish, and that she supposed she was in some way responsible, and that I should probably consider moving out. At some point in the ensuing numbness, I found the lighter someone at the office had given me for Christmas. Then I slid open the glass door to the backyard. To make the fire catch I had to crouch low out of the wind, until my head was nearly buried in the bare thin branches, and cup the small flame with my hands. When it finally caught, I took a few steps back and watched the smoke lick at the cloudy sky. Some of the neighbors' windows flickered with the blue light of television, but no one took notice. Joanne was already upstairs, mending a skirt and talking on the telephone with her sister. The wind whipped the fire but it didn't spread; only two of the bushes had combusted, and even these were beginning to sputter by the time I turned to go back into the house. When I slid open the door, there was Solly, aged five, lips pursed together stoically and both arms wrapped around one of his toys, cradling it to his chest. He didn't look at me and I didn't look at him, but I caught a glimpse of what he was holding before I went upstairs to pack my things. It was his fire truck.

The kitchen in Siskin's New Orleans apartment had been rimmed by a six-inch wood molding that protruded from the wall about five feet above the floor. It was lined, entirely, with empty wine bottles. Two deep, they formed a castle facade of green glass. After Siskin left for work in the morning—he was a public defender downtown—I'd linger in the kitchen for an hour or two, drinking coffee and losing myself in the melodious French of the labels as the light streamed in, its color that of shallow water. Whatever panic had impelled me to come there on a whim had just as whimsically deserted me; I was left feeling more than a little superfluous, dawdling over the morning paper, nibbling crackers, and wondering just how in the world I was going to set myself straight.

The last day of my visit, Siskin returned from work and discovered me in approximately the same position in which he had left me that morning. "Listen, Heshie," he said. "If you're going to run off and be irresponsible, it seems to me you could be doing a better job of it than this. Where's your *je ne sais quoi?*"

"Tell me something," I said. "Why all these bottles?"

"I like to drink."

"Yes, but why keep them afterwards? That's what I'm wondering. The question has engaged me all day, in fact."

Siskin went to the refrigerator and pulled out a beer. The top twisted off easily in his hands. "I like to have something when I'm finished," he said. "I never believed in this go-with-the-flow shit. I like to have a record of my experiences; otherwise it all floats away. Upstairs in the attic there's a plastic laundry bag filled with every condom I've used since 1971. Want to see?"

"Thanks, no."

"I've got baseball cards that go back to Di Maggio. I've got Feller, Vander Meer. Want to see the cleats I wore in Pony League? I'm a fucking museum here."

"How do you like your job, Ernie?"

"How do you like your wife, Hesh?" Siskin drained the last of his beer, then placed it carefully on the recycling pile in the pantry. "Look, you can stay here as long as you like. You can sleep in that chair, if you're so attached to it. I'm happy to see you. Honest. Just don't go asking those questions of yours, trying to make me dissatisfied. I've got everything I want. I'm the most happy fella."

"I'm leaving tomorrow, anyway," I said, and, in saying it, understood it to be true.

"You don't have to."

"Yes I do. Back up there's where I left my *je ne sais quoi*. I'd better go find it."

Siskin looked from me to the floor, his expression blank. "And if you can't?"

"Then I'll have to pretend. It's a common enough trick."

"That's the old Crimson spirit," he said, bringing his hands together. "Hell, let's go over to the Quarter and celebrate. I've got something there I've been wanting to show you."

The something turned out to be a man named DeShaies, who operated a narrow tattoo parlor next to a liquor store. When we arrived, he was stretched out in what looked like a barber's chair, snoring softly, while around him the sweet clarity of the evening waged a losing campaign against the gloom of his store. He was deeply black, thin, broad-nosed, about forty. A transistor radio in the corner was tuned to opera.

"The man's an artist," whispered Siskin, pointing out the assortment of needles and dyes on the scarred counter. "Hesh, I know it's kitsch and all, and it turns off the ladies, but I can't help it. I've got to have one."

I thought it would be smarter to wait until he sobered up, but Siskin shook me off. He roused the tattoo artist from his nap, the two men slapped hands casually, and then I had to sit and endure the next hour and five minutes as Siskin bared his back to the needles. The surface of his skin popped with color, bloomed into a field of bright red flowers, but his face remained gray, somber and intent, his studying-for-finals face. DeShaies looked sleepy and impassive, his eyes no more engaged by the labor of his hands than those of a toll collector on the highway. I had had more than enough to drink for my own lids to feel droopy. Before long I fell into a half doze. The evening darkened. Against the backdrop of the window, the two of them seemed to be one thing gliding to the music, one skater on a frozen pond, making slow, imperfect circles.

And then with a sad flourish Ernie Siskin stood up to reveal a great colored design that stretched from shoulder blade to shoulder blade, runny with blood. "Well?" he said. "What'd I tell you? Is he an artist, or what?"

"What is it?"

DeShaies lit a cigarette and exhaled deliciously, looking over his handiwork. My question, he let me know by his tone, did not offend him. "What's it look like?"

"*Mother of God,*" gushed Siskin, craning his neck to examine himself in the mirror. "*Mother of God!*"

"I'm not sure," I said, in all honesty.

"*Mother of—*"

"It's a map of the world, man," said DeShaies, with quiet authority. "Map of the world."

And so it was. Now that he had named it, I could see, running across my friend's narrow shoulders, great bleeding continents, their mountains and plains described by the uneven, bumpy topography of his spine and musculature. North America looked big, an engorged bull, its horned Canadian head lowered menacingly toward the Old World. The Arctic cowered under his hairline, and Africa hooked south like a vertical pistol. Far away across the landscape of his body, Australia lay in a tranquil ocean of flesh behind one rib cage. It looked like a lovely spot to hide out.

"You hear that?" yelled Siskin, beaming. "A map of the world."

But when we drove to the airport early the following morning, Siskin moved with a perceptible hunch, squinting in the limpid daylight. He tried to help me carry my suitcase but had to quit; he was obviously in great pain by the time we arrived at the gate. "Are you going to be all right?" I asked.

"No problem," he said. "A bit of an itch, that's all. An occasional stab of acute discomfort. I'm already getting used to it."

"Another item for the Siskin museum?"

"And not the last, either. Still room for other planets, you know. I can bear a lot of weight. Can you?"

I blinked.

"Forget it," he said. "I'm just talking. Don't look so serious."

We shook hands and said good-bye. In the end, neither of us bore up very well. I went home and set the hedges on fire, and Siskin, some months later, was hospitalized with knife wounds from two street punks in a mugging. One had been a former client. I called him in the hospital when I heard the news. I had to resist the temptation to ask him what part of the map, exactly, had been sliced open by that junkie's blade. About this period in my life I have certain gaps of memory—much of what transpired between Joanne and myself remains a blur, as does my original inspiration to take off for New Orleans in the middle of an average week—but Siskin and the runny imprint of the world on his back stayed with me; that and the expression on Solly's face as he clutched his plastic fire truck. They were, looking back, the two people whom I missed living with the most, despite—or possibly because of—the fact that they were so much more immersed than I in the world of toys.

*   *   *

When the visitor rang my buzzer, I was dressed only in gym shorts, reading over the Walker file on a drizzly Saturday afternoon, two days after my ill-fated poker game at Charlie Goldwyn's. The sound jolted me. It seemed particularly insistent, willful, as though the buzzer, so infrequently employed, was giving voice to its own long-harbored resentment. Through the peephole I could make out a pair of tinted glasses, a glint of teeth, and not much else; but I had, as I unbolted the door, one of those violent glimpses into the future that precede a disaster. I saw dark, scudding shapes that I understood to be engines of change, agents of confusion. And then sameness.

And then I met Arthur Gordon.

He was only about five foot eight, in his mid thirties, well tanned, with long, thick blond hair combed straight back, forming a short, flippant wave at the nape of his neck. His dress was casual—faded jeans, denim shirt, corduroy jacket, and worn leather boots—and fit him snugly at his broad shoulders and narrow hips. The sole trace of southern Californian ostentation were the blue-tinted glasses, which were of expensive make, and were large enough to cover a good portion of his cheeks. But below them was a youthful, sharp-featured lower face, with a mouth that showed you all its teeth and a strong, lean jaw that announced itself with such boldness and charm that it was all I could do to restrain myself from shutting the door upon it. For I did not have it in me to be charmed that spring.

"Herschel Freeman," the visitor said, with an air of discovery.

"Yes?"

"I've been looking for you. My name's Gordon. Arthur Gordon. Here," he said, putting down a valise he'd had under his arm and diving into his wallet. He slipped out a pale yellow business card and handed it to me. It read simply *Arthur Gordon: AG Productions*. There were two addresses listed at the bottom, one in Los Angeles and the other, which had been crossed out, in New York. Like most business cards, it was a forceful production that revealed nothing. "I'm in film, you see. A director of documentaries. I'd like very much to talk to you for a few minutes, if you don't mind. All right if I come in?"

"You're already in."

It was true; he'd already snaked his way into the foyer, and had come to a stop under the arch to the living room, his back to me. He seemed to be taking in the apartment in one quick pan: the homemade bookshelves against one peeling wall, the scattered laundry, the breakfast dishes still out on the card table, the records heaped over the receiver, bereft of jackets. It was not much of a home, I realized, looking at it through a stranger's eyes, and what it reflected of my life—the disorder, the inattention to detail, the transience—were all of the things about which I felt least proud.

"Forgive me. It's just that I'm glad to have found you. I spoke with your wife several times, only there was some problem about your address. . . ."

"We're separated," I said.

"Ah." He nodded in the preoccupied way one receives old news. "All right if I smoke?"

"If you like."

He withdrew a pipe and a pouch of tobacco from the valise and went through the ritual of tamping and lighting. The pipe's bulge gave an agreeable force to his chin, a higher order of seriousness. "Can't help myself," he explained. "A weak, filthy habit. Sheer self-indulgence. But there you are." He looked pointedly at the sofa, which was covered by the files I'd brought home from work. Politely, he added, "I hope I'm not interrupting important business."

"It's business," I said, "but it's hardly important."

"Ah," he commented again. "Well, may I sit down? I'd like to fill you in on the project."

"What project do you mean? I don't follow."

"Look, I'll explain. Let's just sit down, and I'll tell you a little about myself first, so you'll know I'm not some Joe off the street. I mean, you should know what you're getting involved with from the outset. That's only fair."

"Mister Gordon, I'm afraid I have no inten—"

"Arthur. Please. We look to be about the same age. Why be formal? You have any coffee, by the way?" He grinned apologetically. "I'm full of addictions. I can hardly keep up with them myself."

Was it just that I was lacking good company? That the case I was researching depressed me? Or was I already, even then, flirting with an idea of renewal, nudging open the door to a different future, a more agreeable mix of self and circumstance? At the time, there was no way to know, nothing to go on but instinct. Mine told me to do what I did, which was to clear the papers off the sofa, make a pot of coffee, fix a couple of sandwiches, and listen without interruption to Arthur Gordon's long, allusive, even meandering introductory remarks. The fact is that I appreciate excellence in things, and he was, clearly, an excellent talker. His voice was full of rhythm and pitch; his ideas were passionate; he moved along quickly. There were aberrations, of course. He tended to circle his own meaning at times, and would occasionally trail off into an ellipsis for no apparent reason, as though seduced by a promising thought and then abandoned. He seemed accustomed to speaking of himself in the third person, a biographer tracing developments, filling in gaps of motive and causality. He spoke of his childhood in Canoga Park, California; of his degrees from Yale, Columbia, and the American Film Institute; of his influences and mentors; of American history. He used bits of French, German, Spanish. He used the names Welles, Corbusier, Adams, Foucault, Wiseman. They began to blur. Four times he used the name Abby. At some point I stopped hearing what he was saying and began to listen to him talk the way I listened to the voices on the radio, the way I listened to my colleagues in court—that is, fairly absently, registering more the peaks and valleys than the even plain of the content. I had no idea what had prompted him to confess so much to me, or what he expected me to make of it. I merely sipped my coffee and nodded, trying as best I could to keep alert.

". . . the ironic part, of course, is that I actually *like* the Coast. It suits me, I think. Everything overt, grabby, inspired by light. Sort of a land without shadow, if you know what I mean. But the point is, I'm prone to restlessness. I'm a restless person. Sometimes I fall into brooding spells that go on for weeks. The Germans have a word for it. *Grübelsucht*. Know any German?"

The monologue, which had commenced with a great rush of wind, paused briefly, an overcrowded rush-hour bus making a token attempt to pull up to the curb. I was fascinated; also outraged, and slightly intimidated. Later, it would be clear to me that this was precisely the reaction he was looking for.

"It doesn't matter," he went on. "Language isn't all that interesting, inherently. And for practical purposes, the European ones are insignificant. Now, the Chinese are onto something, maybe, with those ideograms. Make the image the axis around which the thought coheres. I've been meaning to study it, when there's an opportunity. Spend some time over there, maybe. Until I do, I should probably shut up about it. Abby says I'm pedantic when I'm insecure with a subject. Or a person, for that matter. What do you think?"

This time the pause seemed genuine: I was being asked for an opinion. As this was my first encounter with Gordonian dialectics, and I was growing more irritated than intrigued, I succumbed to impulse and told him the truth. "In my opinion, insecurity isn't your problem."

"What then?" he asked, leaning forward eagerly.

41

"I think you're full of shit."

"Ah," he said, now for the third time. Something like delight spread across his broad, smooth cheeks. Only it wasn't delight. His lower lip slid out from his upper, he leaned back, his legs crossed, and with a hairless finger he explored the crack between the sofa cushions. I sipped my coffee and watched. It was almost a parody of thoughtfulness, and there was something so naked in the performance I felt half ashamed of myself for provoking it.

"Of course, I don't even know you," I said, recovering. "Could be Abby's right, whoever she is."

"She's my wife," he said. Then, earnestly, "Also my best friend. And a remarkable woman in her own right. I think you'd like her."

I nodded agreeably, though it occurred to me that the odds of this weren't so hot.

"By the way," he added, digging into his jacket pocket, "*your* wife mentioned something about your boy having a birthday. I brought a little gadget here I thought he might like. Check it out."

It was a kaleidoscope, one unlike any I'd seen. The cylinder was only about five inches long and made of a smooth fine-grained wood. At one end, two acrylic lenses rotated from a metal hinge. It was beautiful. I knew immediately that Solly would love it. "I'm sorry," I said, "but I don't think I can accept this."

"Please, don't stand on convention. Just take a look. It's very simple, but it creates some remarkable effects. Just raise it to the light."

I lifted it towards the window and held each lens steady so that the picture was clean: five slender green leaves in front, shadowed by five wider, red- and violet-hued flower petals in back. It was strangely calming. I rotated the lenses in a slow, easy circle, until the colors softened and began to lose distinction, forming pentagonal splotches and blurs, suggesting shapes without defining them. After a while, the tight frame fatigued my eye, and I had to put it down. "That's a fine gift," I said. "Thank you. It wasn't necessary, or even appropriate. But thank you."

"I like it too." He beamed. "I see all sorts of things when I look at it. Street scenes, landscapes, profiles. Extraordinary stuff."

"Sure," I said. "I can see how you would."

"What about you? What'd you see?"

I shrugged. "I really just looked at the colors."

He nodded, though he seemed, for some reason, vaguely disappointed. "Well, it takes practice."

Suddenly I was tired of him, ready to be alone. "You've been here for half an hour, Mr. Gordon, and I still don't know what it is you want."

"You'd like me to get to the point, yes? I mean, you're a busy man."

"That's right."

He looked pleased. "Fine. It's just that I wanted to spend some time together first. Give us a sense of each other. See if we can work together."

"On what?"

"On this."

He pulled open the valise and extracted a legal-size manila folder, stuffed to bursting with paper. "Take a look," he said. "It's all here. Well, not everything. But the beginnings. The seeds, if you will. Check it out."

I opened the folder, placing my coffee cup to one side, and began to leaf through its contents. There were dozens of Xerox copies of articles and an assortment of photographs, many of them yellowing with age. I didn't read the texts or the captions; I merely looked over the faces, the queer lightweight suits, the features of the landscape in the background. As I did, the sensations that afflicted me were much like those I'd experienced only a few minutes before, as I revolved the lenses of the kaleidoscope: a slowing, a distance, a blur of stimuli. My face must have gone utterly blank, because Arthur Gordon came off the sofa with a look of alarm. When he was satisfied that I was all right, he rested his hand on the arm of my chair, peering over my shoulder intently as I turned the pages in the folder, as though we were two old classmates lingering over a high school yearbook. It was not until I saw my own face—nine years old, grinning awkwardly at the camera as I stood, stiff and self-conscious, in short pants, at the hip of a tall, lanky, distracted-looking character on San Francisco's Fisherman's Wharf—that it even dawned on me whose life I was surveying.

I closed the folder.

Arthur Gordon immediately became very busy. He paced in a circle by the window. He refilled his pipe. He wiped his glasses. I sat there watching him. A block away, some jackhammers made their rough music.

"Well?" he said finally.

"Not interested. Sorry."

"Not interested? How can you not be interested when I haven't even told you what the project is yet?"

"I've been told I lack curiosity."

I had, too. Joanne had put it in the top three of what she called my "blank spots"—along with ambition and morning horniness. I do not like to make love in the morning, as it happens. One of those small, perfectly legal offenses that contribute to the demise of a marriage.

"I must say I'm surprised, Mr. Freeman. That is your last name, isn't it?"

"You already know it is."

"It's hard to be sure with you. You're the evasive type. Tough to pin down. It's written all over you." He bit hard on his now unlit pipe and turned to the window. He seemed to be listening for something; his head was cocked downward. "That a finch? Listen."

"I don't know," I said.

"I like to know their names. You see, I *am* a curious person. I like to dig into causes, origins. I like to get my names straight, know what I mean? Like yours, for instance. You did say it was Freeman."

"That's right."

He nodded. "Cheap joke, that."

I drained the last of the coffee before I responded. "I was eighteen. My taste in jokes wasn't very refined."

"Yes, I'm the curious type," he continued, as though he hadn't heard me. "So when I'm researching a project and I run across something interesting, I follow it up. I like to see where things lead. Like, for instance, a distinguished physicist leaves his lab for a doctor's appointment one morning in 1958, and he doesn't come back. And then its nineteen years later and he *still* hasn't come back. This excites my curiosity. This has some texture. Never mind that he wasn't a big shot, that he never won a Nobel Prize or a medal of honor. That's for the big-money people. Me, I'm an independent. I look for more intimate stories, quality material. I don't want larger-than-life; just the thing itself. Okay, so where is he? Let's say he defected, as a few of them say. To me, that's melodrama. Hollywood spy crap. I wouldn't touch it. But what if he's still around? What if he just dropped out? What if a man in the prime of his success just up and changed his life? Man the maker remakes himself? I'm talking Homo faber, Hesh. Homo faber."

There was a pause as he gathered his breath. I rose, picked up the coffee mugs and sandwich plates, and took them into the kitchen. Gordon followed.

"You can't go somewhere from nowhere, Hesh."

I turned on the water and began to rinse the dishes. I worked slowly, letting the hot water ease down the backs of my hands.

"Do you want to hear my theory of gravity, Hesh?"

I gave each dish a good careful scrubbing with the soap pad before putting it under the water.

"My theory of gravity is that the only thing that keeps you from spinning off the planet is your past. It's heavy at times. I won't deny it can get oppressive. But it's all you've got, dammit. Without it you think you can fly, but you can't even move."

"Do me a favor," I said. "Hand me that towel."

He balled the dish towel in his fist. "I've already written to your mother," he said.

"Get a reply?"

"Not yet; no."

"Don't hold your breath."

"Look," he said, "tell me the truth. He's not really dead, is he?"

I took the towel and wiped my hands with it, then pressed it to the back of my neck. It was already too warm and sticky for May. "What do you want?" I asked.

He looked surprised. "Want? I want to make a film. About Project Y. About the birth of the present era. But mostly about him. About the man who baby-sat the bomb and then walked away. About what happens to a gifted man who sees the energies of, ah, achievement surpass the energies of, ah, fantasy, if you will."

"I, ah, won't."

He followed me back into the living room, frowning openly when I tried to hand him his valise. "But that's what we all want, isn't it? To swing people over to our idea of history?"

"Listen to me for a second. I just want to be left alone. That's what I want. The sum and the specifics."

He shrugged. "You're born into it, pal. That's the way it happens."

"What happens?"

He shrugged again and turned away, his head cocked to pick up the sounds of the birds outside, fluttering over the promenade. "Maybe it isn't a finch, at that. I'm strictly an amateur at these things. Abby's a whiz, though. You should meet her. Why don't you swing by the hotel tomorrow? She'll be flying in at four. We can have some dinner, chat about things. I'd like to show you some of my work. The point is, I'd like a chance to persuade you, and quickly. There are other projects I'm neglecting, you see."

"Tomorrow's impossible. I'm seeing my little boy for dinner. It's my night with him."

He nodded with exaggerated respect, with an air of complicity in such things that seemed utterly false. He was a childless man: It stood out in him, in his own childishness; it all but distinguished him. "Tell you what," he said. "Here's where I'm staying. If you feel like it, drop by. We'll be there at least a week."

He pulled on his sport jacket and patted his pockets, nodding to

45

himself, and followed me to the door. There, abruptly, he turned, and made straight for the coffee table. I saw him place the little kaleidoscope back in the center—it had been in his pocket. Then he gave me a solemn handshake and was gone. I went to the window. A rented Plymouth was parked unevenly against the far curb, and as he pulled away, I could hear the engine roar under his foot.

Chapter 5

The grim truth about my relationship with my son Solly was that I did not know very much about being a father. By legal training and by disposition I was inclined to look for precedent, but when it came to the complicated business of paternity I had one fundamental research problem: I had virtually no memories of my father at home. I had memories of him in his lab, leaning so far over his instruments that the chalk spilled from his pocket. I had memories of him in town, trudging through the heat from one store to another on his dolorous errands, my mother's endless lists crumpled between his long and narrow fingers. I had later memories of a recital we attended at the big cathedral in Albuquerque, of the campanile near his office in Berkeley, of Fisherman's Wharf on Thanksgiving. But at home we had somehow missed each other, following two divergent paths which intersected, occasionally, at the somewhat stationary point of my mother. It was interesting to me that I remembered him as a violent man, though I could recall only one single act of violence, when I was five or six and he broke his clarinet over the furnace while arguing with my mother. He was occupied at all times with any number of things beyond my ken: That was my dominant impression. And it did not serve very well as a primer for my own fatherhood.

I tried to compensate for this with my son by indulging most of his whims and by acting as though I knew precisely what I was doing when I was doing it. It was the same strategy I used with my clients; only with Solly, especially since the separation, the results were more obscure. For one thing, he was shrewd enough to manipulate me into thinking he was pleased with me when he wasn't, and, when it served his purposes, vice versa. For another, he was only seven, and moody as weather.

The night after Arthur Gordon's visit, however, he was in good spirits. We had spent the afternoon watching a ball game on television. Then we

47

had a pleasant dinner in one of the Lebanese restaurants on Atlantic Avenue he likes so much. Because he also likes to play catch, we went over to the promenade afterward and played catch. It was a brilliant spring evening, with the breeze coming off the water in languorous sweeps and the air soft and weightless in the failing light. From the promenade we had a magnificent view of lower Manhattan, its stone and metal and glass, the spires clustered like notes in a frenetic aria. The people of the Heights were out in force—walking their dogs, jogging, strolling arm in arm—and among them, I thought, Solly and I made a good impression, a father tossing a ball to his son, members in good standing of the conspiracy of well-being that crept over the city on the first warm spring evenings and made it seem, for a few hours, a rather wonderful place.

As evidence of his good mood, Solly kept up a steady commentary, as we tossed the ball back and forth, on some of his recent insights into the idiosyncrasies of adults. "That Alan," he informed me, "sure eats a lot of nuts. He even eats them for *break*fast."

"C'mon, throw the ball already. It's getting dark."

"Do *you* eat a lot of nuts?"

"No. Sometimes. Hey, throw the ball."

Apparently my answer dissatisfied him, because the ball's arc carried it some feet above my head. He let out a vicious little laugh. "You'd better go chase it," I said, "before it plunks into the river."

"I'd better go chase it," he repeated, delighted, "before it plunks into the river."

He scampered off, knees pumping high, in pursuit of the softball, repeating my strange sentence over and over to passing strangers. The ball did not plunk into the river, as it happened, but came to rest under a deserted bench.

"Can we go do the bridge now?" he asked, when he trotted back.

"No. It's getting dark."

"Come *on*." He pushed out his chin. "It's my birthday," he offered hopefully.

"That was last week."

"If it was last week, how come you gave me that present today?"

"I told you. That was from a friend who just got into town."

He considered this, tilting back the visor of his cap. "If he's a friend, how come I don't know him?"

"He's not your friend. He's my friend."

I could see the next one coming. "If he's *your* friend, how come he gave *me* a present?"

"Shut up, Solly."

"If I shut up . . ." he began, and his features contorted into a smile so rich with the joy of rational inquiry that I was moved, for the first time in weeks, to miss his mother, "can we go do the bridge?"

We go do the bridge.

Doing the bridge consists of walking along the bike path until we are at a point we consider dead center. There, our backs to the rushing traffic, we lean over the railing as far as we can. Normally I anchor Solly around the waist and he leans down toward the water and yells things at the top of his voice. It is a game we discovered one Saturday morning when my car broke down and we had to wait on the bridge for the tow truck. Pretty soon we'll have to stop. It is, after all, dangerous, and a little stupid. What Solly doesn't know is that now sometimes in good weather I walk the bridge alone on my way home from work. I loosen my tie and take off my jacket, and by the time I've made it halfway across, something inside me has begun to come loose, too; the cold conditioned air of the office goes out of me in heaves, and I smell the moist vapor of the water below, which blows up like steam. With the jumbled lights of the skyline behind me and the low geometry of the Heights in front, I linger at the railing and breathe so deeply the breath seems to originate in my toes.

"*Ai-ai-ai!*" shouts Solly. "*Ai-ai-ai!*"

His body goes slack and he dissolves into laughter. I pull him back onto the surface of the walkway and hand him his glasses. "That was great," he says. "Let's come back tomorrow."

"Tomorrow," I remind him, "you've got school, and I've got to go to work."

"If I skip school, will you skip work?"

"No."

"How come?"

"Because sometimes it's important to go where we're supposed to go. You're learning all that stuff about plants and trees you told me about at dinner. That's important information."

He looks skeptical. "Really? How come?"

"Because it's true."

"Oh."

"And I've got some very important cases I'm working on," I say.

"Really?" He is willing to take me at my word, but he would prefer confirmation. "Who says?"

"Remember Charlie, who came to the ball game with us that time?"

He screws up his eyes, incredulous. "That fat man!"

"Right. The fat man. He's my boss. What he says goes. And he says the stuff is important. Not that he really believes it, of course. It's just a little game we play, Charlie and I."

"Like Capture the Flag?"

"Exactly."

We walk the rest of the way back to Brooklyn in silence, and there goes unspoken between us a certain idea about games, which is that they are a lot of fun on weekends, and maybe once in a while during the week, but that they have their limits, like everything else. Important information.

The next morning Jerome and I were in the library going over *Nichols v. O'Brien,* on the right of paraphrase, when the fat man himself walked in. He headed straight for our table, his face pale and uncertain, almost embarrassed, and when he mooned up at me out of those deep tumultuous eyes I felt a feather of hope: He'd come through, he was okay, he was going to take care of me the way he was supposed to, and everything would be well. "Lunch, Hesh?" he asked.

Jerome, just to kid him, said, "We'd love to. What time?"

"Is he kidding?" asked Charlie of me.

"Is he kidding?" mimicked Jerome to himself, moving his notes to the adjoining table.

"Doesn't he have something better to do?" asked Charlie, lowering his voice into a stage whisper. "Whatta you guys *do* all the time, anyway? You bill a lot of hours, but you never seem to be working. What's that?"

"Gorman. *Copyright Protection for the Collection and Representation of Facts.*"

"Walker?"

"That's right."

"Coming along?"

"Slow. I don't think we'll win, if that's what you're asking."

"Of course that's what I'm asking."

"Well, it doesn't look good. The man's a plagiarist. There isn't a single original page in the whole book."

There was an audible gasp from Jerome at the next table, with whom, apparently, kidding went only so far. "Not that that makes any difference, of course," he said quickly. "Don't worry. Hesh here's a pessimist. We've got it in the bag."

Charlie nodded in approval, and my gaffe was allowed to crawl off into a corner and die a quiet death. Making an allusion to a client's guilt or innocence was a sign of boorishness; it showed a lack of perspective, an unhealthy absolutism. Had Charlie been someone else—Walter Todd, say, or Bill Webber, or Henry Flaherty—I would promptly have been given a stern lecture. Later, in a discreet fashion, some of my more important cases might have been redirected to other associates. But Charlie was Charlie, which meant that he'd hardly been listening. "Can we talk, Heshie?" he asked me now.

Jerome, his eyes small with worry, touched my elbow. "You want me to hang around?"

"That's okay," I said. "I'll be fine. Go get some coffee or something."

He left reluctantly. Charlie, watching him amble down the corridor, shook his head. "That kid a queer?"

"I don't know," I said. "What do you have to do to qualify as queer?"

He let my question, and the tone behind it, sail right past him. "You, on the other hand . . ."

"Me what?"

Charlie waved his wrist disarmingly. "Some people are of the opinion that he's the reason you picked up this year. That when he takes off, you go back to the lotus position, or whatever the hell you do when you're supposed to be logging billables."

"And you? What do you think?"

"I'm not sure. Frankly, I'm on the fence. I'd like to see us win Walker a fat settlement. I'd like to give you Crown. I'd like to bring you in on this uranium thing for Eastern—"

"No way, Charlie. It's a bad idea."

"Why? What's the big deal?"

"I just don't want to get involved in that," I said slowly. "There are personal reasons. I don't want to go out there."

He nodded tentatively, not willing to press the point. "You're angry about poker, is that it? Heshie—"

"It's not that. And let's drop it, okay?"

"Okay, fine. You feel strongly. I respect that." He drummed his fingers against the tabletop; some internal generator was picking up speed within him. He was getting oiled, beady. "Ah, the hell with it. Let's have lunch."

"What time?"

"Time? Now. Why wait?"

"Charlie, it's ten-thirty. There won't be anyplace open. Besides, I've got work to do here."

"You *are* sore at me, aren't you? Because of poker. Listen, Heshie, I apologize. I was in bad shape that night. That fucking Al was on my nerves. Plus there's been a lot of tension between Lorraine and me. It's a difficult period all around. But don't worry—I'm still on your side."

The excruciating thing about Charlie Goldwyn was that, in the end, he seemed to have no side of his own. Rather, that in the voraciousness of his appetites, he enveloped all sides at once, gobbled them up and spit out the pits as he elbowed his way through life. Now he scratched his thick wrist, glanced around impatiently at Mrs. Phillips, our phlegmatic legal librarian, and stirred with the force and density of a man who can eat lunch whenever the hell he wants to. But it turned out that he was restless with another sort of hunger altogether.

"Heshie," he hissed, taking hold of my forearm, "I'm going nuts."

For what must have been the first time in weeks, months, I laughed out loud. "I know, Charlie," I said.

His jaw fell open. "How can you know? I haven't even told you her *name* yet."

There followed a moment in which we both sat erect on opposite sides of the table in silence, as Mrs. Phillips hovered over her desk, licking her fingers to turn pages and eyeing us resentfully. There went that buzzing again in my left ear. Maybe *I* was going crazy.

"I can't believe it myself," said Charlie, unconsciously massaging my forearm in his big fists. "Frankly, I haven't been up for much of the old *amore* these past, well, months anyway . . . and Lorraine, she's got her own *meshugas*. But this is different. This is real. I'm talking about a new *life,* Hesh. Oh, Christ, I don't know." His brow clouded with despair. "I'm a family man. I love Lorraine. What am I doing? Passions are dangerous things, Hesh. Temporal. I'm going to wind up broiling in hell."

"Maybe you should tell me what you're talking about, Charlie. Otherwise it's difficult to respond."

"Fine," he said gratefully, as though I had just given him license to fulfill his most improbable dreams. "Look, you know that uranium case for Eastern we were just talking about? This past week, there's been a new wrinkle—a countersuit filed by the local Indians. Reservation land, holy places, the whole *megillah*. They want to renege on all the agreements and kick us—Eastern, I mean—the hell out of there."

"Any chance?"

"You're kidding, right? Anyway, we had a meeting last week with some of their staff counsel and the court mediator down in Foley Square. One of them's this little thing, maybe thirty years old, brown as a walnut, black hair. And fierce. A regular mustang. Twenty minutes don't go by before she calls me a pig and storms out."

"Well," I said. "It sounds like love."

Charlie ignored me. "Okay. So a few minutes later I go out to the john. And there she is. She's so pissed off she's kicking hell out of the water cooler. She's also crying. Loudly. What could I do?" he asked. "I take her to lunch. Listen, she's had a tough time of it. Life for those people is no stroll in the park. Two brothers are alkies, one's in jail. Mother died young. Plus this is her first big case and she wants to make good. She doesn't trust her colleagues any more than I do. They're just out to make a bundle. Of course, so's most of the tribe, so she's in a tough spot.

"I listen. Hesh, she's dark, with these wide cheekbones, like a Mayan. Cute figure. Something happens to me. A chemical reaction. I was eating fish. Then I was patting her hand. Then I was asking for a date. We're going to the Museum of Modern Art tomorrow. Hesh, I went home and gave Lorraine the tumble of her life. I've probably had eight, ten orgasms in four days. Wet dreams. I can hardly eat. My whole body's turning liquid. I'm going to hell any day, I swear to God."

He looked miserable. My heart went out to him for about ten seconds, then it turned right around and went out for myself. When was the last time, I wondered, that I'd been so feverish over someone? What toll did it take on a man, to live without passions? Somehow, the more time I was spending with Charlie Goldwyn, the closer I was coming to certain realizations about Herschel Freeman.

Charlie, nearly spent and sweating heavily, eyed the white crescent of his thumbnail. "I know I've been erratic lately. Not in top form. The hell of it is, I don't know whether I'm about to get better or worse. Either I'm chasing shadows or, so help me . . ." He trailed off into a dark alley of his own imagining, the vein in his neck pumping visibly beneath the folds of flesh.

Mrs. Phillips cleared her throat, as though for punctuation. We both looked up, though Charlie did so slowly, with only a mild, abstract curiosity toward the surrounding world of lawyers and texts. It was as if his confession had cleansed him; as if, now that he had an outlet for his anxiety storms, he was free. It required a passive role from his confessee, a blank, unblemished wall off which he could bounce his racquetballs of monomania. But this was hardly new. It had been going on for some time now, six or seven months—over poker, lunch, drinks, chats in the corridors, even occasionally in the bathroom ("Come make piss with me," he'd entreat. "It'll give us a chance to talk")—and in that time I could not recall Charlie ever asking me a question about myself and waiting to hear the answer. And I had let him get away with it. And now the big moose was infatuated with a little leftist Navajo, and I saw it all coming: the ascent and the decline, the midnight-oil monologues, the two-dessert bemoanings. His life was at a crossroads, he'd tell me. He was torn, he was tormented, his soul writhed like a leper. And then he'd train those big wet bag-heavy eyes on me in search of the word. What was it? Absolution. No. *Stay*. That was it. *Stay*. It was for me to anchor him to Pinsker & Lem the way I anchored Solly on the bridge. He could be as wild as a boar around me and I'd keep him fixed because I needed him. And then I saw it clearly, for the first time: I was not his anchor. He was mine. We were each other's.

I wiped my palms on my pants and raised them to the table. "I wish you luck, Charlie."

"Luck? I need a miracle." He looked at his watch, his mood lightening. "I gotta run to a meeting. Listen, tomorrow's racquetball, yes? Then I take you to lunch. I owe you one, for bending your ear." He stood; with one finger, he wiped the moisture from his upper lip. "You see? I'm turning to jelly. Soon there'll be nothing left."

"I think you've got some time yet."

"You finish that Gorman. Do a nice job, and I'll talk you up big. Pretty soon, Heshie, you'll be running this place, and I'll be off picking flowers in the desert. Stranger things have happened."

And with that, he swept past Mrs. Phillips, who, stacking books, watched him exit with an expression of malevolent satisfaction. When he was gone, she turned to me, without bothering to rearrange the lines of her face, and above the filling shelves her eyebrows swooped like gulls, as if to say, you too, you too.

Chapter 6

January 1944: At Night Some Angels Work

It is on a bone-cold Saturday night two weeks into the new year, and an hour before her debut performance in a very amateur production of *Arsenic and Old Lace,* that Ruth Orlinsky Friedmann, twenty-two years old, takes the first drink of her life. The bourbon, brought in from Albuquerque, is being handed around in paper cups. Quite honestly, she would prefer some cold water, or seltzer, but there are laws of supply and demand in Los Alamos that baffle her even now. She casts a look around the backstage area of the rickety wooden auditorium, sees the others toasting merrily. Suddenly she can't remember her lines, can scarcely remember, in fact, her own name. With horror, she realizes that she is afraid, and in the wake of this realization she does what people who are afraid have been doing since the beginning of time: She takes a deep breath, grabs a bottle off the table, and pours herself what she assumes to be a medium-sized drink. In fact she pours herself a double, a real belter, and downs it in two hasty gulps. Then the heat rises up and spreads through her chest like a grass fire, and Ruthie Friedmann, with a soft flutter of surrender, begins the first day of her second life on the Mesa.

Not that her first life has been so terrible. She remembers the way it began, the mystery of those urgent late-night calls to Eli from men in Berkeley and Chicago, men with Middle European accents who were, in their ponderous way, unfailingly polite to her on the phone. Some kind of new work to end the war; she didn't know what. Not even Eli seemed to know exactly what it was about; not then. There was the year they spent in Berkeley, and that had been interesting—so pretty, the wood cottages fronted by flowers, the freckle of sailboats on the bay when the fog lifted.

55

Life there had a slow, European—or so she imagined—grace, and she had just begun to settle into it when they were suddenly shipping their things to a place she had never heard of in the Southwest. It was weak of her, she knew, to loathe change so. In fact, looking back, she had to admit that even those first months in New Mexico had a certain, well, glamour to them. The area was so raw and beautiful; they went for hikes in the canyons, rode mules up the slopes, peeked into caves—heady stuff, for a Labor Zionist girl from Pelham Road. On one excursion, she remembers, she and Eli drew off from the others and made love in an abandoned mine. Outdoors! It had been their first time, and this prompted in them a kind of abandon, a noisy vaulting of an invisible barrier she had never even known was there. Later, when they'd brushed off their trousers, she made him promise—a teasing, throaty, sexual promise—to take her back there at least once a week, in good weather. That was close to a year ago, she realizes now. She sips at her bourbon, tries not to make a face. So much, she thinks, for early promise.

But she's not blaming anybody. One thing she has learned in her short, unhappy life as an adult is not to blame people for things beyond their control. The Project subsumes all responsibility; it is a collective enterprise, an international effort, democracy at work. You have to do what you can, Eli tells her, with the available materials. She sips more of the bourbon, and looks around at the other women backstage in their costumes, most of them her age or thereabouts, just as afflicted by dirty laundry, homesickness, and boredom as she is, trying to raise their collective morale with a little liquor, a little theater, a little flirtation with the single technicians. She tries to nurture the ember of this thought into a genuine flame of sympathy, of affection. But she can't.

She does not fit in, and she knows it. She gave up on the Mesa Club after one joyless evening spent discussing how to improve relations with the Spanish-speaking people on the Hill. A fiesta was suggested. Another wife, in a flurry of giggling, ventured that an orgy would be more fun. Don't judge, she told herself, and promptly judged. They were frivolous people, filling their hours with gossip in the commissary, while half a world away people were being blown apart and gassed. Around them she felt so clogged, so heavy, so . . . *Jewish*. Of course, many of them were too. But they didn't seem so to her. They seemed bland and smug, as though they'd traded it in for something. But what? Flushed, she excused herself early that evening, rising stiffly, unable to keep the distaste from turning down the corners of her mouth, unable to avoid the line of their eyes, these women of the club, these well-intentioned, unfocused women with whom she shared her life against her will. "My husband is with the baby," she added at the time, hoping it would explain everything, if even to herself, though she knew she merely sounded girlish.

But that was before: before her neighbor Ellie got the flu and convinced Ruthie to take her part in the play; before the most recent water shortage compounded her diaper problem to the point of absurdity; before Eli began to disappear into his lab in the middle of the night; and, most important, before she started work on her second backstage bourbon. Now, she thinks giddily, it might all change. Now she might have some fun. Now the days and weeks will pass in precisely this manner: hazy at the edges, cloudy and warm at the center, with half-remembered lines written by someone else echoing in her head. Yes, it's all right now. She's all right. One of the girls.

"There she is. Ruthie, hon, come here a sec, won't you?"

By the door to the bathroom, Sally Flynn, one of the organizers, is busy juggling two different piles of mimeographed paper. A tall, severe-looking woman, she has a loud bray even when sober, which she isn't. But tonight her outsized voice washes over Ruthie like a sponge, soothingly complete and generous, rubbing out imperfections, attending to the details.

"This is the finale," she says. "Got it? We wait till the coffin's wheeled onstage, we count to three, and then we launch into the chorus line. You know how they kick their legs at Radio City?"

She nods. She knows, all right. And her legs, though not long, are nicely shaped—better than most of the other girls'. Hasn't Eli always told her so, cradling them around his hips at night?

"Be a dear and run a copy of these to the other girls, will you? That's a lovely dress, by the way. Perfect. And what's that you're drinking? Bourbon?"

"I think so," murmurs Ruth, reaching for the song sheets. The moment—the evening, in fact—has a magical, childlike quality for her. She might be back in the fourth grade, eagerly lending her services to the teacher in exchange for a benevolent pat on the head. Teacher's pet.

"Well, give me a quick snort." Sally commandeers the cup and throws back half its contents, her neck rearing up like a stallion's. "Ugh." When her eyes return to Ruth's they are moist, but undimmed. "You're a peach. Now go on your way. I've got a zillion things to look after. See you at the party?"

Party? Of course. You can't very well have an opening-night performance without a cast party, even if—especially if—opening night is closing night too. But no one has invited her. Somehow this information, which isn't new, which is actually the kind of information she has grown accustomed to over the past months, has, now, an unusual power over her. She feels the blood pumping in her wrists, an angry, insistent, bourbon-fueled rhythm, and her front teeth clamp down hard on her lower lip as she wanders around the backstage area, passing out Sally's mimeos and exchanging the occasional break-a-legs with the other wives. Party? The whole *thing* is a party. She takes in, as though from a great distance, the entire bright, chattering ensemble, all from good schools, all married to young powerhouses, their lives colored red now with the adventure of their enterprise. No, no one knows exactly what it *is* in the Tech Area that keeps their husbands occupied so late into the night, that makes them stare for inordinate lengths of time at the ceilings, or mutter to themselves, or take two-hour walks through the rain. It's known simply as "the gadget." But they suspect it will be, when it's ready, something large and furious, some instrument of war that plays notes previously unwritten, and you can tell it excites them. They are having the time of their lives. It is a long and agreeably messy party, and they don't want it to end. This is their adventure, their one true romance, their movie. And they don't want the lights to go up, not quite yet. . . .

Every party has a pooper that's why we invited you. . . .

And then something occurs to Ruthie Friedmann, which, because she is unused to the effects of two stiff drinks, she attributes to inspiration: *She* doesn't want it to end, either. Not, she thinks, because she shares the other girls' innocence; but because she knows hers has already evaporated, and she cannot imagine what her life will be like back in New York without it. It strikes her that she has joined the party, after all. It's almost a comfort.

"Are you all right, lovey?"

Startled, she turns to find Annette Burke, wearing a man's suit and a fake white beard, looking at her over a script. She is the wife of a senior theorist, matronly and sarcastic, and one of the few who do not share in the gossip at the commissary.

"I'm fine, thank you."

"Your makeup's running. I couldn't tell if you were laughing or crying."

Ruthie puts one hand to her cheek, which she is surprised to find damp, damp and hot. Oh, God, what now? Has she lost control entirely? "I was laughing," she announces, forcing the words out. "It just . . . it just all struck me as so funny all of a sudden."

"You mean all these silly women getting so excited about a silly play?"

There is an edge to the older woman's voice that sounds vaguely satiric, but her eyes, beneath the paint, are not unkind. Ruthie feels her lips begin to quaver; she has to bite down hard again with her front teeth to keep them steady. Oh no, she thinks. Not you. Not a friend. Not here, not now.

"I guess that's what I mean."

"Poor girl. You're a little like me, I'm afraid. Ever notice these little productions of ours are always comedies? I'd give my teeth to try a *real* play. But young people today have no flair for tragedy, do they?"

Ruth wants to agree, but does not trust her own powers of articulation at the moment; besides, she is not certain whether Annette Burke means some subtle indictment of *her*. Her eyes fall to the music sheets in her hand. "Did I give you the finale?"

Annette Burke sighs, nodding at her script. "This'll do me fine. They kill me off at the beginning of Act One. Why stick around?"

"But there's a party of some sort. . . ."

"Isn't there always?" Annette smiles. "Me, I'm having a party of my own. A fat Dickens and a couple of hot toddies. Daniel goes off and blows that horn or chases the WACs or whatever he does at those things, and I get some peace and quiet."

"That sounds wonderful," says Ruth. "Eli plays too."

"Music?"

Ruth blushes. "Yes, of course music. But he's been so busy lately. After the show he'll want to go to sleep early, I'm sure."

"Come, then. We're on Bathtub Row. Have the whole place to ourselves."

What she wants to say is thank you. What she wants to say is maybe you are my one chance to straighten out what has begun to go awry inside me. What she wants to say is that whatever a hot toddy is, she'll have a double.

What she says, however, is, "I'm sorry. I have the baby," and then she looks away with a surge of what she hopes the older woman will think is embarrassment but that she herself knows to be shame.

Annette Burke regards her frankly for a moment. Then she steps back and, seeing a hand wave from stage left, says, "I think it's about to start."

The performance, so far as she can tell, is a smash. Sure, there are muffed lines, and tentative staging, and a couple of the scenes must be ad-libbed or cut short; but the house is full, the laughter and applause copious, and once they have begun, even the threadbare sets seem imbued with the magic of theatrical invention. In the confusion of scene changing, one of Ruthie's big lines is lost, but she doesn't let it throw her.

She feels, in fact, remarkably controlled under the lights, with all eyes upon her. She wonders briefly if perhaps she might have some talent, after all. A sweet, slow clarity seems to overcome her onstage; the poise she has been lacking these past months now rises to the surface, lending grace to her movements, resonance to her voice, making her feel as she knows she must look, crisp and polished, like a plum buffed to a shine. She feels, acting the role of an ingenue, incredibly like a promising young woman with the best things in life still before her. Above all, she feels happy. She is certain that Eli, in his seat on the far aisle, can sense this, but each time she peeks out from the side curtain to catch a glimpse of his face, something distracts her—a pretty dress in the front row, the smoke from someone's pipe, a whispered cue onstage. There is so much movement around her that she barely has time to catch her breath, to savor the taste of her triumph, before they are all rushing back onstage for the finale.

A black coffin is wheeled into the center of the stage. This takes the audience somewhat by surprise; already standing and reaching for their coats, they quiet and settle down again expectantly. The first uptempo strains of the jazz band, with portly Daniel Burke on saxophone, rise up from the makeshift pit. Then the women of the cast, minus Annette Burke, flood the stage, hastily arranging themselves in a ragged chorus line, their skirts hiked up daringly above the knee. It takes a moment or two to coordinate their knee kicks into a wave, but once they've gotten that straight, and are already breaking up with laughter at the thought of what is transpiring, and Sally Flynn has, with a demonic wink, opened the door of the coffin to reveal its contents, the girls join their voices in song:

> *If you knew Oppie*
> *Like we know Oppie*
> *Oh, oh, oh, what a guy . . .*

> *At physics theory*
> *He's got no peer, he's*
> *The brains be-hind Project Y . . .*

> *So let's have no nay-sayers or malarkeys—*
> *Leave that to the krauts and nips and darkies . . .*

Darkies? Ruthie hardly knows what she's singing. The words, held up by the girl next to her, are tumbling straight from her stomach to her mouth, making no evident detour at her brain. Inside herself she hears a *ping,* like the *ping* when their Ford cracked a piston once on the road to

Santa Fe. Something, she knows, is driving her engine now that is going to take its toll later, that will hobble her somehow in the future; but meanwhile, the music wheels and swoops, and it feels so nice, so enlivening, really, to keep singing, to sing and kick her shapely legs. . . .

> *In Greek or Latin,*
> *There's one Manhattan—*
> *Shout it loud; don't be shy.*
>
> *If G-2's near us,*
> *Don't let them hear us—*
> *Pass that bourbon and rye.*
>
> *People say that Oppie's quite a feller—*
> *Even Groves and little Eddie Teller*
> *Say they love Oppie*
> *Like we love Oppie . . .*

And there he is—sitting up in the coffin, some fifteen feet away. Gaunt, clean-shaven, smiling out of his thin-lipped mouth while the one steel-blue eye Ruthie can see from her view of his profile remains cold and does not blink once, she is certain, in the ten or so seconds she stands there watching it, her mouth open, her breath gone, and the chorus proceeding, as choruses will, without her.

> *. . . 'Cause Oppie won't say* die!

Much later, after several additional drinks at the cast party (where, true to form, and despite her best intentions, she hangs back against the wall, watching dear sober boyish Eli play a series of duets with Harry Frisch), Ruthie races out of the Lodge, afraid to be sick in public. When she gets outside, however, she discovers that she isn't as nauseous as all that. Huddled in her parka, she leans over, takes a few deep breaths, filling herself with the cold night air. The sky is clear and close; it smells faintly of sage, but the coal from the furnaces hangs in it too. Still, it is a relief to be outdoors, alone, away from the din of the party—to which, she reminds herself, she was never invited, really, in the first place.

It seems to Ruthie that she is walking pretty well, considering she is drunk and wearing heels. Because it's all coming so easily for her tonight, she decides to allow herself a solitary adventure. She walks north, toward the higher ground, into the thicker junipers, and the disquiet in her stomach eases back from its assault on her throat.

Soon she begins to hum. Exactly where the tune originated, she isn't sure—perhaps her father taught it to her years ago, coming home from *shul*, or perhaps it is one of Eli's own compositions—but it has an agreeable, a sort of jaunty melody to it, which suits her present mood, and she can hum it and walk and breathe in the blended air all at the same time, and there are the endlessly jumbled patterns of the stars around her, the blinking lights of a thousand galaxies. She lets her eyes roam, wishing she knew the constellations. It seems a mark of her ineffectuality that she doesn't. Oh well. She can imagine, after all, and now she imagines herself a native, returning from a hunt in the mountains of Jemez, trailing a load of game. Back at the pueblo there will be dancing, drums, the aroma of roasting meat. And how they'll dance!

But she's being silly, she knows it. Still, she likes it here, just now, on the edge between what is wild and what is cultivated, where the night sounds ring out untempered all around and she can hum her mindless tune—

A stab of pain goes through her shoulder and she hears a small, futile cry. There is something in front of her. She steps back and reaches out to test the space with her hands. Cold barbed wire. A fence. The cry, she realizes with some wonder, was her own voice.

Squinting in the dim moonlight, she can make out a sign: DANGER—PELIGRO—KEEP OUT.

Staring at it, rubbing her shoulder, her breath bunching visibly around her, Ruthie's cheeks go hot once again with the consistent and relentless injustice that characterizes her life on this cold planet. As a girl she was fenced off from the boys at *shul*, consigned to the balcony with the bald women, the widows—the meek serfs in the rigid feudalism of the Orthodox. Very well, that was tradition. But later she was fenced off from going to college—her only ambition for herself—by the demands of her ailing parents. And that was filial responsibility. And now the fences are proliferating, and there is one between her and Eli, and one between her and the other girls, and another between her and the mountains, and another, it is beginning to seem, between her and something larger than any one of those things, something inside herself. . . .

She wants. She wants so much she doesn't even *know* anymore what she wants, what is genuine hunger and what is the reflex of wanting. And it is this last uncertainty, this final fence, that sobers her now; that will, she knows instinctively, require a great deal more bourbon than she's yet tasted, a great many more long moonlight walks, to get through. And even then . . . ?

Hands gripping the cold wire, she peers through the trees, deep into the Technical Area, at the single blue unblinking light of what she has always assumed is a water boiler. But now it does not look like a water boiler, nor does it really sound like one. It hums and churns, a parody of her own inner noises, a comic performance. It is something else.

A chill runs through her. She should be with someone, she thinks. Someone, perhaps, with a flair for tragedy. Because she has a story she would like to tell, a story she remembers from her youth, which now seems so far away. It is the story of the two rabbis. First there was Rabbi Mendel, who was young and headstrong. He boasted that in the evenings he saw the angel who rolls away the light before the darkness, and in the mornings he saw the angel who rolls away the darkness before the light. And then, the story goes, there was his teacher, old Rabbi Elimelekh, who replied: "Yes, in my youth I saw that too. Later on you don't see those things anymore."

It's quite a good story, she thinks to herself, and she wishes there were someone around whom she could tell it to. Because the truth of it is, when she is all by herself, she is not entirely sure of the point.

Chapter 7

"Now this one was a tough shoot. Terrible conditions, but I think we pulled it off rather neatly. Check it out."

From my soft, low-slung chair in the Gordons' small midtown hotel room, I checked it out. This entailed watching the television screen, across which a blond woman in a white lace dress rode bare-saddled on a white horse. It was an autumnal scene, craggy shore, darkening sky. The woman's mouth was open and loose with pleasure, presumably because of what she'd eaten that morning for breakfast.

"Notice that cutaway to the lighthouse. Took forever to get that right."

Exactly what combination of motive and circumstance had resulted in my presence in that room on that evening I could not account for. Boredom, of course, played its part—it had been a while since I'd spent an evening with someone other than Gorman, Nimmer, and their fellow apostles of copyright law. But there may have been other things as well, things awakened by the sound of Abby Gordon's voice when she'd called early that morning to invite me. Her tone seemed to be layered with ironies and expectations that she herself wasn't even aware of, and nothing in it was what I would have predicted from the wife of the earnest, pedantic, denim-clad de Mille who was fiddling with the rewind button of the video recorder at the end of the room. So much for surprise number one.

Surprise number two was what I had been viewing on the television screen for the past hour. Hard hats wiping their brows on bulging forearms and taking long drinks from sweat-beaded cans. Young mothers admonishing their children, then marching off to the laundry room with a basket of soiled clothing. Sleek models in skimpy gowns straddling the hoods of cars from Detroit. Grown men squeezing toilet tissue in supermarket aisles the width of highways. Pens that wrote on marble.

Cheese crackers that made one's houseguests howl like wolves. The images shimmered across the screen like heat ripples. The edits were quick and pointed. After ten minutes I was impressed. After half an hour I was ready to race out into midtown in search of the nearest market; I was ready to buy.

Arthur Gordon was clearly a very talented director. He had also, clearly, done nothing over the past five years but commercials. Having made this discovery, I sipped some club soda, watched the screen with a respectful attention, and chastised myself steadily for having landed, yet again, in a place where I did not belong.

When the show was over, the three of us sat quietly adjusting our eyes to the room's harsh light. I was in an armchair, still dressed in my cobalt-blue suit. Arthur was perched in front of the television, tamping at his pipe. Cross-legged in the center of the double bed, Abby Gordon examined her knees with a concentration so intense it suggested the neurotic. I had done my share of checking *her* out too. She was a long and supple woman of thirty, her pale skin touched by sun at the cheeks and olive green at the limbs. Her frame was narrow, small-breasted, and angular, and had she chosen to carry herself differently she might have had a model's beauty. But there was another, yielding, quality to her, a slight drawing in of the shoulders, a hesitation at the corners of her small, unripe mouth, a lack of force around her eyes—which were neither as large nor as brilliant as her husband's, but had a delicate, finicky light to them—and a casual limpness in her fine long faded-brown hair that made her risk seeming colorless, or of some hue so subtle that it shone only under special conditions, under certain arrangements of light and shadow. The clothes she wore—a beige sleeveless T-shirt and simple khaki shorts—did nothing to enhance either her beauty or her reticence. The shirt, I thought, might have been a little big for her, because there was something undernourished about her bare shoulders that night, something that made you want to put your arms around them.

But I didn't, of course. Instead I said, to her husband, "I like your work."

He actually blushed. "Really? I mean, you don't have to give idle compliments. I'm not thin-skinned."

Like hell he wasn't. "No, I mean it. Very vivid. Makes me proud to be a consumer in this great land of ours."

Probably this last sentence betrayed some of my true feeling, because Arthur's eyebrows straightened, and his wife leaned forward protectively. "Oh, these are just for the money," she said quickly. "Plus you get your feet wet, of course, experimenting with technique. Commercials are actually a very good training ground, you know, for getting your feet wet. . . ."

Her voice trailed off when she realized she was repeating herself. It seemed to be a party line, of sorts; at any rate, she was looking at her husband when she resumed. "Our real projects we shoot on our own time. We have enough to live comfortably, for a while, anyway. So now we can give them our full attention."

"Our?"

Arthur explained. "Abby and I have recently begun working together. As a team. She'll be producing, plus doing some of the writing. That was her specialty in college," he added.

"I wrote poetry," admitted Abby, fumbling with her sandals. "It wasn't very good."

"Bullshit. You had real potential. If you'd stuck with it, who knows—"

Abby shook her head, closing off what was obviously a tired discussion. "Would you like some cognac, Hesh?" She smiled wanly. "Duty free."

"Odd expression, that," said Arthur. "Duty free. Sort of the ultimate temptation, no?"

"Thanks," I said. "I would."

She rose and went to the corner of the room, bending over a suitcase that had been laid open across the arms of a chair. For one or two seconds, her husband and I each had a view of the milky half-moons exposed by the climb her shorts performed up the backs of her thighs.

"None of us," said Arthur, "is duty free. But that doesn't seem to stop us from trying, does it?"

"Say when," said Abby, pouring the brandy into a sanitized water glass.

I wasn't much of a drinker, so I said when quickly. Arthur took a larger portion, which he drained most of in a single swallow. As though some threshold had now been passed, he unbuttoned the second button of his shirt, pulled a joint from his pocket, and lit up with one rip of his lighter. He inhaled twice deeply, then gestured to me.

"Ladies first," I said, to allow me time to consider whether this was really such a great move for a member of the New York bar.

"I don't . . . indulge," said Abby with a wry shrug.

"This is true," agreed her husband, blowing out a jet of smoke. "Abby does not indulge. Not herself, anyway. It's part of what I prize in her, the way she saves all her indulgence for others who need it more. What they call an unselfish person."

"Oh, stop," she said, shrugging again.

"It's true and you know it. You're an unfathomable creature. Like the unicorn and heffalump."

I watched her as he spoke. Her eyes were on her sandals. Her fingernails were short and worn. It took no great stretch of the imagination to think her unhappy.

"Me," he went on, "I run another way entirely. I indulge everyone, and require everyone to indulge me. Things are tough out here in the fire storm. Let people do what they want, know what I mean?"

I took a hit of marijuana, watching a light flare up in the smoke. My eyes burned. "I don't know," I said, in a half squeak. "Everyone seems to do what they want, regardless."

Abby's brows wrinkled over her glass. It had been a cryptic statement, and I supposed she was deciding whether or not it merited pursuing. "I'm not sure that's true," she offered. "In fact, I know it's not. For me, anyway," she added, to soften it.

"Of course it's not," said Arthur, brandishing the joint. "Look at *you*, Hesh. From what you've said, it's obvious you don't do *any*thing you want. You hate your job, your home life's a mess, you've got no time to yourself, no creative involvement in anything. And you're miserable. I can tell just by looking at you."

"Can you?" I asked, bristling.

Abby leaned forward again in what I was coming to recognize as her protective posture. "I think what Arthur means is that we've all had to make compromises to get on with things, but—"

"That's not what I mean at all."

"Well, then, what *do* you mean?" Her patience was beginning to show its seams. "Tell us."

"I will. Just let me take one more hit off this. . . ." He finished and then stubbed out the joint. "I mean," he said, "that I used to be like you, Hesh. It's a classic thing among gifted children, you know, to wind up with an undemanding position in an uninteresting field. In my case, I nearly went into academics. At one point there, I had an offer at U-Mass, American Studies. Tenure track, good hours, pretty campus. I almost took it, too. I'll tell you why I almost took it, though the reason is obvious. I was afraid. I was afraid to find my own limits. I could have taken that slow-death chickenshit academic job and gone right on believing what I really wanted to believe, which was that I didn't *have* any limits. I'd tell myself that somewhere inside me was a giant, only conditions weren't right. Then at a certain point things would turn. Bad dreams. Divorce. Show up dead drunk at colloquiums. We know the signals. This was about seven, eight years ago, this offer. I'd be tenured by now."

"So what happened?"

My question seemed to be right on time. Arthur rubbed his smooth jaw and grinned. "Can't you guess? I met Abby."

Let's fast-forward a couple of hours. We are sprawled over floor, chair, and bed, having worked our way through more than half the cognac, two more joints, Arthur's (unfinished) student film from AFI—a thirty-minute documentary on the rise and fall of Spiro Agnew, titled *Bullet-head*—and a discussion of Central American politics. The time is 2 A.M. I am supposed to be at work in six hours, and it occurs to me only now, and somewhat dimly, that no word has been mentioned of the project I was ostensibly invited here this evening to discuss. Which is fine with me. It is doubtless part of the reason I've been enjoying myself so much. Tonight, it seems, I have been having a good time with some interesting, unconventional people, and no one has brought up such matters as briefs or appellate courts or voluntary disclosures, no one has sought advice on private schools for their children, no one has tried to sell me on mutual funds. It hits me with a throb of pot-stoked emotion that I have not spent an evening like this since before I was married, when I used to spend *every* evening like this. And then, tracing the line to the present, that I am no longer quite young enough to refer to myself as a young man with prospects.

Some of this must show on my face, because here's Abby Gordon gazing at it with what might be sympathy or what might be a commensurate disappointment of her own. I am more than a little taken with her. She looks lovely and haunted and besieged by doubt, and there is no question but that she is just my type. There is in her, I suspect, a kind of depth that comes from long acquaintance with solitude, the kind that only-children and expatriates have. But perhaps that's too romantic. Perhaps she is merely, as I thought at first, neurotic; a woman of slippery moods. She has been listening to me talk about Solly, but has allowed the subject to lapse, probably out of exhaustion. We are left looking at each other in the room's softened light, as Arthur, curled on the floor, one hand resting casually between his legs, lets out the faintest and most pleasant of snores.

"I'd better go," I say.

"Yes."

I realize with some injured vanity that she has been preoccupied. "You look very tired."

She shrugs. "Jet lag. It always takes me a week to get over it."

I rise to go. Suddenly all the air seems to have gone out of the room. "Will I see you guys again?"

The "you guys," which did not exactly roll off my tongue, has its intended effect: We both glance over at Arthur, sleeping his untroubled sleep, his pink mouth even more boyish than usual. "Poor Arthur," she says, and sighs mysteriously.

"Poor everybody," I say, feebly.

She makes no comment. When we arrive in the doorway she hovers there, resting her bare upper spine against the frame's cool metal. For a moment she gnaws at the nail of a finger, then checks herself, holding her hand back and staring at it crossly, five errant children. "I don't do this anymore."

"What?"

"Bite my nails."

"Oh." I am stumped for something intelligent to say.

"We'll be in town for another several days. Arthur's lining up some seed money, and I'll be over at Columbia, doing research."

"So you're going ahead with it."

"It's our project," she says simply. And then, perhaps remembering what the true purpose of the evening was supposed to have been, she gives me the hardest, most resolute look I've yet seen from her. "Yours too."

"What makes you say that?"

"He's your father."

"So what?"

"You can't go somewhere from nowhere, Hesh."

For the second time that evening I am reminded that the Gordons are a married couple who share certain verbal expressions. But which of the two, I wonder now, coined them in the first place?

"I'm not trying to go anywhere," I say.

She smiles. I have offered her a straight line for a joke that will inevitably be on me. She has the good manners, at least, to allow a neutral pause before going on. "Maybe you'd be more content if you did," she suggests mildly.

"I'm afraid I've given up on contentment."

"Too bad," she says, and looks down at her feet for what seems to be a long time. Then, deliberately keeping her voice light, as though to underscore, or possibly negate, her words, she mumbles, "I'm afraid I haven't."

And with that she pecks my cheek, a feathery tight-lipped kiss, and bids me good night.

"If you don't have fingers," my mother once told me, "you can't thumb your nose."

Naturally she was a little tight when she said this, sitting in the dark cool of the kitchen in her beloved adobe house, smoking a cigarette and listening to the news on the radio. But it was the right thing to say at the time—she had a gift for ethical maxims, a Talmudic sixth sense— because I'd been about to accuse her of being a drunk. I was twelve or thirteen, an idealist of sorts, and when I returned from school to find her dreamy over a glass of melting ice, all my frustration with the texture of our family life rose up in me like a bad meal. But her voice, heavy with her origins, and the absurd picture her words summoned, disarmed me wholly. It was a piece of advice that I must have considered, and rejected, several hundred times in the twenty-odd years since I'd first heard it.

I thought of it now, in part because I was a little tight myself. It took me a good portion of the two blocks to Seventh Avenue before I found my walking legs and before the revolving wheel in my head ceased its sluggish whirling. Late as it was, I felt no desire to go home. Brooklyn would be slumbering at the other end of the subway line, its sidewalks vacant under thick foliage, its bars and nightspots padlocked until morning. Manhattan, on the other hand, was a different story. It pulsed and crackled, rumbled and hummed. Manhattan wanted me to stay up late, to walk the streets, see the sights, take part in her nocturnal industries. She was a lit jukebox, a sequined stocking, a twitching ass. She wanted me to stay. To play.

The night was hazy with spring. I turned south on Eighth Avenue, against the sidewalk traffic, the black girls in their hot pants, the bleary cabbies leaning over their hoods, checking out the *Post* beneath the garish yellow halo of the Port Authority. It was optimistic of me to be walking there, considering the hour, but I felt a queer sort of invulnerability. I was tall, groomed, and white, dressed in a tailored suit. My briefcase swung in wide arcs. Choose your weapons.

"Yo, mahn," called a skinny island kid at the corner of Fortieth Street. "I got what you want, mahn, everything you want, mahn." The words ran together musically, up and down a tiny scale of notes, effortless. His frame, leaning out of the shadowed doorway, was so reedy and still he might have passed for something inanimate, a piece of scaffolding. He looked fourteen, nervy, and bored. I bored him. The city bored him. His own hands in his own pockets bored him. As I walked past, I heard him hiss something—a greeting, a remark, a judgment—but it was not meant for me.

The sanitation workers were on strike again; the sidewalks swelled with garbage in ripped green bags. The smell filtered through the street and into my nose, and with it, some of the romance began to leak out of my adventure. I was beginning to feel vulnerable, sluggish. I wanted to rest. Where was everyone going to rest? Beneath my feet, a train roared through its black tunnel, following its charted path downtown. The taxis whizzed along the straight, smoky avenues. The metal arrows pointed south. It was a whole island of one-way streets, a perfect grid of them. But tonight it was late, and they all seemed headed south, the grid webbing with cracks and fissures, dissolving into shapelessness, into stillness, into the water that surrounded us. In New York City you didn't need a map to know where you were headed. The numbers told the whole story.

In the mid thirties the sidewalks emptied out. I walked past the darkened Garden and through the garment district. I felt numb with weariness, and my feet were pinched in my shoes, but I did not hail a taxi. I only hailed taxis when I was in a hurry, or trying to impress upon myself the notion that I was a man of the world. And I was past the point, just then, of impressing myself with any gesture I could think of.

In Washington Square there was laughter and the smoke of marijuana and incense. SoHo was poised and quiet. The clubs in Tribeca spilled people from the boroughs out onto the sidewalks, where they had to contest with the refuse, as though engaged in rites of initiation. I moved east through Chinatown, dark and narrow, past the windows where the ducks hung in rows from metal hooks, denuded, slender, and beheaded. Then south again, down and down, down . . .

A full ninety minutes after leaving the Gordons' hotel room, I found myself at the corner of Nassau and Pine. The district was ghostly, a movie set, ridiculously dense with buildings. An occasional pigeon hopped and pecked in the gutter; otherwise there was no movement at all. Leaning against a streetlight, I craned my neck to take in the tall concrete-and-glass receptacle that contained me so effectively for most of my waking hours. A few scattered windows were illuminated, leapfrogging the dark tower. The lights, though playful, seemed potentially significant, as though they might have been transmitting a coded message to the inhabitants of another tower, in Chicago, or Los Angeles, or London. The world is a litigious place, Charlie was fond of saying. And it is very, very small.

I crossed the deserted street, feeling no particular desire to go inside.

71

Neither did I feel any particular desire to remain where I was, or to go back to Brooklyn. Aside from the view of Abby Gordon bending over a suitcase earlier that evening, I could not remember entertaining a specific desire in some time.

The lobby, as usual, was cool and well lit. The floor gleamed with polish, like fresh ice. The large abstract expressionist paintings on the eastern wall loomed over the place in their full dimensionality, immense with latent energies. Whoever had purchased them, I thought, had intended precisely this—this light, this hour, this mood. Everything seemed to fit, to be in place, including Jimmy O'Connor, the night security man, who sat at his desk beside the main elevator banks, blinking at me sleepily over his console as though I were an old and not particularly involving movie.

"Whattaya know, Mr. Freeman?"

"Not much, Jimmy," I said. "How goes it tonight?"

"Quiet and slow. Slow and quiet."

"Anybody up there?"

He leaned back, scratching his solar plexus. "Coupla associates. Young fellas, like yourself. And Mr. Goldwyn, I think. Hey, 'dja hear the rumor?"

"What's that?"

"About his condition. They say it's terminal."

"What is it?"

He frowned in annoyance. "What am I, a doctor? I'm just telling you what I heard."

"How many years you been here, Jimmy?"

"Sixteen last October."

I pressed the elevator button and waited.

"You like it? Working here, I mean."

He look at me guardedly over his shoulder. "I like it fine," he said.

"You like me, Jimmy?"

"I like it fine," he repeated stubbornly, until the elevator yawned open to carry me away.

Chapter 8

Charlie Goldwyn was reasonably certain he was not going crazy. True, it had been days since he'd been able to stomach solid food. There was also the matter of his recent behavior, which Charlie knew did not reflect well upon him. After all his stentorian bellowing, his cyclonic mood shifts, his fits of unprovoked weeping, you could hardly blame people for doing what he was sure they were doing—that is, making comments, snide remarks behind his back when he got out of the elevator. He knew his wife was miserable, that he was driving his adult daughter to therapy, and that his accountant—clucking his tongue at the sight of Charlie's diminishing assets—was threatening homicide. All this Charlie knew, and it pained him.

At least, he *thought* that was what pained him. On the other hand, he'd been drinking two cases of Diet Pepsi a week; that could have something to do with it. And there was the pressure here at the firm, with the old man leaning on him to clear up personally some of the backlogged caseload. That uranium suit in New Mexico was getting messy, for instance; he'd have to figure out a way to cope with it, but not now, not with the proxy fights and takeovers and leveraged buy-outs stacked up past the window ledge in his office. He needed time. He needed to concentrate. He needed more Pepsi. It was three in the morning, and there was so much to do. For the past couple of hours he'd been barking letters into his Dictaphone and simultaneously, through the network of speakerphones, riding herd over those few eager-beaver associates he'd managed to rope into an all-nighter. They weren't such bad kids, either. That pretty Yalie with the flat chest was holed up at her desk, combing depositions. Chicago was in the library. And Stanford—where was Stanford? Had he sent him down for more soda?

They were good kids, all of them. You had to treat them well, of course, to get their best work. That's what separated Charlie from a clod like Webber. Sensitivity. Knowing how hard to push, when to let go. That was the secret. He was loud, he was tough, he could at times be brutal—but they knew that underneath he had a heart. He was not some goyish cold fish like Walter Todd, with the elegant suits and manicured nails. Charlie checked his own nails and laughed out loud. Filthy! Uncouth! And so what! It was he—Charlie—pulling in the plum clients, handling the mergers, running the Management Committee. Fat Charlie! Loud Charlie! Lord Charlie!

No, he wasn't crazy. He pushed back his chair and, heels resting on the corner of the imposing walnut desk, crossed his thick legs. Below him slept the darkened city: quiet, tame, not even putting up a fight. He was not in such bad shape, after all. Because he knew what he wanted, and nothing, he thought, stood up to you when you knew what you wanted. And it had long been his business, his obsession, to know. It went way back, to the battles he'd wage on the asphalt playlot of P.S. 111, to the grubby little apartment over the deli on Tenth Avenue, with his old man so feeble he could hardly pound in a nail or fix a fuse. Charlie caught his own reflection in the dark glass of the window. He saw nothing in it of that veiny little Old World dreamer, and that white rice-paper skin, those moist black ineffectual eyes. And good riddance. He had erased him, supplanted him. He had made himself into his own father, become a man of force. He had grabbed hold of the reins and pulled himself up, high up, toward the splintered light and the thin heady air on the upper floors of Nassau Street. Here. Among the tallest of the spires. With the stars, the stars so close he could practically scrape them with his knuckles. He was doing fine, he thought. In fact, he was doing terribly, terribly well.

Okay, you gave up certain things. He did not have a great number of friends, for instance. Hell, he did not even have a *small* number. But never mind. You made your choices and you tried not to complain. You played the hand you were dealt. You made your bed and you slept—

But the phrase stuck and turned sour in his throat. It had an unwholesome sound to it. It sounded, actually, very much like something Lorraine had said, in anger, the night before. What had set her off? Oh, yes. She had said it because they had been having an argument. Because, before their argument, he had been writhing in bed, unable to sleep, his heart—that sturdy, albeit overworked, warrior—pounding out tribal rhythms in his chest, as though to make clear to all sides the lines of battle: duty to the north, desire to the south, and everything between a demilitarized zone of suffering. Yes, yes, that was it. She had said it because he, Charlie Goldwyn, fifty-seven years old and two hundred eighty-one pounds in his Jockey shorts, wanted to have an affair.

Because of the kind of man he was, he could not hide this simple fact from himself. Nor could he stop, once the verdict was in, from blurting out the whole thing to his wife. So be it. He had long known that the sole common denominator in the various equations of his life was a lack of self-control; it had made him, for better or worse, what he was. Indeed, he had come to regard this aspect of himself almost fondly, the way a young boy might regard a shaggy, omnivorous sheepdog even as it chews up his best tennis shoes. But just what was it chewing up now?

"Thirty-four *years*, Charlie. You want me to feel sympathy?"

Lorraine, dry-eyed, laughed a short laugh. They had been sitting up in bed—*their* bed—with the bed-table lamp on, the one they'd bought together on Canal Street in 1965. Charlie, naked, covered only by a sheet, reached out to finger the strap of his wife's nightgown, an old habit. She smelled good, familiar; a little more meat on her bones, she'd be a knockout, even at her age. Plus, he loved her: That should count for something. Only the geography of it was all wrong. The sun of affection still warmed him in the north, but below the Mason-Dixon line in his chest winter had set in, and the clouds stretched, gray and ominous and unbroken, as far as he could see. Still, he did not want to cause pain. Not to her, and certainly not to himself.

"Don't get excited," he said, though it was he himself who was flustered. "I'm just telling you what's on my mind. A fantasy, they call it. I haven't done anything yet."

"How decent of you."

"The President of the United States has fantasies of this nature. I read about it in a magazine."

"Please, spare me. You didn't even vote for him. You're not even a Democrat anymore. That's how far gone you are."

He sat up straight against the headboard, to indicate to them both that he was in earnest. "Don't they mention mid-life crisis down at the New School?"

"Charlie," she said, and almost smiled, "you went through your mid-life crisis ten years ago."

"I did?" For a moment he had no idea what she was talking about; then, when he remembered, he grew irate, indignant; feeling himself, for a change, in the right. "That was a prostate infection. I was in the hospital. Besides, Ellen had just gone off to college. Leaving the nest—a difficult thing for all concerned. You said so yourself."

"All right. Don't shout at me."

"Shout? I don't shout. I just want the record clear. Is that so terrible? Am I such a terrible person?"

He hated her for the way she kept him waiting for an answer. It's sunny and dry in New Mexico, he thought to himself. He could have a garden, raise cactus, horses. . . . There was no telling the things he could raise.

"Let's go to sleep now, Charlie," Lorraine said eventually. "We'll talk tomorrow."

"I love you, Lorraine. That's the goddamned truth."

"Tell me tomorrow, honey, okay?" She reached for the lamp, flicked it off. The sight of her performing this simple ritual filled him with anxiety.

"I'm turning to liquid. I swear to God. My whole system's going to pieces."

"Go to sleep," urged Lorraine, and she twisted under the covers into a curl, her back to him.

But he hadn't gone to sleep, of course. Instead he'd turned over and over, like a rotisserie chicken, his back aching, his stomach rumbling from all the carbonation, and tried to bring back into focus the chimera that was tempting him to gut the machinery of his life.

Lucy. Loo-see.

Two hours in the Museum of Modern Art, surrounded by Picassos, Matisses, Kandinskys—a man could be expected to feel an aesthetic thrill, he told himself, even if he could not, an hour later, remember a single piece he'd seen. Except for one: a little brown cubist number, with cheekbones you could cut your finger on, and a mane of caviar-black hair which gave off an electrical charge when he brushed against it. And brush he had, repeatedly, unable to hold himself back. It was all he could do, in the end, to keep from shouting, right there in the middle of the sculpture garden: I am in the grip of something! Something larger than I am! Something sweet and merciless and strange!

But he hadn't shouted. Had hardly even spoken, except to mumble what few wisps of appreciation for modern art he'd managed to pick up from a lifetime spent accompanying Lorraine to openings. In a way, though, they hadn't really *had* to talk. They hadn't even had to look at each other. Because it was right there in front of them, plain as day. They fit. There was a charge between them. They complemented each other perfectly. Big, small; light, dark; young, well . . . middle-aged. Like ying and yan. Or wait—yin and yang? He'd have to remember to ask Lorraine which was which.

Whoops. Okay, he'd leave Lorraine out of it. He'd talk to Hesh, get his advice. A sensible young man, even if he lacked energy. Still, he was young, with-it; he'd understand. Because it was important to separate the issues here. This was not, in his opinion, Fidelity v. License. This was more complex, requiring a more subtle approach. Think of the depositions he could take on this one—Dante, Shakespeare, D. H. Lawrence, John O'Hara. The library—the *public* library—was full of them. And look at the precedents: in New York State alone, a list as long as the phone book! Don't talk to me about binding contracts or good-faith agreements, Your Honor. Let the jury decide. They're human too; they have a nose for the complexities. The worst, the very worst they could rule is . . .

That word again. No, he was not insane. Just excitable. Possibly high-strung. Occasionally maybe even teetering over into the neurotic. Like when he'd started to cry in the elevator on the way back to her hotel room. That, he recalled with a shudder, was a little neurotic. Or when he stole those stockings from her drawer, slipping them into his briefcase while she was in the bathroom—okay, *more* neurotic. And then, after she'd already closed the door and said good night, after her wistful, tentative glance as he retreated, in some agony, backward down the corridor, heels dragging friction from the carpet, the way he'd raced back and begun to croon—was it "Good Night, Sweetheart"?—through that closed and impeccably solid door . . . Oh God, he *was* crazy! A nut case! A big, stupid, clumsy oaf chasing a firefly! And for *this* he was planning to abandon the woman sleeping so evenly, so reliably, beside him? They should send him to Bellevue!

But that was last night's anxiety. Now he was alone, in his office on the fortieth floor, busy in a world of clear causes and predictable effects. He was, after all, a man of some influence, one who was able to arrange the surrounding clutter into a shape that worked in his interests. He was supervising a load of over thirty cases, he had associates combing the entire Federal Supplement and all fifty titles of the Annotated U.S. Code, he had spent half an hour that morning on the phone with an under secretary of state, whom he now knew firsthand to be a boob. . . . Charlie Goldwyn could do whatever the hell he wanted. And right now he wanted to court Lucy Johnson.

The same Lucy Johnson who was, at that very moment, on the red-eye back to Albuquerque.

And then he heard a knock on the door, and saw Herschel Freeman standing there with a tired, uncertain look on his face, as though he had just walked the length of Manhattan in the middle of the night—and Charlie Goldwyn heard the thunderclap of an idea. "Come on in, Heshie, for Christ's sake. Have a Pepsi."

"What are you doing here, Charlie?"

"Working. What's it look like?"

Freeman remained in the doorway, that same abstracted look on his face. Jesus, he was a self-absorbed person, Charlie decided. You could hardly talk to him half the time. "And you? What brings you in? Can't sleep?"

"You might say that. I've been walking."

"Walking to or walking from?"

It was just a casual remark, something to pass the time, but Hesh seemed to think he'd meant something subtle by it. He took his time thinking it over, and finally, dropping into a chair, said, "I'm not really sure."

"I know what you mean," said Charlie sympathetically. But he didn't. Nor did he really think he wanted to. "So tell me, how's Walker? Under control?"

"Sure," Hesh said vaguely. "No problem."

Charlie nodded. "Good, good. Think that paralegal of yours could finish it up without you?"

"I suppose so. It depends on whether they'll settle. I can't very well send a paralegal into court, can I?"

"Of course you can't. Don't be so crabby. What's the matter with you tonight, anyway? Wife problems?"

Freeman winced. Too late, Charlie remembered the man was separated. Well, it wasn't *his* fault. "Okay, new subject. How'd you like to take a little trip with Uncle Charlie?"

The younger man smiled for the first time, as though at a private joke. "I don't think so. Thanks, anyway."

"Aren't you even curious where?"

"No."

"No?"

"Okay," Hesh said wearily. "Where?"

"New Mexico. Land of Enchantment."

Hesh stirred. When he spoke, his eyes were smaller, harder. "Oh? A business trip, is it?"

Charlie cursed himself for his transparency, his damnable blurting. To compensate, he straightened in his chair and looked angry. "Of course, business. Where are we right now, Bermuda? What kind of person do you take me for?"

"I don't know. What kind of person are you?"

The two men's eyes locked and held steady. Charlie warned himself to

78

stay calm. It was late. Not long ago, Freeman's wife had left him. Plus there was that poker game the week before. Charlie knew he hadn't behaved well that night, had been abusive and childish. But wait—whom was he feeling so apologetic toward? This punk? This *associate,* with the lazy manner and ironic remarks? Now Charlie was angry, but for real this time. "I'm a senior partner. That's the kind of person I am."

"Meaning what exactly?"

"You went to Harvard. Figure it out."

"Charlie, don't do this. I'm tired. I'm real tired. I've got a lot on my mind. Let's just say, for personal reasons I'd rather not go."

Charlie laughed. "You got girl problems, Heshie? Join the rest of the race. We're all miserable swine, when you look close. Flailing away in the mud, eh?" He was aiming for jovial heartiness here, but it wasn't working any better than before—Freeman glared at him with uncharacteristic intensity. Okay, he counseled himself. Ease up. Keep it friendly. Softer. "You don't *have* to come, of course. I can always take Fitzie, or Hugh. . . ."

"Good idea. They know more about mineral rights, anyway. Didn't Fitz work on that Westinghouse suit?"

"Sure," Charlie agreed, tossing his wrist.

"Or how about Marge Keller. She's the best litigator you've got—you told me so yourself. And she wears those fetching black stockings. I'd say she's the perfect choice."

"Perfect, huh?"

"Absolutely."

Charlie lit a cigar and leaned back, thinking: You act powerful, you feel powerful; you feel powerful, others sense it—incremental, artificial change becomes actual, qualitative. This was the way it worked. You run the self like a business. You've got to advertise the product. "You know, Heshie," he said, "I'm beginning to think you don't have much respect for your own abilities. What kind of attitude is that for a prospective partner?"

"Charlie," said Hesh. "I'd like to point out a couple of things you're overlooking. One, I've been doing nothing but copyright law for the last year and a half. Two, I've been doing it *well,* which may not count for much around here, but it makes me feel a little better at night when I go back to Brooklyn. Three, I know none of the background on this case. Four, if I *did* know it, I'd undoubtedly be on the side of the plaintiffs—"

"Don't play the man of conscience, Hesh. It's three in the morning and I'm full of Pepsi. I might throw up."

"All I'm saying is, I'm not right for the job."

Charlie lifted his cigar from his mouth and leaned forward. "Are you finished?"

The other man was gazing thoughtfully at the portrait of Pinchas Lem above Charlie's head when he answered. "Just about. I'm just about finished."

"Good. Now let me point out a few things *you're* ignoring, my friend. One, I'm flying to New Mexico on Monday. It's a big case, it could get out of control out there, and it needs the handling of someone who knows hardball. Two. I have some personal matters to attend to, which might distract me at times. So three. I need someone there I can talk to. Fitzie's no help—I think the only place he gets hard is the shower at the Y, if you know what I mean."

"Don't be ridiculous. He's—"

"Let me finish. We're speaking frankly, yes? Okay. Frankly, Hugh is Walter Todd's boy. They're very chummy, and I won't take a chance. And Keller—Keller's terrific. Hardworking, good personality. Gotta love her. But she's got a *cunt*, know what I'm saying? I won't be able to talk to her. Hell, I won't be able to have a *drink* with her. I know myself, Heshie. I'm a man needs to talk. I'm going through a little crisis here. But I'm going to come through, dammit, and you're going to help me. Because if you don't we both know what's—what're we up to?—four."

"Let me guess. I get a big promotion and fat raise, and we all take a house together in the Hamptons."

"Wise guy." Charlie snorted. "Look, this is in your interests too. Change of scenery, change of luck. You gotta learn to take risks, Heshie. Otherwise you're just treading water."

A silence welled up, as each man digested this last statement in his own fashion. Above them, Pinchas Lem hovered, jowly and alert, gazing at the opposite wall with a look of unmitigated ill humor. It was the look he'd trained on witnesses in cross-examination; it was also the look he'd trained on his protégés, particularly those, like Charlie Goldwyn, whom he'd favored. He had been a nasty old buzzard, and an excellent mentor, Charlie remembered, and he suffered a moment's temptation to fly out to Maui and see him, listen to his war stories the way he used to, lay out his own problems, and be forgiven. Only, he felt so tired all of a sudden. . . .

After two sleepless nights, with nothing in his system but chemicals and tobacco, Charlie Goldwyn was being hit by wave after wave of exhaustion. He felt no desire to continue the conversation; he was not, in truth, even certain anymore that *he* wanted to go to New Mexico. With the side of his hand, he rubbed one fleshy cheek, feeling the stubble. His lids drooped. Christ, he was a mess. A fat, lonely mess. Abruptly a warmth rose in his chest toward Hesh Freeman, sprawled brokenly across the chair on the other side of the desk. The poor guy's wife had left him. Wasn't that an awful thing? And yet he was always so nice to Charlie, listening to his troubles, keeping him company at lunch, taking him seriously. Why not give the guy a break? Throw the case on Fitz. Stick around and forget the whole thing. A silly exercise in infatuation. They should teach a course in it, he thought, at the New School: Warding Off Death 101. Hell, he'd buy some stroke magazines, or lose some weight, maybe join a gym. . . . There were all sorts of things he could do.

But Hesh was getting to his feet. What was that he was saying? ". . . need a few days, at least, to wrap things up."

He would go along. It had been inevitable. Just as it had been inevitable that he would fold up his cards in poker. Incremental, artificial change becomes actual, qualitative. Assumed power becomes lived power. That was the nature of the sport.

But now, wait a minute. Because the funny thing was, he himself was not entirely sure it *was* a good idea, or that he even still *wanted* to go, that he could still *get* himself to go.

". . . Tuesday, Wednesday, more like it. That soon enough for you, Charlie? Charlie?"

Too late, too late. But he could still explain, couldn't he? A whim, a joke, an insomniacal discussion, entirely hypothetical; you shouldn't be so literal, you shouldn't necessarily think he *meant* it, of course, it was just a game between friends, like poker, or racquetball, or litigation. He should say something, he should really say something right now, he only had to open his mouth. And his eyes too, of course, he really should open his . . .

"You son of a bitch," he heard, but the voice was far away, underwater maybe, and then he was alone.

Chapter 9

"How nice."

These two words, and only these two words, constituted my wife Joanne's response to the news of my impending trip. Their brevity was compensated for by the eloquence of her inflection, which was as flat and dark as tar. Unfortunately, I was calling from my apartment on an aimless Sunday afternoon, and I'd had it in mind, when dialing the number, that there might be some sympathy in store for me at the other end of the line. "It means I'll miss the next couple of Little League games, at least."

"Don't worry about it," she said, as before.

"I'm not worried about it. I'm just telling you."

"Okay. You've told me."

"You know, Joanne, sometimes—like right now, for instance—I have a hard time believing we're really adults."

This time when she replied, some of the edge had softened. "I know you do, Hesh. Maybe that's the difference between us."

"Score one for you."

"Please. It was nothing. Had my eyes closed, in fact."

I gripped the phone a little harder. "So who'll be coming to the games, you or your friend?"

"His name is Alan. Alan Copeland. And you'll be relieved to know that Solly adores him. They're becoming very close."

I do not appreciate gross insensitivity in anyone, so I allowed a measure of bitterness into my response. "Sweet of you to tell me."

"I'm just telling you," she mimicked. And then, "Oh, Hesh. I'm being a bitch. Every time we talk, I turn into a bitch. Let's stop, okay?"

"Stop talking?"

"Stop bitching."

"Okay."

In the wake of this treaty, there seemed, for a moment, nothing further to say. Finally, Joanne made the effort. "You don't sound so great. Are you okay? Do you miss me?"

"No and yes. In that order."

"I'm sorry."

"About which one?"

"Hesh . . ." She sounded pained, though whether from annoyance or something else, I couldn't determine. "I think I should give you over to Solly. Agreed?"

I could hear her calling Solly to come in from the backyard, making a familiar song out of the syllables, repeating it for the sheer pleasure of its melody.

The next voice on the line, however, was hers again. "My God, Hesh, will you *see* her? I didn't . . . it didn't even register—where you were going. What are you going to do?"

"I'm not sure, Jo. It'll be about an hour's drive, I think. Probably I'll—"

Off the line, Solly clamored for attention. "Is that Daddy?" I heard him ask.

"Sweetie, be quiet for a sec. Yes, it's Daddy." Then, to me, "I'm sorry. What were you saying?" Then, to him again, "I said be *quiet!*"

"I said I wasn't sure. I don't know if I can handle it right now."

"Hesh, it's been *years.*"

I didn't say anything. Now that I had the full weight of her concern, I was no longer sure I wanted it. But I liked the feeling of sitting there, staring out the window at the gray East River and listening to her voice.

"Well, do me a favor," she said. "If you get out there and for some reason you need to talk or whatever, call me, okay? I mean it. Tell me you'll call me and for once you won't try to be all proud and self-possessed. Tell me."

But there are so many things I *already* want to tell you, I thought to myself. So many fragments you get used to sharing at odd moments of a life together; so many scenes, unfoldings of plot or character that, having sat through much of Act One in adjoining seats, you could be counted on to understand. I thought of someone I'd run into recently at a movie, of a letter I'd received from a college friend, of the Eugene McCarthy button that had turned up on the floor of my closet. I thought of the hard, knobby, adolescent firmness of her breasts. Of—

"Still there, Hesh?"

"I'll call you," I said.

"Well, good. Then here's Solly. And have a good trip." I could hear Solly ask, "Where's he *going?*" and her reply: "Ask him yourself."

And then his voice, breathy and querulous on the line: "Where you *going?*"

"What happened to Hi, Daddy?"

Murderous silence. Finally, in a small, constricted whisper: "Hi, Daddy."

"Is that Hi, Daddy as in Hi, Daddy, numero uno on my personal hit parade?" Oh God, I thought, listen to *this*.

"Mom!" I heard him complain. "He won't tell me where he's *going!*"

"Okay, okay. I'm going out west. New Mexico."

"On purpose?"

It was one of his favorite questions, and it sounded, as always, charged with the metaphysical. "Uh huh," I said.

"Coming back?"

"Uh huh. We still have that ball game we're going to, remember?"

"Okay."

"I'll bring you back a present, okay?"

"Okay." After a moment, "What present?"

"I don't know, pal. Something great, though. Maybe something made by Indians. There are a lot of them out there, you know. Thousands."

The vagueness of this number somehow did not impress him. Or else he was in one of those moods when the world seemed entirely too serious a place for someone to address him as though he were a child. "How many thousands, exactly?" he asked.

Unfortunately, numero uno on his personal hit parade did not know the answer to that question, and told him so. And then this person began to sound a little funny on the telephone, like he'd caught a bad cold, or like a swallow of milk had gone down the wrong way. After a moment, the person said, "Solly? I think I have to go now, okay?"

"Okay."

The boy waited, but there was no click. Well, did he have to go or didn't he?

"Daddy?"

"I'm right here, pal."

In a whisper: "You gonna marry Mom?"

"I don't think so, Sol. We tried that already. Now we're going to try not being married. That way we'll see which we like better."

"Okay."

"Hang up the phone now, okay?"

"Okay," the boy said.

But in the end, it was not his job to hang up the phone, and so he didn't. He waited until there was a click on the other end, and then he listened to the drone on the line that followed, the way he'd listened that time at Sandy Hook back in August, when his father had brought a conch shell over to their blanket and told him that if he kept it to his ear long enough, he would be able to hear the ocean's roar. He had listened and listened, the boy remembered, and still he was not sure when what he was hearing was the ocean, and when it was everything else.

Just when I had begun to think my ability to please others had sprouted wings and taken off for good, I found myself face to face with the Willie Mays of pleasure, Arthur Gordon. It was Tuesday. Six days had passed since I had visited him and his wife in their hotel room. In that time he had been, he told me, extremely busy, which was why he had suggested that Abby have dinner with me the night before. It had been a quiet, unambitious evening his wife and I had spent, neither charged with sexual tension nor lacking in it, an evening of calm appraisal. For the most part we spoke of neutral subjects—politics, film, the law—and when the meal was finished we said good night without even a hand-shake. Which did not stop me from feeling now, as I watched Arthur sip a frozen margarita in a trendy Village restaurant, the slightest twinge of guilt. *We're all swine*, Charlie Goldwyn had declared, and I had few reasons to doubt he was right.

It was difficult, watching Arthur now, to imagine him asleep in the fetal position on the floor of his hotel room. In fact, it was difficult to imagine him asleep, period. His energy was prodigious, hypnotic. It created a crackling force field around our table—the waitresses fussed about, chatting and animated; the maître d' snapped his fingers; and young couples at the bar glanced over at us intermittently, wondering which movie or television show or rock group we might belong to. Arthur Gordon, I had to admit, had a certain style, a brisk ease. Even I was affected by it. The enervation he'd aroused in me at first was gone; in its place was the kind of amiability a man feels when he has let drop the compulsion to exert his own will in any particular direction. If there were forces out there determined to make me their plaything, then let them come, I figured. What was there to gain from obstinacy? Why not relax and enjoy the ride?

Arthur, interrupting his own monologue, gave me a suspicious look. "What is it with you? You seem different. Drunk? On one margarita?"

"It's just funny, that's all."

Immediately he looked pleased with me, as though I'd said something

85

enormously clever. "Yes, it *is* funny. This table, for instance. It's too small. Notice how the plates and glasses look huge on it. All to suggest an image of American abundance. A cornucopia."

"The food's lousy, though."

"Of course it's lousy. It's bland and overpriced. You look at the menu and see wild eclecticism, ethnic surprises. Then the food comes, and it's of a uniformly low quality. This is what keeps us from confusing the experience with traditional forms of eating, right? We have left functionality behind. That's the point. If you want functional, you go to a diner, or to someone's home. But this, this is spectacle. This is entertainment. Check out those people at the bar, for instance."

They were mostly young, in their twenties and early thirties, in suits and skirts, fledgling tans. As they sipped at drinks, their eyes roamed about the place ceaselessly; they seemed to be looking for clues to a puzzle. There was loud, frequent laughter.

"This is their night out," he said. "This is their culture. We're in their movie, delivering their dialogue, moving their props. Lean back and laugh. Spill your drink. Go ahead—it's in the script."

"It's just that you sound so delighted with it all."

"What should I do, weep? Stamp my feet? Of course it delights me. I have nothing but affection for dying civilizations. Spengler hit it right on the nose—as death comes after life, civilization is the inevitable destiny of culture. It's a wonderful time to be alive."

"If I were in a different mood," I said, "I'd say that sounds like the fashionable cynicism of a director of commercials."

"Ah." He blanched. "Possibly, possibly. But it doesn't stop there, you see. I'm trying to work *with* it. It's one thing to say the whole thing's a movie and throw up your hands. It's another to go ahead and made your own movie-*within*-the-movie. I'm not saying it changes the final outcome, of course. But it might."

"I don't see how."

"You're being naive, then," he said sharply. He pushed aside his plate and brought out what must have been his only pipe, tamping it calmly with his thumb. "Use your imagination for a moment. Think of a movie theater as a modern temple. There are a number of similarities, after all. It's grand; it's poorly lit. It relies on a certain acoustical resonance and certain flourishes of language and color for its impact. It features icons, which we worship. Brando. Cooper. Monroe."

"Worship is a strong word."

"Women killed themselves over James Dean. Or is killed too strong a word?"

I made no reply to this.

"Anyway, bear with me. I think of the experience as religious, you see, because it involves awe, displacement of ego, transcendence. A good movie, in my opinion, forms a *completeness* that envelops us. It puts us there inside of it, breathing inside of it, eating popcorn inside of it, whispering to our friends inside of it—living, in other words. But *what* are we living? The energies, the vocabulary of images—they aren't our own. We are subject at that point to the will and obsessions of the director. It's like we're trapped, chained within the perimeters *he's* chosen. We can't escape, either. We wouldn't even think to. Don't you get it? The movie is a construct so godlike we don't even experience it as a construct. We're shaped by it without knowing it *has* a shape. And so we're made happy."

He finished his margarita and signaled the waitress for two more. The candlelight flickered on his tinted glasses as he moved his weight back, crossing his legs at the knee.

"*Sieg heil,*" I said.

He smiled tolerantly. "I'm not saying it's a good thing, of course."

"You're not? I seem to be getting the wrong impression, then."

"Look," he said. "I'm just saying that this is the way power manifests itself today. Constructed forms. Look at architecture. No, better—look at information. Information shapes. For instance, who do you think invented the atom bomb?"

I didn't answer, and he didn't wait longer than a second before continuing.

"I ask that rhetorically, because I know all the conventional answers from my research. You could say Szilard. You could say Hahn and Meitner, the Curies. You could say Bohr, or Fermi, or Oppenheimer, or Bethe, or Teller. Or, more accurately, that all of them had a part in it. But you'd be wrong. I know who invented the atom bomb, and when, and how. One man."

Again I said nothing, merely waited for him to finish.

"H. G. Wells invented the atom bomb. In 1914. He wrote a novel called *The World Set Free*—a novel read, years later, by the aforementioned Szilard, not long before he worked out the idea of how to sustain a nuclear chain reaction. Now, where is the genesis? How do we trace it? We can't—it's underground, subliminal, windy like the *zeitgeist*. But that's my point. Information *shapes*. In subtle, and not so subtle, ways. That's why we're so obsessed with it now. Information theory. Information management. Information manipulation, coding, decoding, access, storage. That's where the money is, where the technology is. The best brains in the world work for who? Bell Labs. IBM. TRW. Those are the elites. Compared to those guys, the bureaucrats in Washington are lawn furniture." He paused, drew hard on the pipe, but it had gone out.

Instead of lighting it again, he laid it gently in the ashtray, so that none of the tobacco spilled from the charred bowl. His plate had been wiped clean. There was none of the spendthrift about Arthur Gordon. "There's no cynicism in this, Hesh. I've been looking into it since I was twenty-two, when I spent a summer writing ad copy in New York. My assignment, interestingly enough, was the Xerox campaign. Irony upon irony—writing copy about copy machines that would itself be copied by my boss in the cubicle down the hall, so he could keep his dull job. And where did *my* ideas come from?"

"You copied them."

"That's right. From other ads. Very quick of you."

"Lucky guess."

"Well, anyway, it was a bad scene. Very bad. But I tried to learn something from it, at least."

At that moment I grew bored with his earnestness, his pedantry; it seemed to me that I was being condescended to. "As opposed to me, for instance?"

He smiled coyly. "You tell me."

"Know what happens if I mishandle a case, Arthur? A firm goes under. People lose their jobs."

"Du Pont goes under? Westinghouse goes under? U.S. Steel goes under? Or do you mean the little people?"

"I mean that we have other clients too, who suffer real, direct consequences. It's not some entertainment factory and it's not sales. It demands intellectual rigor and a lot of hours. Really, if I've given you the impression I think it's all meaningless, that's only a mood I sometimes fall into. I'm not ashamed of what I do."

He brought his hands together and clapped quietly. Golfer's applause. "Bravo. I apologize for being so flippant. So tell me, why do you hate it so much?"

I was looking down into the streaks of color—browns and greens and reds—still left on my empty plate, when I replied, "Sometimes I wonder if it isn't just that I don't like to work, period."

"Bullshit. Work, the right work, is self-evidently good."

"That," I said, "sounds insufferably Protestant."

"Now, now," he said, and smiled a deliberate smile. "No name-calling."

At this point we both leaned back, stuffed with the meal and our own words. Around us silver clanged and conversations cross-hatched into indecipherability. A tray of four used champagne glasses toppled to the floor when someone on his way to the men's room bumped a waitress. Almost no one looked up.

Now that we were resting, it occurred to me once again that no mention had been made of the Gordons' documentary. Or had we in fact been discussing it all along?

"Hi there. Sorry. I got held up."

It was Abby Gordon, floating toward us in a sleeveless white dress, flipping the hair out of her eyes with the fingers of her right hand.

"You ate already, I see," she observed, sitting down at the table's third chair without looking directly at either one of us. She sounded disappointed.

"You told us to go ahead and eat without you," said Arthur, picking up his unlit pipe. "At least, that's what I remember you saying this morning."

"Did I? Oh, it doesn't matter." Settling in, she sat forward, a preoccupied smile on her face, and turned to me. "What have the two of you been talking about? Me, I hope?"

It took me a second to understand that I was being flirted with, by which time Arthur was already answering for me. "Of course you," he said. "What other subject is there?"

She dimpled on cue. In that dress, with her Mediterranean necklace and her air of languid good humor, Abby Gordon struck me for the first time as a dangerous woman. She seemed, in the course of a day's work, to have rearranged some internal decor to her own satisfaction, and the success had taken her into a comfortable looseness I hadn't noticed the previous night. Perhaps she had still been jet-lagged then. Or perhaps she was acting a bit now. But for whose benefit?

"My God, look at this place," she said, swiveling in her chair. "We're all going to wind up in *New York* magazine. How's the food?"

"Unspeakable," chirped Arthur contentedly. "But we managed to speak about it, anyway."

"Maybe we should go," I suggested.

"Do you really want to? I was hoping for another margarita, myself. How's that sound, Ab?"

"I'd like that. I'm not really hungry, anyway. I grabbed a bite at the library."

"How'd it go?"

"Wonderful. I dug up at least three new sources to try in—" She

89

stopped herself suddenly, and an embarrassed silence descended from the ceiling to oppress us all. "Sorry about that," she said, to no one in particular.

"We'll talk later," said Arthur, reaching over to pat her hand.

There was an awkward silence.

"I feel like a four-year-old," I said, "whose parents spell out the words so he won't understand they're talking about him."

Abby glanced quickly at Arthur, who seemed lost in contemplation of his napkin. Then she turned to me. "We just . . . we didn't want to keep bringing it up, Hesh," she said, rubbing a spot on the tablecloth between our plates. "We don't want to press you."

"That's right," Arthur echoed. "We don't want to press you."

"Look, I said I didn't want to get involved, and I meant it. That doesn't mean I need to be treated with kid gloves. I'm as curious as the next person. I really don't mind hearing about what you're doing."

I'd made myself sound a good deal more certain about this than I really felt, so I added, "Up to a point, that is."

Arthur Gordon treated me to another in his continuing series of "Ah"s. "And what does that mean?"

His chin moved toward me winningly. "Listen, Hesh, with all due respect. I like you. I mean, we both do. We've got a rapport here. I think we all sense that." His eyes fell from mine to a point closer to Abby, as though he were waiting for her to second him. But she didn't. "Only, you're a bit of an equivocator, know what I mean? With us, a project of this nature, 'up to a point' gets tricky. If we talk to you, we involve you. If we involve you, we'll want to ask you things. It's no good for us if you flit back and forth. It'll just divert us, throw us off. That's why we've been avoiding the subject entirely. You're a grown man, you know what kinds of things we're after. Why should we press? I don't want your cooperation under duress. I'd rather go it without you."

Abby sipped some water, shrinking into herself somewhat. "Why don't we change the subject?"

"It's too late," I said.

Arthur eyed me warily. "Why's it too late?"

And then I made my confession. "Because I'm going out there, that's why."

I have never been one for holding hands. My palms sweat heavily, for one thing, and for another I have long and erratically knuckled fingers— broken several times over in my high school football days—about which

I'm self-conscious. As a result, I'd made a choice fairly early in life to be hands-in-pockets when I go for a stroll, though in moments of intimacy or cold weather I am not above draping one arm around the shoulders of a female and hugging her into the warmth of my torso. Joanne had quickly grown disillusioned with the whole business, contenting herself on occasion with three fingers on the underside of my bicep; for the most part, however, we walked as two separately contained beings. Which I suppose, looking back, we were.

With Abby Gordon, though, I was holding hands. It hadn't been my idea in the first place, but then I didn't object to it, either. The real blame, I thought, should lie with Arthur, who had mysteriously taken his leave on our way out of the restaurant, with the explanation that he was dead tired. "Don't let me spoil things," he'd urged, flagging a cab. "You two have fun. Show her some of the sights, Hesh. Poor Ab's been working too hard."

Poor Ab, I thought, as we turned the corner onto Sullivan Street, did not seem very poor, or very tired, and from the way she directed our steps she knew the city at least as well as I did. But I let her lead me as she wished, through Washington Square Park, past NYU, and onto Bleecker Street, where we sat at a sidewalk café and drank cappuccinos among the college students and the people speaking in foreign tongues.

I took another good look at her. Her hair hung loose and was dark at the roots. Her eyes were hazel, with something black in them, and set fairly wide apart beneath her placid brow. She wore no makeup that I could see, and her only jewelry was a necklace from Majorca, a thin arrangement of beads and stones in dark colors that gave off no shine under the light from the streetlamp. Her expression was opaque; she kept the sort of time she was having to herself—except once, when something full and green leaped up to flare in her eyes as she took a bite of pastry. A moment later it was gone. She was no easy girl to read.

I told her so. She blushed, as if I'd paid her a compliment, and with the infusion of color her face seemed to take hold of its own beauty and put it on display. "That's funny. I've always thought of myself as terribly transparent. You're probably just out of practice."

I smiled at this, because she was right.

She brought her wrist up to stifle a yawn. "You're tired," I said. "I'll put you in a cab."

"No. I just need to walk. I need to keep moving. I only get tired," she said, "when I stay still."

"Me too, I think."

"Is that often?"

"Often enough," I said. I thought of the green light in Siskin's kitchen and found my limbs, even now, growing heavy. "Shall we?"

And then we were strolling again, the sidewalk maples playing hide-and-seek with the streetlights, the first balmy whiffs of June in the air, and Abby Gordon's cool fingers found my own. She squeezed. Immediately I felt transported to a simpler time, a time so simple, I knew, that the source could not be experience but only some hopeful desire, a time of unambiguous allegiances and burgeoning possibilities, when the touch of another's flesh seemed as open-ended and mysterious as the stars. I did not know any longer whether there had ever been such a time for me, or whether there ever could be. When you came right down to it, I did not know very many things about myself at all. But I knew that the touch of Abby Gordon's hand made me wobbly.

On Hudson, we turned and walked toward the river. The sun had long since set, but the haze over Jersey still held its purple hue, the last gasps of twilight. Seeing it, Abby stopped, let go of my hand, and gave out a small groan of recognition. "Oh, how lovely."

"It's only Hoboken," I said.

"I know that," she said. "It's lovely anyway. And it's not nice, you know, to trample on a girl's enthusiasms."

"Sorry. Like you said, I must be out of practice."

She turned and, lightly, touched my jacket. "Hey, I was only teasing. Besides, you're right. I was being breathless. I've probably had too much to drink."

"You only had one," I reminded her. And myself.

"For me, that's enough. But you must think I'm a terrible lush. Every time you see me I've been giddy."

"I wondered," I said, "if that was just from drinking."

She made her little shrug, frowning, her bare arms veined by shadows of a wire fence. Above us, the moon smeared against a stray cloud.

"Don't play with me, Hesh," she said after a while, her eyes on the river.

"I could say the same to you."

"Then why didn't you?"

"Because I think I like it."

I hadn't intended to say that; I hadn't intended, in fact, to say anything. The blood crowded into my face, and I lowered my head, letting the exchange dangle in the air between us. Again I had been guilty of equivocating, it seemed. I did not *think* I liked it; I *knew* I liked it. Perhaps it was just the idea that she—and, it seemed likely, her husband—obviously *wanted* me to like it that gave me pause. I did not mind being led by the hand, but I had no wish to be led by the nose.

In any case, I felt impelled to change the subject. "You know, I used to dabble in writing myself, once upon a time."

She brightened. "Really? You didn't say anything. Poetry?"

"Fiction, I'm afraid."

"I bet you were very good."

"You'd lose. Actually, I found that I had very little to say."

"I don't believe that. Everybody has things to say. Some are too critical and unforgiving of that side of themselves, that's all. It blocks them up. I know: I'm the same way." She looked off toward Jersey again, musing. For a moment I was certain that the conversation had turned back to her, that we had just touched upon a yawning emptiness inside her that would have to be addressed right then; but whatever it was, she mastered it quickly and turned back to me. "Is that why you went to law school? Because you gave up writing?"

I nodded. "It was 1969. I'd already spent seven years in college."

"Seven years?"

"It took me a while," I said, "to settle on a major. By the end I was sick of dodging, sick of odd jobs, sick of novels. I wanted the freedom to do what I wanted."

"And once you had it?"

"Guess."

"I don't have to guess. It's the oldest story in the world."

"I suppose it is," I said.

We crossed the street and turned our backs to the river and to the moon, which cast its pale light upon it. I put my hands in my pockets, found them empty, and felt the shoulders of my jacket stretching from the weight. I decided that the conversation must be over; that, finally, whatever had been exchanged between us had been, in her eyes, fairly banal. Perhaps in my eyes too. I slowed a step, ready to put her in a cab and get out of there, when that hand of hers, for the second time, snaked its way into my own. "Your father," she said, "was a handsome man. You have the same eyes. So dark they almost make you nervous."

"My mother would agree, I'm afraid."

"It's all very interesting, you know. This research we're doing. Can I say that?"

"You can say that."

"I mean, the facts are so powerful, just by themselves. There are so many ironies. For instance, there's the fact that Heisenberg—you know who Heisenberg was?"

I nodded.

"Well, evidently he and Niels Bohr were at a conference in Copenhagen back in—was it 1941? Anyway, they went for a walk together, and Heisenberg tried to assure Bohr that the Germans *didn't* have the bomb, that they weren't even close. Only, there was a misunderstanding. Bohr thought he meant they *did* have the bomb, or were en route to it, at least, and when he came back and reported this, it gave momentum to the whole enterprise. I mean, imagine: If that message had been communicated correctly, everything might have been different."

"That's very interesting," I said.

"And there's what happened to Oppenheimer, those terrible hearings when they took his clearance away, and there's that spy business with that man Klaus Fuchs, which was connected to the Rosenbergs, and oh, yes, there's what I was reading today, how they tested the first hydrogen bomb in the same spot, the *exact* same spot, where the *Pequod* went down in *Moby Dick*."

"No kidding," I said.

Her hand tightened in mine. "Remember that description, 'O trebly hooped and welded hip of power'? Well, it's remarkably close, isn't it, to the logo for atomic energy? The three hoops, welded? I got chills. It almost makes you believe in prophecy, doesn't it?"

"Yes, it almost does."

"Oh, and"—she was clutching my hand, carried away by her discoveries—"and guess what they called the computer. That first one, the one they designed to help produce the hydrogen bomb. Guess."

"I couldn't possibly."

"Oh, try," she urged.

"Okay then." I furrowed my brow. "Let's see. MANIAC?"

She stopped in her tracks, appalled; it was the first time, I think, I'd seen her shaken up, and the observation excited me. "So you *do* know! You know *all* of this! You're just playing with me!"

And then I found that I was shouting, "Of course I know, dammit! You think a few days in the library collecting trivia is what the thing is about? You think that's all there is to it?" A bitter taste was in my throat, of old and soured coffee. I blamed Abby Gordon for it, and for a couple of other things besides. "And for the record, if you really don't want me to play with you, then stop standing so close, stop holding my hand, stop making me—"

"Fine," she announced, stepping back and away. "I will."

"Fine," I echoed. "Then let's get the hell out of here."

But it wasn't fine, not even close to fine, and the here I wanted to get

out of referred less to Sheridan Square than it did to a general condition
that, in the charged silence that now overcame us, was only intensifying.
This would never work. In less than a week, I'd be in New Mexico with
Charlie Goldwyn, and the Gordons would be in Los Alamos and vicinity
for interviews and landscape shooting. We were bound to see each other;
I'd as much as promised it that evening.

But I'd never pull it off, not at this rate. Whatever quantity of on-again,
off-again flirtation with Abby Gordon I had it in me to perform, I doubted
it was very much more than I'd performed already.

I stepped out onto Seventh Avenue, waving my arm like a semaphore.
I'd put her in a cab and be rid of her. If we couldn't get along when we
met up in the Southwest, I'd deal with it then. Meanwhile, find a cab. Go
back to Brooklyn and forget about it. She bit her nails. She flirted with
strange men. She had small breasts. She was married. She was full of
despairs I couldn't even guess at. Only, where were all the cabs?

"Hesh," she called from the sidewalk.

I pretended that I couldn't hear her, that the city's noises had
swallowed hers up completely.

"Hesh, listen to me. I'm a mess just now. I'm in the air, really. . . ."

Hold on, I thought.

"Hesh."

This time I turned. Her mouth was open but she wasn't speaking, and
her brow had hatched lines of worry so deep it seemed possible to lose
things in them. At the sight of her framed against a rusting metal fence—
her long olive face in the dim light, her shoulders bent in, her elbows
collapsed against her ribs, her entire body threatening to close upon itself
like a folding chair—a mew of desire rose up from the place where the
fluids tossed inside me. I was helpless to stop it; I could only muffle it a
bit on its way out, as it moved to bridge the ten feet that separated us. I
waited, then began to walk toward her determinedly. The sound had
been naked, unmistakable. She would turn away and that would be the
end of it.

But she held her ground. And looked miserable. And when she spoke,
her voice was as low as a cough. "Remember what you said the other
night? Well, it's not true. People don't do what they want. At least you and
I don't. At least not . . ."

And then, as though what we were doing followed inevitably from what
we were saying, as though our purposes were as clear as day, as though
we were the kind of people for whom decisions like this were perfectly
commonplace, we leaned into each other and kissed. She was a tall
woman and so it required relatively little in the way of choreography.

People continued to thread around us on the sidewalk, taking no special notice; it was the Village, after all. And the kiss lasted no more than a moment. It almost didn't happen, it was so brief and uncomplicated. In a way, it had felt more intimate to be holding hands.

"At least," I said as I released her, "we seem to *know* what we want."

"Oh?" She touched her hand to her neck and looked at me with something very like disappointment. "Is that such a giant step?"

"Knowledge is power, Abby."

She shook her head; beneath the fine swaying curtains of her hair, her mouth turned flat at the corners. "Beware the chain of monsters," she said, cryptically.

"Am I being insulted?"

For a moment she looked bewildered, as though we were as inexorably strange to each other as two alien species. I tried to draw back, but her fingers held the sleeve of my jacket. "No, no," she said. "It's from Valéry. 'Every man drags after him a chain of monsters . . .' There's more, but I can't remember it now. I have it written down somewhere. I do that sometimes, write things down. It keeps me sane."

"Are you sane right now?"

She let her breath out slowly. "I'm afraid so."

"Then whose monsters are you worried about, mine or yours?"

We let go of each other at approximately the same time.

"All of them," she said evenly. "Every goddamn one."

Part II

LAND OF ENCHANTMENT

Chapter 10

March 1944: The Mouth of the Furnace

Eli Friedmann cannot sleep, though he seems to be forever lying down. At night the winds blow incessantly—icy blasts of dry air, which seem to suck the life from the earth itself—sending dust clouds whirling over the Mesa like dervishes. Sirens bellow and wail. It has been a long, severe winter, and as usual, the water supply has not been able to cope with demand. Two months ago his lab caught fire. If Max Baker hadn't seen the flames from his dormitory window, all their work—minor, even peripheral as it might be—would have turned to ash. Of course, as Baker reminded him, the work was being duplicated elsewhere. If not their implosive lens, somebody else's. What was the difference, in the end, with matter so ripe and eager to turn to ash, anyway?

The sweat trickles and pools beneath his armpits, teasing his skin where it is most sensitive. Eli pulls back the sheet with a groan. They keep these apartments too hot. Too much coal in the furnace. He has to speak to the fireman about it. Maybe he should go do that right now, he thinks—get up, put on his slippers, and go downstairs. It is the right thing to do, under the circumstances.

Quietly, so as not to wake his sleeping wife, he struggles to his feet. Her mouth open on the pillow, facing him, she breathes shallowly, noiselessly, as though unwilling to impose herself on the fragile silence of their shared bed. As he looks down at her, something tightens in his chest. He sees she is afraid. She is afraid even now. He has only to say boo and she'll be up, dressed, packed, and on her way back to New York in an instant.

And then the hardness drains away and leaves a residue of guilt. He has done everything wrong. He has brought her to this place, he has given her a child, and now, as part of some irreversible process he does not as yet understand, he has abandoned her.

Or has he?

Hasn't she *let* herself be abandoned? Hasn't she, in fact, *sought out* abandonment? Her affinity for loneliness is incredible—she works at it, he's sure, as hard as he works at his lens, and with better results. He turns to take in the bare, functionally furnished apartment, which looks stark and inhospitable in the malignant vapors of night. This, he thinks, is *her* Tech Area, her place to tinker and refine her sense of dread, calculate the depths and shapes of her innumerable longings. It's all wrong. It's unfair. He is twenty-five years old, his career star is rising, and he has a wife who is afraid of him.

She murmurs softly, sleep-fogged. Oh, yes, he thinks, I fear you too. How many weeks has it been since they have risen from bed at the same hour? For how long has he been the first into the kitchen, scrambling eggs and tending as best he can to the baby? He is on the run, and he knows it. Not from her lovemaking, exactly (though, if he is to be honest with himself, he has to admit that the raw insistence of her desire, her awful neediness, her desperation to fill herself with his seed, as though to populate the barren planet she carries inside her, has a hand in driving him away, in making him feel pinched and miserly with his own flesh). But the reflex that sends him scrambling all those eggs and changing all those diapers is less of the body than of the will. He does not—*cannot*—listen to her dreams. A man is beset by enough demons in the course of a night; where does it say in the marriage contract that he must contend with those of his wife too? Especially when they are so profuse, so shadowy, so unforgiving?

When he was younger, when he had more energy, when she herself seemed more capable of mastering her emotions—then it was different. They'd lie awake side by side as the sun laced through the curtains, and she would recall her dreams, and together they would make connections to recognizable phenomena, ferry rides to the opposite shore. Occasionally her eyes would go slick with tears; more often, confession led to intimacy, intimacy to passion, and their joined bodies spiraled through the jumble of sheets and blankets. But that was before.

Now when she wakes she is already crying, or crying out, or pummeling the pillow with her small fists, her face gone bleary and white, her dark hair bunched and gnarled; already fighting, already losing, already negotiating the terms of surrender. He looks at her now with some surrender of his own. What is he to do in the face of such discontent? What note has not already been played, what drum not pounded, in this endless fugue of unhappiness? He never promised her happiness! No one has the right to expect it! He only promised to love her! Love her . . . Has he done even that?

He flees the bedroom, pulling a cold towel around his waist, and goes into the bathroom to take a shower. The wood floor is littered with laundry; the acrid smell of diapers assaults him. From the baby's room, a cough. He closes the door. There is a faint gurgling from the pipes, then a short trickle of warm water, then nothing. The head of the shower exhales dryly.

Eli Friedmann moans. In his frustration, his sense of things going beyond his endurance, his contempt for his own limits, he lets the towel fall from his hips and reaches down to yank at the one thing left in his narrowed world that will stay still for him, yanks so hard he doesn't know at first whether the sounds escaping his constricted throat are of pleasure or pain, are material or spiritual. He doesn't know. He doesn't know. There is so much, it occurs to him, that he doesn't know. It is difficult work, all of it, and it's hard, so hard to know. . . .

A drop escapes him. A leakage.

Five percent will work. Better to make it three. Safer.

He keeps going, rocking back and forth, heel to toe. Cut down on the leakage. Three percent, tops. Maybe two. The detonators must fire symmetrically. It must be exact.

He hears something behind the door. Ruthie?

A blur of white. A low cough.

Ruthie?

Implosion.

When he is finished, he pulls on the pants and shirt he wore the day before and goes into the baby's room. He can hear, running beneath the stillness like a counterpoint, the distant roar of the building's furnace. Too hot. No wonder the baby catches so many colds. Who can cope with such extremes? What system can stabilize under such conditions?

He leans over the crib, above which hangs the mobile he fashioned out of paper airplanes and coat hangers the week his son was born. The string jiggles; the planes dive and arc, blithe in their circumscribed motions. Motion is easy, he thinks, when you're bound by physical law. The true test is what happens when you're not, when possibility replaces certainty, when wave replaces particle. When morality itself embodies quantum logic.

Another cough. A weakling, this boy. With his pale skin, button nose, and puffy, hooded eyes, his son might be a caricature of his wife. The

101

powerlessness, the need. Who can tell how he'll evolve? Which tendency will win out—spontaneous development or genetic pattern? Does Eli even possess the patience, at this point, to find out?

It's so strange, he thinks, being a father. You look down at this assemblage of chromosomes, this pastiche of plasma and water, this tangled circuit of synapses, and you wonder what mystical strength empowered you to create such a thing; was creation the inspiration of love, or was it the other way around?

At least, that's what *he* wonders. How other people handle such things, strike the thousand balances parenthood requires, he has no inkling whatever. It's all ad hoc, uncontrollable; he has to try so hard not to be sloppy. He is forever aiming for a precision that seems beyond him. At the lab he has to do everything twice or he does not trust his results. When he composes music, the same. Every line, every note—twice. He isn't good enough. He isn't a natural, even as a parent. When he wipes the excrement from his son's behind, he uses so many strokes, approaches from so many angles, that the boy cries out from the soreness. When he tries to give him a bath, he spends so much time checking the temperature that by the time the boy's in the water it's too cold. The whole business exhausts him. If he doesn't begin to hoard his energies somewhat, there will be nothing left for the work.

But he's still young, and it can change. Everything, he thinks, is elastic, in flux. There—another cough. The boy is uncomfortable. Just pick him up and draw back the blanket. Just hold him for a moment, lend a sense of weight, the density of presence. There. Bring him to your shoulder, juggle him gently, shush him in a whisper even if he's not making any noise. Sibilant sounds. Constancy. Shush . . .

A puff of wind sends the airplanes diving again, a rhythm that lulls the father if not the son. If he could only sleep, it would help; he'd be less tense around the house. But the place is so goddamn hot. Then go, he thinks. Go tell the fireman. Assert. Provide for your family.

He rearranges the crib's blankets and sets down the baby, hearing in his own voice—the repeated shushing—something young and cowardly, something that makes him feel like a callow boy playing at adulthood, at life itself. And then he buttons his shirt and heads for the stairs.

In the basement, Carlos, the fireman, sits with his shirt off in a slatted wood chair, munching an apple and staring moodily into the coals. Built thick and low to the ground, unshaven, with a red bandana tied loosely around his wide, stubbly neck, he looks to Eli like a cartoon Mexican bandit, a grubby, unsavory creature who takes your gold and then shoots you for the fun of it. And what, Eli wonders briefly, do I look like to him? *"Buenos días,"* he attempts, in his lame Castilian Spanish.

Carlos grunts, raises the apple to eye level in a halfhearted salute. His eyes shine dully in the glow of the furnace.

"¿Qué tal esta noche?" Eli goes on, straining, forcing a smile. *"Bueno?"*

Again, the smaller man grunts. He is either a simpleton, or an aristocrat, or else he simply doesn't understand. Perhaps he's a Pueblo from Tesuque, or San Ildefonso, one of those oppressive, impoverished villages that supply the maids and janitors of the Hill. He should learn to talk to these people, Eli thinks; make himself at ease with them. But he has been ill at ease with so many, for so long, he hardly knows where to begin.

Discouraged, he finds he cannot manage another smile, as Carlos, mumbling to himself and giving vent to his body's gases, looks away. Eli sees the man's gaze come to rest on a crinkled paper bag, twisted at the neck, propped to stand on the workbench a few feet away. Of course: a bottle. He's waiting for me to leave so he can finish the bottle in peace. It's okay, Eli wants to say, and then hears himself saying it.

This time, the words register on Carlos's face. "Okay?" he asks, blankly.

"Yes," says Eli, nodding his head with vigor. "Okay."

Carlos leans back and smiles, revealing a good set of yellowing teeth. The word seems to have put him on familiar ground—he addresses a few soft "okay"s to the basement ceiling, enjoying himself. A courtship has begun; the first gift has been unwrapped and found to be just fine, thank you.

Eli takes this opportunity to sit down on the workbench, two feet from the paper bag. He knows he must look odd, sitting there in a half-buttoned dress shirt, slacks, and slippers in the middle of the night. The cement floor is strewn with coal and paper—screen magazines from the PX, candy wrappers, greasy government-issue napkins. An orange sheen is cast by the open mouth of the furnace. Carlos gnaws his apple contentedly, his lips making neat smacks. An odor rises from him, sour, fecal. A leakage.

Eli leans forward to say what he has come to say. Before he can begin, however, the fireman, alert to some obscure internal mechanism, straightens, tosses the core of the apple into the furnace, and rises to grab the shovel. Heavily, deliberately, he plunges it up to its neck into the black coal pile, grunting with the exertion, his stubby body slick with sweat. He tosses in one load rather carelessly, some of it spilling onto the cement, and then bends to the pile to take on another.

Eli, watching him work, says nothing. It is as though, now that he has made the trip to the basement, his mind has switched into neutral; he cannot, for some reason, think clearly. He feels dull, slow, unable to stand, unable to talk, unable to sleep. Stasis. There before him is the plodding laborer, and upstairs somewhere the heat is streaming through the vents, and though he understands that a connection exists between these two phenomena that is essential to all physics, to life itself, he is momentarily confused as to its precise nature. Blinking back exhaustion, he tries to summon his scientist's eye, to watch as Baker, for instance, would watch: with one equation noting the transfer of heat energy, and one that calculates the amount of spilled coal beneath the furnace mouth. But there is Carlos, too. The human variable. He who fights death; and dies.

At some point Eli drifts off. He and Ruthie are on the roof of her father's apartment building, watching the elevated subway float past the chimneys. Ruthie smells of bread. From a nearby church, a blast of organ music. He reaches out to her, folds her into his enormous hand. . . .

Shrieking.

What? What have I done to you now?

And then he is awake and hears the fire sirens in the distance. Immediately he tries to count backward, to the blast he heard in his dream. "How many?" he asks Carlos automatically.

In the slatted chair, Carlos yawns and stretches. The sirens have stopped. "I think five, six," he grumbles.

"Tech Area?"

Carlos nods impassively. "No enough water. Bad business."

"I suppose the SEDs will take care of it."

"Bad business," repeats Carlos, with a look of distaste. He eyes the shovel and sighs, gathering his weight forward.

"No," says Eli quickly. "Too hot."

"Too much?" Carlos muses. "No think too much."

"Yes. Too much. It's too hot upstairs."

"Too much?" Again Carlos considers the idea, cocking his head, shooting a glance of assessment at the furnace. His body leans invisibly in that direction. One fleshy hand, black with coal dust, floats up to pull at the amoeba of his earlobe. He looks around the cellar. This is his nightplace, the clutter his clutter, the rules and procedures his to dictate. That Rita Hayworth stuck to the wall over the worktable is his; she keeps her eye on him as he works and sleeps, reminds him what it is to be a man. The Anglos in their white coats with their soft white hands and soft white wives, what could they tell him about work? While his people dig in the mines until their backs spasm, breathing the foul clogged air, the Anglos move in clouds of chalk. And always they want more. "I think okay," he decides aloud, and bends to his shovel.

Eli is on his feet. "Not okay. I just told you—"

"Carlos do his job, mister." He grips the shovel in his black hands. "You go upstairs. Everything okay."

"But that's what I'm trying to *tell* you," Eli stammers. "Everything's *not* okay. I have a child, a wife. It's too hot, I tell you."

"Your wife not have problem. She tell me."

Fists clenched, Eli comes forward and, in his anger, pounds himself in the thigh. "You don't even know who she *is,* you little drunk!"

Carlos stiffens. "No, mister."

"Don't give me that. I know what—"

"No, mister." Carlos, defiant, plunges the shovel into the deep coal and stands poised at the mouth of the furnace, his lips curling into a sneer. "Your wife I know."

Ruthie? What a ridiculous . . . what an incredible . . .

"Little lady. Skinny. Black hair . . ."

Yes, black, he thinks. Deep black.

"Ruthie I know, mister."

That coal is so deep and black.

Of course, he could be dreaming again. That's entirely possible. His eyes, which ache from the dust, are closed, and he sways somewhat as the fireman's voice rumbles on. He must be facing the furnace, he thinks, because he can feel the heat of it on his cheeks, and he sees blotches of scarlet and orange where his lids are pressed limply together.

". . . little lady and little baby. But big bottle, mister. She leave it here sometime. She tell me, too hot or too cold. She tell Carlos. . . ."

Again, in the distance, Eli hears the sirens, the shrieks and echoes in the canyons. The wind, he thinks dully. It had better die down, and soon. The flames could so easily spread.

Chapter 11

"When I die," crowed Charlie Goldwyn, surveying the wreckage of our area of the 727's first-class compartment, "they're going to bury me in paper."

Outside, the sun was brilliantly lucid in the midwestern sky. Below us the farmlands of Kansas yielded almost imperceptibly to the desolate reaches of the lower plains. Beyond, the slow fade to the Texas prairie. I had not been west of the Mississippi in nearly twenty years, and the hard expanse of the landscape struck me like a blow to the head. But that was outside. Inside, covering the seat between us and much of the floor, was everywhere the product of human endeavor, the piles and piles of papers—briefs, memos, files, clips—that accrue when man files suit against his fellow man. And when that suit has a long, tangled history, involving a couple of dozen lawyers in three states, countless millions of dollars, and a fair portion of the *Fortune* 500, and when it is being managed by two people as distracted and unprepared for the task as Charlie and myself, the profusion of paper itself becomes a landscape of sorts, one that, in its disorder, its absence of level ground, its sheer bulk, is as awesome and incomprehensible as the great mass unfolding some thirty thousand feet below us.

"God help me, Heshie," said Charlie. "I love my work."

This was all too true. Charlie had not gotten where he was at Pinsker & Lem by turning his back on unwieldy cases. Rather, he fed on them; matched their unbalanced weight with his own, biding his time, confident—and why not?—that at any moment he chose, he could rear up like the lethal beast he was and swat them into submission. He had let the OTG suit sit on his desk for three months, he told me now, while all around him partners were pulling their hair and screaming at their speakerphones. This went on until the night before the first hearing, whereupon he and one associate whose name he could no longer recall had holed up in the conference room on the forty-first floor, taken the phone off the hook, ordered a couple of pizzas and a case of Diet Pepsi, and knocked out a line of attack so brutal and sweet in its simplicity that they had won dismissal in less than an hour. "Only problem was, I'd promised Lorraine an April in Paris. The goddamn thing was over in January. So we went to Miami instead. I really hate Miami. A regular hole. Sprained my ankle playing tennis that trip. A disaster."

"It's because you don't limber up, Charlie."

"Lucy says I need to learn how to relax. She thinks maybe TM." He yawned, his mouth a grand cavern.

Considering I'd never met the woman, I was coming to be very familiar with what Lucy Johnson thought about things. Also with the extravagant yawns that invariably accompanied mention of her name, as though the effort of fitting the alien syllables to his own voice was too much for him. But the explanation, I figured, was simpler than that: Charlie was just nervous, feigning casualness. It seemed he had reason to be nervous. Lucy Johnson, he told me, was not returning his phone calls. Nor was she answering his telegrams, or for that matter the psychic emanations he appeared to be sending her as our plane winged west. Halfheartedly he looked over a brief, and tried to engage himself in a question of waived privilege regarding the documents signed by the Navajo ranchers the previous spring—documents that would, I assumed, be our immediate focus—but after ten minutes he took off his reading glasses and, grimacing, rubbed the reddened bruises at the bridge of his nose. "What if she's out of town?" he demanded of me. "What if she's engaged to some stud with a pickup truck?"

"You hardly know her, Charlie. I think you should be prepared for anything, including the worst."

"The worst," he muttered, looking past me, out the window, at the serene azure sky. "This is the worst already. I'm all strapped in. I can hardly think."

With his meaty hand, he reached out and grabbed a passing stewardess by the elbow. "Hey, when do you get a meal around here, anyway?"

A pretty standard-looking airline blonde with a flat midwestern smile, the stewardess appeared to be new to first-class service. She looked at Charlie blankly, as if he were a terribly inaccessible bit of abstract sculpture. "Sir?"

"A *meal*," said Charlie. "Is that too much to ask?"

"But sir, we served lunch an hour out of Kennedy, remember?"

"Yeah," he said, with what passed in him for patience. "But that was noon eastern time. Now it's noon *western* time. See what I'm saying? How's a man supposed to coordinate himself, physically, if he doesn't put his stomach in sync?" He waited for the logic of this to sink in, and then went on: "Now, my colleague here"—he jerked his thumb at me—"he's on an important case for a blue-chip law firm. He can't afford to screw up. Me, I can wait till we land in Albuquerque, no problem. But he's got a sensitive constitution, this guy. So how about you bring him another steak and baked potato. Ranch dressing on the salad. I'll make sure he eats it all."

She turned to me, her eyes flickering once and then going hard. "We're out of ranch dressing. You'll have to take Russian."

"Fine." Charlie grinned. "And don't forget dessert."

When she'd moved away, Charlie laid a benevolent hand on my knee. "Ah, Heshie. We're going to make some team, the two of us. Tell me something: Do you forgive me for dragging you out here?"

"Sure I do."

"You say sure but you're an ironic sonofabitch, and I want to know you mean sure. You mean it?"

He looked me over, bearing down with his full courtroom stare, searching my eyes for impurities of affection. What he saw I can only guess. But he had reasons of his own to find me sincere when I repeated, "Sure I do."

He leaned back and gave vent to his relief. "That's the ticket."

"Besides," I went on, "I've got some personal matters of my own to look into."

His gaze went squinty. "What kind of matters?"

"Well, my mother lives out here, for one thing. And my f—"

But he was already talking. "Because we've got a lot to do out here, Hesh. This case is no piece of strudel. Can't have you running off at all hours doing personal business. This is major work here. I've got twenty associates back on Nassau doing discovery. Can't let them down. It might be all our jobs, if that bastard Todd gets his way."

"What does Todd have to do with anything?"

"He's a killer, Heshie. The man's cool, but psychotic. It irks him that he's older than me and his blood's blue, but I'm the one with the clout on the committee. He wants me to fall on my face. He's even trying to steal my associates."

"You've lost your mind, Charlie."

"Have I? What do *you* know? What have *you* accomplished?"

"What's the difference? I can still see foolishness when it's in front of my face."

"Bullshit. You don't see shit. I'm trying to do you a favor, show you how it works with us. A little poison in the system, a little character assassination. Rumors of incompetence or bad health. It doesn't take much to woo a client, you know. By nature they're stupid and fearful. A little doubt in the right places goes a long way. I know what I'm talking about."

I reviewed what I knew of Walter Todd. Oxford scholar, elegant dresser, old-money family. Also, from what I'd heard, the best brief-writer in the firm. But he was strictly a behind-the-scenes player—no courtroom phenom, no hustler of clients. Walter Todd gave one the impression that the law was a gentlemanly sport, practiced behind thick, fine-grained wooden doors in hushed, thoughtful tones by men who had attended school in Cambridge and New Haven and who went sailing on Saturday afternoons. He was the only man I'd ever met who regularly played croquet. I knew this because I'd played it with him, back in March, on the singular occasion of my being invited to dinner at his Connecticut estate. We knocked the balls around his front yard for the better part of an hour, as his wife readied salmon steaks in their gleaming kitchen, and in that time we spoke with awkward formality of theater, film, and novels, finding, as we did, that we had virtually nothing in common. The entire evening was a little baffling, as latent with unfamiliar ritual as our croquet game, which ended in a draw. At least, Walter Todd called it a draw. I couldn't say for certain that he didn't win.

He won my admiration, though, merely for the way he avoided all mention of the firm. And he was a conscientious host, a true presence, filling wineglasses and nodding gravely over his hooked white eyebrows, his skin smooth and tan and, save for the liver spots on his hands, youthful. After the meal, which was excellent, we went into his study for the requisite brandies. An expensive dartboard hung over the fireplace, striped with browns and blacks. Three fat quilled darts drooped from its bull's-eye like a hairy appendage. When Todd pointed it out to me, I had the feeling he was trying to please me with the sight of it, its aptness and full earth tones in the quiet room. The board itself looked barely used; it seemed to hang there for no better reason than that his guests might expect it of him. Certainly he showed no particular skill, flinging the little spears with more velocity than accuracy. Nor was he any good at keeping score. In the end, we simply stood there at stiff attention, throwing the darts and then fetching them, dutifully following the grammar of the occasion.

After a while, he began to talk about his son, who had taken time off after law school some years back to join the Peace Corps. He spoke in a flat Yankee voice, with little of the heartiness he'd tried to display over croquet, and I must have listened well, because three months later I was able to recall almost everything he said. He told me his son had returned from Guam, stepped into a perfectly good associateship with some Boston Brahmins, and stepped right out again before collecting a single paycheck. "He went to Kenya this time. He lasted six months. I wired him some money and he came home. It was a difficult adjustment. For a while he ate nothing but fruit. He ate fruit and watched television a good deal. But I wasn't particularly worried. He was applying to a number of very good graduate programs in a number of very interesting disciplines. Twelve in all. He was accepted, I might add, to all twelve. Michael was an exceptionally bright young man. Even his suicide note was thoughtfully chosen. Have you read much Hawthorne, Herschel?"

"Just *The Scarlet Letter*."

He turned back to the dartboard, his expression almost wistful. Perhaps he was regretting having ever purchased the thing, or, perhaps, not having purchased it sooner. "Terribly gloomy writer, but quite instructive. There's a story he wrote about a man who leaves his home and then, much later, returns. Michael underlined the last paragraph. He propped the book open with the empty bottle of Seconal. I won't burden you with the quote itself, though you can look it up, if you're curious. It says a great deal, I suspect, about your particular generation."

Just to say something, to alleviate some of the coldness in the room, I said the first thing that popped into my head. "It's funny about my generation, isn't it? There's always been so much to say about us. Possibly the main thing there is to say about us is how much there is to say about us. If you follow."

Walter Todd's white eyebrows knotted in some confusion, for which I could hardly blame him. But then he did something strange, unexpected, something that endeared him to me forever. He let go a good round belly laugh, doubling over and slapping his stomach, his fine, sculpted face flooded with so much color I feared for a moment he was having a stroke. "Good Lord!" he exclaimed, upon recovering his breath. "You've got something there, all right. Indeed!"

Following which, like the good host he was, he fed me another glass of brandy, showed me his greenhouse, and escorted me to my car, somewhat pleased with us both, I think, for having risen to the occasion so nicely. At the sight of my battered Toyota, however, he frowned as if from genuine pain. Politely he inquired as to its mileage and repair history, nodding with interest as I replied. Had it not been for the three Mercedeses parked in front of the garage, I'd have taken him for a prospective buyer. As I catalogued the car's historic misfortunes, he shook his head, heavy with sadness. "I see," he said. "Uh huh." Finally, he broke down and allowed as how there were many fine cars on the market that year, and that his "young people" at the firm were particularly fond of the Subaru. I thanked him, promised to pursue the issue, and sped off, thinking that Connecticut was neither so foreign nor forbidding a place as I'd always imagined.

Recalling that night in March and that long half hour spent before Walter Todd's dartboard, I found it difficult to imagine him a killer at all. On the legal pad in my lap, I jotted "Hawthorne" in the top margin, above a page reference in the Federal Supplement that Charlie had asked me to check. It seemed I had some real library work before me.

The stewardess sailed over, bearing a second lunch.

"That's okay, Miss," Charlie said, relieving her of the tray. "I'll pass it along. You're a good girl."

"We were out of ranch," she said again. "I had to give him Russian."

"Fine, fine. Tell me something—what's that say?—Cindi? Tell me something, Cindi. How old's your father?"

It had taken her most of the trip, but finally she knew what tone to take with Charlie, what tone he had wanted her to take all along. "Now, now, is that any kind of question to ask?"

Charlie nodded happily. "Do me a favor. The man's at least sixty, right?"

"Fifty-two," she said brightly, as if to a small homesick boy. "Isn't that nice?"

"Nice," mumbled Charlie, pulling at his napkin.

She hurried away down the aisle, as Charlie, mumbling something I couldn't catch, tucked his napkin into his pants and cut his steak. Daintily, he raised the fork to his mouth and, holding it there for a second, observed, "I've got my appetite back—you notice?"

But when I glanced over a moment later, he seemed to be chewing his lunch with no particular relish. He even offered me a bite, which I refused. I had a feeling that it would take more than a full stomach to align me with time once we landed.

Chapter 12

Members of the Academy, esteemed colleagues, fellow Americans . . .

Are you working, little Nagra? Can I get a level? Am I speaking too softly? Test. Test.

If you don't work, we're shot before we shoot. Ha.

Okay, there it goes. . . . Test . . . Test . . .

This is Arthur. Audio notes re project status, June 3, 1977. Dictating in Room 130, Trinity Motel, Los Alamos, New Mexico. Eleven-fifty P.M. Must speak softly, because you're sleeping, Ab, curled up as always with your back to the wall. So to speak. You do look tranquil, love. I'm tempted to join you, but then who would be making the record of our progress? Someone, you see, has to look to the future.

Hold it—let me check the levels. Okay, fine. I've got what on this reel— about twenty minutes? Okay, then. Onward.

Our current status: problematic.

Money first. As I told you the other day, Ab, the Endowment came up with ten thousand in seed money. But they want—I should say insist on—seeing something on film before they'll approve the rest. Okay then. So I submitted a budget of three hundred thousand, which Mel tells me will be approved, no problem. Pending, he says. Pending what, I say. They want to make sure they like the look of the seed reel first, he says. Politics! Mel made then one of his typical off-color jokes about the industry and then an irrelevant and somewhat offensive comment about my choice of subject matter, the implication being that the area has already been done to death by every hack who ever heard an air raid siren. Exactly, I said, and walked out—probably a little too melodramatically, considering how much I'm relying on his support. Actually, he's quite a good administrator. I should call him tomorrow, just to smooth things over. Will you remind me?

112

Look at you over there. My God, my life. What are the odds of us working out, at this point? Where are you now? Spain? New York? What am I going to do?

Work. Talk. Love. You'll be happier when you're writing, of course. But there's a ways to go yet. You didn't realize the script would come last, that we'd have to slog our way through, first, looking for our angle. You actually know very little about this business, don't you? About me, possibly. Trust in the process, love; let things develop. My sweet lady. Are you getting this? Are you safely in the black, little arrows?

Good. Then let's see where we are.

Friedmann, Eli. Born 1919. See notes from Lemann interview, May 27, Columbia University. We can do something, maybe, with the connection to Einstein here, that being the year the solar eclipse proved the relativity theory correct. Or, I don't know, maybe that's too pointed. I mean, we start off stretching like that and we'll look silly. It'll sound like we're making it all up. What do you think? Scratch the whole idea? Just born 1919?

Next.

Bronx Science, honors. Plays in orchestra. We'll use those photos from the school yearbook, of course. And that one of Ruth Orlinsky, the one that shows her pretty smile. Three, four minutes is plenty for childhood. The early stuff is inherently boring, in most cases. If they want that shit, let them go to the library and read Proust, right?

Next.

Attends Columbia 1937–41. Marries in '40. Grad work. Then grad work at Berkeley until winter '43. Check notes from interview with Anderson, May 25, Chock Full o' Nuts. Works on neutron emission under Szilard. Not considered first-rank physicist. But I don't remember who said that. Better write to both Lemann and Anderson to confirm.

Then here. Los Alamos, spring '43 until late '56. Works in Ordnance, then Theoretical Division. Fission program, then thermonuclear design program. Comes up slowly through ranks. Never seems to make it to highest level. Why not? Christ, we've got a lot of interviews to do. Call New York tomorrow too, to check the mail. I've got half a dozen people in Livermore I'm expecting replies from. I hope they'll talk to us. Thank God I have you along. You'll charm them. You charm everybody.

And speaking of which. Son, Herschel, born August '43. Late '40s, transfers divisions, works on Super, other classified projects. Separates from wife and son, summer of '49. Stays till '56. Then three semesters at Berkeley. Then disappears. God knows where or why. What is this, a detective movie? How am I supposed to find him? Ten thousand fucking dollars! Can't even hire an investigator.

113

The key man, obviously, is Hesh. We've got to get him in on this, get the private dimension, the psychology. There's an affinity between the two that'll leap right out of the frame, if I can get him right. But he's slippery—he requires delicate managing. I don't want him to freak on us. Maybe, Ab, between the two of us, we can steer him along, hit the right note. What say?

Okay, then.

This is all ducking the real question, of course. The question being who gives a shit. That is the question, isn't it, Ab? Who gives a shit? Or as Mel would say, how will this play on the subway? The chances are fairly good, I suppose, that whatever this film will have to say will be said to an audience already aligned into predictable camps, and will be just another fallen sixteen-millimeter tree in the great black celluloid forest. Am I getting cynical, or just tired? Maybe the answer is the old saw about art being therapy. A little exorcism of the commercial demons. But it's a regular minefield, this one. The odds are I'll make him too sympathetic and get it from the left, or not sympathetic enough and get it from the right. The odds, let's be honest, are that I'll never pull it off, period. So hard to make history visual. It's lucky that the locations are dynamite out here. So beautiful and open. Sort of romantic, don't you think, Ab?

Yes, well . . .

Found a great little ditty someplace . . . where is it? This notebook's a fucking mess. . . .

Ah, yes. Here. Check this out, Ab. *We have tended to assume that the machine and the human brain are in conflict. Now the fear is that they are indistinguishable.*

That's good, right? I think it'll play nicely. A touch of class. Of course, I have no idea who said it. We'll probably wind up getting sued. Well, there's always Hesh, if we need a lawyer.

Okay, well, almost out of tape. Time to stop. Stop talking so much. You've stopped—why can't I? What is it you want, anyway? You're like this tape, aren't you? You're blank and you want to be filled, right? Can we make something together? Can we?

We're going to make it, Ab. First we'll do this film. You'll see how it works, what it *is*. Just pictures, that's all, one after another, a serial arrangement of frozen compositions. Patience, love. It's going to synthesize the way it's supposed to. And we're going to come through, Abby. If you wait for me we'll write the script together, in the fall, with plenty of time, plenty of money. Eat, sleep, work, love—we're after a synthesis, babe, and we're going to get it. Word and image. Master shot and close-up. Light and shadow. If it doesn't come out right at first, we'll get it in the editing.

Nobody cares about what you cut away, after all.

How much time left?

Are you still there, Abby? Are you still moving, little arrows? Are you getting it all, my pretty Nagra?

How much time left?

Members of the Academy, have we passed the test?

Chapter 13

The drive from Albuquerque to Santa Fe is, for the most part, an exercise in sameness. Same flat reddish-brown, sage-studded earth to the left; same low, muscular, chummy mountains to the right. But at the apex of a June dusk, the clarity of the light and the cool velvet currents in the air lend each stretch of landscape the kind of incandescence that gives sameness a good name. It worked a spell upon me. Zooming along the open road in a metallic-blue Chevy I'd rented at the airport (Charlie, naturally, had gone for the Lincoln), I felt free, infinitely new, heady with relief to be out of the city, the paralyzing sloppiness of New York. I was even beginning to feel glad I'd come.

That day the two of us had put in some quality work at the office of our local affiliated counsel, Sullivan and Peck. It was one of those small, relaxed, soft-cornered establishments that big-city lawyers dream about in their midnight catnaps, a place of manageable dimensions and thinkable consequences. The staff were a cheerful and unaffected bunch, flattered to be of service and eager to accommodate even our most whimsical demands, such as Charlie's insistence that the secretary assigned to him call him Doctor Goldwyn. "You've got to set yourself apart," he told me. "Otherwise you get lost in the shuffle."

The *Hindenberg* would have been easier to lose in the shuffle, but it was Charlie's parade, and so I said nothing. I was a little demented myself. We were driving rented cars, spending the firm's money. We were large men, big guns from the East, people to reckon with. Traveling on business. The phrase conjured up associations of power, sex, expensive restaurants. All the years I'd spent ducking thorny cases had meant ducking extended trips like this; I was starting to think I had missed something.

After dinner Charlie went off in a cloud of cologne in search of Lucy

Johnson. I spent an hour doodling on a legal pad in front of the television, in a state of acute indecision. There was no need to hurry. I would be there for at least a week. I should spend a couple of days, I thought, just getting acclimated.

But when I found myself staring open-mouthed at an interview with a celebrity I'd never heard of, I roused myself, took a sip of water, pulled on my jacket, and went outside.

An hour later I pulled off the highway and into the parking lot of the San Antonio de Padua Convalescent Home, in Santa Fe. I suppose that I looked, as I stepped out of the car, fairly dapper in a jacket and tie, and I walked with none of my customary slouch. But my smile had something manic in it, and my eyes felt smaller than usual and slightly itchy.

Confession: on the drive north, I had, for no good reason and a surfeit of bad ones, smoked one of Arthur Gordon's joints. It had been a dumb thing to do, and the only testimony I would give in my own defense is that the entire visit seemed so foolhardy an enterprise, so futile a gesture, that I was sure nothing I did could possibly make it worse. But of course it could, and I had. And now, standing in the parking lot, putting drops in my eyes, my face lifted to the huge desert sky, I experienced one of those flashes of paranoia familiar to adolescents of all ages. The cars, I was certain, had their glass eyes on me, the local gendarmes were just around the corner, and had I the stomach to turn a few degrees south, toward the grid of windows overlooking the parking lot, I would find there a geriatric Greek chorus, shaking their gray heads in judgment and chanting a primeval dirge.

I had not seen my mother in nine years, and I was stoned.

I had not seen my mother in nine years because when last we'd met—in Chicago, on the day of my wedding—we'd had a rending fight. She had not been impressed with Joanne's looks, or her intelligence, or the smug piety of her prosperous Reform Jewish family and their prosperous synagogue, and she did not think she would be able to sit through the ceremony, feeling as she did. My mother told me all this in her low, petulant voice as she worked her way through a bottle of, to her tastes, inferior vodka. And then my tie snagged in my rented collar, and I was sure I'd never be able to breathe properly again, and suddenly—as sometimes happens on landmark occasions—my perspective on myself went black and absolute. I was not certain she was wrong about Joanne; I was confused as to exactly what bonds life expected me to form and maintain in my years as an adult; I was midway through law school, which I loathed; and I had no idea whether my father, whose name I was

117

not allowed to mention even had I wanted to, was alive or dead. The one constant in my life, aside from a ubiquitous sense of unreality and claustrophobia, was my mother, and it seemed fairly clear to me at the time that she did not really wish me well. She loved me, of course, fervently, but in her disappointment with me, with herself, with us all, she was unable to make the leap into generosity; she simply wouldn't budge.

And so I did what I had never thought possible: I kicked her out.

And she went.

Back to her snug adobe house in the hills of Santa Fe. To her job teaching first grade. To the books and bottles and the blintzes she regularly burned. We had always been furiously obstinate, the two of us, in our domestic tug-of-war, and we had never been very good on the phone, anyway, so it did not surprise me when she'd hang up on me or when, after a year or so, I stopped calling. Nor did it surprise me that she never answered the letters I sent, or cashed the checks—let alone flew to New York to see the grandson whose yearly growth I recorded for her in photographs. Nothing, in hindsight, had been much of a surprise, including the day of my wedding. There are relationships in a family that seem never to mature, and there are relationships that mature too quickly, that call for too many adjustments too early. As I watched her exit the synagogue that Sunday morning in Chicago—still slender, tangled hair abundant and black, gait as unmannered and pleasure-starved as ever—I sensed that there was a failure in me, too, to let go. Instead of sending her away, I should have gotten good and drunk with her, danced a *hora* with her, engaged her dybbuks and golems with my own. But I had done it the easy way, and she had let me. Or, more likely, vice versa.

Several years ago her health had deteriorated, according to the one relative—my aunt Ethel—I kept in contact with, and my mother had wound up here, in San Antonio de Padua. Built in the local manner—two stories of white adobe and brown trim, with small square recessed windows of brown glass—it stood on the northeastern rim of town, about halfway between the square and the Sangre de Cristos, at the end of a cul-de-sac lined by new homes. When I approached the front door it was eight-twenty. The sun's descent had taken it to a point just below the roof, so that the adobe, framed by violet, looked like the bud of an enormous flower. A solitary walker, its metal handles smudged with fingerprints, waited on the brick porch for somebody to summon it to service.

At the reception desk, a slim Indian girl in a white uniform showed me her large white teeth. "May I help you?"

"Yes," I said. "I'm looking for a Mrs. Friedmann. Ruth Friedmann."

"Is she a patient?"

"I believe so. Yes."

"Just a moment, please." She bent to open the top drawer of her desk, extracting a long manila folder. The top sheets were a computerized roster. I followed her eyes down the column of names, unable to make them out upside down, my eyes still itchy from the smoke. When she straightened and looked at me over the desk with her soft, inquiring stare, I fought an impulse to run. "I'm sorry," she said. "I have no listing for Ruth Friedmann."

A wave of relief broke inside me.

"Maybe if you describe her to me?"

"Short woman," I said. "Olive skin. Bad liver."

The girl shook her head. A lottery ticket peeked from her vest pocket. "I've only been here a week, though. Maybe Mrs. Rosenthal can help you. She's the evening administrator. That's her office over there." She pointed down the corridor, to an open door.

"Thank you."

"If she's not there, she may be in the Music Room. There's choir rehearsal tonight. We've been invited to Taos."

When she smiled at me again I felt warm, expansive. For a moment I thought she meant she and I had been invited to Taos, on some honeymoon trip for the innocent. But she meant the choir, of course. I was in some shape. All those hours with Charlie Goldwyn were paying off: Now we were neck and neck, sprinting loopily toward the asylum. I willed myself to thank her and get my rear end down the hall.

The walls of Mrs. Rosenthal's office were populated with smiling seniors afloat in the pool, gathered around the piano, playing bingo, blowing out row upon row of birthday candles; but she herself was not in. A framed diploma next to the filing cabinet awarded a master's degree in social work to one Deborah Rosenthal. I read it over carefully, finding in it a peculiar comfort. There were, I imagined, Deborah Rosenthals in settings like this the world over, administering to the infirm with soothing manner and ready Polaroid, tempering fate's viciousness with mercy. It was warming to know that when the debauch of youth had broken you into pieces and scattered you on the floor, there existed an army of Deborah Rosenthals to sweep you into dustbins like San Antonio for the duration. Indeed, I was tempted to cash in my chips and sign myself over to her right then. But she seemed to be busy elsewhere.

From a distant room, the tinkle of a piano, a chorus of joined voices. "Raindrops keep falling on my head." My mouth felt dry, cottony. No sign of Mrs. R.

I tiptoed down the corridor, passing huge calendars of events, three paintings of horses, some Indian weavings, and a nearly life-size crucifix. A courtyard on the left offered an unpromising arrangement of cactus and pebbles; it was uninhabited, at that hour. Up ahead I could hear the muffled music of the choir, pressing onward, to Taos and beyond. A darkened hallway stretched off to the right, quiet, gloomy, shot through with dusk. I decided to follow it.

The rooms ticked by, symmetrically ordered, on both sides. All looked more or less exactly the same: two beds with neatly tucked corners, reading chair, floor lamp, television. The carpets were a uniform weave of dissonant colors that, taken together, nearly canceled each other out. The air-conditioning hummed steadily. Every room was well lit. Every room was empty. I could have been wandering through a display room, a diorama, a dormant factory of beds and toilets. This was what it looked like before you put the people in, and this was what it looked like afterward—in between were only interludes of pain and small pleasures; they would not last long. It was like entering an apartment building through the basement, discovering all the mechanisms: the boilers, meters, pipes, furnace valves. These were the true inhabitants. The native species. The people upstairs, the choir across the courtyard, they came and went, like so much decorative art.

Two cardboard nameplates hung on each door, fixed with thumbtacks. Simon and D'Angelo. Kravitz and Sherman. Jefferson and Boudin. Life puts you in pairs; you can't escape it. In the end, even the dreariest and most reluctant wallflowers are dragged, in couples, down the ramp of Noah's leaky ark. Yarmovsky and Bronston. Kane and Carr. Lieberman and Paultz.

I had decided that the hall was completely deserted until, in the second-to-last room on the right, I happened upon two women in ludicrously gay bathrobes, watching television. One of them, so obese she seemed to have taken root to her chair, waved to me casually. Her slippered feet were propped on a hassock, her cigarettes littered the ashtray; she looked strangely regal. The other lay curled on her side atop the unwrinkled bedspread, her thin veined feet crossed at the ankles. Lost in the light of the television, she did not turn toward me when I came into the room.

"You lost, sugar?" the heavy woman asked, not bothering to turn from the television. Her accent sounded Brooklyn. Borough Park.

"I'm looking for a Mrs. Friedmann," I said.

"No such person here." She touched a finger to her tongue, checking for tobacco. Her cigarettes were unfiltered. "You sure you got the right name?"

"I think so. Do you live here?"

"I'm down the hall. Myra Epstein. With a *y*," she added sternly, as though I should have been writing it down. "Are you a doctor?"

I was at a loss to decipher any motive in her question other than the standard one for Jewish women the world over. I admitted to being a lawyer.

She shrugged. "Same difference."

"I suppose so."

"Did my son send you? Because I'm not changing my mind. He's not getting a penny, the *schnorrer*. You got a light?"

I reached into the pocket of my jacket and found the matches I'd used to light the joint, back in the car. I was thinking that I could have used, perhaps, a little more.

Myra Epstein held my wrist in the cool folds of her hand as she puffed at the flame. Then she released it slowly. Leaning back, she exhaled languidly. We gave each other the once-over for a moment, and she made something that resembled a smile out of the loose puckered fruit that was her mouth. "You didn't come to see me, did you? I can tell from your face. What's the matter with your eyes, by the way? They look funny."

"I'm just tired. I flew out from New York, you see."

At the mention of my adopted city she folded her arms loftily, the cigarette dangling from her upper lip like a walrus tooth. "Ach, that place," she said. "Everybody says it's the greatest city in the world. The museums, they say. The theater, they say. Do you want to know what I think on the subject?"

It amazed me to find that I did.

"The whole *farchakdet* place could slide right into the Hudson and we'd all be better off. I'm saying that and I've still got family there. Let it slide away, or give it to the colored and the Spanish, who'll get it soon enough, anyway. I haven't been there now in what?—four, five years. The humidity, whew. Then there's the bugs. Crime. Subways. Once I saw a lady my own age get stuck in one of the turnstiles. Nobody came to help her. The animals were throwing things at her, calling her names. She had a bag from Bloomingdale's taken from her. Nobody would help. I bet you ten to one she's still there, that lady."

121

I considered, and rejected, the idea of asking what she herself had done to lend aid to the victim. I found myself looking at the woman on the bed.

"You know a real classy city? Denver. Denver, Colorado. I was there last Passover, with relations. It's a mile high, did you know that?"

I shook my head vaguely.

"Every morning I waited for the nosebleeds to come, but they never did. You watch *60 Minutes*? They did a program on Denver once. What is it with you? Why do you keep staring at her? Let the poor lady watch her program in peace."

"What's your name?" I asked the woman on the bed.

"That's Mrs. Orlinsky," Myra Epstein answered for her. "We're friendly, the two of us. We watch television together." She narrowed her eyes suspiciously. "I thought you wanted Friedmann."

I went to the doorway and looked at the nameplate again. Orlinsky. No, I hadn't smoked anywhere near enough of that pot, I thought.

Myra Epstein now cast her unsympathetic gaze directly on me—my sweating face, my drooping shoulders, my fuzzy attention toward the woman with whom she watched television—and evidently did not find much to trust. "Say, what kind of lawyer are you, anyway? What kind of lawyer comes at nine o'clock on a Thursday night? Maybe I should ask to see some identification."

I let my breath out slowly. "I'm her son," I said.

"Oh, and what's this Friedmann business, may I ask? A son doesn't know his own last name?"

"It's a little complicated, Mrs. Epstein. I wonder if you'd mind leaving us alone for a few minutes."

"I very much *would* mind. I'll stay right here with my friend, thank you. You just go ahead and conduct your business. Pretend I'm not here. I won't say a word." As evidence of her sincerity, she stubbed out her cigarette and directed her full attention at the television.

I went to the foot of the bed, so that my face was just below my mother's line of vision, and touched her gently on the ankle. She looked shrunken, jaundiced, the bones of her face prominent, stretching the yellow skin so tight the capillaries showed through like measles. Her hair was thin, mostly white, though there were discordant black streaks on top. The dark recesses around her eyes were deep as wells; the pupils themselves were washed out and trembly in their fluidity. She looked pale and infinitely, infinitely small. My mother, I had to remind myself, was not yet sixty years old.

"Ma," I said in a tight voice. "It's Hesh, Ma."

No response. Her gray eyes blinked dully.

"Ma," I said again. "I'm here, Ma. Mom . . ."

Myra Epstein did not say a word, as promised. But her tongue clicked knowingly a couple of times, and she made some noise moving the position of her chair.

"Mom? It's Hesh. Mom, it's Hesh. It's Heshie, Mom."

I was no longer very stoned, but to my ears my voice seemed distant and full of hope. It had no relation to anything I'd heard myself sound like for as long as I could remember.

"It's Heshie, Mom." I brought both hands together around her ankles, and held on. They were surprisingly thick; also smooth, cool, veined like marble. "Mommy?"

Very slowly, in a kind of ballet, her eyes floated from the television to me, and from there to the hands on her ankles. And there she let them rest.

"Oh, Mommy. Oh Christ, Mommy."

"You won't get much out of her, young man," said Myra Epstein. "She's not what they call a verbal person. She's a very good listener, though. That's why we get along so well. Me," she acknowledged, "I'm oriented that way. Towards the verbal. Nothing I can do about it."

"Have you ever tried?"

I wanted her to scream. I wanted her to scream at me and then, when she was done screaming, maybe I'd wake up and find myself somewhere else.

But Myra Epstein would not accommodate me. Her finger dabbed once again at her tongue, in fluent control. "Mr. Sarcastic," she said. "That's what New York does to you nowadays. I feel sorry for you, if you want to know the truth."

"How long has she been like this?" I released my mother's ankles and then faced the unpleasant task of deciding what to do with my hands. For the moment, I put them in my pockets. "Is she always this bad?"

"What do you care, anyway? You're not here. I'm here all the time. I'm the one who cares. You? You talk through your hat."

"You don't understand, Mrs. Epstein."

"What's to understand?" She lit another cigarette—this time she lit it herself, without any gallantry—and waved away the smoke. "She's always been quiet. Not one of those social butterflies in the chorus. A serious person. Since the last attack, she's quieter, that's all. People don't change much, in my opinion. They just get more so. Are you really the son?"

I nodded.

"Any children?"

From my wallet, I withdrew two pictures of Solly: one as a baby, the other taken the year before at the Central Park Zoo. Myra Epstein held them in her lap as she looked them over without comment. My mother, I observed, continued to watch my hands, following their movements even now that they had released hold of her ankles. She watched in a kind of dreamy wonder. Her breaths were audible, regular.

"You've got good-looking genes in your family. That's a nice thing." Having extended this much of a compliment, Myra Epstein felt impelled to qualify it. "Of course, there are other things that count, you know. Environment gets involved. My grandson Howard was a delightful person until he went to college. Then he started in with the rock music. Now he wears an earring. He wants to live in Holland, he says, so he can bicycle everywhere."

"That doesn't seem so terrible," I said, looking at my mother.

"Sure, you can say that. You're the lawyer. Where's your wife in these pictures, by the way?"

"Mrs. Epstein, no offense, but I'd really like to be concentrating on my mother right now. I haven't seen her in a long time."

"Is that my fault? I should feel bad for that?"

"It's nobody's fault," I said. I liked the sound of the phrase. An immaculate concept. "Nobody's fault," I repeated, ducking my mother's stare.

I went over to her dresser and yanked open the top drawer.

"Hey," said Myra Epstein, "what are you—"

There they were. Twenty, maybe twenty-five envelopes addressed to Mrs. Ruth Friedmann, Santa Fe. In my own handwriting. Each seal as perfect and unbroken as fresh ice.

I turned back to the bed. My mother regarded me with slow, almost curious concentration. Her eyes seemed to be skating. Her nostrils flared; her gray lips went tight. It looked more like discomfort than recognition, but there was no way to tell. "It's me," I said loudly. "Hesh. Can you hear me?"

Finally a quiver seemed to run through her, and then another. Her cheeks became flooded with color, and her wrists twitched once, oddly, as though from an electrical charge.

"That's right. Hesh. *Heshie*, Ma. You *hear* me?"

I strode back to the dresser, threw open the drawer, and grabbed a fistful of the envelopes, ripping them open with my fingers on my way to the bed. Some of the contents spilled over her lap, others onto the floor.

There were photographs, notes, checks, invitations, announcements, birthday cards, hasty crayon drawings. A storm of paper. A blizzard.

"Look!" I barked.

In her thronelike chair, Myra Epstein squirmed, her flesh trembling with emotion. "Why don't you leave her *alone*? What's she done to *you*?"

"Shut up!"

I was tearing through another batch of envelopes, my mother watching me with mute fascination, my bad ear flooded with static. I felt high, low, full of fear, and vaguely nauseous. When I found what I was looking for— a picture of Solly taken the year before, standing on the bridge in his baseball uniform, his cap pulled down too low over his eyes, so that most of his face was in shadow; an inept picture, really, with only a distant likeness to the boy I knew him to be—I crouched by the headboard, so that my face was only inches from hers, and cradled the picture in the palm of my hand, directly before us. A milky scent rose from her scalp. "Solomon," I whispered fiercely.

It had been her father's name, a name the sound of which I had always loved, its three rounded syllables like a series of verdant hills, and something loosened inside me as I pronounced it. Perhaps I was merely light-headed from the marijuana, because I felt a certain slippage, an unhinging; the borders of time itself began to loosen a little, to weave, like a bicycle chain slipping free of its gears, and I suffered a mad and ghostly vision of being present, somehow, at my own birth: this bed, this room, this light, this woman, this child. . . . It was all light and air around us, I wanted to tell her, tell us both, and we had only to close our eyes and jump, to be free. . . .

But our eyes weren't closed. Not mine, not my mother's, not Myra Epstein's, and especially not Deborah Rosenthal's, which were wide and clear and somewhat lacking in mercy, I noticed, when she insinuated them between me and my mother a half minute later. "I think you'd better come with me," she said, her gaze moving from the overflowing ashtray to me with equal disapproval. "Visiting hours were over some time ago."

"For a second there I thought he was crazy," explained Mrs. Epstein. "He started running around throwing paper in the air. I've never seen such a thing."

"You can tell me all about it later, Myra. I'm sorry if you were disturbed. This should never have happened."

Suddenly—perhaps from the sight of my mother tracing her index finger over the picture of the small boy on her lap, or perhaps because she was no stranger to crazy herself—Myra Epstein softened, and ventured a word of defense for a fellow traveler. "We had an interesting conversation. This man is from New York. They've got unusual ways of doing things, that's all."

"So I see," said Mrs. Rosenthal wryly. Then, to me, "Will you come along now, please? Will you get up from the floor and come along, please?"

I was on the floor because I was hastily gathering the envelopes that had fallen beneath the bed; now, feeling more than a little sheepish, I stood up and faced the triad of older women with whom I was sharing this nightmare. My mother's expression was still benignly curious, though not so very different, in truth, than it had been when she was watching television.

"I'm her son," I told Mrs. Rosenthal. "I just want to give her back these letters that fell on the floor."

"Son?" At least forty, having worked in a nursing home for, I imagined, some dozen or so years, Mrs. Deborah Rosenthal was pretty unflappable, doubtless accustomed to finding the relatives of her charges in postures stranger than this. A hint of boredom stole into her calm, coppery eyes. "If you're her son, I'm sure you'll agree that her best interests are most important."

"Yes," I said, and tucked the pile of envelopes into the angle formed by my mother's torso on the bedspread. She made no sign of satisfaction or lack of it. I touched my lips lightly to her brow, feeling bone.

"Are you ready?"

I forced myself away from her and followed Mrs. Rosenthal out the door. The hallway was still deserted. "Very nice having met you," I heard Myra Epstein call out behind us in a rush. "It's the humidity that does it. I used to be from there myself, you know. . . ."

On the wall of the administrator's office, the seniors no longer seemed to be quite so smiling and carefree, but appeared strained in their enthusiasms, as though trying too hard to please the photographer. The room felt chilly. Sitting on the wrong side of the desk, I experienced another stab of adolescent paranoia—I'd been caught smoking in school, and now I was going to get it. The chair dug into my back like a reproach. "I'm sorry if I broke any rules," I said. "I didn't know. I just wanted to see my mother."

"It was inappropriate, and foolish, to see someone in her condition without consulting me first."

"I didn't know anything about her condition. I had no idea how ill she was."

She smiled a condescending smile, wondering, no doubt, what in the world I did have ideas about.

"How ill *is* she?"

"Your mother," she said, "is in a delicate position. Her organs are weak, except for the heart. Her motor skills have deteriorated since the second stroke. And she tends to be withdrawn, mentally. Especially these past months."

"I'd say, having just been with her, that's an understatement."

"The point is, Mr.—"

"Freeman. Herschel Freeman."

"The point is, Mr. Freeman, your mother has not been responding as well as we'd hoped to treatment, and visitors, it seems, are something of a hazard for her. Of course, given the right circumstances, they could make all the difference in her attitude. There's a great deal about her condition that we don't entirely understand. But really, this kind of carrying on—"

"Excuse me," I said, "but has she *had* many visitors?"

She took her time answering, to let me know how little she appreciated being interrupted. "Well, there was her sister, of course, but not very recently. Chicago is such a long distance. Oh, there have been others, through the last couple of years. But not very many. And invariably your mother would be distraught afterwards."

"Any idea who these people were?"

"I'm sorry."

I could not tell from her voice whether or not this was true, or how much, if anything, she knew of our family history. A half-pint container of milk was on the desk blotter in front of her. She leaned forward now to open the spout. Her features, as she sipped the milk through a tiny straw, relaxed somewhat, and for a moment I had a glimpse of a fifteen-year-old honey named Debby Rosenthal, reviewing her notes in some lonely, well-lit corner of a high school cafeteria.

"Can I at least ask where the money's coming from to keep her here?"

"Why, the Lab, in part. And the state pays the rest. Surely you knew that."

I shook my head. "We haven't been in touch in some time, my mother and I. In fact, I didn't even know she'd gone back to her maiden name."

"Oh, that's been several years already. Since the divorce."

"Wait—what divorce?"

She looked at me blankly. "Why, from her ex-husband, of course."

"I didn't . . ."

"Oh, this was two, three years ago. I was here when she signed the

127

papers. I'm afraid it was a difficult experience for her. She's still far from being an old woman, you see." She studied me for a moment. "Are you feeling all right, Mr. Freeman? Do you need to lie down?"

"I think maybe some of your milk, if you don't mind. I'm very thirsty."

"Go right ahead."

She pushed across the container of milk, watched me finish it, and waited as I crumpled it and threw it in the garbage can beside the desk before she commented, "It seems this visit was a shock on all sides."

I was tired, so tired I could barely nod my head. The drive back would be long, dreary; I'd have to stop for coffee. I'd never get to sleep.

But Deborah Rosenthal's plans for me were moving in an opposite direction. Suddenly she perked up, her eyes going bright, her mouth twisting into its practiced official smile. "Will you be coming back tomorrow?" she asked. "Because it strikes me that you really *can* do her a world of good, you know. You can make a great deal of difference in such a case as this, provided, of course, you don't upset her. She's so easily upset."

"I don't think I'll be able to make it tomorrow," I said. "But maybe in a few days. I'm in the area on business, you see. Maybe in a few days."

"A few days?" She lost some of her brightness; she looked, for a moment, regretful that she'd given away her milk to me.

"As soon as I can," I said.

"Well, then." She stood and reached out her hand to me. "Please see me first next time, Mr. Freeman. Visiting hours, by the way, are over at eight o'clock. We ask that they be respected."

"Of course."

"Good-bye then."

"Good-bye."

On my way out I tried a wave on the young receptionist, but she was chatting with an attendant her own age and did not see me leave. My eyes were itching badly. At the car, I paused to put in some more drops. I had to stand there for a full minute, blinking, until they cleared. Above me the white peaks of the Sangre de Cristos glimmered like a holograph.

On the drive back to Albuquerque I thought of Denver, Colorado, of a city a mile high.

Chapter 14

"I wish you'd stop saying that," objected Dr. Donald Ziobro. "I don't understand what you mean. I don't think *you* understand what you mean."

Abby Gordon cleared her throat and began again. "I mean, it must have been difficult for you to continue with your research after that. After V-E Day, that is. Once the ethical base had been eroded."

"What are you talking about, young lady? We were in a war with Japan in the Pacific."

She felt his hostility like a physical force; it vaguely sickened her. "Yes," she said, "but they didn't have fission. The whole point of the project was to beat Hitler to atomic weapons, wasn't it? And once he'd been beaten, didn't that call for some kind of reevaluation?"

They sat, the two of them, on opposing sides of a formica table in the coffee shop on Trinity Drive. It was a gray Saturday morning. The physicist wore a light plaid flannel shirt, blue jeans, and hiking boots; his presence nevertheless seemed to Abby as severe and formal as the clouds looming outside. His round face was heavily lined, both from age and from the frequency and intensity of his frowning, and his craggy features were spotted with dark pores. Sipping black coffee and staring impatiently across the table, he appeared to be making a show of his curmudgeon-liness, as though living up to some moniker she had no knowledge of; she wondered if he practiced in front of the mirror before he left the house. Some choice for her first solo interview! She thought of all the exuberant, amiable faces she'd passed since coming to Los Alamos, all seemingly unthreatened by such a harmless thing as a camera or a tape recorder. Why hadn't she picked one of them to interview this morning? Only, how many of those boy wonders had even been born in 1945, let alone worked, as Ziobro had, on the implosive lens alongside Eli Friedmann?

"I didn't allow myself such sentimental notions," he said. "I didn't at the time, and I don't now. What is this ethical base you use like a bludgeon? Was it unethical of the apple to hit Newton on the head? Who says science grows from ethics? The thing was technically sweet. It worked. That was the thing that mattered."

Abby, though her pocket tape recorder was running, jotted the words *technically sweet* into her notebook, in part to give herself something to do, in part to make sure she remembered them. "But surely there's more to it than that."

"Yes, most people would like to think so, wouldn't they?"

"But even Oppenheimer expressed guilt over it. That famous line: 'I have become death, shatterer of worlds.' "

Ziobro made a face. "Please."

"Then you don't agree."

"I have no wish to knock the man. He did a brilliant job. Possibly nobody else could have done what he did. But he wasn't a saint, or a martyr, either. A colleague of mine once said that some people express guilt to claim credit for the sin. I think you know what I mean."

"Then you agree it was a sin?"

"Young lady, you're twisting my words. My view of the world is complicated enough, I hope, to make such questions meaningless."

"And Dr. Friedmann?"

"A private man," Ziobro said with a shrug. "Difficult to say."

"You don't want to talk about him?"

He moved his head, but she was not sure if he meant anything by it, either way. "We weren't close. The whole thing makes me uncomfortable, frankly. It's a tricky thing to render a man's life. I hope you and your husband understand that."

Abby nodded carefully.

Ziobro leaned back; some of the lines in his face were losing their tension under the narcotic of reminiscence. "I loved it here, I'll say that. I still do, naturally. But then it was like something out of Plato, an ideal city-state. Here I was a nobody, a junior scientist out of Johns Hopkins, and I was exchanging ideas with men who were names in my textbooks. Fermi. Hans Bethe. Do you know about Bethe?"

Was it a test, or was it merely a rhetorical question? Which one *was* Bethe, anyway? There were so many names, and it wasn't her field.

But he was going right on. "This was the man who wrote the equation that explains why the sun shines. An amazing physicist."

She glanced out the window at the outline of the sun, a ghostly circle obscured by a thin layer of cirrus. She wanted to ask him how such a simple

thing could be so complicated it required an equation to make it compre-
hensible, but thought better of it. She should really listen with more
concentration, she thought; she was missing half of what he was saying.

". . . Yes, an extraordinary time. And we did a damn fine job under
difficult circumstances, in very primitive conditions. I think we just
about all felt that way."

"Even after Hiroshima?"

He folded his napkin slowly and laid it next to his coffee cup. She was
losing him, she thought. He wasn't even going to answer.

He was looking out the window again when he finally spoke. "They
should not have dropped it in the center of town. That was a mistake.
There were military establishments that would have been more appropriate. But the truth is, we were relieved the thing worked. It hadn't all
been for nothing. Two billion dollars, several years' work, all those
reputations at stake. We were so afraid it would fizzle, and then how
would we have explained ourselves?" He crossed his legs, groaning
faintly. "Eli and I and some others were more interested in Fat Man,
anyway. That was the implosion device used at Nagasaki. When that one
worked, we knew we'd pulled off something terrific."

His satisfaction, his ease, set her off. At least, that's what she told
herself later. "I'd say you got quite a bargain. A hundred thousand dead
Japanese was all it took to make you feel terrific. Some people require
much more than that."

Ziobro, without moving his head, let his face close down with irritation.

"I"m sorry," she attempted. "All I meant was—"

He lifted his hand to cut her off. "Listen," he said deliberately.
"Invasion of that country would have killed this many. Napalm raids like
we were already running would have killed that many. It could be
debated endlessly. I'm sure there are academics who spend their days
and nights doing that very thing. But it was a military decision, do you
understand? That wasn't our job. We were making breakthroughs that
had intrinsic value and we were following them to see where they'd lead.
We weren't monsters and we weren't devils. We were—are—scientists.
It's our duty, and our passion, to find out how the world works. To pursue
knowledge, to discover, and to share our discoveries with those around
us. I thought you understood that. Why must there be this endless
knee-jerk revisionism? This country is so unintelligent, so whimsical in
its ideas. Why can't people leave the past alone and go on trying to make
the world a more hospitable place in the present and the future?" He rose
to leave. "Now, if you'll excuse me, I'm taking my wife for a hike this
afternoon."

131

Now that she had blown it, now that it didn't matter anymore, she felt some justification for what she said next, for her own timid self-righteousness when she called out after him, "Because no one's sure there'll *be* one. That's why."

He stopped and half turned, so that he was looking out the window, at the Valle Grande beyond, when he replied. "How silly. They've been saying that since the invention of fire, and look at us now."

Abby watched him go. He had a pretty springy step for a man his age, she thought. In the wake of his departure, in fact, she felt a measure of admiration for him, and a concomitant revulsion for herself. He'd been right—she had conducted herself vaguely, unprofessionally, and he'd merely treated her accordingly. She was no good at this; it was all too clear. Let Arthur do it. It was his project, after all. His. When she was honest with herself she knew that, fundamentally, she cared very little about the events of three decades ago. Her interest, as usual, was in herself. Wasn't she just using this documentary, using Arthur, to get a writing credit, so that she might get more work on her own? In that case, she thought, she must have already decided to leave him. But she could not remember making any such decision.

One kiss with Herschel Freeman, however pleasant, was not the whole story. On the other hand, since returning from Majorca the previous month, she had not found herself even capable of *looking* for the whole story. She could almost feel herself drifting, feel the first subaqueous tugs of the rapids that lay ahead. Something in her had begun to give up; now she wondered if she possessed the strength, or the patience, to fight it. Maybe that was why she'd blown it with Ziobro. Who was *she* to judge *him*? At least he'd applied himself to accomplishing something, instead of flitting from one thing to another the way she had. He wasn't so bad, really. She wished he had stuck around longer, so that she could ask some other, more pressing questions. Did Ziobro see a therapist? Was Ziobro haunted by such phantoms as "personal fulfillment"? Had Ziobro ever spent an entire morning mooning to himself in a strange coffee shop, the way she was doing now?

What was it Arthur used to say? If you're going to act, you've got to learn to ignore. Another line from Valéry. And she'd given Hesh the impression that *she* was the one who read and noted such things. Not that she was lying, of course; she *had* read Valéry, and Ortega y Gasset, and Baudelaire, and plenty of others. Only, more often than not, at the suggestion (the insistence?) of her husband. Her tutor. Her mentor. Her great love. Who believed in her.

Why? She could hardly remember.

Because he believed in himself. And what was she, really, but an extension, a reflection, of him? What was she but his creation? What else?

In fact, Arthur reminded her a little of Dr. Ziobro. The same ability to focus on the problem at hand, to take action in a burning house. Even with all their nocturnal bickering, he'd been lighthearted and undistracted that morning when she drove him to the airport. He had a meeting in L.A. with some prospective backers. It would go well, of course. He was so good with money people because he was so unfailingly optimistic, because he believed in himself utterly. And now it was this very quality, this strength of purpose, that she found so intolerable in him. Because the truth of it was that she did not know if *she* believed in him. Because she did not know if she believed in anything. That was the fact. She only knew that she was thirty years old and she wanted to be happy already. Was that such an ignoble thing? Were you only happy if you were making something?

Then do it, she told herself. Make yourself something. Write a script. Get a job. Have a baby. Take a lover.

She looked deep into the perfect bowl of her coffee cup.

After a moment she fished in her purse for change, then went to the pay phone in the back of the diner. The number he'd given her was scribbled on a small strip of yellow paper, torn from a legal pad. The line rang twice, and then a woman's voice answered. "Sullivan and Peck. Just a moment, please."

A faint serenade played on the line as Abby Gordon took a deep breath and called herself two or three unflattering names. When the woman came back to ask with whom she wished to speak, Abby pushed the name out forcefully. What *is* this ethical base you use like a bludgeon? she asked herself.

And then she heard his voice on the other end, gruff and preoccupied and very nearly as mood-ravaged as her own. "Freeman."

She held her breath. If he didn't hear her, she could still hang up the phone and nothing would have started.

"Hello?"

But that was simple weakness on her part. A tendency toward flight. She had to overcome it, and she might as well start now. "It's me," she said.

There was a pause. He didn't know who she was. He kissed women on the street all the time. He was busy fucking someone right now.

But his voice this time sounded smaller. "Abby?"

"It's me," she heard herself say again.

"Where are you?"

133

"Los Alamos. I had an interview. Oh, Hesh, I—it didn't go well. *Nothing*'s going well. All of a sudden I feel thoroughly incompetent at everything"—she was blurting it out, talking too fast, saying too much, but now that she had begun she found it all but impossible to stop—"and I'm all alone in this creepy town, and I think I'm about to go insane."

Another pause, as she fought for breath. Wasn't he going to say anything? Was she going to have to keep on babbling like this forever? Now the waitress at the counter was giving her the eye. She'd heard that "creepy town" remark, or else she just didn't care for the sort of person who took up a table for two hours on a tab of fifty cents.

"Listen, Abby," Hesh Freeman said finally, "do you have a car?"

"Yes. We rented one."

"Would you like to drive down to Albuquerque for dinner tonight? I'll be tied up until around eight. Is eight okay?"

"Yes," she said, thinking: What will I do until eight? "Yes. Eight's just fine. Hesh?"

"I'm right here," he said.

But she could hear other voices in the background; he must have been in the middle of a hundred things that lawyers were busy with all the time. She half whispered, quickly, "Arthur's in L.A. for the day. He comes back tomorrow."

"I see," he said slowly.

You see *what*?

The operator chose that moment to come on the line and request more money.

"Abby? Look, give me your number and I'll call you back in two minutes. I want to switch phones, anyway."

Without her reading glasses, which she'd left on the table, she had to stick her nose right up to the white strip under the phone dial when she read the number. He hung up without saying good-bye.

She went back to her booth and sipped at the cold coffee left in her cup. There was her notebook open in front of her, and the pocket tape recorder Arthur had given her for her thirtieth birthday. One thing she particularly liked about doing the film was that she got to use it. A great little machine, she thought. She turned it on, rewound the tape, and listened to the interview again. It had not really been that terrible. Some of it might even be of use. That business about Oppenheimer, for instance. And that expression Ziobro had used, *technically sweet*. And she'd get better, undoubtedly, as she went on. It was valuable work, very valuable. And between the money from the Endowment and the funds Arthur was off raising that day, they'd have the resources to do a really thorough, quality job. Who was Ziobro to lecture them, anyway? A nasty old hawk, a truly odious man. He reminded her a little of her own father, back in Concord, New Hampshire, who had sold his small shoe factory to the government so the poor bastards who went to Vietnam could be shod. Hadn't that been a technically sweet arrangement? Wasn't that what it was all about, in this culture—sweets? Wasn't the whole complex of military and industry, all the machinery of commerce, just some confectionery Disneyland driving the entire miserable country into a diabetic coma?

She remembered that her system could not really accommodate three cups of coffee.

To slow herself down, she began to write. Once begun, the words came of themselves, spilling from her pen into the notebook in wanton profusion. She had only to move her wrist to see it happen. Words and words. They built to lines. Lines built to pages. The small circles described by her writing hand widened sinuously, like smoke rings, until they began to enfold her.

The window in Barney Peck's Albuquerque office looked out over a baseball diamond used by the local American Legion team. The grass shone a brilliant green in the midday sun, and was empty, save for one teenage boy, shirtless, in faded cutoffs, who was practicing with his Frisbee. He would fling the silver disk high in the air, it would travel twenty or thirty yards, from center field to second base, and then tilt back in the direction it had come from, softly, steadily descending to the hand that had launched it. It was a splendid thing to see, the silver glinting in the light against the unblemished blue of the sky, making languorous arcs, moving so slowly it promised to allow you to participate in geometry itself, and it made the ten minutes I spent standing there shouldering the receiver, waiting for Abby Gordon to pick up the phone, a slightly less deadening experience.

She had mumbled something about her reading glasses; it seemed entirely possible that she'd gotten the number wrong. Whether or not this was the kind of error to which Abby Gordon was prone, I had no idea. I knew so little about her. Only that there seemed to be a sense of shared affliction between us, a communing of uncertainties. It had brought us together, to some extent, but it seemed just as likely to keep us apart. An image floated to mind and stayed there: two children on a seesaw, neither trusting the other to fully cushion the ride. The matter deserved some thought. Unfortunately, I was sharing Barney Peck's office with a full-blown psychopath in the throes of lovesick depression, and opportunities for reflection were in short supply.

135

Charlie Goldwyn, as was his habit, had thrown the place into a mess, conducting campaigns of discovery on all fronts simultaneously. In the matter of *Navajo Nation* v. *Eastern Oil,* we had already produced a stack of interrogatories two feet high, filed no less than thirty Requests for Admissions and double that number of Requests for Production of Documents, to say nothing of the time and resources expended in responding to discovery requests filed by the plaintiffs—and we were just getting started. The trick in discovery is to get all the information you possibly can while at the same time divulging as little as possible to the other side. Charlie's tactic, however, was to go one better. Because the other side was understaffed and already being stretched to their limit, his strategy was to swamp them in paper—produce such voluminous documents in response to their interrogatories, padded with so many irrelevancies, that they'd lose the forest for the trees. It was an exercise in public secrecy, in message jamming, a vicious battle in the protracted combat of information that is litigation. And it couldn't fail to succeed.

All of this made for a good deal of noise. Squadrons of associates were chatting garrulously into their Dictaphones; an army of secretaries clattered away at their IBMs, committing it all to paper; the boys in the copy room were sweating through their T-shirts, trying to keep up; and the post offices in two cities buzzed like hives. Beneath all this surface verbiage ran a steady percussive rustle of tender. Everyone was being paid by the word, in effect, and the word was *uranium*. It made us all busy and proud. Ours was the kind of strategy that big, rich firms delight in, for it manhandles the notion that under the law of the land they have no more clout than poor, small ones; and, under different circumstances, it would no doubt have delighted Charlie Goldwyn.

But discovery on his other case—*Shakespeare, Dante & Goldwyn* v. *The Enigma of Lucy Johnson*—was not going nearly so well. For one thing, it required much long-distance driving. Her office was in Crown Point, near the Arizona border, a good hour's drive from Albuquerque. A *bad* hour's drive, I'd found out the night before, when undertaken at midnight, after a long day's work, on a stomach bloated with Mexican food and beer, with a passenger who insists on listening to country music turned up loud to drown out the bombastic thunder of his own tormented heart.

I myself would never have gone along on the trip, of course. But we had a meeting scheduled in Gallup early the next morning, and Charlie—sly, grotesque Charlie—had insisted we would do better to discuss our strategy out in the night air, under the benevolent light of the stars. I'm as foolish as the next subordinate, I suppose: I took him at his word. It was only when I saw the sign for the Crown Point turnoff in the Lincoln's headlights that the real purpose of the expedition revealed itself to me. And by then it was too late.

"Why, look where we are, Charlie," I said. "Crown Point. How'd that happen, I wonder?"

"Y'know, Heshie," he said quietly, "I hear this is quite a little town."

"No fooling. Too bad it's so late, and we have to get back."

"Don't be such a schoolboy. Let's find a nice local dive and I'll blow you to a beer. Howzat sound?"

"Goddamn you, Charlie. What do you need me for?"

"Now don't get mad. It'll be a nice quick trip, I promise. Just keep your eyes out for"—he rummaged in his pocket, extracted a scrap of paper, and flipped on the overhead light to examine it—"a Kayente Drive."

"I think we just passed it."

"That's okay. Take your time. It's just a little town. We'll circle around."

I found the blackness past the windshield oppressive, so I kept one eye, as I drove, on the man in the passenger's seat. I watched him run a comb through his thinning hair and then lick a palm to smooth down his sideburns, like a fat jungle cat readying for the kill. He took off his tie and loosened the top button of his expensive Italian shirt. He drummed his fingers on his hammish thigh. In the space of two minutes, he raised fidgeting to a form of art. Finally, with an interest so keen it nearly broke my heart, he examined the length and cleanliness of his fingernails, shaking his head unconsciously at whatever portentous message he found hidden in those white, rounded moons. Had Lucy Johnson only been there in the car, instead of wherever the hell she was, she would have been, I thought, a goner. I said as much to Charlie. He giggled once nervously in response and rubbed his hand over the spot where his breath had fogged the window.

After another minute, he grunted. "There it is. Pull over."

The house was not a house but a trailer, and not much of a trailer at that. Two cinder blocks served as a front porch, their ragged gray dimensions illumined by a bare yellow bulb of meager wattage. The yard looked stumpy, neglected. The only adornment anywhere on the property was a satellite dish, about fifty feet east of the trailer. It must have been in working order—the lush vulgarities of television music were audible even across the street, where I pulled over. "Something tells me we're not in Kansas anymore," I said.

"I don't get this," muttered Charlie. "I don't get this at all. I took her to the Museum of Modern *Art*, for Christ's sake. This doesn't figure."

"Well," I said casually, "I guess it's time to go back."

But Charlie was already lurching out the door. "Just sit tight. I'll be back in a minute." He vaulted over the rocks that marked the perimeter of the yard, and disappeared inside.

The moon was half full, its darkened portion still visible in outline. I tuned the radio to an all-night news channel, but it was difficult to make out what was being said, especially with the late-show music coming from the trailer. The Lincoln felt big as a house around me. I leaned my head back against the seat and, for a brief moment, let my eyes fall closed. The subliminal cacophony of the night animals welled up like a hemorrhage.

"Yo, Heshie! Come in and be sociable."

Charlie, his head lit monkishly by the yellow bulb, was waving at me from the cinder blocks, the door of the trailer open behind him.

But I did not find, when I entered, Lucy Johnson. Instead, amid a squalor fully equal to that of the exterior, sat a leathery little man in blue jeans and T-shirt, leaning back in a patched BarcaLounger, the soles of his raised feet caked gray with dust. His nose was long and straight, his hair a mane of snow, and his eyes were wide and hard and black. He looked, for some reason, more than a little happy to see me.

"This man's name is Popo," Charlie roared over the television.

I nodded, took a step forward, prepared to shake hands, only Popo made no move to rise out of his position. A bottle of Jim Beam and three 7-Up glasses were on the card table beside him. "Have a drink?" he asked me.

"I told him we were representing Eastern Oil, and he got very friendly," Charlie informed me. "He's very eager, Heshie, to have a drink with us."

"I'm only sorry I didn't get a chance to clean up the place," said our host. "Nobody told me you all were coming."

"So what happened to your girlfriend?" I hissed to Charlie.

"Later," he said. He had appropriated the remote control for the television, and his big fingers moved over its surface until they found the mute. In the sudden quiet, he turned back to Popo. "Now, Mr. Johnson, you were saying something about that business with your land."

The Navajo, pouring out three stiff drinks, grinned with equal parts satisfaction and irritation. "I told you what I told those other men. The ones that brought around that piece of paper. I'm more than happy to sell. This is allotted land; I can do whatever the hell I want."

"Of course you can," agreed Charlie. "So, in other words, when that agreement came to you, and you signed it—"

"In ink, mind you."

"In ink, and you read it over—and you understood exactly what it was you were signing, is that right?"

"Course I understood," snapped Popo Johnson. "I can speak English as good as any white man. Better, I'll wager."

"Of course you can. I didn't mean to imply—"

"Look, I'm not trying to cheat nobody. I just want what's coming. Uranium, from what I hear, is a valuable thing, but I got no use for it here. Let them come and get it, I say."

Charlie nodded and murmured, as though to himself, "Too bad some of your neighbors didn't understand what they signed. It would have made things so much easier."

Popo Johnson leaned forward and, with a proud lunge, swallowed the bait, hook and all. "Oh, don't let them fool ya. They understood, a good lot of them. They're just trying to drive up the price of the settlement. Those scare stories about radiation in the water don't fool me, mister. It's all a money game. Everybody around here just wants to play. Not much else to do, is part of it. Plus screw the white man, of course."

"Of course," Charlie agreed.

"We know how to screw, mister. We've learned that much, all right."

Charlie's head was bobbing up and down as though someone had overoiled the hinge in his neck. "Now, Mr. Johnson, I wonder if you'd be so kind as to entertain a couple of our colleagues later this week. They'd be very grateful if they could come out here and write some of this down. How's Thursday? You busy Thursday?"

"Hell, I ain't busy. Let 'em come and take down whatever they want." He gulped at his drink and smiled craftily. "It's a free country, ain't it?"

I turned my back on this conversation and looked around the trailer. Above the neatly made single bed, an assortment of yellowed photographs were taped unevenly to the wall. All of them showed men in uniform. "Were you in the war, Mr. Johnson?"

He looked past Charlie and down his imperial nose at me. "Sonny," he said, "you got no idea."

"Well," said Charlie, brushing his palms against his slacks, "guess we'd better get—"

Popo Johnson leaned forward, his chair folding into a right angle. "I was a Codetalker. That mean anything to you?"

"No."

"Heroes of the Pacific, four hundred of us. The Japs couldn't break it. Used Navajo, you see. Drove them damn near crazy, poor Japs. Know what we called the Japs. *Ana'i.* Called the bombers *ginitsoh.* Sparrow hawk. They must have thought we were Martians. Or geniuses. Couldn't break it." Haltingly, he rose out of the chair and came forward to the rows of pictures. He seemed frail, tentative in his steps. "Here, let me show you. . . ."

"We really shouldn't take up any more of your time," declared Charlie, looking at me meaningfully.

"No?" Popo stopped in midstep. "Well, maybe when you all come back, eh?"

"That won't be us, Mr. Johnson. It'll be other men. Colleagues."

"Oh sure," he said vaguely. "I remember you said that."

When we shook hands, he tilted into the space between us awkwardly. "That first word you used," I said. "What did that mean?"

"What, *ana'i*? It's what we called the Japs, like I told you."

"But is that what it meant? Or was it only gibberish?"

He shook his head, his dreamy white hair. "No, not that at all. It's an old saying. It means 'the enemy.' "

Out on the empty street, I thought about the day we'd spent, and the sound of Charlie oiling testimony from the man in the trailer, and I did not feel very pleased with the course of my life. "Let's get out of here," I said.

"The wrong Johnson," said Charlie with a shrug. "Well, like I always say, you do what you can with what you get your hands on. That'll make one very pretty deposition."

We got into the car. I touched my foot to the gas and heard the Lincoln rev up and roar like a lion.

"You're a good lawyer," I told Charlie, and he didn't look at all surprised to hear it.

The next morning was a hectic one; by the time I got back to Barney Peck's office, I was frazzled and already dreading what would undoubtedly be a long, enervating afternoon. When I was at my very worst, when my blood sugar had sunk to its lowest ebb and the paperwork on my borrowed desk had reached its greatest height, I received the call from Abby Gordon, which ended so mysteriously. Then I had a tasteless sandwich, a couple of tasteless phone conversations with New York, and spent the next several hours noting the documents that had to be mailed to the plaintiffs before noon the next day.

Around six o'clock I gave the list to one of the Sullivan and Peck secretaries, instructing her to round up as many of the documents as she could find. She was a plain, humorless young woman who evidently felt employed below her station, because she did not agree very gracefully to do it. "But this is gonna take me two *hours*," she complained, stamping her feet below her IBM.

"So what?" I rejoined, in my best Manhattanese.

"Mr. Peck promised to let me leave on time tonight. I've got an appointment. Can't you give it to somebody else?"

Something washed over me then, something like weariness, something like disgust, and I felt myself giving in to a conditioned response I had never fully given in to before. "Listen," I said softly, "your name's Mary, right?"

She nodded unhappily.

I brought my hand up and, gently, pushed an errant string of dry blond hair off her cold forehead. "Mary, my name's Hesh. That's what I want you to call me."

"Okay," she said cautiously.

"Now, I'm sure you have a busy and abundant life outside this office, Mary, and I don't, God knows, begrudge you your appointments. But I think you should know, Mary, that this is an important case, important enough to bring Mr. Goldwyn and myself all the way from New York, and we've been working very hard on it. The truth is, Mary, I don't enjoy working very hard, and I'm not having a great deal of fun out here, and right now—right now, Mary—I'm on the verge of taking it out on you. Do you understand?"

She nodded. She may even have been listening. It didn't matter.

"So here is what I want you to do. I want you to take this list and go compile these various documents. Then I want you to bring the pile back to me and smile your most alluring smile, the one you use on all your favorite appointments, and I want you to say, 'Hesh, I do not resent you for making me do this.' If you can pull all of that off, Mary, I think we're going to be good friends. Do you think you can pull that off?"

When she glared up at me this time her eyes were wet behind her glasses, and two front teeth had emerged to bite down hard on her colorless lower lip. She did not say a word. At a certain point I realized that she was waiting for me to go back to my office, that she wouldn't move a muscle until I was gone. When I saw myself reflected for a moment in the lenses of her glasses, beads of sweat popped out on my forehead and my bad ear began buzzing with static. It was no great trick to recognize the look of a partner.

An hour later Mary pushed into my office, waving my list like an enemy flag. "I can't find them," she said flatly, taking care to stand a good ten feet away. "Almost all of them are missing."

"That's impossible. Check the interoffice memos for the last couple days. Maybe they were sent to New York by mistake, along with the copies."

"I already did, Mr. Freeman. Twice."

"Okay, what time is it—seven? Check with—"

It had been a rhetorical question, but Mary took the opportunity to inform me, icily, "It's seven-*thirty*. No one's around. They've all gone home."

"They have?"

"Yes, Mr. Freeman."

The set of her chin made it clear that she would go to her grave before asking me again for permission to leave. An apology wouldn't help matters, I knew, but I took a shot at one anyway. "I'm sorry for keeping you so long."

"I don't mind," she said tonelessly.

"Well, I'm sorry," I heard myself repeat, my voice more gruff than I'd have liked. "Okay, I'll see you tomorrow. Have a nice evening."

"You too, Mr. Freeman."

She turned on her heel and strode out, literally bumping into someone just outside the office door. There was some straightening of clothes, and then Abby Gordon came in, rubbing her elbow, and drew to a stop not far from the spot occupied by Mary a minute before. Women, it appeared, were not eager to come very close to me.

"What's the matter with her?" asked Abby.

"One of her superiors has been browbeating her."

"Why?"

There was nothing hidden in the question; she merely wanted to know. But I chose to answer suggestively. "He must have been angry about something else. The term, I believe, is displacement."

Abby's eyes hardened and her lips disappeared. I was really in fine form, I thought. I could hardly wait to see who would walk through that door next for me to antagonize.

But the tension lasted only a minute. She defused me by taking two steps forward and flopping into one of the room's two swivel chairs. Her face was shiny with color; her dress, as usual, was a simple summer cotton. However she'd been feeling when she called, she was no longer feeling the same way. At least, that's what I assumed from her appearance; I wasn't really sure. Beneath the serenity of her expression there was something that made her inscrutable—she seemed to be enjoying a private knowledge, savoring her own self-involvement, as though she'd only recently awakened from a cathartic and easily deciphered dream which she felt no great urgency about sharing. Her mood could not have

142

been more different from mine, nor felt so immediately abrasive, had she just won a fortune in the lottery. "I think I must have read the number wrong," she said mildly, at the precise instant I decided she hadn't. "I didn't have my glasses with me."

"Sure," I said. "I understand. No big deal."

"I know it's no big deal," she asserted. "But I wanted to apologize, anyway. In case you waited."

The baseball diamond below the window was now alive with teenagers in expensive uniforms. You could hear the chatter of the infielders in Barney Peck's office.

"Is that why you're here? To apologize?"

"Partly," she singsonged, all of a sudden as blithe as a schoolgirl.

"Abby, you're beginning to make me crazy, you know that?"

"Then let's go have dinner," she said. "We'll get along better after we've eaten something. Come."

She put out her hand, and I rose to take it. I was already half gone on her. A cheer went up from the baseball field—someone had hit a long line drive, and the left and center fielders were giving chase. Abby and I went over to the window to watch the play. The two boys in the field were running as fast as they could, their elbows and knees pumping hard. Base runners were scooting around the bases. Framed by the symmetrical clarity of the diamond, the movements of the players seemed as awkward and ineffectual as those we experience in our worst nightmares. Against the quality of that backdrop, I wondered, how inept would the contest between the two of us have to appear?

We went in my car. The sky was dulled by haze and the traffic was thick. It took some time to find the restaurant, a Mexican place recommended by my colleagues at Sullivan and Peck. It was a small adobe setup with a cactus and fern garden in the back for outdoor dining. Immediately it struck me as vulgar, foolishly romantic, a grade-B *film noir* hideaway in which to contemplate transgressions. But Abby, looking around, seemed charmed. "This is lovely," she said. "It's one nice thing about money, isn't it? Being able to eat wherever you want."

I didn't answer. The menu was eighteen inches high, and I buried myself in it. The waiter came over with the margaritas we'd ordered, but we let them sit.

Abby pursued the topic. "I always thought, actually, that it would be a mark of personal failure or something if I ever found myself eating out at places like this."

"And now?" I asked, not managing to sound terribly interested.

"And now," she said, "I don't know. I'm not so cavalier about marks of personal failure. I try not to even think in those terms. I suppose it had something to do with turning thirty and, I don't know, starting to realize this was *it*, and I'd better start enjoying myself. I've always been such a sacrificial type. It's very tiresome, really. Lately I've been feeling almost, well, decadent." She giggled softly. "Not turning into my mother seems to be a harder job than I ever thought. I guess it's that way for everybody."

I took a long sip of my drink.

"I mean," she went on, "I've always had such high expectations of myself. It's only recently that I've begun to realize I may never meet them. And that that's okay. In fact, it's kind of liberating." She reached for her margarita, avoiding my eyes, her mouth showing lines of strain. Liberation, from the look of things, did not much agree with her.

I figured I'd let her go on like this for about another hour, by which time any attraction she'd ever held for me would have dissipated completely, and I could relax and enjoy the meal. The food came, and it was surprisingly good. I tried to concentrate on the *rellenos,* instead of on Abby's nervous philosophizing, only she would not let up; it was as though there were a series of psychic scabs she could not refrain from picking at. She chattered on compulsively all the way through the meal and well into the coffee, not even registering, I thought, the fact that I was barely participating. I felt something mounting in me. It was a feeling so intense I had to cover my mouth with my hands to keep it from showing.

". . . In fact," she was saying, "I think that's what maturation is all about. Learning to give up your self-consciousness, to accept that the things you thought were absolute are only relative. Otherwise there's no peace. You're continually fighting your own ideal—"

"Shut up."

"Wha—?" She looked stunned.

"Shut up."

Her face froze, her eyes locked on her coffee, and the only sound in the room, it seemed, was the roar of my own pulse.

"No more, Abby, okay? You've made everything crystal clear. We're into overkill at this point. Enough."

Slowly, numbly, she wiped her hands on her napkin. "O-kay," she murmured, in that spooky blithe singsong, and then pushed back her chair, slung her shoulder bag over one arm, and headed for the door.

We had come in my car, and so I didn't hurry. There was plenty of time to peel two twenty-dollar bills from my wallet, lay them over the check, and saunter toward the exit. I was as close to feeling good about myself as I'd felt all day.

All of which lasted until I stepped out into the parking lot and found no Abby Gordon slumped against the locked car door.

I went after her. For fifteen minutes I drove up and down the same stretch of road, cursing us both in a steady monotone and beating the hell out of the dashboard at every red light. In the unfamiliar jumble of buildings and alleys I could find nothing. The windows were all darkened for the night or else flooded with blinking neon—either way, I could not see in. The blind chasing the blind. It wasn't until a taxi cut in front of me, pulling through an intersection, that I had an idea of how she had managed to flee, and of where she must have gone. Undone, I thought, and perhaps for the best.

There she was at the Sullivan and Peck office building, bent over the hood of her car, the contents of her shoulder bag spread before her like the pieces of an elaborate puzzle.

I parked and ran over. She didn't turn at the sound of my footsteps on the asphalt lot. Her shoulders were moving in jerks; the light from the street was strong enough to reveal that much.

"I can't *find* them." She was sobbing quietly. "I've *looked* and *looked*."

I moved to take hold of her shoulders from behind. "Abby," I said.

"I can't figure out where I *put* them."

I turned her around. She went along compliantly, but would not lift her face. "Listen to me," I said.

"What do you want," she muttered.

"I couldn't let you keep talking that way. I couldn't listen to another word about how much you were lowering yourself, and what a failure you felt like, and how decadent and relativistic an experience it was to be having dinner with me—"

"I didn't *say* that! I wasn't even *talking* about that!"

"You were too, dammit, and you know it. You're fucking yourself around, and you're fucking me around, and I'm not going to stand for it. Do you understand?"

No response. Her shoulders in my hands were like stones.

"Now do me a favor."

After a moment she said, in a small, dispirited voice, "What."

"Say something sweet to me."

She fidgeted, and her mouth twisted unpleasantly, but I held on to her and waited her out. Thirty seconds passed. Finally, she mumbled something inaudible in the direction of my shirt.

"What's that? Didn't catch it."

"I said you're very sweet."

"Thank you. So are you."

145

These admissions seemed to drain the life out of both of us. We stood leaning into each other, Abby's back pressed against the door of her car, her fingers loosely clutching the sleeves of my jacket. Whatever else we may have been that night, we were not courageous people. In the distance of midtown, a siren whined its message of license and injury. Abby cleared her throat. "Hesh?"

"I'm right here."

"Why do we keep playing these games with each other?"

"Isn't it obvious?"

"Nothing to me is obvious," she said, her voice growing heavy with self-involvement. I could get tired of her. I tried to hold on to that thought. "Tell me."

"It's because we're afraid of what happens when we stop. Remember? That chain of monsters business."

She looked up at me now without any apparent difficulty. "Do you know that Henry James story about the man who waits?"

"No." Henry James! What was I *doing*?

"He feels that some very special, very private destiny is going to come his way. He tells a woman about it, a friend of his, a soulmate, really, all about it. It will be wonderful and fulfilling, this life, when it comes. And he waits, and waits. . . ."

"And it never comes."

"Is that how you'd have written it?" She cocked her head, finding, evidently, something in my version that reflected poorly on me. "No, it comes. It comes, all right. Only, at the end of his life he realizes that he missed it. That he'd been looking in the wrong places. Because it was her, his friend to whom he confessed everything. This person he made an audience of. She was the thing that would come to him."

I remembered now that I had yet to look up that Hawthorne story Walter Todd had recommended to me. I was going to have to start reading again, to keep up with these people. "I'm a little dense these days, Abby. In other words?"

"In other words, maybe not doing is more monstrous than doing."

"Not if doing is a symptom of weakness and decadence, it's not."

Her eyes left me and flickered toward the street. "You have a cruel streak in you. I don't like that."

"I'm just trying to keep things straight, Abby. Right now at least one of us should. Later, it'll be harder to pull off."

"You say that with such ominous conviction. But I doubt you're right, really. I think you're just hedging your bets."

Of course, this was true of both of us, and as we drove to my hotel in separate cars, the ten minutes alone seemed ample time for one or the other of us to back out. I was reasonably certain that she would and I wouldn't. I was even hoping it would play out that way. But then I remembered the scent of her hair when I'd held her, creamy and apricot, and there was her silhouette in the rearview mirror, sloping, angular, hair splaying fluidly over her shoulders—and she did not seem any sort of threat at all; she seemed like a precious gift.

Inside, we fell into opposite chairs. Abby looked around the room with a sort of wonder, as though she had never seen a hotel room before. Perhaps one has never really seen a hotel room until one has entered it with the purpose of committing adultery. The light thrown by that particular taboo tends toward the surreal: It softens the meticulous arrangement of the furniture, even as it heightens the substantiality of certain links with the outside world—the phone, especially, seems suffused with menace, but the television hides portents of a larger drama, and the windows, well, are windows, and cannot be draped heavily enough to obscure their function.

We sat, then, under the klieg lights of our mutual self-consciousness, on a set that had been designed thousands of miles away, in some tall glass tower, to achieve precisely this effect, this rupture of refuge from home. We had traveled, the room told us, from the world of actual places and actual things to a purer place—a system of controlled internal references, of room service and top-drawer Bibles and cable television, of Magic Fingers and bathrooms ribboned with hygienic paper, a system that fed happily on our money and on something of our self-respect as well. It buckled the will. I had not slept with a woman in the twenty-seven months since my separation from Joanne, and it might just as well have been twenty-seven years: I felt numb, lethargic. All I could think to do was talk, and I didn't want to talk. The issue we had left back in the parking lot was not going to be resolved by conversation. On the other hand, it wasn't likely to be resolved by what we were about to do, either.

All of this deliberation occupied but a fraction of the time it took me to rise to my feet. We met in the middle of the room, at the foot of the bed, and turned in to each other with a kiss. Slowly, slowly, we fell. With my eyes closed it was weightless and airy, a romp through space. We kissed for quite a long time, not so much passionately as tenderly, as though establishing something we had wanted to be sure of first. Then I took off her dress. I peeled the straps gingerly, like the skin of a fruit, and when she was naked I traveled the length of her body with my lips. Abby was hard in some places and soft in others; she was a series of surprises; even the small sounds she made when I tasted her were a surprise, and as we moved I turned my ear to her belly and listened, but they sounded far away, private, exclusive. I turned her over and nibbled at the fine lengthy slope of her back. The lower I moved, the higher she arched toward me, until I was literally biting her, and she was literally crying out, but in an arrhythmic, muffled way that frightened me. I wanted to slow down. I wanted to break it up somehow, with a joke or a look. But the feel of her, the tight downy skin, carried me away, and before I could think to stop myself I had slipped inside her. It was warm, it was an ocean, it was flow and flow and flow, and for a short time I lost track of her completely in the winking lights of my own sensations. But she brought me back. When I stopped moving she made a noise like *ifth* through her teeth and began flexing her inner muscles. She would not let me soften. She kept me inside her and there was something dogmatic and stubborn about the way she held on until I was hard again. Then she slid away and moved on top of me. I watched her as she took, felt the heat of her grinding down at my center. This time she finished first; I had to hold her at the flare of her pale hips as I moved from below, for she was jerking awkwardly and I had no idea where she might go. It was not really so good for me, that second time.

Above me, she was giggling softly, her eyes bright and damp, her slender arms crossing to hug herself around the waist, making a cradle of her own limbs.

"A good joke?"

"I was thinking I had a new way to describe it. A man taught it to me this morning." She saw the look on my face and added, quickly, "It was part of an interview. I mean, it was just something he said."

"What was?"

She smiled down at me from the ceiling. "*Technically sweet.* That's what it was."

It took me a moment to find my breath. In another room, the phone made its shrill ring. We listened to it without moving. It rang ten times. Between the fifth and sixth rings, I decided never to sleep with her again.

"Please," she said. "Please don't pull away."

"Abby, you don't seem to appreciate the difference between pulling and being pushed."

She took a while to digest this, and when she spoke again, I had the sense that she had moved onto another subject. "I liked it better a few minutes ago," she mused, "when there *was* no difference. Didn't you?"

"Yes."

"Can I just lie here like this, on top of you? You won't feel smothered?"

"I won't feel smothered." I reached up and, with my fingers, stroked her damp backside. I could not figure her out. Her breathing went slow, regular; it seemed to take her very little time to get comfortable. I knew it was important to not ask many questions, but I ventured one, anyway. "Are you staying the night?"

"Yes."

"And Arthur?"

"He's flying in tomorrow at eight. I have to pick him up at the airport."

"Are you going to leave him?"

"Yes." She said it quickly, as though she'd been waiting for it. Her weight shifted. "I'm not too heavy; you're sure?"

"I'm sure." And then, even though I'd gone well over my allotment of questions, even though the conversation had already plunged me so far into confusion that my scalp itched, I cleared my throat and asked, "How do you feel?"

She nuzzled down, her mouth smeared against my shoulder. "Tired," she murmured, and I had to content myself with that, because she was instantly asleep.

I hadn't had a full night's rest since arriving in New Mexico, and this was not going to be the one to break the string. For many hours I lay beneath Abby's cool weight, feeling each involuntary tremor as she negotiated the path of her dreams. Above me the pebbly stucco of the hotel ceiling picked up shards of light from the street and glittered like a makeshift galaxy. Occasionally I'd shift my own weight, trying to relax, and Abby remained melded into me, but in the troubled depths of her slumber she seemed as far away as ever. I felt utterly alone, beyond comfort, severed of every connection. My eyes roamed the anemic sepia light, settling at last on a cheaply framed rendering of an Indian pueblo on the opposite wall. It was badly done, a jagged, washed-out pyramid of muddy adobe, the black doorways empty of life and abandoned by art, and yet its very bleakness spoke to something in my spirit that had accustomed itself to hollow structures.

It was only much later, at the foot of morning's summit, that I drifted into sleep.

Chapter 15

July 1945: The Road to Alamogordo

All afternoon, it seems, they have been heading down.

To Eli Friedmann, rattling along with four other men in a dilapidated army vehicle, his entire tangled consciousness seems to have mysteriously straightened into lines—lines that link theory with execution, the private with the public, an individual past with a collective future. Straight lines. Reason contradicts, asserts that the lines of nature are always curved. But there are moments, he thinks, that subvert reason, and this is—will be—one of them.

The road ahead shimmers in the dreary July heat. The weather falls on them like a lead apron, bending them inward, each man counting backward to zero in his own fashion. Straight lines. In March they finished the lenses, in April the detonators, the initiator on May 1. A week later, the first test of the complete lens assembly. Straight lines. Out there somewhere in the margins, a president has died, an Army has surrendered, wire gates have been flung open to reveal skeletons piled like refuse in their nightmare sanitariums, and though there have no doubt been straight lines sketched on that blueprint too, there has not been time to study them. The Mesa itself has become a closed system, implosive, its core compressing inward upon itself, turning supercritical. Even the weather—the heat, the furious hail, the electrical storms— seems to be part of the process, part of the same dawning tempest.

If by your art, my dearest father, you have put the wild waters in this roar, allay them.

So many fathers, he thinks to himself. And all of the same baby.

He glances over at Max Baker, who's reading, his lumpy face nodding to the vibrations of the car, his cheeks sunken and marked by stubble.

150

The work of the past five weeks comes off him like an animal scent. Five weeks in the Omega hutment, pushing the pieces of bomb metal together, charting the progressive multiplication of neutrons. Tickling the dragon's tail. Eli watched him one morning, maneuvering the deadly metals with the blade of a screwdriver amid a clutter of radiation counters ticking like metronomes, and about the only expression that graced Baker's features as his hands moved closer together was an untempered, almost defiant moroseness, one that seemed to have no particular object. It was merely Baker's look. He's wearing it now. He was wearing it earlier today, when he mounted the hemispheres inside the capsule and bade the others touch it. It resembled a watermelon, a watermelon coated with uranium, and when Eli put his hands to it he felt the generous warmth inside, the warmth of a tiny malignant sun. "Hot," crooned Baker. "Hot and sassy."

But now Baker is reading, and McNulty on Eli's left is asleep, and in the front seat the Pope, Fermi, is quiet, and the driver, a young man Eli doesn't know, is quiet also. They are all summoning their strength, he thinks, because the time is close. Everyone knows it. Even those people back on the Hill—people like Ruthie—who are still in the dark, even they know the time is close. Still, he wishes they knew what he knew. It gave him a lonely feeling back on V-E Day, watching the celebrations, knowing that it made no difference, that it was too late to stop it; too late for everyone, for himself as well. They wouldn't, they couldn't, and above all they did not *want* to. A border had been crossed, from duty to passion, and from there to something else, and now the clock is ticking and he is glad. The lines are straightening out. It's a parade. A reverse parade to zero.

> From this crude lab that spawned a dud,
> Their necks to Truman's axe uncurled,
> Lo, the embattled savants stood
> And fired the flop heard round the world.

The verse, and others like it, have been circulating around the Lab for weeks. No one's sure who's responsible, but Eli suspects Baker. Little games. Of the men in the car, Eli alone has resisted the betting pool on the gadget's yield. He's no gambler; that much about himself he knows. Though lately other things, too, are becoming clear. His talents in physics are more reliable. No longer does he need to labor over the same set of equations for two weeks before mastering them. Perhaps all these months of structure—the discussions and colloquiums, the informal

151

patter in the cafeteria, lectures in the company of giants; yes, perhaps even the little games themselves—have begun to pay off. He can hold his own. At night, in his quiet lab, he has begun to make notes for some original designs. Nothing revolutionary, but the seeds are there. The chronotron has emerged from one of them, and though he holds no great hope for its feasibility, at least the idea has been accorded some respect. Also he's made a sketch for a lens more compact and reliable than their present one, one that will be quicker and cheaper to assemble. He has begun to focus, to concentrate, to chart his path. Straight lines. What he has been building, he senses, has in fact been building him. He feels a rush of intoxication, thinking about it.

"Excited, Herr F.?"

Baker, eyeing him sideways, has his number. "I suppose I am," he admits, keeping his voice low.

Baker nods sleepily. "I'm having a vision," he says. "A very happy one."

He does not elaborate further. He doesn't have to. Already, in Max Baker's dry, unsmooth face, there is a trace of what will happen later, and if Eli does not yet know with any empirical certainty the wheres and hows, the what, at least, is clear. Baker's vision is of a thousand shadows, the flickering forms of the dead, and he is happy because he knows he is on his way to join them. It has become his occupation, his mission, to join them.

Here's how it will happen. It will be September, during the transition. He will be sulking because Herr O. will not allow him to fly over and see, firsthand, the casualties of Japan, and there will be a slip—if it *is* a slip—of the screwdriver, and then a blue ionization glow will bathe him in the dragon's fire, and the vision will be complete. If you're as fast and smart as Baker, thinks Eli, you can catch your own shadow.

But now they are driving down for the test in the unholy white light of noon, and the tranquillity of their private visions is shattered when McNulty, shaken rudely awake by a flaw in the road, blurts out in his childish voice, "All I can think of is the damn thing won't blow, and we'll be stuck here forever."

"It'll blow," says Baker. "But we might end up here forever, anyway."

The driver, whose name Eli doesn't know, glances at them via the rearview mirror. His eyes reflect a hopeful blue sky. "Look at it this way," he reasons. "If it's a dud, we'll have proved implosion's impossible. Happy ending for everybody."

"What about those son of bitches in the Pacific?" asks McNulty in a whine. "What's their happy ending?"

Eli has leaned back against the worn cloth seat of the car. His eyes are closed, his muscles marshaling for the long night ahead. Thus he has no idea what Fermi's face looks like when he turns around and says, "I invite bets against, first, the destruction of all human life; and second, just that of human life in New Mexico."

"Zero and zero," says Baker, after a pause. "Won't happen."

"Well," says McNulty, "for the ignition of hydrogen, you've got to factor at least—"

"My *God*," cries the driver. "My *God,* what are you saying? How can you *say* such a—"

But the next voice is Fermi's again, precise, European. "It would indeed take a miracle for the atmosphere to ignite. . . ."

"Well then, *Christ,* why didn't you—"

Eli's eyes remain closed, but it doesn't make any difference, because the man they call the Pope has turned to face the road ahead—the straight, undulating, heat-battered black line—when he completes, with no evident sternness, his thought:

"I calculate the chance of a miracle to be about ten percent."

Chapter 16

"He was joking, right? The man wasn't serious."

Dr. Cyril Stone, meteorological division, Los Alamos Scientific Laboratory, shrugged a half shrug. A tall, pudgy man in his mid fifties, with wire-rimmed spectacles, bushy brown hair, and a permanent five o'clock shadow, he seemed to be enjoying the attention, the opportunity to reminisce, to speculate. He especially seemed to be enjoying the V formed by Abby Gordon's long, tanned legs as she bent toward him with a rack of lights. His dark cheeks glowed furrily. "It's hard to say."

Arthur Gordon, holding a sixteen-millimeter Aaton camera to his naked eye, pressed the point. "Well, what did the others say?"

"None of us said anything. The man was the Pope, you understand. Already in the pantheon. He could calculate the speed of a bumblebee with one glance. Of course, he might have been joking. Then again, he might not have been. My eyes were on the road. And the sky, which was beginning to get cloudy. And not necessarily in that order." He smiled in the direction of the camera. "I want to emphasize that what I'm telling you is one man's response. We were all under incredible pressure. A thousand things on our minds. I'm just saying that I, personally, have never forgotten that moment. It was, I think, the first time I stopped to realize what we'd set in motion, this beast we'd unlocked. In that regard, the test itself was an anticlimax."

Arthur moved in for a tighter shot. I could hear the camera's drive motor whir and hum. "Go ahead," he said cheerfully. "What did you do when you arrived at the site?"

Dr. Stone's mouth puckered as he looked over his fingernails. "Very little, as it turned out."

"Oh? And why's that?"

"My job was to predict wind conditions. There was some concern, you

154

see, that fallout would drift over Amarillo or Albuquerque and be dumped by the rain before it could dissipate. It was a legitimate danger. My job was to help advise the general on postponement."

"And did you?"

"Never got the chance. The general called us in and then dismissed us immediately for not predicting rain in the first place. If we screwed *that* up, he said, he'd be damned if he'd listen to anything else we might have to say."

"He had a point," said Arthur mildly.

"Oh, sure. Of course he did. Do you happen to know the population that would have been affected? Neither did I, at the time. That's why I shut up and left with the others. Later we got lucky, if you want to call it that."

"What do *you* call it, Doctor?"

Another half shrug from Stone. "I call it what happened."

"Yes," said Arthur. He lifted his eye from the camera and turned in my direction. "How's the level?"

"Fine," I said. "Steady."

At least, I thought it was holding steady. The arrows on the Nagra's monitor seemed safely in the black. But my training as a sound man only went back as far as ten o'clock that morning, and so I wasn't certain. The Nagra made me uneasy. Holding it seemed to implicate me in a form of detection, a preoccupation with the sound of things at the expense of everything else. Even silence came through the earphones as a sound of something, a stylized arrangement of white space. I had to stop myself periodically from holding my breath so as not to appear on the tape. Arthur had assured me this wasn't a problem. He'd shown me how to carry it, how to set the levels, how to keep track of the time remaining on the reel. He spoke of each feature with the proud affection of a parent. He had emphasized the need to concentrate on manipulating the boom without distracting the subject, and he had mentioned something about "wild sound" that had escaped me completely. I nodded, anyway. For Arthur I would move a mountain, walk through fire, erect a bulding. Five days ago I had slept with his wife. Moral irregularities of this nature make one eager to serve.

He had called me at work the previous afternoon, a few days after his return from Los Angeles, and some forty-five minutes after I confirmed that at least half the discovery documents requested of us by the Navajo attorneys were indeed missing. The prevailing opinion at Sullivan and Peck—many of whose employees regularly attended church on Sunday— was that there had been some inadvertent misplacement of the materials, and everything would be straightened out shortly. I had a different take on it. As Myra Epstein had observed, people from New York have their own way of going about things; I saw in this the hand of Charles Goldwyn.

All of which might go to explain why when Arthur called, inviting me along on the next day's interviews, I did not say no. I even offered to help. Which was how I came to be working with the Nagra, and wearing earphones, and making virtually no eye contact with him or with the woman who I needed to keep reminding myself was his wife. As the interview progressed, I kept one eye on the little arrows, pulsing back and forth in the black like mild, easily assuaged pangs of hunger, or lust, or conscience. *A sound man,* I pronounced to myself.

"It was very strange," continued the meteorologist, "having nothing to do that night. I remember drinking coffee and eating some chow, and nobody really wanting to go to sleep. The test was scheduled, originally, for four A.M. Bainbridge, Kistiakowsky, and some of the others were at Point Zero, arming the thing."

"What did it look like, Doctor? Without its housing, I mean."

"Why, like an orange. A peeled orange. At least, that's what they told me. I never actually saw it."

"Who told you?"

"Well, Eli, for one. He was up there too. Oppie was worried the rain might damage the circuitry, so they sent Eli and Baker up to baby-sit the gadget until the test. Baker spread out his bedroll and took a snooze. Strange character. Quite sad, really. Eli told me later how *he* passed the time. He'd brought his flute up with him, strapped it to his leg, under the pants. None of the accounts mention this, by the way. At least, none that I've seen. They'd have made more of it than it was. He just liked to play. Later, when I had the chance to get to know him a little, I saw that was how he relaxed."

"Hold it." Arthur lifted his eye from the Aaton and turned toward me. I didn't know whether he was concerned about the level, or was out of film, or had to go to the bathroom, or what. He looked at me quietly, and something worked in his smooth jaw. Then he turned to Abby. "You all right, Ab?"

"Fine," she said quickly, and shifted her hands on the light pole.

"Want to take a break?"

"No."

He nodded to himself, satisfied. "All right, Doctor. Can I ask you, though, not to take off that sweater?"

Stone smiled. "It's so warm. The lights."

156

"Yes, but it'll screw up our continuity. I mean, you'll appear on film to be wearing two different outfits. We don't want to confuse the viewer. Do you mind?"

"Of course not." Stone chortled and pulled the sweater back on with a show of sportsmanship. "Fine, fine. Where were we?"

"The night of the test. Dr. Friedmann and Dr. Baker, up in the tower. The flute."

"Oh, yes."

"Do you remember, by any chance, what piece he said he was practicing?"

"No. I wasn't there. I didn't hear."

"A shame. Well, then, how about later. The test itself."

"Well, we drove over to the control station, which was just a concrete bunkhouse. It was full of people—army people, physicists, psychiatrists."

"Wait a minute. Why psychiatrists?"

"The general thought there should be psychiatrists around. To calm people down, I suppose."

"How quaint," Arthur said. He was talking, I thought, at least as much as Stone, as though driving home the point to all of us: *It's my movie.*

"Well, we were lying there, in very dim dawn light, wearing our dark glasses. Someone, I think Dr. Teller, passed around some suntan lotion. I didn't take any—it seemed absurd. It was a cool night. I mean, how powerful could the gadget *be*?

"So anyway, Sam Allison, a very nice man, was doing the countdown. It was an eerie thing. We'd leased the frequency of a local radio station, but because of the delay, they'd already begun their morning program. So, as Sam counted, you could hear—"

"Music," I heard myself say. "Strings."

Stone nodded. "Why, yes, that's right. It was Tchaikovsky, in fact. The Serenade for Strings. How did you know?"

The Aaton whirled toward me. I looked down automatically at the floor. I could hear my voice come through the headphones, faintly. "I must have read it somewhere."

There was a pause. Arthur lifted his eye from the camera, blinked, and then turned back to Stone. "Go ahead, Doctor. The countdown."

"Well, there we were, none of us sure what to expect, Fermi ripping up pieces of paper—out of nervousness, I thought, though later it turned out to be an experiment. When Sam got to zero, he jumped back from the microphone a little. Like he was afraid the blast would come right through the circuits. And then after that first blinding flash you could see the fireball. It was one of the most aesthetically beautiful things I have

157

ever seen. The colors were intensely realized, green and yellow and scarlet. It climbed—God, it climbed—and kept climbing, and the clouds turned pink and red, like a sunrise. For what seemed like a long time there was no sound at all. Then a kind of thunder. It echoed all over the place. It was . . . well, it was huge. I had goose flesh. I had it all morning. It was worse an hour or so later."

"Why's that?"

"Silly thing, really. I was back at base camp with some of the other fellows, and Oppie pulled up in the car. I'd never met him before, so I was curious to see him. It was nothing; he was about twenty yards away, getting out of the car; I couldn't even see his face. But . . ." He rubbed his brow with a handkerchief; he kept it balled in his fist as he continued. "But the way he *walked*. It was . . . he was so . . . assured. Supremely at ease. It reminded me of a conductor's bow at the end of a performance. Absolutely chilling. I'll never forget it."

"Dr. Stone, if you don't mind, I'd like to get back to—"

But Cyril Stone wasn't finished. He was working something of his own into this, giving shape to a kind of history. It was his scene, after all, and he knew it. "Because I thought to myself, how marvelous, to be at ease like that in this new world. Because it was, you know. New. And I didn't—"

At that moment, someone knocked at the door. A man entered the room, a young man with short hair, wearing a plain blue blazer. The clearance badge on his lapel was of a different color than any we'd seen since arriving on the grounds that morning. "You've got a phone call, Dr. Stone," the man announced to all of us.

Stone looked at Arthur and made a face of apology. "Go right ahead," said Arthur. "We don't mind waiting."

"It won't take a moment," said Stone, and followed the man in the blazer out the door.

"Let's cool the lights, Ab," Arthur said. "How are we on film?"

She checked the pack. "Two more magazines. Is that enough?"

"No problem." He set the camera down in its sponge-lined aluminum case, then did a series of quick knee bends. When he was finished, he said to both of us, "Stone's a pussycat, isn't he? Ever meet him before?"

"Not that I remember," I said.

"Did you know about all this, by the way?"

"The flute? No. It doesn't surprise me, though."

"I thought you said you knew *everything*."

The voice, sharp and petulant, had been Abby Gordon's, but her eyes were turned away, her hands busy adjusting the height and angle of the lights. It had been neither a question nor an accusation, but a kind of lament.

"I know what I know mostly from reading the accounts, same as you. I was two years old at the time, remember?"

"You don't have to get defensive," she snapped.

"Then don't be offensive."

Arthur stood near the window, hands on hips, following this exchange with only a distracted interest, which was no more, really, than it deserved. His tinted glasses hung from his neck on a brown leather strap. Now he put them on, peeking through the window curtains, and whistled softly between his teeth. The green Jemez Mountains loomed above us, but he was not whistling at the landscape. "Incredible," he said. "What a night it must have been."

I felt the weight of the Nagra pulling on my shoulder.

"Imagine. The pregnant pause before transgression. The half-life ticking away beside you. Five kilograms of plutonium practically between your legs. One private encounter, then boom. Quite a night, eh?"

"Arthur," Abby complained, "I'm getting hungry."

"I wonder what he played. I very much wish I knew what he played that night. A lullaby by Brahms, maybe. That would work. Or, hey, maybe some Sousa. Halftime on the playing field, et cetera. Think he knew any?"

"Any what?"

"Sousa."

"No. I doubt it. He was partial to the Europeans, I think."

"Sure. Who isn't?" He stuck his head through the curtains again, looking from behind, like a portrait photographer snapping a picture. Aside from that one look we'd exchanged some minutes before, he had kept his face from me. From both of us. "What do you say, Hesh?" I heard him ask through the curtain. "Running around the old haunts give you any ideas?"

"Sorry. Everything's different, you know. Nothing's where it used to be. This wasn't even where the Lab was, in the forties. And everything's so settled, so domestic. Just another company town."

"That's good." I heard him laugh. "A company town. I want to get that on film later. Yessir, you're proving to be a big part of things. A central figure, all right."

"Isn't anyone else getting hungry?" asked Abby.

"Everyone, love. Everyone's hungry. Aren't they, Hesh?"

I didn't say anything, not even when he came out from behind the curtain and walked toward me.

"A born sound man, you are. Full of hidden potentialities. I can't wait to get you on film. They'll eat you up. Those big hangdog brown eyes. It's your baby, this film. I'm just trotting along watching."

"Are you on something today, Arthur?"

"A few lines of powder, now that you mention it. The effects, I'm afraid, wore off long ago. Coke adds life, according to the song."

Abby Gordon made a snort of disgust.

"My wife, of course, does not approve. A regular Puritan, isn't she, Hesh?"

"Please," she said quietly. "Let's not."

"Fine. Name-calling, it gets us nowhere. Sticks and stones. Speaking of stones—"

The door opened, and the meteorologist came back in the room. But he did not resume his former position behind the desk. He looked a bit subdued. When he cleared his throat to speak, it sounded like heavy gravel being loaded by shovel. "I'm afraid I have to go now," he said. "I have a pressing meeting."

"Just a few minutes," said Arthur easily. "I'd like to go over some—"

"I'm sorry. I really am." Stone glanced at Abby, who was staring at him with open incredulity, and in deference to the pleasure her legs had given him, he tried to smile. "I've enjoyed talking to you. I really have."

"But why do you have to *leave*?" she demanded. "It's been going so well."

He smiled hopelessly.

Arthur moved forward, placatory, nodding his head up and down. "That's okay, Doctor, that's okay. Can we possibly, though, schedule another session? Maybe day after tomorrow? You're really giving us some wonderful material."

"I'm very sorry." Stone moved sideways toward the door, his face a mess of conflict.

"Well, thank you," said Arthur, giving his hand a firm shake as it traveled past him. "Thank you very much for your time."

"Yes, *thank* you," called Abby loudly. "Thank you *so* much."

His hand on the doorknob, Cyril Stone chanced a look at me. His gaze was strangely deferent and solicitous. He seemed to find something specific in my face that engaged him. "Have we met before, young man?"

"I doubt it," I said, busying myself with the Nagra. "I live back east."

He nodded abstractedly, giving in, doubting his own intuition. I watched the light leave his face as he repeated, "I'm sorry," and then he walked out the door.

At the window, Arthur now had his hands on his wife's pointy shoulders, massaging them steadily and crooning her name into her ear. Her eyes were closed tightly, as though she were casting a spell. "It's all my fault," she moaned. "That silly fight with Ziobro. Now no one will talk to us."

"They'll talk," he said. "They'll talk plenty."

"How do *you* know? How do *you* know anything?"

There was something ferocious in the set of her mouth as she wheeled about. The arrows of the Nagra were jerking off the meter—I'd forgotten to turn it off. I did so now. I should get out of here, I thought. I had my own business to attend to. On the legal pad of my conscience, there was a full outline of the responsibilities I'd left dangling in recent weeks—my job, my son, my mother, my future—and I had better, I knew, attend to them. Only, the Gordons had their way of keeping me in their orbit. Arthur, even as he was ministering to his wife, let his eyes travel wearily in my direction, letting me see, with only the barest effort to conceal it, just how exasperating that day—and who knew how many others?—had already been, and just how little promise his current enthusiasms seemed to hold.

But by then she had turned to me. "What do you think? Have I blown it for us?"

As always with Abby, I felt in the words an expectation of complicity with her private despair, an invitation to draw her close with a touch, to make things whole.

"Well?"

"It's hard for me to say, Abby."

"You're some pair," she said, as we bent to gather together the equipment. "Both of you think you know everything, but when push comes to shove, you're both just little boys with runny noses. What am I *doing* here, anyway?"

"You're working on a project," Arthur said mildly.

"Fuck the project."

"Abby, calm down." He said it coldly, in a lower register than I'd heard him use before. I noted the change.

So did she, apparently. "Sorry," she said, and tried to mean it. "Bad mood. Don't mind me."

She went back to the window and, in a gesture that made her look a bit like a child herself, leaned her forehead against the glass. Her shoulders were drawn in, waiting for comfort, the way they'd waited for comfort the other night in the parking lot; the way they'd been waiting, in fact, since I'd met her, and no doubt since well before that. I took a step toward her and then took a step back. Arthur packed up the Aaton and snapped shut the case. "So," he said, "should we hit the road? It's a long drive to the site."

"What are you talking about?"

He looked surprised. "Didn't I tell you on the phone? I want to drive down to Trinity. Look around Ground Zero, get some footage. It'll be one of our primary locations, after all. I want to see what the camera does for it, and vice versa."

I felt an awkward sensation, a tightening. "I've never been there before," I said. "Isn't that a remarkable thing?"

"Then here's your chance." He paused by the door, waiting. "I kept seeing cutaways," he said. "The whole time he was talking, I was seeing the cutaways. Here's this perfectly upright citizen talking about the *weather,* for God's sake, and we'll be cutting to mushroom clouds, scorched earth, piles of rubble. Put some Tchaikovsky on the sound track. Nice." He looked reluctantly around the room, wiping his glasses with a fold of his shirt. "You know where they got countdowns from? I mean, the concept of them? From a movie."

"I had a feeling you were going to say that," I said.

"One of Lang's silents, when he was still in Germany. *Die Frau im Mond.* Woman on the Moon. I mean, who says life doesn't imitate art?"

"Nobody says that," said Abby, attempting a smile. "Not in this century."

"Right," he said. "Well, let's get out of here, what say? Why don't, since we'll probably stay over and Hesh'll want to come back, why don't we take two cars? We can caravan."

"Fine," I said. "I'll follow you."

But out in the parking lot Arthur surprised me by suggesting that Abby ride in my car. "That way you won't have to take that long drive alone both ways. What do you think?"

"Okay by me, if it's okay with Abby."

Abby's voice, however, was flat. "I don't mind," she said, and ducked into the Chevy. As I put the car into gear, her husband gave a little wave of encouragement, tracking us with his stare until we pulled away, but if she saw it, she did not let on. Nor did she do anything to raise my hopes about the coming drive. "Please keep quiet," she said, and then for a long while said nothing more. Her right arm dangled loosely out the open window; her left, taut like a sphinx, rested over the Nagra in its jacket.

I let Arthur pass us going out of the parking lot, and we followed him across the bridge and through town. There was a lot of new wood-and-glass housing of the sort being built in prosperous communities from southern California to the Hamptons, with BMWs and station wagons in

162

the driveways and shiny basketball hoops over the garages. There were ripened gardens, trees planted two decades before which had grown tall and splendid, and there were, as there had always been, views of the canyons. They were like deep cuts, blood-red sacrificial slivers offered to the immense altar of the sky, dry and steep and wasted, and I knew they would film well, because there was practically no living thing to which they did not stand in contrast. Posed against the canyons, the manicured houses looked absurd, toylike.

When we passed the building that contained our old apartment, I slowed down the car. But the place was much changed, of course. It had been added on to at both ends and repainted, and the landscaping looked different too, except for one full-bodied ponderosa pine around back, which I remembered climbing with the McNulty boys. I hadn't lived there very long, and so I was a little surprised to find myself moved by the sight of it. It seemed to me—it had been seeming to me since the visit to my mother—that memory, perhaps, in its size, its ephemerality, its negative energies and its pockets of velocity, was not unlike the atom; that it possessed within it the potential, should one of its own neutrons be captured by a hardy nucleus, for fission. Maybe that was what I was feeling now: the rumblings of a chain reaction of my own. There were doors being flung open, glass breaking, walls shaking off their plaster. Countdown.

I looked over at Abby, who was staring straight ahead. Woman on the Moon.

The sun was hot through the windshield, and the sky was blinding and clear. The clouds would come later, toward evening, and with them the rain. I knew about the weather in this place, its moods and habits. I knew so many things, all of a sudden. I followed the road down off the Mesa, the road that wound its way like an intestine into the belly of the canyon, and as I descended into the full heat of the afternoon I had a series of recognitions, a storm of memory. I remembered a set of blue teeth, a spindly organ shell, a Ford, a suitcase, an alien driveway. I remembered the last time I'd driven down this road. This light. This smell. This quiet. I remembered. And it did not, in truth, seem so very long ago.

Chapter 17

September 1949: The Scientific Method

I am already six years old and no stranger to adversity when my mother shakes me awake one morning and tells me we are leaving Los Alamos and moving to Santa Fe. Instinctively, I sniff her breath for liquor. But there is only the sour musk of coffee and, from her armpits, another smell, slightly floral, which I know to be something she exudes on her own, some essence. Whether other people—my father, for instance, who is already gone; he normally leaves at daylight—notice this smell, or associate it, as I do, with unhappiness and self-doubt, I'm not sure. I am only six, after all. There are limits to my understanding.

For instance, I do not entirely comprehend the need for my parents to separate. True, they do not get along very well, but from my scattered observations of life on the Hill, most couples get along no better—except at the parties, where there seems to be a great deal of hugging and kissing and pronouncement of affection. It is only afterward, when the ties get loosened and the shoes come off and the bedroom door is left carelessly ajar, that the fights start up.

There was a party just last night, it so happens, in the McNultys' apartment, below ours, and from the sound of things it was quite a wingding. Through the floorboards came occasional whoops of laughter, much jazzy music, and some syncopated stomping I took to be dancing. Lying in bed, I could, from long habit, picture my father tinkling moodily at the piano, his gaze abstracted, as one or another of his colleagues endeavored to loosen him up with some bawdy jokes; and my mother, drink in hand, laughing a bit too loudly in the kitchen, straining her neck forward a little too far to catch some wisp of gossip from the women she privately despised. It was an unpleasant picture; to blot it out I began to whistle through my teeth along with the music.

164

"Maybe you should close your eyes, lovey," said Mrs. Burke, peering in at me from the doorway to my room. My mother's sole confidante, she is a solidly built, white-haired matron given to sarcasm, hot drinks, and fat novels. She appears to have no great fondness for me, or for children in general. In some people, the capacity for private amusement is so great that the demands of social discourse merely serve as the backdrop for the parade of their own idiosyncratic passions. Mrs. Burke takes me in stride; she performs the duty of baby-sitting with a kind of gallant geniality indistinguishable from boredom. I perceive it as part of a larger strategy directed toward my mother, to whom she seems fiercely attached.

"Go to sleep," she urges.

"I am asleep," I say, which doesn't feel like much of a lie at the time.

A shriek vaults through the floorboards. Mrs. Burke, still in the doorway, sniffs in disapproval. "Janet Sommers. That silly bitch."

"Silly bitch," I agree.

It is not so difficult, really, talking to adults. All you have to do is listen. Mrs. Burke smiles and comes forward to sit at the edge of the bed. "You're all right, lovey," she says. "You've got a future."

Her weight bends the mattress, so that I have to prop myself up on one elbow to avoid falling into her lap, which is large and deep. As long as I have the ear of a sympathetic grownup, I decide to clear up something that's been troubling me. "Who's Stalin, anyway?" I ask.

Mrs. Burke arches an eyebrow. "Never heard of him."

"Yes you have."

"Why do you want to know?"

"My mom says he's the reason we're staying here," I say. "He had some kind of test, and now we have to stay."

She just sits there, heavy and grave, nodding her head like a doctor. "And what did your father say?"

"He said we'd stay anyway. He said he likes it here."

More nods. "Do *you* like it here, lovey?"

I shrug. Were I more precocious, or less tired, perhaps I'd manage to express some of the confusion I really feel over the matter. Like, dislike— the truth is, I have no standard of measure for such things. Aside from one trip to New York to attend my grandfather's funeral, I have had no opportunities to explore any other sort of life. Thus I take my cues from those close to me; specifically, my parents, who appear to be split on the question. I know only one thing for certain: I do not like the split itself. It afflicts us all, individually and as a unit. It has somehow become the overriding fact of my life.

"When's he going to finish that thing, anyway?" She is staring off into the corner of the room, at the hull of the model organ—the spindly wooden frame and the tangled circuit of stretched wire—which has occupied my father's evening and weekend attention for as long as I can remember. Lit by a shaft of moonlight, it does not look now to be as precariously balanced or haphazard a construction as it does in the glare of day. Suddenly it looks promising, almost "ready to sing," as my father likes to put it. Soon he will teach me some of his tricks, show me how to make music spring up from the wood and the wire. It is kept in my room for a reason, after all: It is meant for me.

We both must have fallen asleep then, because the next thing I know, big, jowly Daniel Burke is looming over the bed, shaking his wife—who lies curled up beside me—gently awake. "Annette. C'mon, pallie. Come on. Attagirl." His big palm massages her shoulder in a tiny circle, as though he is rubbing a spot out of her sweater. His lips purse when he notices me looking up at him. "Hello, sport," he whispers casually. "What'd you do, slip her a mickey?"

I don't know what the hell he's talking about, so I just blink a few times. We've never had much to say to each other, he and I. A metallurgist at the Lab, he is a blustery and intimidating fellow, uncomfortable with domestic life, impatient with the modulations required by a situation such as this. And yet, staring up into the enormous solidity of his shoulder, the baggy exhaustion of his eyes, I do not feel sorry to have him in my bedroom. "I hurt my thumb," I announce in a whisper, over his sleeping wife. It isn't exactly true, either. I've merely slept on it, and now it's asleep, tingly and numb. I seem to be turning into quite a little liar.

He stands, crosses around to my side of the bed, and sits Indian style on the wood floor. "Give me a look." Frowning, he turns the thumb over in his big callused palm, pressing it above the joint. "That hurt?"

"A little."

"Try to bend it."

I bend it quickly, feel no pain, then flex it very slowly a couple of times, to suggest concentration. The floor is dirty, but Dr. Burke doesn't seem to notice. Still holding on to the base of my hand, he lets out a long sigh that speaks of a weariness as great as the earth itself. "That's good," he says, "that's very good, sport. Someday, you know, we'll be able to do a lot more for people and their thumbs. Why, we'll just bring you into the Lab when it hurts and fit you for a new one."

"A new thumb?" My brows knit in skepticism. "Where'll you get it?"

"Why, we'll *make* it, sport. Whip it right up, then plug it on like an extension cord."

"Will it hurt?"

He smiles. With the moonlight coming in from the window, I can see the inside of his mouth hovering a couple of feet away. It is a wide, confident thing, his mouth—unlike my father's, which is drawn into a grim line most of the time—but I think I can see the gums beginning to pull back from his lower teeth. "Not a bit," he says. "That's the whole point, you see. Your thumb will be a thing that works perfectly. And not just yours, either. Everybody will have them."

"Where'll you put them?"

"Oh, I don't know. You'll be able to take them off when you go to sleep, I guess. Put 'em in the fridge, next to the Coca-Cola."

"I don't think so," I respond, vaguely.

"No?"

Daniel Burke pulls himself up so that he is now on his knees. After a quick glance at his sleeping wife, he clucks his tongue and brings his hands up so that they cover his mouth mysteriously, the way people cover their mouths when they are sharing a terrible and dirty secret. I lean close, expectant. He brings his hands forward in closed fists. When they are just below the level of my neck, he opens them and smiles a crooked smile unlike anything I've seen before.

There, cupped in his hands, looking almost blue in the dim light, are his teeth.

I hear myself let out a little yell. So, evidently, does Annette Burke, who turns over, stretches sleepily, and, shaking her wide head to clear it, sits erect. "Hello, pumpkin," she says to her husband. "Fun party?"

He makes a face. "The usual. A lot of the new folk, you know. Kept getting their names wrong. I'm no damn good at parties."

"Uh huh," she says dreamily.

"Well, you know what I mean."

I examine him closely as he speaks. His mouth looks normal. There are his teeth, snug and white and precisely even, right where they belong. Either he is some sort of sleight-of-hand magician, or else I only imagined that those were his teeth he was showing me, or else I am dreaming, and none of this is real, including the conversation going on at this moment between these two older people who are not my parents but have somehow come to straddle my bed—in which case, I figure, I should really just relax, lie back, and let their banter carry me through the night without trying to sort it all out; because dreams, when they're occurring, do not imply their shape to the dreamer, and this one feels as though it might keep on going in just this manner for an eternity, with the dance music coming up through the floorboards and the light turning everything blue, and people passing around the parts of their bodies like pieces of an intricate puzzle. . . .

And then, dimly, I hear the click of a door.

In the morning, I help my mother load the suitcases and boxes full of kitchen stuff into the Ford. Because she is small, anemic, and by nature disorganized, it takes a number of trips, with a lot of time spent pausing to regain her strength and composure. She is having a tough morning. It isn't really in her to be resolute, to take more than one step forward without a half-step back, and when we are nearly finished I find her sitting at the top of the stairs, smoking a cigarette and looking pensively at the bare walls of the kitchen through the open door. A radio is playing in one of the other apartments—a weatherman is predicting a hot day. Both of us are wearing long pants and long-sleeved shirts, but it is too late to change now, my mother informs me. "Are we forgetting anything?" she asks.

"I don't know."

"Well, let's go and see."

Together we walk through the apartment. It has never been decorated with much care, so we've been able to do a pretty thorough job despite ourselves. The place, furniture aside, looks stripped clean, except for my father's work space and the bathroom, which for some reason my mother refuses to include in her inventory. Perhaps she has left more of herself behind than she thinks. I peek in and find her everywhere: in the sloppy fold of the towels; the long strands of hair contorted into a Rorschach blot on the drain of the shower; the trace of her damp footprints on the throw rug; the empty bottles of pills prescribed by the psychiatrist, who arrived only last year and quickly became so popular with the ladies.

I went to see him once myself. He was a young man with a long face. My mother took me in to see him in his cramped, white-walled office at one end of the hospital, and when we were alone together he asked me to draw him some pictures, giving me to understand that I would do well to comply. So I drew a few things. I wasn't much on drawing, and his crayons were in lousy shape, but I managed to work out one pretty fair rendering of a train station, one cracked egg, and one outline of the organ my father was working on at the time. For some reason these didn't go over very well. The psychiatrist told my mother she should bring me in for another visit, but when the day came I feigned illness and neither of us mentioned it again. Though she went without me, I might add, quite a few times.

When I am done in the bathroom, we go through my room again. My mother snatches an errant sock from the floor of the closet, and some marbles that have found their way under the box springs. As she kneels at the foot of the bed, searching the floor, I wander over to the organ-in-progress and run my finger along the gum-faced plywood of the wind chest. On the workbench beside it are a number of little metal fittings my father has been experimenting with for the ducts. It occurs to me that I have never felt what my father has felt, that I am a stranger to the things that preoccupy him. Deliberately I grab half a dozen of the fittings in my hand and jiggle them softly, experiencing the weight of their collisions.

"Ready?" My mother is standing up and looking around one last time, her chest heaving under her shirt. It's funny: I have seen her cry so many times, in the light of so many mornings, that I no longer attribute the sight or sounds of it to grief, or an acute pain of any sort; rather, I register it as a tic of expression, a chemical reflex, something to indulge matter-of-factly for a moment and then move on.

As for me, my lack of understanding of consequence is coming in handy: This whole enterprise strikes me as a phase of adventure. Building one's future, I'm learning, is like building anything else—you've got to be flexible, willing to sacrifice design to improvisation. My father's organ, for instance, is already shaping up differently from how it looked on the sketches he used to labor over; still, he continues to work through the possibilities with steady detachment, with patience and attention to detail. He calls this approach to things the scientific method. Though I grasp it only superficially at best, it is related somehow, I think, to the test Stalin has taken recently, and to the reason my father needs to stay at the Lab, and it has something to do, probably, with that tall tale Daniel Burke told me about my thumb, and God knows what else—but there is no time, just now, to digest it all; the Ford sits outside, loaded with our possessions, and my mother is at the door, her features composed into a mask of pragmatic determination. "Let's go, then," she says, bringing her hands together into an approximation of cheer, or prayer. "Before we change our minds."

We go. Passing the new hospital, the new library, the new housing, on a freshly paved road that still smells of tar, we are bucking the traffic of history. Four years ago, "the first team," as my father called them, took this same route off the Mesa, and what they left behind was a half-formed organism, successful and notorious for that success and utterly uncertain of its own future. This made it fertile ground for men like my father, men who were gifted and ambitious and dogged, scientific-method types who, by substituting structure for inspiration, found themselves able to make those small leaps of craft and status that determine the trajectory of a career. He had begun as an outsider, and he made adjustments; now the place belongs to him. Because he has never expected much in the way of

169

happiness, he will not do much peeking under the rug of his contentment. Nor will he, with his physics and his music, miss us very much. Or at least no more than when we shared the same apartment.

On the drive out of town we pass the new stadium, still under construction, which will be named for one of the men from the Lab, who was killed in an accident. It is nearly finished. The benches gleam in the sunlight, ascending from the playing field in neat semicircular rows, like waves. The stadium is magnificent, hypnotic. As the car rounds a curve, I turn full around on the front seat to watch it recede against the backdrop of the Jemez Mountains. My last view is of the stadium's back wall, still incomplete; an assortment of unused girders lean awkwardly against the base, which is littered with candy wrappers, yellowing newspapers, and beer cans from the crew's Friday lunch.

"Sit down, *shaynkeit*," says my mother, "so you don't fly out the window."

I remain where I am.

"Please, Herschel." She looks over at me in exasperation and notices my balled fist against the top of the seat. "What's that? What's that in your hand?"

"Nothing." But when I open my hand I find some of the fittings from the organ's wind chest. I do not remember putting them in my pocket before, or grabbing hold of them now. "They're Dad's," I say.

"You shouldn't have taken them. They might be important." Having said this, she winces, and frowns a complicated frown into the rearview mirror.

The stadium is soon out of sight. We wind down the lowest of the finger mesas. The view out the back window is partly obscured by boxes and suitcases, so all I can see are the peaks of the Jemezes jutting up from the Valle Grande. My father once told me how the whole thing was formed: a massive explosion, not so different from the one that lit up the southern sky four years ago. And now Stalin has taken some test over on the other side of the world, and the new men are flooding in to work at the Lab, to figure out a way to cause an even bigger explosion. You get the feeling, growing up in Los Alamos, that explosions are not entirely terrible things; or possibly, that in what we call the terrible, there are other things going on, cycles of birth as well as death, options opened as well as closed. Reality, it appears, gets twisted into a variety of shapes: some good, some bad, some too close to call. Volcanoes blow up, then turn to lush hill country. Cities get built, then deteriorate, then revive. People love each other, then stop and move somewhere else. Everything is liquid motion. Matter comes and goes. It's almost musical.

Of course, I am only six at the time, and have not yet begun to think in these terms, but in a childish, visceral way I have taken a leap of discovery myself. *I am a part of all this.* Winding out of the canyon, away from my father, headed out toward that metropolis of Wild West strangeness called Santa Fe, I finger the fittings of the wind chest and begin to hum.

My mother, hunched forward on the seat so she can see over the dashboard, lets out her breath. Soon she's humming too, though it is not the same song. She hums what she always hums, "Cheek to Cheek," in the key she always hums in—which is, my father has let her know, quite a bit flatter than B flat.

We arrive in Santa Fe just after noon. The house is on the eastern edge of town, on slightly higher ground than the rest. When we get out of the car, I can see the roof of the cathedral near the square, but the glare from the sun is too strong for me to identify other landmarks. I feel woozy, weightless.

My mother has already yanked open the trunk of the Ford, but now, poised above it, she stops and turns her attention to the house. "Look," she urges, and takes a couple of tentative steps onto the property. "Isn't it beautiful?"

It isn't exactly beautiful, this new house of ours. It has a small, con-stricted look about it, and after the wood structures of Los Alamos the muddy brown adobe seems primitive and hasty, more like an eruption of the earth below it than a willful addition, sculpted by men. The driveway is unfinished gravel. The yard is strewn with weeds, rocks, and scrub. The windows are tilted and small, like postage stamps carelessly pasted, and more than a few of the roof tiles lie chipped in the rain gutters. Still, it *is* a house. I've never lived in a house before, and neither has my mother. A diaspora Jew arriving in Zion for the first time, she actually bends down low to smell the ground in the front yard, sighing with audible relish.

"You smell? Isn't it beautiful?"

"Yeah," I say, from my position by the open trunk.

She catches something in my voice, then, something she has been fearing, or expecting, and looks at me over her shoulder through her hard nut-brown eyes, and for a moment I'm sure she's going to cry.

But she doesn't. "Ours," she says, more to herself than to me. It is her customary way of talking.

I reach into the trunk for my suitcase, which is on top because it's so frail and the handle is broken, and when I bring my left hand up to support it from the bottom, the organ fittings spill onto the red earth at my feet. It's just as well, I figure. I have my hands full with projects of my own, and the scientific method has failed us once already.

171

Chapter 18

We drove south through the white desert, through the indeterminate blur. The highway followed the narrow, meandering slice of water that is the Rio Grande that far north, past Veguita and La Joya and Polvadera and Socorro, into the Jornada del Muerto.

The Jornada del Muerto was named by that slim remnant of conquistadores who, three centuries ago, having survived the murderous heat, the Apaches, the scorpions, and the thunderstorms of their journeys, still had the strength such naming required. It was bordered by mountains to the west and east, brown hummocky peaks that shimmered through heat ripples and dust devils, their comforts far way, unreal. The desert floor was rusty with alkali and almost perfectly barren, though there were occasional dots of yucca and sagebrush to remind you that you had not left the planet after all, that there are hells right here that are neither symbol nor metaphor, places that offer death like a mercy, a sacrament. It was flat and arid and still, awaiting pioneers, baking for them in its bleached light, throwing off gusts of hot wind like yawns from a settling beast. It seemed to have a truth it wanted to reveal to us, but it would take its time about it. In fact, that *was* its truth—the time it would take, the malevolent indifference to the animate—and it was entirely a measure of your own strength of purpose what you would do with this truth. My father and his colleagues had gone it, I thought, one better, but that was another time.

I had the air-conditioning roaring full blast to hold back the heat. It created, in the inner world of the Chevy, an illusion of exemption. Sometimes the ground outside looked like an arctic sea, cold and white; at other times it resembled the ash residue of an enormous fire, or clay, or glass. Whatever phantasm revealed itself in that unmeaning vastness, with the windows closed it seemed somehow more rather than less

172

threatening, as though we were getting away with something on our journey south which would catch up with us later. "Wild West," I grunted to Abby.

She made no reply. She had a piece of embroidery on her lap, but seemed to have lost interest in it a few miles out of Albuquerque. Her eyes were closed, her head against the seat, her hands folded into her thighs. The sun bore down from overhead, superimposing the litter of the dashboard—an abandoned crossword puzzle, a couple of plastic pens, and a coffee-stained map of New Mexico—onto the windshield, so that we appeared to be driving into our own pile of refuse. "Careful," she said after a while. "You're all over the road."

"How do you know? You've got your eyes closed."

"I can feel it." She lifted her head, squinting from the glare. "Ugh. Where's Arthur? Can you see him?"

"He was pretty far ahead of me. At least a mile. But I think I caught sight of him a while back."

She nodded. "I lied to him, you know."

"About us?"

She nodded again.

"Think he believed you?"

She made a noncommittal gesture with the flat of her hand. "I lie all the time," she announced. "All the time."

"Don't make it such a big deal, Abby. You've got plenty of company."

"Not Arthur."

"Right," I said, growing edgy. "The last honest man. It's just that he happens to make commercials. But you wouldn't call those lies, I suppose."

"That's right," she insisted. "I wouldn't. Those are just . . . well, representations."

"Excuse me, Abby, but you're both full of shit."

"Physicists, they operate the same way, you know. People like your father. Sometimes they call an electron a particle, sometimes they call it a wave. When they talk about what holds a nucleus together, they say it's *charm*. From the outside, it's easy to call those lies too."

"But those are descriptive of something already there. What Arthur does is something else. He creates an idea for something and then says, Look, there it is. I know all about it. I'm a lawyer, remember?"

Whether she did or did not, she held back her response. We drove on without speaking for another five miles. The light pooled between us on the car seat; it was so strong I was afraid it might damage the Nagra even through the leather case. A buzzard swooped low over a stand of Joshua trees. We passed the ruins of a mine. I had begun to lose track of the afternoon, to float again in time, when I heard Abby draw a breath.

Up ahead I saw Arthur's rented Mustang, signaling a right turn into a gas station. I began to ease off the gas pedal. At approximately the same time, Abby, drawing another breath, pressed her foot against an imaginary pedal on the floor. "Don't stop," she said.

"Abby . . ."

"Please."

"This is insane. We are now passing the border from sanity to insanity. The reality patrol will come after us any minute now, you realize that?"

"Just keep going for a while, Hesh. Please. It's so . . . empty out here. Let's just drive."

"Sure. A joyride. I take them all the time."

"If it makes you this uncomfortable," she said, "I'll drop you off and go on without you."

"Would you do that?"

"You know I would."

"I know nothing of the sort."

"Well, then," she said, sitting up straighter, "this is your chance to find out."

I snuck a glance at the Mustang as we zoomed past the station. Arthur was washing dust off the windshield with a squeegee, his shirt unbuttoned. He could almost have passed for an attendant. He did not look up when we drove by.

"What about the footage?" What about your husband? "We've got the Nagra with us."

"He can do it alone. He'll shoot MOS anyway."

"MOS?"

"That's a shot without sound. He doesn't need us for that, and there will be plenty of natural light, won't there?"

She picked up her embroidery, which she had balled up tightly when we spotted Arthur's car, and smoothed it across her bare tanned legs. If there is any nobility in flight, Abby embodied it now: Her cheeks glowed with a defiant pride, and she sat tall and square in the seat, facing the road dead-on. I looked at her, I checked the rearview mirror, I adjusted my weight, and then a thought bubbled up that almost made me laugh out loud. *Charlie Goldwyn, c'est moi!*

"What do you think it's like?" asked Abby, after a while.

"What?"

"Trinity."

"I told you," I said. "I've never been there before."

174

"But you've got some ideas about what it's like, don't you?"

The ground blasted clean of vegetation. The lizards reduced to carbonized shadows, fossils etched in the caliche by the heat. The dirty desert floor fused into a crater of green glass, a new element. I had some ideas about it, all right. In fact, I'd have liked to see it. Something about the idea appealed to a paternal reflex in me. Perhaps we all have one—a buried impulse to create and transmute, to cheat nature, to synthesize new forms and whisper into their ear some of the secrets of life and death. Trinity beckoned like an inspiration, a genie cooing in her jade bottle. But it was too late. We'd already passed the turnoff for Route 380 and were headed for unknown territory, and so I'd have to wait and see it on the footage, like everyone else.

"Would it be so awful," Abby mused, "if it finally fell?"

"I don't know what you're talking about," I said.

"No?" She scratched at one ankle. "I'm talking about the relief, that's what I'm talking about."

"I think we're getting into a weird area here," I said. "Morally."

"Oh," she said, scratching harder. "You don't say."

"I'm going to have to stop for gas."

"Can't we go a little farther first?"

We went a little farther, and then I pulled into a station in a town called, so help me, Truth or Consequences, just across the river from Elephant Butte.

Abby got out and strolled over to the vending machines as I tended to the car. The windshield was streaked with coppery dust, but when I reached for the squeegee, the picture of Arthur those twenty miles back brought a sour taste to my mouth. In the odoriferous men's room, I slapped cold water on my face and tried to collect my wits. What I saw in that spotted mirror was not very pleasant—my cheeks were flushed with sun, my eyes deep-set and abstracted. I was able to see more of my scalp than usual; it, too, had reddened in the sun. Thirty-four years old. I could not tell whether I looked much younger or much older, but I was fairly sure I did not look my age.

When I returned to the car I found Abby unwrapping a pack of cigarettes as she leaned against the back fender. "Since when do you smoke?" I asked.

"Since today." She crumpled the cellophane, which made a joyless hiss.

"I believe I'll have one too."

We smoked and listened to the engine tick as it cooled, the idling hum of insects, the roar of an occasional truck down the commercial strip. The station attendant, his name stitched fancily onto the patch on his heart, came over in hopes of making conversation, but we sent him away disappointed. We smoked our cigarettes down to the filter before Abby stubbed hers out. "There's a nice-looking bar across the street," she observed.

"So?"

"So let's get something to drink. In fact, let's get loaded, okay?"

"Okay."

"And after that, let's find a Motel 6 and make us some love. Okay?"

"Okay."

"You think we can pull this off, Hesh?" she asked, reaching for the door handle. "Or are we just procrastinating?"

"Pull what off," I said. Then we both climbed into the car to look for a place to park.

At the Motel 6, some hours later, we made a lurching attempt at love. Our sounds, in the ghost-dusk quiet, struck me as exaggerated and hopeful, a performance of passion, if not a rehearsal. At one point I went soft from what I hoped was the liquor, and I felt Abby tighten with impatience, but then she bent to me and brought me back. She moved clumsily when she climaxed, but then I suppose so did I; we were both being very careful, for some reason, not to fall off the bed. Afterward we lay in the tangle of damp limbs and sheets without speaking, and it was only then that it occurred to me to ask her what kind of birth control she was using, and only then that I discovered she wasn't using any birth control at all.

I started to say something—I started to say a whole series of things—but Abby put one finger to my lips and whispered, pleadingly, "Not now, okay? This is the nice part."

Well, yes, it was. So I held my tongue for the moment, and we showered, put on the clothes we'd worn that afternoon, and went out into the twilight. Slowly, teasingly, the sky opened its jewels to us, the constellations emerging like photographic images in a darkroom. We bought some peaches at a stand and ate them as we walked, dribbling juice on the sidewalk. I couldn't stop staring up at the sky. It was everywhere—vast and deep and slivered with light. It would be foolish to attempt to hide from such a sky, and yet I had. I'd been on the run a long time.

We stood there and listened to the night calls of the coyotes. The smell of yucca washed in from the desert. The West, it was a palpable thing; it stirred the evening like a drink. And I knew then that I had stayed away

176

on purpose, too unsettled to chance it, too unhappy in my marriage, too unanchored in my work, too protective of what I'd fancied was my independence to risk coming back. I must have groaned from the thought of it. Abby eased her hand into mine and I clutched it tightly. I'd stayed away, and now here I was, with this fragile, foolish, impulsive young woman, both of us on the lam from that part of ourselves that had grown weary of prudence, of holding up our ends—and I saw that I had not been so wrong in my apprehensions, after all.

"Are we near the border?"

"About an hour's drive," I said. "Why?"

She shrugged. "No reason." We were in front of a toy store, and she paused to look in the window. Her hand left mine in favor of the pocket of her shorts. "I was just thinking that if that's the Rio Grande over there, we must be heading towards Mexico. That's all."

"What are you trying to say?" Something in her manner, her careless posture, her reflection in that window jammed with teddy bears and model trains, made me terrifically impatient with us both. "Are you trying to say you want to go there?"

"I wasn't trying to say anything," she snapped. "I was just curious. Can't I ask a question without you exploding?"

I suffered a moment's weakness then. I approached her, as I assumed she wanted me to, and put my hands on her shoulders. It had cooled off, and her skin was cold, but the flesh was still smooth. "Sorry," I said. "Now tell me the truth. Do you want to go to Mexico?"

She shrugged again. "I was telling you the truth. I was just curious about where we were. It doesn't matter."

"Why not?"

"It just doesn't."

"Nothing matters, is that it? That's the party line?"

"Some party." She frowned. "I'm sorry. That's not fair."

"You're right. It's not." I was boiling.

"Let's not fight, Hesh. Please. I'm here with you because I want to be . . ."

"You want to be *what?*"

"Please," she said, with some pain. "It doesn't mat—"

"I know. It doesn't matter. It doesn't matter if you run off in the middle of the afternoon. It doesn't matter if you get stinking drunk, or conceive a child, or run off to Mexico—"

Abby's face was frozen, white. "What do you mean, *conceive a child?* Who said anything about *conceiving a child?*"

"Unless someone changed the rules on me, Abby, having sex without birth control makes it possible. First there's the fucking, then the pitter-patter of little feet, and soon Junior's in college bringing home loose women for Thanksgiv—"

And then she was crying. It was the first time I'd actually seen her cry, and I found myself watching closely, hoping it would help me understand some of what I seemed to be unable to understand. She leaned against the toy store window, her shoulders pulled up to her ears and the soft irregularities of her features contorting into something wild and inscrutable and broken. It happened so quickly that I had no time to consider what might have prompted it. The misery was private and large; it swept her in waves. I felt flaccid, intrusive, a stranger observing her unguarded. For want of a better plan, I resolved to stand there beside her protectively as she sobbed and coughed. In the window a model train went around and around its model track, tireless in its narrow purpose, and each time it crossed its model bridge it gave a little toot from its model horn which was just audible on the other side of the glass.

I thought of Solly, how light he felt in my arms on the bridge back home, and grew a little misty myself.

After some minutes Abby blew her nose and took my arm. We walked through the remainder of the town's commercial district. When we came to the end, the point where the town left off and the desert began, we stopped and held each other close, and I felt her shivering as though it were my own. "I'm sorry," she said, and wiped her nose again. "You couldn't know."

Her hair had fallen across her cheek like a curtain. I smoothed it back with the flat of my hand.

"It doesn't work with me."

She offered this statement as a finality, with a grin vacant of all else but resignation. But resignation did not come naturally for her; something rose up, the green flashed in her eyes, and she pushed on.

"I don't know why. I'd like to think it's *because* of something. I don't mind a little brutality in my life, you know. I can bear up under a lot, believe me."

"I believe you."

"Thank you. But I don't like capriciousness, and I don't like meanness, and sometimes the randomness of things, the way nature just fucks you over sometimes . . . that I can't . . . that I'm just *fucked,* that's all. I'm just *fucked.*"

At this point, her nose, already chafed from all the wiping, began to run again, and she let it. I didn't have a handkerchief with me, so I reached up with one hand to lift her jaw, and with the back of the other I patted the soft indentation above her lips until my hand was runny with her. It was, in its way, the most intimate act we'd committed yet.

"Have you been to see a doctor?"

She shook her head no.

"Then how do you know it's you? Maybe it's Arthur."

"No," she said immediately. She jerked away from me and turned to face the river, and the mountains beyond. "It's me, Hesh. Because I've had other men too."

This shocked me; I was half certain she was lying, but I kept quiet.

"I've been trying for a year, more than a year. I tried with Arthur. Then I went to Spain, and what the hell, I tried there too. I had what you call flings. I had what you call several flings, in fact. I had the baker. I had the manager of the local bank. I also cried a lot. I'd lie outside, working on my tan, reading poetry, and crying. Is this how it feels? I'd ask myself. Is this a nervous breakdown? It was awfully formless and disappointing. But I thought that if I came back pregnant, then maybe it would have all been *for* something. A romantic notion, I guess. Anyway, it doesn't matter now, if you'll forgive me for repeating myself."

"Abby, none of this means it's you. There are a thousand factors involved."

"I know," she said. "I know all about the goddamn factors."

"Then why don't you go to a doctor and find out for sure?"

When she turned, the tendons in her neck were standing at attention. "You don't understand, do you? I don't *want* to find out! I don't *want* to know for sure! Why are you being so stupid? I've lived my whole *life* believing in possibility—what happens if I stop now? I'm only thirty years old!" She stopped, began to sob, choked it off, and, with a bewildered expression, allowed her hand to travel to her mouth, two fingers gently pressing the lips, as though to shush herself. "Oh God, I'm never going to grow up, am I? I'm always going to be like this. Neurotic and hysterical and selfish. Driving everyone away."

"I'm still here," I reminded her.

"Well, Arthur isn't." She stopped again, as the irony of her statement washed back over both of us; when she went on, it was with considerably less righteous anger than before. "I know you find him comical, Hesh, but he's really very sweet, and good-natured, and sincere. He actually wants to *accomplish* things. Can you beat that? And I've battered him around with my neediness and complaining until he's practically scared to death of me. I'm just fucked, Hesh. You really should stay away from me. I like you so much, though. . . ."

She had begun to cry again.

179

"Oh, God. Do you know what I want? What I really really want? It's so mundane I'm ashamed to say it. A house. Just a nice little house by the side of the road, with a garden and a picture window and plenty of polished wood. Isn't that funny? My whole life I go around thinking I'm something special, and when it comes down to it all I want is what everybody else already seems to have. You used to have one, didn't you?"

"Yes."

"Was it nice?"

"It was nice. But it was too small."

"It was too small, or it felt too small?"

I took a moment to answer. "It felt too small."

"Well," she said, with a depleted sigh, "at least you're honest."

In the morning we drove down to Las Cruces—where it did not escape my notice that another outlaw, Billy the Kid, had been brought down a century ago—had a wordless lunch, and afterward took turns in the phone booth. When Abby emerged, her color was high and her neck was arched combatively. "I left word I was going to Mexico and would be back soon," she said, and left it at that.

I went into the booth and called Shelley Lubin, who seemed happy to hear my voice. She told me that Jerome had gone back to New Haven, which didn't surprise me, and that the word on Charlie Goldwyn was he had encephalitis and was about to punt the Eastern case over to Walter Todd. "True or false?"

"A toss-up," I said.

"What's the matter? You sound troubled. Tell Shell."

"Just a case of the dreads, I guess."

"Is *that* all."

"Do me a favor, Shell, and call Charlie in Albuquerque. Tell him I've got an emergency, okay? It'll take a couple of days. And tell him—tell him I tried to call to explain but couldn't reach him. Will you do that?"

"You can count on me, boss."

"You're the best. I can't tell you how many hours I've spent behind my office door, listening to you type and talk on the phone simultaneously. It makes me proud to be an eavesdropper."

"You're easily impressed," she said. "Hey, where *is* Albuquerque, anyway? Are you anywhere near Mexico?"

"Somewhere near it," I said.

"Why don't you take some time off and go see it. I bet it would do you good. Keep you young."

"I just might do that," I said. "Maybe I'll bring you back some peyote."

"Swell," she said. "Just don't get caught. You're the type that does, you know."

After I'd hung up, I examined the fold of traveler's checks in my wallet. Five hundred dollars and change. It should take us, I thought, about as far as we wanted to go.

Chapter 19

I see motion, said Thomas Aquinas, *and I infer a motor.*

But it would have been difficult to infer anything at all from our excursion into Mexico. We were motion in search of motor; energy spreading itself out to fill a vacuum. We had stepped out of the frame, screwed up the continuity, but good. Even our clothes were different. Immediately after crossing the border, we went to a chain department store in Juarez and loaded up on necessities—underwear, shorts, cotton shirts, toiletries, huaraches. Abby, roaming the cluttered aisles, was having a fine time. On impulse she bought a small, badly potted cactus to bring along in the car, and two pairs of aviator sunglasses for driving. In an hour we had spent a hundred and twelve dollars. Neither of us seemed anxious to leave. We dawdled over the magazine rack, the shower curtains, the sets of cheap dishware. In the camping section I had to argue her out of buying a Coleman lantern and stove. "We're not going to rough it," I said. It was going to be rough enough, I figured, already.

We had no itinerary, of course, no destination in mind except for some people in Mexico City that Abby said she used to be close to and whom she thought I might like. Like, not like—they would serve our purposes. That the distance involved was a thousand miles didn't seem to trouble either of us. What's a thousand miles? New York to Chicago. No large distance. Not for the young-in-love, not for the wayward escapees. Why not go farther, to Peru or Argentina? Why not paint the whole hemisphere red? That was the point of this adventure, after all: an end to halfway measures. Or was it?

First, though, we drove the highway down to Chihuahua, a four-hour trip through the rough, scrubby heart of the plateau, and it took some of the fight out of me right away. The air-conditioning checked out ten miles south of Juarez. We rolled down the windows and tried to breathe

the thick, hot air. It was full of flies from the herds of cattle grazing on both sides of us. Between the glare, and the dust, and a nervous stomach full of the greasy quesadillas from lunch, I tired easily. Late in the afternoon we took a rest in the cool of an abandoned zinc mine. I napped and Abby worked a crossword puzzle. She did them in pen, so when she made a mistake it usually meant crossing out the entire section, or just giving up. Occasionally, when the subject of a clue eluded her, she'd ask my advice, frowning at me over the paper as I took my time forming an answer. If our ability to work together on such things was a test of some sort, an experiment in the joint channeling of our disparate wills, a gambler would have done well to bet against us. But I was not feeling that way at the time. I was in dreamy waters, the sun-tipped shallows. I could feel the heat of Abby's limbs against my own, the smell of apricot through the clouds of dust. South of the Border. The idea had a pleasant taste.

We proceeded on toward Torreón. To keep ourselves occupied we played cassettes on Abby's pocket tape recorder. When that broke, we pulled the Nagra out of the trunk, fit on a new reel, and sang our lungs into it. We sang Beatles, Motown, Gershwin, Sinatra. I did a solo on "Papa Was a Rolling Stone" to fit the occasion, and I let Abby run away with "How High the Moon." There were occasional lapses in enthusiasm, fade-ins and fade-outs of pitch and volume, as though our singing were an accompaniment to some very basic task we were performing with our hands, like kneading bread or scrubbing the floor. It was fitful and spirited and just a bit clumsy, like our sex. All the while, even though its mechanism had jammed, the pocket recorder remained in Abby's lap, her fingers tracing the seams in its casing.

Later, toward evening, we used the machine to try to teach me the language. Abby would patiently intone a phrase in her musical Catalonian Spanish, and I would dutifully repeat it, and then we'd rewind the tape and I was able to hear my own mistakes.

"You've got to be willing to sound foolish," she admonished. "That's the only way anyone ever learns a language. Otherwise you never get anywhere."

"It's no use. Maybe we should try Esperanto."

"Come on. Let's work on the present tense. That's the simplest."

In a way, the present tense was exactly what we *had* been working on ever since we'd met, and it was not, we both knew full well, as simple as all that. Still, that didn't stop us from trying.

Because of the late start, and the shopping, and the napping, and the pocked concrete roads, we made it only as far as Jiménez by midnight, at which point we crashed in a white-walled *posada* that seemed to double as the town's concert hall, or brothel, from the evidence of the operatic howling we heard as we staggered into bed. I could smell fruit rotting beneath the trees outside, which turned my empty stomach from hunger to a vague nausea. The bridge of my nose felt raw from the sunglasses, and my back throbbed dully from the car seat. I wanted to ask Abby to rub it for me, but she fell instantly, soundlessly, asleep. I spent a good hour or two floating, just above wakefulness, in a kind of broody washing tide, listening to the night songs from the ground floor and to the insects as they massed and whined overhead, until they lost all urgency. A ballet commenced on the ceiling, a choreography of skating phantoms, ominously whirling. The last thing I saw looked like me, driving away in a black cloud of exhaust.

In the white light of morning, I woke to find Abby sitting cross-legged next to me on the bed, a sketch pad open on her lap and her hair fallen in discrete lines down the sides of her face. Her eyes were reddened from what I decided was probably sleep; they squinted down on me almost guiltily, then moved to the charcoal drawing, only a small part of which I could make out without lifting my head from the pillow. As she worked, she made *tsk*ing sounds with her teeth which seemed to indicate a mounting dissatisfaction with at least one of us. I hoped it was her. I felt groggy and longed for peace. "Is that supposed to be me?" I asked.

She looked startled. "Oh," she said. "You're up."

"Or thereabouts. Whatcha doing?"

"Just playing. Trying to get a likeness. But it's hopeless."

"Why's that?"

"Because," she said, and looked me full in the eye, "I don't see you well enough. Your features slide around, even when you're asleep. Sometimes you look sweet, and sometimes . . ."

"Uh oh . . ."

"Oh, well," she said, and threw down the charcoal. "It doesn't matter."

"Again with the 'It doesn't matter'?"

She smiled in apology, shook her head as though to clear it, and slid forward to deliver a desultory peck on the lips. "Lover," she sighed slowly, infatuated more with the word, I thought, than with its object.

"Is this us getting up for breakfast?"

She nodded, slid off the bed, and began to dress. I remained where I was, turning the sketch pad around to face me so I could have a look at it. It was a hopeful idea, in a way: I wanted to see myself as Abby saw me, as though that would somehow free us up for some action as yet unimagined, something we would undertake together. But the sketch was hasty, impressionistic; neither mirror nor window. It didn't give me any particular confidence in either of us; in fact, it depressed me.

"Hesh."

Abby was at the foot of the bed in her unbuttoned shorts, her white sleeveless T-shirt bunched around her neck. At first I didn't register that she was getting not dressed but undressed, and that she was undressing for me; but once I'd caught on, and she began to slide toward me, her skin humming and warm and the sound of her breathing rising up in soft spasms, I lost all consciousness of depression and aspiration and buried myself in the long, elegant question mark of her bare neck. She had said the word and now we would make it true—where lovers love must lie love. A choice of tools, the clamor of building, the surrender of completion. We would make us a house. *Ifth,* groaned Abby through her teeth, and then we took our rest. The breeze blew through the open windows; it bore song and heat and fruit. When we left the room, it was afternoon.

We took our time moving south and west along the foothills of the Sierra Madres. When we wanted to stop, we stopped. We hiked, snoozed, loitered in stuffy cantinas, played language games with the Nagra. When in doubt, we drove. The off-roads were hazards, clotted with mud and speed bumps. And everywhere, the dark, heat-flogged children of the poor. They came running alongside us with their animated, resentful chatter, their television dreams flickering in their stares as they chased our gleaming fenders. They frightened me. There was nothing innocent or joyous about them, no quaint local color; they looked recriminatory and poised. It didn't take many years for them to understand what Late Capitalism was all about—all it took was an occasional car like ours, a trickling parade of chrome conquistadores, to show them who lived on the other side of the TV screen. One needle-legged boy, about seven years old, tried to sell us a can of deodorant that looked as if had fallen out of someone's suitcase. This was a few miles south of Durango; we were tired, and as the boy persisted, poking his head in the window to get a look at the intricacies of the dashboard, I felt my mood turn on a pivot. "*Vayase!*" I yelled, and slapped at his hand on the window. The boy grinned hugely. "What?" I said to Abby. "I'm pronouncing it wrong?"

Blanched, she ignored me, called the boy over to her side of the car, and proceeded to talk to him for twenty minutes, buying the deodorant with a thousand-peso note and for all I knew confessing to him, in detail, the full depth and variety of my limitations. When he was gone, Abby muttered something to herself in Spanish that I didn't understand. I let it pass. She settled in to write postcards to her mother and to some friends in Spain, and I drove on toward the dry gray mountains of Zacatecas.

That night we had dinner in a village called El Palmito, on the porch of a small cantina that bordered the graveyard on one side and the county *biblioteca* on the other. We were the only customers. The moon was better than half full, the night sharp and clear. We could see the uneven jumble of the headstones from our table, leaning at erratic angles like magnetic poles under the tangled vines. A solitary cook rattled in the kitchen. A strangeness began to creep over me as I sat there, a sensation of anonymity so pure it was like breathing pure oxygen. When the food came, it too, made me giddy, and I ate ravenously and drank three beers with it. Abby stretched, the hollows of her armpits glowing white under the lamp. Around her the stars swam like fireflies. She looked, I thought, serenely beautiful.

A young girl cleared away our dishes, and we ordered coffee. The feeling inside me intensified as I looked over the mess I'd made of the tablecloth, the flecks of lettuce and the grains of rice. They looked ordered and full of charm. So did the headstones and the wildflowers. So did my companion. Under the table our bare ankles touched, and I heard myself laugh out loud. I thought that perhaps this was why I had come to Mexico: to lose control of myself entirely, to go mad. Abby studied me with amusement as I bent forward, reached for her hand, and massaged it between mine, as though it were in my power to smooth out the knuckles themselves. "What?" she asked.

"Why? Where? How? Who?"

She blushed. "It's nice, isn't it, Hesh?"

"Yes. Yes indeed."

"Very, very nice."

"Surprised?"

She let that one go and sipped at her coffee. "Tell me about your marriage."

"Abby," I said promptly, "let me tell you about my marriage." I paused and shook my head. "What do I say next?"

"Were you close?"

"We were close."

"Too close?"

I shrugged. "In some ways."

"Like you and me?" She smiled gently, attempting no hidden meanings; she accepted something about us as a fact that I had only recently begun to guess at. She was not all blind self-absorption, not by a long shot—it was an easy dodge to think of her that way. Besides, who was I

186

to fault anyone for self-absorption? "I lost track," I said, squeezing her long hand. "That's what happened."

"Of Joanne?"

"Of myself. Of everything."

She lowered her gaze to the coffee. "You're awfully hard on yourself, aren't you? Just like you're hard on your father."

"Look who's talking."

"We're both talking," she said. "But where does it ever get us?" She took her last sip of coffee and then looked up brightly. "What do you say, white man? Let's have us an adventure."

"I thought we already were."

"Oh," she said, "but this is just the beginning," and then she looked away, and despite all her breathlessness, the phrase, when I repeated it to myself silently, struck me as only the most winsome and hopeful of dreams.

The girl came back with her quiet black stare and we asked for the bill. It came to much more than I'd expected.

The night air was warm and still, heavy as marmalade. We walked in a circle through the *zócalo,* past a once-ornate fountain, now dry and chipped, coated in droppings from the blackbirds. From several blue-lit, screenless windows, the theme song from *Hawaii Five-O* filtered around the square. It followed us down the dirt road and back to the cantina, but by the time we reached the graveyard it had muted, become just another voice in the choir of crickets and roosters and burros. I had an idea of what we were headed for, and it thrilled me.

"Here," whispered Abby, and her eyes slid downward. I reached for her and she leaned against me, her small breasts easing back and forth under my shoulder, and in that loud tangled stillness we lay down behind a headstone and had our adventure. The dust rose up and covered us with its blanket; the lizards skated away. The sex itself was fast, brazen, and not very tender. With all the textures around me, I could hardly feel my own orgasm, and Abby, I was certain, was trying too hard to have one.

Abby's friends, Shy and Malla Torborg, did not so much live in Mexico City as live above it. Their villa was in Azcapotzalco, about half an hour north, but their actual residence was in a mere ethereal state, a state bordering innocence and bordering cynicism, maintained by a healthy supply of liquor, drugs, and a self-satisfaction of the sort you find among ideologues, house cats, and compulsive throwers of parties. Our arrival, in fact, interrupted some fairly languid preparations for a party that very evening. It was Flag Day. On the back patio, the Torborgs were in the process of coloring, on large strips of muslin, crayon versions of the Soviet, Cuban, Vietnamese, and Disneyland flags. One of the neighbors' children had purloined the red crayons, however, so they were improvising with other colors, and with blank spaces, and not, from the look of things, having much success. Still, they seemed to be enjoying themselves tremendously.

"Huzzah!" they chanted, when they first caught sight of Abby.

"Return of the prodigal," she said, shrugging, and there was a triangular embrace as I looked on. "And this," she said after a while, "is Hesh."

My name alone seemed to endear me to the Torborgs, and they greeted me as though we were long acquainted, as though my presence required no greater explanation than those four letters. They were happy to see us, to be sure. But it seemed to me their real pleasure was in fact being *seen* by us. I had an intuition touring the small, cluttered rooms of their villa (rented, they claimed, from a CIA man currently on loan to Honduras), that this couple would be a workout. They seemed to rely upon visitors to confer something upon them, appreciation, or envy, or legitimacy. We were to be the new wave of tourists in the curated exhibit they made of their lives. It was a form of role playing that made me balky. I had the feeling we'd be up half the night, and all I really wanted was to lie down.

Still, my thoughts were not all this uncharitable. The Torborgs were attractive people, warm and generous hosts. They beamed at us attentively as we spoke of our trip, their gazes shifting fluidly from Abby to me to each other. Perhaps their ease had something to do with their background. Shy had been a UPI correspondent and Malla a photojournalist; between them they'd been witness to a fair proportion of the decade's wars, coups, famines, and massacres. They let you know in the way they conducted themselves that they had already earned certain points in their own eyes and would take such privileges as they could find without guilt or self-effacement. Their movements were casual and practiced, their speech slow and layered with irony.

"It's lucky you came this week," Shy told us on the patio. Big and well-muscled, with reddish skin and small features, he was handsome in a conventional way. The ease with which his mouth lit into a smile suggested something facile, or merely uncurious. "Next week I'm off to Oaxaca. Travel piece for the *L.A. Times*. Where to stay, what to eat, what kind of suntan oil to bring. Heady stuff."

Loud reggae music began to roll out from the expensive stereo in the living room. Malla Torborg followed, bearing a tray of goat cheese and English crackers, and four more Tecates with limes and salt.

"I was just telling them about Oaxaca," said Shy.

"Sí, señor." She sat on a lawn chair of blue plastic tubing. Tall, almost startlingly slender, she wore sweat pants and a bikini top, which rested loosely over the dimpled serenity of her even-browned chest. Her hair, long and fine and sandy, fanned over her shoulders. She looked smart, sleek, unhurried. I could see why Abby prized her so.

"We'll be going over to Monte Albán, of course," Shy went on. "Quite a site. Got to hand it to the Zapotecs. When it comes to awesome buildings good for absolutely nothing, they were way up there with the Romans."

"Don't forget the Mixtecs," said Malla.

Shy raised his beer to her. "Show-off. But you've got it wrong. They came later." He cocked his head toward us. "Sort of your anal-retentive types, the Mixtecs. Kept elaborate genealogies. Manuscript records of the gods. When they found the Zapotecs' burial chambers, they kept them intact but tossed out all the bones. Their version of spring cleaning, I guess."

"I'd like to see it," mused Abby.

"So hey," he said. "Come."

She ran one finger along the rim of her Tecate and smiled to herself crookedly. "Maybe I will."

Shy leaned back and spread his arms across the back of his chair. "We'll make it a party. Cruise down to Puerto Ángel for the surf and snorkeling afterward. The article should be a snap. In fact, we can all collaborate on it. The majestic ocher-colored mountains and all that."

"That sounds fun," said Abby.

"I like it," said Malla. "We'll bring Juan and Esperanza. Two new friends," she explained to us. "Communists. But they like to play."

"That does sound fun," Abby repeated, checking my reaction with a quick, tentative glance.

"The particular charm of Oaxaca," recited Shy, "comes from its, ahem, juxtaposition of cultures. The area offers many rewards to the aficionado of pre-Columbian art. Be sure to ask for a balcony table at the yadda-yadda-yadda, the best restaurant in town, where a dinner for two, with the drinkable house wine, will cost only twenty of your stinking dollars. Afterwards make sure to climb the yadda-yadda-yadda, famous all over Pochutla for its magnificent view of the ancient Mixtec outhouse and delicatessen, the yadda-yadda-yadda." He smiled at us triumphantly.

"You see? We could write the article without even going there. Maybe that would be more fun."

"No, dear," said his wife, rubbing oil on her belly. "It would be more fun to go. By an infinite margin."

"Well, then. It's a happening. Old friends. New ones too," he said, and turned to me. "You like it, Hesh?"

"What's not to like?"

"You hear, sweets? That rhythm. This man is from the House of David. We were just talking, Mall and I, about how we never meet any Jews down here. You think that business with Trotsky scared them away, or have they all fled to the Holy Land?"

They were high on something, I told myself, and they were Abby's friends. And they were in all likelihood Jewish themselves. So I kept my voice level. "I don't really know. Maybe they require better company."

Abby looked at me strangely. Shy had some more beer. Finally, Malla yawned and stretched. "I feel I should do something," she said. "Maybe finish those silly flags. Or make dinner. Anybody feel like dinner? Or should we just skip it?"

"I really don't care," said Abby pleasantly. "I'm fine right now."

"What time are people stopping by?" husband asked wife.

"Around ten."

"Think they'll bring beer, or should we go to the store?"

"You must be kidding. They're out to break us. I told you last time."

The two of them moved into the house, bantering, as much for our benefit, I thought, as to convey information. We've got our rituals, our private codes, our places of worship, they seemed to be telling us, just the same as the Zapotecs and Mixtecs, and it is for you, our guests, to join us in our ceremonies. That is the price exacted from travelers, a subtle extortion to pay homage to the domestic altar. Even the long, pleasant afternoon, flooded with toning light, seemed to be an idea of theirs, an arrangement they'd worked up before we came. I waited until they were out of earshot before turning to Abby. "I can't stand this," I said.

Her mouth tightened. "I think they're a lot of fun."

"I agree with you. By an infinite margin."

"What's the matter? We've been doing so well."

"We've been alone."

"Well, we can't stay alone forever. That's not real life."

"Neither is this, Abby."

She looked away, toward the thicket of weeds and vines that made up the backyard of the villa. "We don't have to decide anything now," she said carefully. "But I'd like to see Oaxaca."

I didn't say anything. I watched her fumble with her sandal, her bare arms rosy with the light, her face reticent and puckered and intent. What did she want? We kept moving south and moving south, but the border itself—*her* border—kept shifting. And mine?

I would like to say that I enjoyed or did not enjoy the party that evening, but the truth was it had a numbing effect on me that eluded the normal categories. I remember that it had a peculiarly structured quality to it, full of announcements and recitations and organized parlor games. Perhaps it was an attempt at something British in the way of sophistication; I didn't know. In between the formalities there was eating, of course, and dancing, and plenty of hash and beer and tequila. There was also some political quarreling I did not understand, and intermittent laughter like the fire of an automatic weapon.

At one point Shy Torborg recited Aztec poetry. It may have been the beer, or my loss of bearings, or else Shy Torborg was an extremely talented fellow, because I found the verses very moving, and told him so. One was so beautiful that I asked him for a copy.

> Is it true, can it be true that we live on earth?
> Not forever here, only for a moment on earth—
> For the hard jade splinters
> The bright gold loses its luster
> The shiny quetzal feather rips—
> Not forever here, only a moment on earth.

There was a journalist named Anderson, who read from his collection of unpublished essays, "American South." It was a description of watching the 1972 election results in a Nashville bar less than a mile from the Grand Opry, and the prose was merciless and chilling.

A shaggy-looking Jesuit from Philadelphia read from the Psalms in a halting, heavily accented Spanish. When he paused between verses he looked lonely and soft, as though waiting for encouragement to go on. No one said a word. There were candles scattered on the tile floor and the lights were out; a bottle of pear brandy was passed from hand to hand. Everyone listened politely. When he was finished, the Jesuit looked embarrassed, and the woman on my left, who worked in the records department of the French Embassy, giggled and said, "Shit."

Later, Abby began to flirt rather reluctantly with a lugubrious archaeology student from San Francisco. He seemed, from the way he was leaning toward her in the kitchen doorway, to be discovering lost cities in her. The color was high in her cheeks, and her legs, flexed slightly at the knees, looked to be testing a diving board.

"But of *course* there's a point to human sacrifice," I heard him saying across the room. "Only it's magical, not religious."

I watched her mumble a response. He watched her too, keenly, searching for shards, tools, assembling a personality for her from fragments and speculation. We were not so very different, I thought.

The Jesuit's softness was being exaggerated by the brandy. "She's dead," I heard him confide to the French girl, whose eyes were elsewhere. "She loved Randolph Scott. It was sort of an obsession."

"Who?"

I had an odd impulse at this point. I was sitting in the corner, quietly nursing my way through a six-pack of Tecate and feeling things begin to slide away from me. It was not an entirely unpleasant sensation. But suddenly I had an urge to come forward and tell some stories myself. I wanted to occupy the party's center, to share a world—*my* world—full of the recognizable and ineffable characters I knew, all stumbling inelegantly toward grace. I thought of Charlie Goldwyn and Walter Todd, of Jerome, of Shelley Lubin. I thought of Siskin in New Orleans. Perhaps I was a little homesick. I thought of the way Wall Street looks in the middle of the night, when no one is out but the newspaper trucks and the odd exhausted associate, waving his briefcase at any passing car, hoping for a cab. Of the stoned jabber of the boys in the copy room as they zing tall stacks of paper with light. Of the four-foot-high ceramic dalmatian that stands by the window of Bill Webber's office, just beneath the photograph of Webber and the ex–attorney general in Palm Springs, taken a few months before the ex–attorney general's indictment and subsequent conviction. Of the library at Harvard, crowded with girls from Somerville looking over prospective mates. The pictures rolled through me like a tide, but with the jolt of each remembered image the energy to share them leaked away. I felt less and less certain of their relevance to any outside sphere, less confident of my ability, in any case, to speak of them. I had hoped they would make me expansive, but they worked in me a different form of magic; I began to close down.

Malla Torborg, sitting yoga-style on the floor beside me, stubbed out her cigarette in an unpolished conch shell and looked me over appraisingly. "Where'd you get this guy, anyway?" she called to Abby. "Does he always look so dour?"

Abby paused in midsentence to examine me, her face hooded and sleepy, a cigarette in her left hand. "I don't really know," she said, her eyes finding mine and holding on. Something passed between us. She lifted one eyebrow and gave out a diffident chortle. "That's just Hesh, I guess."

It had been a betrayal of sorts, the kind of betrayal I remembered from my deteriorating marriage, and it made me restless to get out of there. I'd get up and go; she could catch up to me if she wanted to. But in the sluggish whirl of the alcohol my resolution faltered, and a phrase washed over me, that pet expression of Arthur's: *You can't go somewhere from nowhere.* For the first time, I thought I understood it. That I had found it. Nowhere.

"Come with me, Señor Dour," said Malla Torborg. "A change of scenery."

She held out her hand and I took it. It was longer, cooler, and drier than Abby's, with high ridged knuckles. A lone silver-and-turquoise bracelet dangled at the wrist. She was light in her movements; as she led me out to the yard I had the sensation of sliding over glass. The overgrown garden gave off the smell of peppers and a perfume of weeds and mulch that made the whirling inside me go just a bit faster.

"It's just back here." We walked through the tall weeds to a tin-roofed shed behind the house. "This used to be our darkroom. Here, let me just get this lit."

We were in a sculptor's studio. The air was cloudy with dust. The white wood floor and walls were speckled with clay, as was the ceiling, which resembled the palest of gray skies in the light of the kerosene lamp. In the center of the room a wide table had been fashioned out of a door and two sawhorses. On it lay a number of art books, an *I Ching,* an ashtray brimming with butts, and a transistor radio. Their shadows wavered.

"Look," said Malla. "This is what I wanted to show you."

She pointed to the far wall, where a series of figures made of clay stood in a line, like a mute dwarf chorus. Each was about two feet high, wide-hipped and square-shouldered, with the jutting broad calves and arms you see in Picassos. The textures were rough—there were pinches and tears in the clay, as though the artist had been working a kind of vengeance on it, determined to leave no illusion of skin, no promise of protection. I wasn't sure if they were finished, though, or even if they were supposed to be finished. None of the figures, for one thing, had heads.

"This is where you're supposed to say something," said Malla Torborg, folding her arms. "Preferably something complimentary."

"Very powerful."

She repeated the phrase without much enthusiasm.

"I suppose I'm wondering about the heads," I said. "Is that very bourgeois of me?"

She had another cigarette in her mouth but had not yet lit it. It waved expressively, an extension of her thin, pale lips, suggesting that she found the question itself a bourgeois one. "You're very self-conscious," she said. "Your rhythms are way off. I can tell just from the way you stand, all scrunched up at the neck."

"Thank you, Doctor."

"Don't get sulky, Señor Dour. I'm trying to be a good friend. I'm worried about Abby. She's all locked up. I love her very much, you know. We go way back. I even introduced her to Arthur, once upon a time. The point is, I'm interested in you."

"No you're not."

She didn't even blink. "You're right, I'm not. But I'm interested in Abby, and I felt like getting out of that room and showing a new person my work. You haven't put up any resistance so far, so why not oblige me?"

"Okay. So what about the heads?"

"I tried a number of approaches, understand. Some were primitive, admittedly. I was feeling my way along. Exaggerating the features. Playing with found objects. I used to take those little plastic eyes out of dolls and stick them onto the clay. It was no good. Too distracting. Then I tried leaving off the features altogether, which was a step forward. Then I went cubist for a while, splitting the heads up, left brain, right brain, that sort of thing. Only that was too retro, I decided."

"Plus all those splitting headaches."

"Making fun? How charming." She wandered over to the row of figures, stopped at the first one, and caressed the unsurfaced angle of the biceps with two fingers. "I had quit work by this time, and we were both living off savings. I took my time, playing with the form. Double heads. Hollow heads. Backward heads. Mixed-media heads. It was agony. I felt thoroughly untalented, a poseur. Every morning I'd come out to the shed and look at my piles and piles of botched heads, and I'd say to myself, Malla, old girl, you're a very sick person indeed. Finally, one day I got really disgusted—I'd just cut my finger on a paring blade—and I went around and gathered up all the rotten heads and buried them in a hole in the yard, where the landlord buried his dogs. And that changed everything. Now I'm a success. The time moves quickly. I have a gallery in the city that sells my work, and another in Santa Barbara that gives me an annual show. Nothing extravagant, understand, but enough to keep me going. End of story. Contentment sets in and the story is over."

She absently fingered the bracelet on her wrist, considering, perhaps, whether or not she wished to retract that last sentiment. Possibly it had defined her life more accurately than she'd intended, or possibly she was more interested in me than either of us had thought. Whatever it was, when she continued it was with greater seriousness then before.

"The days here are nice and long, and I get good sun. We were stuck before, Shy and me. Always going out on assignment, and always bringing back the same story. Half the time the New York editors wouldn't run what we wrote, anyway. They'd send some new stringers down who would see the shit firsthand and immediately get radicalized, and then they wouldn't run their stories, either. There are generations of us down here, pinko stringers who nobody wants to print. Some of them are back there in the house, getting wasted. There's so little else for them to do, you see."

"So that's why you quit?"

She laughed shortly. "There are so many reasons. That's just the one I'm using on you."

"And now? Now you're an artist, is that it?"

"Now," she said, "Shy works on his little pieces and I work on mine. It's just that the pieces are different, that's all. Then in the afternoons we work in the garden. Neither of us has read a newspaper in six months. Everyone thinks we're crazy, or stoned, because we gave up such good careers. I don't care, really. I've got the sun and the clay and it all flows through me the way it's supposed to. I don't give a shit if tomorrow I win a Guggenheim or I drop dead. That may not sound like such an achievement to you, Señor Dour. I don't care. For me, it's the mother lode." She drew close and took the unlit cigarette out of her mouth. "What are you doing here, anyway? This couldn't possibly be your scene."

"Answer me something," I said. "In your dreams, do the people have heads?"

"An ugly question." Something had come in to muddy the lucid blue of her eyes; her lips went down at the corners. I didn't think she would choose to answer, but she surprised me. "Sí, Señor Dour. I see heads. I see angels and insects and everything in between, just like you. But the colors are softening, know what I mean? Got a match for this?"

"Sorry."

"Then let's go back to the house."

She stepped around me easily to extinguish the kerosene lamp, and without a backward glance went outside into the dry weeds. The wind was whistling through the fruit trees, and the haze from the city had

195

dissipated so that the night opened itself above us. It was really a lovely spot. When Malla Torborg slipped into the house, I hung back for a minute, resting on one of the plastic lawn chairs on the patio. I hadn't shaved in three days and the stubble on my cheeks itched. My skin felt raw and stiff, old, a burden—it wanted to come off. I scratched at it for a while, grateful for the activity, and gazed off into the summery darkness.

When I finally went inside, the candles had burned down to their bases, which were pooled in colored wax. Nobody was left in the living room, though the empty glasses and soiled napkins from dinner were still out, the maps of Oaxaca still spread on the bare brown tile, the cigarettes still poised on the lips of the ashtrays and in the cracks of the conch shells, forming presences that flickered in the candles' failing light, a dialectic of silence and waste. It was 4 A.M. I found Abby curled up on the mattress in the little guest room, her right arm thrust high over her face. When I moved under the sheet, she shuddered and mumbled a vague warning. I did not know the colors of her dreams, but I was willing to bet that they were a long way from softening.

For the most part we slept in the sun, confining ourselves to the Torborgs' patio and garden. Occasionally we'd stroll into the shops of Azcapotzalco for more beer, or eggs, or meat, but we maintained a level of idleness even then, speaking little and moving without urgency, as though we were both convalescing from a long and taxing disease. What little was said was about Oaxaca. It is one of the peculiarities of travel that once embarked, you are continually anticipating the next destination at the expense of your present one; though, to be fair, the subject was usually brought up by our hosts, who had not been away from their villa or their little community of party people in some time. I did not participate in these discussions. Instead I bathed myself in Tecate and sunlight, and the vacant pleasures of a novel about pirates by Sabatini.

On the fifth day of our visit I took the bus by myself into Mexico City to see the museums and the Diego Rivera murals in the lobby of the Hotel del Prado. They were profuse, angry, magical, much like what I'd seen of the country itself, and on a scale that made me feel small and outside history. When I was tired of looking at them, I went across the street to Alameda Park and opened the book I had bought that morning in the English-language bookshop.

The book was *The Portable Hawthorne*. I read the story "Wakefield" twice, and when I came to the end the second time, I took out a pen and underlined the passage Walter Todd had recommended to me back in Connecticut, a commentary on the follies of sons everywhere:

Amid the seeming confusion of our mysterious world, individuals are so nicely adjusted to a system, and systems to one another and to a whole, that, by stepping aside for a moment, a man exposes himself to a fearful risk of losing his place forever.

Later, beneath the vines of the Torborgs' patio, sipping a Tecate in the last light of Monday—the first urgent nudge of the new week's elbow—I thought of the various forces that had shaped and described my life, and felt myself grow bloated with a useless nostalgia. I shut my eyes. There I was in Barney's, buying my first suit, in preparation for my first job. The feel of the cloth, the smoothness, the slopes and contours, the neat unbroken lines. "This'll last you a lifetime," the salesman had said. There was the closet where I hung it; there the new house; there the leafy disorder of the new neighborhood. There were the kids on bikes, the dogs on leashes, the roar of a thousand lawn mowers in the weekday twilight. It was all there. Everything but me. I had moved away, and away. I was motion itself—an experiment in the repulsions and attractions of orbit. And now, I thought. What now. The elements of a choice were emerging, and I had never, I knew well, been half so much the chooser as the chosen.

It was close to eleven and we were making love in the Torborgs' bedroom while they spent the night visiting friends in the city. The sex was not going so well. I was on top of Abby and was conscious of the effort required to excite her, so conscious that it would require a good deal more, I discovered, to excite myself. I felt thick, slippery, full of useless weight. There was nothing in our movements of the simple syncopation of love. At least, that was how it seemed to me. Nonetheless, I was indulging the conceit that Abby was having a better time of it.

Until I saw her face. Her face held an expression of great purity. It contained none of her usual lewdness, no flashes of light from her inner spaces. It contained, instead, a focused wonder: Her eyes, wide open, seemed to be tracking the slow progress of something above us—a scorpion, I thought immediately, in a panic, a scorpion or a spider or some other form of crawling death that leaked from the walls at night. "Hey," I said, "what is it?"

She didn't say anything. It was getting closer, whatever it was; I could hear the measured intake of her breath beneath me. I made up my mind to turn over, to face it squarely.

When I spun over onto my back I did not see what I expected to see. In fact, it took me a moment to realize what it was I was looking at, and

197

in that moment my own expression took something of a beating, and then went slack. I watched it happen. Abby watched it, too. She had been watching all the time. It was easy—the mirror above the Torborgs' headboard had to have been at least three feet square.

"Well?" she asked coolly. "What's the matter?"

I didn't say anything.

"I didn't put it there, you know. I just happened to notice it, that's all."

I sat up and rubbed one knee with the knuckles of both fists. I could feel the agitation rising in each of us.

"Well, what did you *expect*?" Her voice pitched high on the final word, as though it were bobsledding away from her, from her original meaning into a much wider and more daunting one.

"I didn't expect anything, Abby," I said quietly.

"Oh, don't give me that, Hesh. You expected everything. So did I. Two peas in a little pod, that's us. Two watchers and waiters. You were watching me, and I was watching you, and we were both watching us."

She slapped the wall above our heads, as though to dispel the fog that stole in with our use of the past tense.

"Too bad," she said. "Some people get off on this. How come we don't?"

We stared at each other for a moment then. Not at ourselves in the mirror, but across the bed, at each other. Then, at almost the same instant, we said what we needed to say next.

"I'm going back."

"I'm not going back."

We hesitated, sorting out the overlap, making sure that there had been no mistake. It became terribly quiet. I looked at her, her bare skin spotted with sweat, her knees drawn up to her chin, her lips locked tightly together as she began to rock herself, summoning from her center of gravity her full powers of self-possession even as I felt my own deserting me. She was lovely, I thought, but I needed to get up. I needed to move. I felt myself drowning in waste.

I stood, balancing my weight against the springs of the mattress, my genitals slapping awkwardly against the insides of my thighs. Abby glanced up at me with mild interest and continued to rock herself. Seen from above, she was a stylized arrangement of curves; she was flesh and bones and hair; white oval shapes and spills of shadow. Then I looked up. I had plenty of time to think about how I was going to do what I was going to do, and then to do it, and as I did it I found the time to marvel at how much time I had to think about it. There was my right hand, balled into a fist, and then it traveled along an arc to a point where it became two hands, two hands hurtling toward each other, magnetic twins. And then there was an explosion of glass. A shattering. The larger pieces broke against the headboard and slivered, raining down on us as we ducked our heads and covered the backs of our necks with our arms. Abby screamed once, more out of surprise than terror, then choked it off. She held on to her neck with both hands, her gaze trailing over the ruined bed with some of the same intensity and wonder that had been there before, as though it had happened of itself.

And then the phone rang.

Our eyes met and there was the barest hint of amusement. Of perversity. Abby, careful not to cut herself, shifted her weight forward toward the edge of the mattress. "Well," she said. "The charm dissolves apace, to quote the bard. Here we go, then."

But she didn't move, not at first. A pulsing commenced in my throat. *Don't. Don't. Don't.*

The ringing finally stopped and we each took a long breath. Then it started again.

"Your hand's bleeding," she said, and lifted herself away.

She went into the other room and picked up the phone, her voice low in greeting. After a while I began to clean up the bedroom. I had to get down on my knees to do it. As I worked I lost track of the time, so I do not know how long their conversation went on—it might have been ten minutes or it might have been thirty. There were some cuts on my knuckles, but they didn't hurt and so I ignored them.

When she came back into the room, the phone pressed against her bare hip, I could see that she'd been crying. "I'm not going back," she said for the second time. She said it quickly, in a defiant whisper, and then the lines of her face began to shudder. She held out the phone and turned away.

I took the receiver—still damp from her skin—and lifted it to my ear.

"Hesh," said Arthur, with a cool and level ferocity. "I found him."

199

Part III

THE ORGAN BUILDER

Chapter 20

Arthur Gordon had been having a bad dream.

His car had blown a tire in the desert. When he opened the door to get out, he found that his legs, too, had lost their shape. They were congealing into a kind of pudding, boneless and soft, and they would not support his weight. He waved for help, and as he waved, the pudding crept up past his waist and chest, past his shoulders and neck, until finally even his head had gone formless, mere runny pudding in the hot desert sun, and he'd awakened with a loud cry to find himself alone, in the motel's flabby bed, lost in a tangle of sheets.

It had been, he thought later, the kind of dream that ruins some men for the next day and inspires others, and until his interview with Henry Lytell in the coffee shop of the Trinity Lodge, he had not known for sure which it would be. But now he knew. Now he had some real material to work with, and quality material, as any artist knows, is what is required to build the actual out of the possible. He was on his way.

He had been put onto Henry Lytell by Cyril Stone's secretary, with whom he had spent a harmless Friday evening at the most pricey restaurant in Los Alamos. She was a plain, yielding, good-natured girl, really, with a weakness for flattery no worse than most people's, and as the violinist knocked off some Strauss to go with their second bottle of Mouton Cadet, she had told Arthur Gordon about the impending visit of Princeton's Chair of Theoretical Physics. He was, she said, a brilliant scientist, an able wit, a now outspoken advocate of disarmament, and a man who had once worked on a project—which project exactly, she didn't know—with Dr. Eli Friedmann.

Arthur had not been obligated to sleep with her, he knew, and yet he had done it, anyway—as much to punish himself as to reward her. That explained Friday night. Saturday night he slept with her with approximately the reverse in mind, and Sunday, well, was Sunday, and he did not want to be alone. He had left her before dawn and returned to his motel room, where he made some notes, banged his knee against the Aaton's case in the darkness, and fell into the nightmare of pudding.

Lytell he liked right off. The physicist was in his late fifties, stocky, with a doughy, pockmarked face. A salt-and-pepper goatee, squaring off his long chin, lent him a somewhat rabbinical air. For most of the interview it harbored the stray crumbs of a cheese danish. It would have made a nice picture, Arthur thought, had he only had the opportunity to get the man on film. But his crew—and his Nagra—were off somewhere in Mexico, and he hadn't had the time or the cash to hire a new one. He'd have to make do, even if it meant jotting down notes like some refugee from *The Front Page*. He could always come back for the footage.

"I should explain at the outset," said Lytell, "that virtually nobody outside the scientific community knew, or to this day knows, about Urizen. That's neither here nor there, of course, as it's now in the public record. But it might explain why you haven't run across it so far in your research. It was a very odd enterprise, a one-of-a-kind. Even now, talking about it, it's difficult to imagine that we had the nerve to try it. But perhaps I should start off with some background first."

"Yes, please."

"Well, I suppose it goes back to Weimar Germany, to the establishment of an operation called the Space Travel Society, Verein für Raumschiffahrt. Do you want me to spell that?"

"That's okay. I know German."

"Fine, then," said Lytell. "Well, the VFR began in 1927, in Breslau, when nine young visionaries got together to conceive and develop the liquid-fueled rocket. I don't have to tell you what a spectacular achievement it was, especially when you consider it was done entirely without government assistance. Von Braun joined the group in 1930; three years later, Hitler terminated the project. If he hadn't, who knows. The war might have ended differently. As it was, the rocket program—the V-2, I mean—played a major role in it, though it was disastrously expensive, really out of control. He'd have done better to leave the original group alone. Then we'd *all* be speaking German.

"Well, then, it's now 1958, and a group of us living on the Coast, who knew each other from working here—I'm talking about myself, Lars Nugent, Piet Harnick, Eli, some others—we're attending a reactor colloquium in San Diego. It's a nice environment, we're sitting around in someone's hotel room, shooting the breeze. We get to fantasizing about work we'd like to do, sort of daydreaming aloud. Three days later we're still talking, still dreaming. By the end, we've taken it into our heads to set up something along the lines of the old VFR. We're going to build an experimental laboratory, loosely organized, not like here or Livermore. Free of government interference. An amateur operation. And no weapons work, either."

"But wasn't that what you all had in common? Working on nuclear weapons?"

"Exactly. I misspoke myself. We had weapon design in mind, all right. But not for conventional purposes. For a very *un*conventional purpose, in fact." He picked up his fork and, holding the base to the table, swung it on an axis, like a compass. "Our idea," he said, "was to build a spaceship that would be fueled by nuclear bombs."

"A spaceship," Arthur repeated slowly.

"It sounds crazy, doesn't it?" He laughed heartily. "In fact, it wasn't crazy at all. The conventional wisdom as regards manned space travel was—in fact, still is—the sort of chemical rocket designed by Von Braun and his crew. I don't mean to knock it, but it can't take us very far. It's not feasible, economically, for going any further than the moon. I don't mean to knock the moon, either, of course, but it's rather a limited quantity, isn't it? Nuclear fuel, on the other hand, carries a million times as much energy. Our ship was going to be simple, simple and cheap, with a flat steel-and-graphite bottom that would carry a couple of thousand fission bombs of graduated range. These would be dispensed down a shaft, one at a time, through a hole in the bottom of the ship. Know where we got the design?"

"No idea."

"A Coca-Cola machine!" he crowed. "We'd just blow those bombs out of the ship with a little compressed nitrogen and—bang!—detonate them about a hundred or so feet below. Start with a tenth of a kiloton and work our way up to the big boys. It would only take about two hundred kilotons, you know, to get a ship that size out of the atmosphere. We were talking about Mars, young man. Mars by '66. Then Saturn. A lot of possibilities with Saturn; all that water. Saturn by '70. Even Pluto wasn't out of range. And comets, of course. But we disagreed on that. On so many things, really."

"And that was Urizen?"

"That was Urizen."

Oh Christ, thought Arthur, where's the Aaton? How to get down on paper the look on this man's *face*?

"Nugent and I went to General Dynamics with the proposal. We were hot properties at the time, from our work on the H-bomb. Whatever we wanted, they were ready to give us. One million, two million. They didn't care if we *were* crazy; they only wanted us to be happy. The whole country did." He sipped at his coffee moodily before commenting, in an entirely different tone, "We've all abused each other so terribly, as a result."

"It must really be something," Arthur said, "to have that kind of funding."

"You have no idea how something it really is. A stepladder to your mind's attic, where all the best visions are stored. Of course, there were a lot of visions in circulation at the time. Everybody was on the gravy train. Cyclotrons, accelerators, particle hunting. A lot of us who weren't building bombs at the time were after the unified-field theory. This was sort of an agreeable detour, though just as grandiose. Another speculative search. Only ours *worked*."

And the Nagra, thought Arthur. He'd trust the research a lot more if he had it on tape. But the recorder was with Abby. So was Freeman. So were half his traveler's checks. In a panic, he looked at the top of the page and found he could barely read his own notes. Some director! Some project! Maybe he should go back to commercials, something he knew he could do well. But wait, the man was still talking—

". . . quite a Xanadu, really. There were thirty of us, with all the time in the world, the ocean at our backs. We didn't go in for compartmental-ization like you see here—we were a team, pooling our talents; each of us did a little bit of everything. And there was no need for secrecy, either. So what if the Russians caught on? There was plenty of room in the galaxy."

"Were they interested? The Russians?"

He smiled. "Who knew? We were too dizzy with the idea of going to the stars. Naturally we were all itching to be on the first ship. There used to be contests over little things. The reward was always a ticket on that first ship. I can't tell you how exciting a time that was for me."

"I gather that something went wrong, though. I mean, you're still here."

"Yes, I am. How very true." His eyes flickered toward his watch, then moved back to the interviewer. "But nothing, you see, *went* wrong. The prototypes all worked. We had the backing. Even Von Braun—who, in a way, had the most to lose—even he admitted we were on to something. Every night the stars looked closer, more accessible."

"What, then?"

"It was 1963. Does that suggest the answer?"

"Kennedy?"

"Well, yes," he said. "In a way. The limited test-ban treaty. It stopped us dead in our tracks; there was no way around it. We couldn't very well test our equipment underground."

"So what did you do?"

"We were all crushed, of course. Everyone scattered to their respective universities, to work on problems that suddenly seemed quite banal."

"And Dr. Friedmann?"

"I don't know. Honestly, I'm not stonewalling. I lost track of him completely."

"When?"

"Soon after he returned to Berkeley, I think. But I can't be sure. It was a messy time. Frankly, I got out of there in a hurry. It was too painful to stick around." He scratched some of the crumbs out of his beard thoughtfully. "You have to understand about physicists. In a number of ways, we're like musicians. We work with counterpoint, cadence, rhythm. These are, of course, abstractions, and they occur, for the most part, inside our own heads. We're quite solipsistic, by and large. It makes for a different kind of working friendship, in human terms, than what most people are used to."

"Of course," said Arthur. "I understand. Really."

But Lytell was not really listening; he leaned forward, impassioned, and Arthur Gordon recognized something in him that had been subdued up to this point, a flash of the activist on the stump. "You see, we were a restless crowd, our group. When you create something, as we'd done here in the forties, there's always a danger of becoming trapped by your own invention. We were extremely conscious of this danger, having built the bomb. Clerk Maxwell warned about it a hundred years before. Systems tend to enclose those who devise them. That holds true in all realms. Lately I've been traveling around the country, along with some other people, warning about the same thing. Everything's become so specialized, and the entire complex support network of government and industry has become so entrenched, that the young scientists today are closed in. They can't see outside anymore, or perceive the general relevance. It's quite sad, really. But it's more than sad. It's frightfully dangerous." He took a breath and leaned back. After a moment, he looked at Arthur, still scribbling in his notebook, and asked, "Did you get all that? Is it helpful?"

"That's an understatement, Doctor. But I wonder if I could ask one more question. A stupid one, probably."

"Stupid questions are how we learn," Lytell said generously.

"What would have happened, do you think? I mean, if the test-ban treaty hadn't put a stop to you?"

Lytell took his time forming an answer. "I don't really know," he said. "But the fact is, we never solved the fallout problem. The machine's exhaust, if you will, was lethal. It's indeed possible we'd all be dead by now."

He would have to shoot him, Arthur decided, in a medium shot, and he would stay with it through the entire story. It would defy the conventions of scene, throw off the viewers' expectations of cutaways and edits: a long take, a single camera position—he'd use the tripod—and the interviewer as silent witness. Intensity would come from the artlessness, the simplicity, the absence of response. Perhaps the entire film would run that way—a series of monologues around central themes, a blend of historical recounting and character profiles, the public and the personal, the historical-determinist model and the great-man model at once. It would get at the big issues, questions of history. What was history, anyway? What was invention? Was history itself an invention? How much *vérité* in the *vérité*? Oh Christ, he thought, this is too big for sixteen millimeter; we're going to have to blow it up to thirty-five.

He laid out three lines of coke over the cover of a Rand McNally map and let his mind swim with possibilities. An hour wasn't going to be long enough. Which meant they were looking at feature length. Which opened up new markets. He could try it at the festivals—Venice, say, or Toronto. He wasn't necessarily confined to television at all. Only maybe, for the development money, he should stay with the station. That would be the classy thing to do.

Meanwhile, he needed to get Lytell on film, before he overexposed himself on the lecture circuit, and before the Lab got to him and warned him away from the Gordons. It was a miracle nobody had pulled the strings yet back in New York, nobody had canceled the seed check. Abby was costing him, he thought. She was costing him plenty.

He looked down at the three white lines, thinking that there was no real point to doing them. They'd only make him manic, and he was already manic enough. He breathed deeply of the room's chilled air and thought about calling somebody. When he gave that thought up, he did one of the lines, anyway. Then he looked over his notes. It made sense that it was the Germans who started the whole thing. Always ahead of their time. Music. Space. Film. Nothing neutral or passive about the Germans. They knew about dread, how to fight it. You either create or you destroy. Two sides of the same coin.

But there were other ways to fight dread, of course. He was looking at two lines of it now. And Abby—wherever she was, no doubt in Mexico

City with the Torborgs—she was doing her version of it too. The Spanish Shuffle. The Majorca Two-Step. Freeman, though, was the master. What was it his ex-wife had said about him, back in New York? "When push comes to shove, leave it to Hesh to find a way out." Well, he'd found one now, but it couldn't last. If there was anything about his wife Arthur Gordon knew with certainty, it was her intolerance for the ambivalent. She looked for clarity and willfulness in her playmates, a known quantity to anchor the equation of her life, an equation in which she herself was the variable. No, it couldn't possibly work with Freeman. That was why he'd been happy to throw them together in the first place. Two variables wouldn't factor. Very unlikely. He had only to wait.

But Arthur Gordon hated waiting.

He dialed the number of Freeman's legal office in Albuquerque. The secretary gave him to an asthmatic-sounding person who seemed to be upset about something. They had a short and not very coherent conversation, which left Arthur back where he started. The Torborgs.

He dialed Mexico City, hung up, then dialed again. The line was busy. For more than a minute he listened to the signal, each pulse of it a wave from what seemed like deepest space. Woman on the Moon.

He did the remaining two lines and decided that there would be plenty of time to call later, from the airport. He had some stops to make first.

From the closet he brought out both traveling suitcases and packed up the room. With Abby's clothing he was gentle, smoothing the wrinkles as he tucked each item into the suitcase, fingering the sheer material of her panties as though for the first time. He felt a limp throb in his groin.

Voice-over, he thought: *Of course, there were a lot of visions in circulation at the time.*

When he was ready to leave, he stood at the door and looked over the room for things he might have left behind. Eight-second wide-angle pan of motel room, he thought. Hand-held camera. MOS.

One suitcase he dropped off at the front desk, with a brief note. The other he loaded into the trunk of the rented car. Then he climbed in, raced the engine, and gunned out of the parking lot.

His head felt light and full of music. Voice-over, he thought: *There's plenty of room in the galaxy.*

Propelled by this cheerful notion, man and machine flew off down the Mesa.

Chapter 21

I drove all night. The sky was black and endless. The road fell away, a pale wavery ghost in the headlight beams. In my haste I had left the map behind, but it didn't matter: Everywhere I looked there were signs pointing me north. It was funny. I hadn't remembered seeing so many signs on the way down.

I drove very fast for a very long time. To stay awake I had to play games with myself, tell myself jokes, make myself promises. The wind whipped at me through the open window, throwing my hair around. When I ran a hand through my scalp I could feel the particles of glass trickle onto my shoulders like a gentle rain. Fallout, I joked. But could not coax a laugh.

On the radio I was able to pick up the megawatt patter of the border stations to the north. The jocks were raucous, big-throated men, outlaws from the FCC and its impositions of public service, news, and fairness, and you could hear the existential fury in their raps, the tension of the border, the crossings and recrossings, the endless transformations. I remembered listening to Wolfman Jack at night, every night, in high school, XCRF out of Ciudad Acuña. At night renegade Mexico came in, stealing over the airwaves and under wire fences. A clandestine filtering, a hidden tide. It was hard to feel safe listening to those X stations, 100,000 watts blasting at you from the hot south. Muddy Waters. Carl Perkins. Howlin' Wolf. You'd lie in bed, listening, smoking cigarettes, twitching with restlessness, and in time you came to understand what the jocks were saying—that restlessness was not a symptom of some adolescent malaise but the thing itself. And it would not pass.

The sky thinned, paled, then swelled into morning.

At the border they took away the cactus Abby had bought in Juarez— it had been sitting untended on the back seat for close to a week—and asked me what else I wished to declare. The official wore a blue uniform and smelled of coffee. He yawned and leaned against the door lazily, his thick arms folded. His eyes took in the Nagra, the litter on the dashboard, the ashtray. I could hear the tired motor idling roughly. "That's all," I said.

"Nothing else?"

"Just me."

He yawned again, stood back from the car, and waved his wrist at the official in front of me, signaling that I was free to move on. I put the car in first and it immediately stalled. The quiet hit like a shock; numbly, I turned the key and pressed hard on the gas. The motor strived and whined, but did not turn over. I was so worn out and depressed that I started to laugh, helplessly, compulsively. I sat there laughing, slumped against the seat, until the car behind me began honking its horn and a posse of uniformed men began muscling their way toward me. Everyone was in a hurry, you see, to make it for lunch in America. But we all had to wait, because the engine was flooded. Five long minutes, poised on the border, while the sun gathered strength over Texas.

I went straight for Santa Fe, not even stopping in Albuquerque to change my clothes. It was seven o'clock—the evening news was rolling credits—when I entered my mother's room and persuaded her to come for a walk.

I say persuaded, but it wasn't any kind of effort. I merely showed up at the door of her room and, without a word, inclined my head toward the metal walker leaning against the bathroom door. Myra Epstein was not present, and I was all business. My mother, meeting my eyes, made the barest nod of agreement—a gracious bit of deference she might have learned from Scarlett O'Hara—and swung her unsteady slippered feet off the bed and onto the floor. I rushed over to help. She bent her weight against my forearm for just an instant as she adjusted to being vertical, but then her hands gripped the walker's handles, she pulled herself erect, and together, my arm poised loosely around her waist, we stepped haltingly into the corridor.

At the door to the courtyard she stopped and scratched at the pit of her elbow. The sun was beyond the walls, and the air, though fine and clear, was chilly. "Are you cold?" I asked her. "Should I run back and get you a sweater?"

She didn't answer, but her eyes swept over me in a new way. I took off my sport jacket and arranged it to cover the thin material of her bathrobe. It draped across her shoulders comically. She ran her hands over the material, her mouth pursed in a flippant line as she made her skeptical assessment. It would have been in character for her to make a remark about the quality of my jacket, but my mother, from the look of things, had given up remarking altogether.

In the courtyard we walked in a slow circle around the stands of cactus, following the path of white pebbles in the failing light. We were alone there. The sounds we made were muffled and thrown back on us by the surrounding walls. My mother moved steadily, occasionally emitting a sort of dreamy grunt from the exertion. She was much stronger than I'd imagined from her appearance; whatever her condition might have done to her, it seemed to have been done with her cooperation, perhaps even according to her rules. It was disappointing, in a way. I had expected to be in control of our time together, to take charge, be of service—but it was not like that. She let me hold on to her, but not because she needed my support, or wanted it. It was something very different. It was an act of indulgence.

It hurt me to see this. But it was true: I had been her good boy all along. Eventually, despite all attempts at rebellion, I had done what she wanted of me. She had wanted me to be an "independent professional," as she put it, and I had become one. She had wanted me to dump Joanne, and I had dumped her. She had wanted me to reject my father, and I had rejected him. She had even wanted me to participate in her own abandonment, and I had gone along with that. Always for reasons that I thought were my own. But they were not my own. None of our reasons are our own—we take our shape from others, and we do it young. And now it seemed that we have come too far to do it any other way. I could not change the rules on her at this late date; she wouldn't be a party to it.

At least, that was how it seemed to me at the moment. A little later, I was not so sure. We were taking a breather on one of the stone benches that lined the courtyard, and as we settled in I reached into my shirt pocket for the chocolate bar I'd bought from the machine in the lobby. I hadn't eaten anything all day, and I was practically faint from hunger and fatigue.

At the sound of the wrapper tearing, my mother, who had been staring absently at the ground before her, turned. Something happened in her eyes when they spotted the candy. They narrowed, and the light in them hardened; the moist vagueness went out of them and was replaced by a dry enthusiasm. Her hands came together as though pulled by magnets. They made a soft, puffy, clapping sound.

Suddenly I felt flooded with her, and with all her doomed simplicity. She was just a girl, I thought, a girl who loved candy. A girl who'd conjured life as an all-or-nothing proposition and who had taken her stand on the latter. A girl who had remained a girl, and would die one, gladly.

"Oh, you're the one," I said out loud. "You're the one, all right."

She blinked apathetically.

"I should tell you all about her. Her and your good boy. You're the one to tell, aren't you?"

She made a feeble gesture toward me with one wrist. As gestures go, it was vaguely rhetorical: it did not expect to find its object. It was merely a flotation, a bit of personal theater, one that I'd seen from her a thousand times before. She'd reached for me that way when I was very small and needed my chin wiped or my knee bandaged or my fears salved. She'd reached for me that way on the drive from Los Alamos to Santa Fe, when I stood on the seat to watch the Mesa recede through the back window. And, some years later, when I'd return from school to find her sprawled on her bed, her hair all over her face, her first-graders' ragged stick-figure drawings all over the floor, a glass of melting ice pressed against her forehead. It was like something out of the movies, that repertoire of gestures, all speaking of the same things—the thirst and the unwillingness to quench it, the need and the recoiling from it, the large place she'd made for the myriad of things absent. And me, I was a quick study. I'd learned how to keep things I wanted at bay, to reach and not find. Yes, I was her good boy, all right. I'd learned how to hole up. We all had. My father had holed up in his lab, my mother in her bottle, and me . . .

Oh God, I thought. I needed to go back. I needed to go back to the beginning. I needed to start again. It was going to be a big project, and I was going to have to begin and begin and begin . . . and meanwhile, there was still so much to *attend* to.

"I'm going," I announced. "I'm going to go."

Her eyes were fixed still on the candy bar. I unwrapped it and gave her half and we chewed our pieces noisily, licking the last traces from our fingers. Then, after a minute, we rose. This time when she leaned against me to grip the walker, she did not pull away so quickly. She looked me over. I could hear an agitated whistle in her breathing. Her lips fell into their flippant line, but then, for a moment, they wavered, and seemed on the verge of something else. I had the idea that she was either seeing me for the first time or, what was more likely, seeing my father *in* me. And for once the sight did not summon disapproval alone, but an equal and naked regret.

Chapter 22

Propped up by three synthetic pillows, Charlie Goldwyn listlessly eyed the tray the nurse had set before him, and felt something stir uneasily in his stomach. The world, he'd long known, was an inhospitable place, as willing to break you one way as another. If a man wasn't careful, he could find himself flat on his back at the very moment of his greatest triumphs, cut down at the very instant he feels least mortal. All this knowledge, Charlie thought, should lend him a certain largeness of perspective—an ability to see things whole, and to see his own small place in the wholeness. But the truth of it was that there existed in him a substantial gulf between awareness and behavior, and that gulf had consequences. There was also a gulf between strategy and execution, and *that* had consequences. And then there was the gulf—in fact, the black, howling abyss—between his undernourished superego and his rampaging id, and that, too, had consequences. All of which amounted to this: He was in the hospital, tripped up and pinned to the mat by the vagaries of his own precipitous heart.

He stuck a fork into the wrinkled baby peas on his lunch tray, but before they were halfway to his mouth a wave of nausea rolled through him. He felt lost, dizzy. His eyes whirled about the room, unable to catch hold of solid forms. Everything was white. The walls were white. The bedding was white. The personnel uniforms were white. The ceiling, at which he stared for hours on end, tracing the weblike imperfections in the panels, was white. And now, when he looked down at his lunch, he saw the creamy blob of his mashed potatoes overrunning everything else, gobbling up the fish sticks, the peas, the carrots, a glacier in fast motion; the same way, he knew, that Walter Todd was at that very moment making inroads into his power at the firm, taking his clients to lunch, sweet-talking the committee, turning associates against him, sending him condescending telexes about his "western vacation" and Christ knew what else.

Oh, it was bad. It was downright shitty. Once the old man found out about his attack, how many minutes would elapse between the condolence call and the reassignment of the Eastern case to Todd? And how much longer, once the process had been set in motion, before his entire power base at the firm had eroded and toppled like some blighted oak?

A fist clenched in his chest. His breath caught short. For the love of Christ, he didn't want to, he couldn't—

But the pain subsided, and with it the panic. Charlie closed his eyes and tried to fix on something pleasant. There was Lorraine, for instance, in the mauve camisole he'd brought her from San Francisco a few years back. She was good to him. Always, when he'd been laid up with something, there was Lorraine with her hand on his forehead, cool as a plum. There was Lorraine, cooking his meals, laughing at his jokes, massaging the soreness that gathered at the base of his neck from the tension of sitting still.

True, she had her faults. She tried too hard to be highbrow, with those night lectures at the Met, the piles of *Smithsonian* and *New York Review of Books*. And then those parties with the finger food and the white wine and the chat about modes and deconstruction. Not destruction, like you'd think. De-construction. Try and figure out the difference, with your mouth full of sour asparagus. And she bored him, sexually. Of course, he probably bored her too. Thirty-four years. The *sound* of it was boring. But what was sex, anyway? A small part of the day, at best. A swelling, a heaving, a great warmth—then you're back out in the cold again. There was a hell of a lot more to life, Charlie Goldwyn told himself, than a little novelty in the sack.

Especially for a man who weighs two hundred and seventy-eight pounds and has just made a thorough ass of himself chasing a piece of tail around half the state of New Mexico—a big, ugly, rust-colored place, unfit for a civilized person in the first place—and to what end?

This. Floating in a sea of white.

But a man shouldn't be too hard on himself, Charlie thought. You chase, you don't chase; possibly it all comes to the same thing. And for a moment there, he had soared high. But for the ringing of a telephone, he might still . . . well, never mind. It had been a lesson, of sorts. He was developing, at this late date, a grudging respect for the accidental, a stumpy little fellow who wanders in from the sidelines to blindside you, just when you look to be free and clear, sprinting for daylight. Respect, yes, but no affection. He would not as yet surrender himself to it. He was certain that whatever happened, you had to live your life as though there was no such thing as accident. Otherwise you were licked before you started.

"Can I come in?"

He opened his eyes to his visitor. Herschel Freeman.

The man looked different to him. Tanned, purposeful, he seemed to wear his light summer suit more casually than usual; he almost seemed handsome. Probably it was just because Charlie himself felt so wretched and immobilized, but the bile rose in his throat. He hated Freeman, in that moment, for his youth and trim figure, for the cavalier way he treated the firm, the law. And he feared him too, for the same reason, and because somehow, even with all the man's damnable inertia, Freeman was stronger than he was, the way that certain plastics can be stronger than metal. But something else rose in him too, a depth of affection was tapped, an acknowledgment of mutual need.

Charlie waved his wrist, an intimation of vigor. Freeman remained where he was in the doorway. Charlie waved again. "Come in, Heshie," he said, and heard the gravel of phlegm in his throat. "How'd you find me?"

"Barney Peck. But it wasn't easy. He said you swore him to secrecy."

"Had to," he said, and struggled to raise his head on the pillow. "If New York finds out, they'll have me on early retirement before you can say Jack Robinson. Todd would like that. I have enemies, Heshie." He waved at the lunch tray before him. "The man who cooked this, for instance."

Hesh paused by the side of the bed and reached out tentatively with his right hand to pat Charlie on the shoulder. "Peck told me what happened, Charlie."

"He doesn't know what happened," Charlie snapped. "Nobody knows what happened. Even I'm not too sure. So don't go understanding things too quickly, all right?"

"All right," said Freeman evenly. "How do you feel?"

"Like I'm in a cage."

Freeman smiled. "That seems to be going around, lately."

"What, I should feel sorry for *you*? Is that what you're trying to tell me?"

"I'm not—"

"Poor Heshie Freeman, who takes off for Acapulco in the middle of the biggest case he's ever worked on and leaves the whole operation in an uproar? Wait, let me get out a hankie. I'm dissolving in tears."

The associate sat down in the chair by the bed and ran his hands along

216

his thighs. "I'm sorry about what I did. It's very complicated. If I'd known about all this, I'd have come back right away."

Charlie waved again. "Sure. Fine. Don't mention it. Why argue? You don't argue in a hospital. You make nice in a hospital." He thought he could feel his strength deserting him. "So tell me, how's Peck bearing up?"

"Well, he's worried. He's off his serve in tennis, he says, and that seems to be a bad sign. On the other hand, I think he'll be more than a little pleased to see us go."

Charlie didn't say anything. He was aware of the laboring thuds inside his chest, and listened to them carefully, as though trying to decipher a code.

"Did you hear what I said, Charlie?"

In the next room, someone coughed twice, violently. A woman down the hall cried out for a nurse. Downstairs, on the street, an ambulance siren whined. Charlie Goldwyn gritted his teeth. Pound on, he thought. Pound on, pound on, or join the conspiracy of whiteness. "I found her last Thursday," he began, "when we sat down in chambers."

"Who?"

"What do you mean, who? How many hers am I trying to find out here?" He mastered his irritation before going on. "Right away I knew the score, from the looks going around the table. There were smirks, knowing winks. I knew I'd been set up."

"Set up? What are you talking about, Charlie?"

"I'm trying to tell you my discovery. It was a *game*, Heshie, y'see? A setup. The old Mata Hari. All those hours I spent tracking her down meant that much less time on the case. Engage the affections of the opposition, then do an end run. Oldest game in the world."

Freeman shook his head. "It seems awfully unlikely, when you consider that—"

"Seems, shmeems. I'm telling you how it *is*. I knew it inside of five seconds, I tell you." He paused to recover his breath. "Okay, well, I'm a sucker. Had to give them credit for shrewdness. So just to show there were no hard feelings, and maybe to be a little perverse in the bargain, I invite her out to dinner Saturday, anyway. I hate to eat alone, you know that."

"Yes. That I know."

"Two drinks and she starts telling me how confused and depressed she's been. She really *likes* me, she says. She's only been avoiding me because she's so confused. I don't believe her, understand, but I say okay, and order more drinks. By the time the fish comes she's running

217

down her boyfriend and tossing around her hair. I'm trying to be nice, paternal like. Half of me says she's playing with me even now. The other half wants to play too. I feed each half a couple more drinks and pretty soon we're on the way to her apartment with her head against my shoulder."

"Charlie, relax, okay? You're supposed to be taking it easy."

"Sure," he said, "no problem. But let me finish the story, okay? So we get inside. Very tasteful. Sort of collegy, with the cat piss and the bricks and boards and dance posters. Just fine. We sit on the sofa and have tea, like *Masterpiece Theatre*. She tells me straight out that she's not going to sleep with me. It would be leading me on, she says. Can you imagine? She's worried about leading on a fifty-seven-year-old man."

"Who is acting like a fourteen-year-old kid."

He cocked his head. "Point well taken. But my desire for her, Heshie, has wings. I fly across the room and kiss her. She sort of resists, but Uncle Charlie wears her down. I get her pants off and I'm on top of her hearing trumpets and just about to go in when the phone rings. Bingo, I lose my hard-on. Strangest thing; maybe from all the booze. Anyway, I keep trying, but the phone's still ringing, and it's no good, and she's telling me to get off. Next thing I know my chest is on fire and I'm lying here with Barney Peck leaning over me. With his asthma, I thought we were *both* dying."

But that's not it, really, he was thinking, even as the words fell from his mouth. I'm not even sure I *did* have a hard-on, in the first place. And the phone, when it rang, it didn't actually *cause* it, you couldn't say it *caused* it. . . . He always sounded so much more certain of things, when he told a story, than he really was. . . .

"Why don't you call Lorraine, Charlie? The doctor says from the look of things you'll be out of here by the end of the week. You want me to call her for you, say when you'll be home?"

"I'll call her later," said Charlie. "I'm going to take a nap first. I'm tired."

"Good idea." Freeman rose to his feet.

"You better get back to the office and bone up, Heshie. You've got that hearing Monday in Santa Fe. You'll have to handle it yourself."

"I'd rather turn it over to Peck, Charlie. I don't know what kind of job I could do right now, given everything."

"You'll do fine. You're a high-priced attorney with a blue-chip firm. We bill Eastern a hundred fifty an hour for your services. They can afford it in spades, of course. But we've gotta keep up our image."

"There's hardly any time to prepare."

"Don't worry about it. I read the depositions. The woman they're bringing in to testify is half crazy. You'll eat her for lunch."

For a moment, Herschel Freeman stood beside the bed looking very much like his old familiar indecisive self. But then, after some internal consultation, he shook his head and raised his chin to Charlie gamely. "Okay," he said.

"Good."

"But listen. After this hearing, I need some time off to look into personal matters. Agreed?"

Charlie grimaced. "You just went to *Mexico*, for Christ's sake. What is this with you? You chasing a girl?"

"No," Freeman said. "Look, just tell me yes or no. If it's no, I'm going to quit right now, and you can handle the hearing yourself."

Charlie tugged at his ear. "Okay, okay. Just make sure you win. If he grants that injunction, Wiener over at Eastern goes through the roof. When he lands, we're both in hot water. And Heshie—"

"What?"

"Mum's the word about my little episode. Todd will use it against me. I'm not ready to move to Florida, understand?"

"You're paranoid," the younger man told him.

When he'd gone, Charlie leaned back against the pillows' cool bulk and shut his eyes. One hand rose to lie over the western portion of his chest protectively. Yes, he thought. I *am* paranoid, and thank God for it. It was the way you kept your force in this world. Once you stop painting things with your own colors, the whiteness surges up and overwhelms you. He understood this with the certainty of law.

Chapter 23

Outside the federal courthouse in Santa Fe, a new hotel was going up. From the cafeteria on the first floor, where I sat over a cup of weak coffee, I had a view of the workmen pounding away on their girders, tool belts hanging jauntily at their hips. They were lean, broad-shouldered men, their bare backs a deep brown in the morning light, their hair black and slick with sweat. Someone had said they were Mohawks. The Mohawks were fearless builders. They'd riveted together half the high-rises in Manhattan. It was easy to picture them in the midtown sky, skipping lightly, plank to plank, up and down the tall skeletons of the city. Like me, they were hired guns, a subcontractor's dream. I tried to think of other similarities between us, but failed. My mind had gone blank. It would have done me good to eat something, probably, but I had picked up some kind of parasite in Mexico, and my stomach was queasy and in constant motion.

There were about a dozen people scattered throughout the cafeteria, most of them lawyers. Two were sitting at the table behind mine. One had the haggard, well-fed look of a partner. He was complaining about a judge to his young companion. The partner, as he went on, began to raise his voice. It grew loud, and then louder still, and then, incredibly, it did not diminish—it threatened to rub the very paint off the walls. The other man—I took him for an associate—lowered his own voice to a whisper, as if to compensate. In this fashion their conversation seesawed on and on. I listened, of course, and was amazed to find my sympathies lining up against the associate. He was the one who had yet to find his place in the world. The partner had been doing his job long enough to internalize a code of behavior that dictates certain idiosyncrasies, such as the one of at all times speaking in a sonorous voice, as though you are eternally competing for the fragmentary and impersonal attention of some black-robed higher authority in some frenetic courtroom.

More simply, of course, lawyers are accustomed to being heard, and conduct themselves accordingly. I cleared my throat, looked at my watch. A jackhammer went to work across the street. For a brief moment, the din outside and the din inside converged like two fronts of air, and the static kicked on like an electrical storm inside my left ear. I was all alone, and I had to make good. It was not the sort of occasion to which I normally rose.

I thought for a moment of the headless sculptures I'd seen in Azcapotzalco, the touch of that rough, rounded surface, and a chill ran through me; I felt cornered.

And then there was a hand on my shoulder, and someone was asking me if I was Herschel Freeman.

I turned to face a dark young woman with straight, deeply black hair that fell to the small of her back. She wore a stiff blue suit with a white blouse buttoned all the way to the top, and was unadorned by jewelry. There was a little brown smear of a birthmark on her cheek, and her mouth had some of the intensity and humorlessness of an idealist. She set down her new briefcase so she could better shake my hand, though I had put it up as much in defense, really, as in greeting. "I am plaintiff's counsel," she said. "Lucy Johnson."

"I don't believe this," I stammered. "It's like meeting a fictional character."

Her next question gave me hope. "Which one?"

"I'm not sure. I'll have to get back to you later on that."

"Our case is about to be called," she said. "Shall we walk over together?"

As we left the cafeteria, she moved to the left so she could hold the door for me. I saw her glance back over her shoulder at the lawyers strewn about the tables. Her lips came together primly; she might have been a grade school teacher watching her students at recess. She looked hard and attractive and so serious as to render me dumb.

"I've heard a lot about you," she said, matching me step for step down the corridor.

"And I you."

"I was at the hospital yesterday, after your visit. Charles was so relieved that you could step in for him. It seemed to calm him down. He's very excitable."

"Yes. A regular Krakatoa, that Charles."

The birthmark twitched once; the effect was not without its charm. "The truth is, I came by to ask you a favor," she said. "I'd like to ask you to go easy on the named plaintiff."

"The old woman? Why?"

"She speaks no English, and she's also very excitable. I'm not asking you to do anything to harm your case, of course. But it would be indecent to press her too fast or to make her look foolish. I assure you, Mr. Freeman, she isn't a fool. It's a question of culture."

We came to the door of the courtroom. I could see through the window that the place was nearly deserted. "Look," I said, "I'm a lawyer. You can't ask me not to try to win."

"I'm only asking you to let the case be judged on its merits. Is that so strange a request, in a court of law?"

I didn't say anything. I didn't want to sound cynical, and I didn't want to sound glib. I also didn't want to lie. It left very little, really, to say.

"I have to join my colleagues now. But can I tell you something Charles said about you, first?"

"Please do."

"He said the only thing keeping you from being a brilliant public-interest lawyer was a lack of public interest."

"Charlie said that?"

She nodded. Abruptly, she seemed uncomfortable; tired of my company, perhaps, or merely preoccupied with what lay before us. Now, when she spoke again, it was with an air of formality. "We'd better go. They're about ready for us to state our appearance."

The hearing had been called to settle the first of some half-dozen motions brought by the other side. This one asked for a preliminary injunction against our client, Eastern Oil, to enjoin the opening of a uranium mine on reservation land. The plaintiffs were claiming that to open the mine would cause irreparable damage to the local water supply. This was because the process, *in situ* mining, pumped acidic chemicals into the mine to dissolve uranium. The danger was that the chemicals, and/or the uranium itself, could bleed into the reservation's water table. Or such was their claim. It was going to be a tough call, since the process in question was relatively untested. I would have liked about three more weeks to review the merits of the case for myself, but the judge had turned down our request for a delay. Besides, I had been with the firm long enough to understand that my opinion in such things didn't matter. It simply did not count.

The first hour or so of the hearing, Lucy Johnson and her colleagues from the Peoples Legal Services introduced written scientific and engineering evidence depicting the dangers and potential health hazards of *in situ* mining. Their presentation was orderly and assured, and even though I had before me three sheaves of commensurate written evidence depicting the relative safety of the same practice, I was by no means certain ours was more convincing. I had other reasons for concern, also. Several times the plaintiffs referred to discovery documents that had mysteriously disappeared. This prompted the judge—a silver-haired, drawling patrician—to direct an occasional withering glance in my direction, and prompted me to find a sudden interest in the lines on the backs of my hands. Charlie, it seemed, had been a naughty boy. It might have been carelessness or it might have been arrogance—for whatever reason, he seemed to think we would get away with any number of legal barbarisms before we were through. And he was probably right.

For the remainder of the presentation, I fidgeted uncomfortably at the defense table, scratching my elbow, looking over my notes, and shaking my head to clear away the static in my left ear. No one seemed to notice all this activity—there were less than twenty observers, all from the reservation, apparently, and they had the good manners to keep their attention focused on the main event. The room glowed with an unfriendly yellow light, a light that brought out some of the incongruous modernity of the old courthouse's interior—the thick beige carpet, the teak-paneled walls, the synthetic upholstered chairs—and a light under which even the healthiest complexions looked sallow, jaundiced. There was also a muffled clanging sound that came through the walls. At first I thought it might be the workmen's hammers across the street, but as time went on I came to accept it as an inhabitant of the room itself, a flawed mechanism in the ventilation system which sounded at regular intervals like a clumsy hidden metronome.

We broke for lunch. The four counselors for the plaintiffs went off together in a huddle, whispering among themselves. The observers filed out and headed for the cafeteria. The stenographer picked up her small machine and backed through a door behind the judge's chambers. The last person out of the courtroom was a young white man in a gray suit, who smiled at me in a collaborative way when he caught my eye. I thought I must have met him before but I couldn't place him; anyway, my mind wasn't on it. We had a hundred and five minutes for lunch and I spent the first hundred and two of them seated on a toilet in the cool, blue-tiled bathroom, waiting for my stomach to settle enough so that I might eat something. I'd been sleeping badly and at one point I might have dozed. A roar of water in the adjoining stall startled me, and I hurried back to the courtroom just in time to receive a malevolent glare from the judge. "A nice lunch, counselor?"

"Yes," I said. "Thank you, Your Honor. I apologize for being late."

"Very well," he said. "You may proceed, Ms. Johnson."

Lucy Johnson stepped forward in her crisp blue suit. Interlacing her fingers so they formed a cat's cradle, she called the named plaintiff to the stand.

Sarah McShane was a Navajo in her mid or late sixties, a stout, leathery woman in a long black dress bedecked with turquoise jewelry. She was trouble. There was something grand about her, a sense of command, of monumentality; she was a stern, big-breasted matriarch, her brow wrinkled with deep arroyos, her lips full and ruddy and contorted. She looked like a walking incarnation of Mother Earth. When she took the oath she made the unfamiliar words into small explosions of suffering and hardship; when she sat, her bearing suggested such dignity and self-possession as to make the rest of us look like hunchbacks. The judge, too, was clearly impressed. He sat up straighter himself, and in an unconscious motion smoothed the hair behind one ear. He might have been preening himself to ask for a date.

At the same time, the translator stepped forward and took her position just to the right of the witness chair. She was a round young Navajo girl in a plaid dress, somber beyond her years. When she opened her mouth, I could see the pink edge of her tongue for a moment as it curled against her even teeth, but after that it disappeared, and she inclined her head toward the witness chair deferentially.

Lucy Johnson nodded once to the judge, then turned to her witness. "Would you tell the court, Miss McShane, why you and so many others of the Navajo people are seeking to halt the sale of your land to Eastern Oil?"

There was a short pause as the translator repeated the question, in Navajo, to the witness. Then the old woman spoke a few words in a murmur, directing them to a point on the floor a few feet in front of her. Her tone was almost bored; the explanation seemed to be so obvious as to beg articulation.

"It is a holy land," the translator said.

"What makes it holy land?" asked Lucy Johnson.

Again the pause, the low bored murmur, then the translator's response. "We live on it. We dance on it. We bury our dead in it. It was ours and they took it away and then it was given back to us." The translator addressed her next words to me. "The Great Spirit does not want the land dug up. He cares nothing for your uranium."

There followed a long and somewhat discursive question-and-answer session on the subject of the Navajo people and their attachment to the land under discussion. Halfway through it, I knew the judge would never grant the injunction. His eyes were rigidly fixed on the old woman, and he nodded his head from time to time in a sort of sympathetic encouragement to go on, but I suspected that this was more for entertainment value than anything else. The presentation itself was fairly dramatic, but the singularity of it—those murmurs and long pauses, and then the words of this elder stateswoman issuing from the pink mouth of a girl whose face had not entirely healed from the ravages of acne; the displacement of language and meaning—worked increasingly against it as the afternoon waned. I could read in the judge's expression a certain willingness to respect the personal, so long as it did not implicate legal action, especially the sort of controversial, drawn-out action that granting their injunction would be sure to inspire. The whole business made me uncomfortable: with the witness, with the judge, with the other side; above all with myself, for what I was about to do. I felt the way I imagine a young actor feels rehearsing his lines for a badly conceived play, knowing, with the intuitive clarity of youth, that the drama has neither the depth required of tragedy nor the self-awareness of farce, and wondering how the choreography of his life—the thousand small non-choices that make up a destiny—has brought him to this low ebb where no amount of energy or craft can redeem the production.

Lucy Johnson, at some point, sat down, and there was a collective clearing of throats. In the witness chair, Sarah McShane looked proud, expectant, undimmed by the harsh yellow light of the courtroom. I could have looked at her all day.

"Mr. Freeman, are you with us?"

The judge had taken care to inflect his voice with only the thinnest veneer of sarcastic impatience, guessing from the cut of my suit that I was the kind of attorney upon whom no suggestion would be wasted.

"Your Honor?"

"It's your witness. Would you like a recess? You seem under the weather."

An interesting way of putting it, I thought. Yes. I am under the weather. Who isn't? But I was already shaking my head no.

"Very well, then. Proceed, if you please."

About what follows I will add little to the court transcript, except to point out that my participation in this transient and dispiriting episode was full, conscious, and at times nearly animated. I had spent only a fraction of my time as a lawyer in court, but I knew the effects it could have on a person. There is a power at work in a courtroom that is so dark, so malignant, as to suggest the occult. Once you have stated your appearance for the record, this force tightens your sphincter, quickens your pulse, lends guile to your words, puts bombast where before there was meaning, and will not let you rest until you have won some kind of victory, however small, however personal; carved some tiny niche into the stone face of authority. It is as close as many of us will ever come to a combat zone. I have heard stories of lawyers who become hysterical in a courtroom, who laugh or cry uncontrollably, who break into an impromptu jitterbug or turn almost catatonic. I have seen Charlie Goldwyn sweat through three different suit jackets in a single afternoon in Foley Square. I have seen Walter Todd only on one occasion in a courtroom, and I remember he sat through the entire proceeding with an expression of consummate distaste, rising periodically to question a witness in a soft, impassive voice, and then resuming his seat with a solemn bow that was wasted on everyone present but the bailiff and myself. If the world is everything that is the case, as the philosophers say, then the courtroom is where everything in the case is the world. It is a crucible, a carnival, a rodeo show, a tag-team wrestling match. It's no surprise that the justice angle gets lost sometimes. Still, as major spectator sports go, the law is no more of a crapshoot than anything else.

I looked over the list of questions on my legal pad, grabbed the top document off the stack on the desk, and rose to my feet. The questions I was careful to address directly to Sarah McShane, in part because this seemed to be the professional thing to do and in part because I did not trust myself to keep things straight if I allowed the process of translation to distract me. "Miss McShane," I said, holding up the document, "do you recognize this piece of paper?"

She glanced tentatively at the paper and made a noncommittal nod, which the translator relayed as a no.

I crossed to the other side and waved the document before the plaintiff's table. Lucy Johnson's eyes flickered over it, then over me, with no great interest. "Your Honor," I said, "I submit a signed contract between Sarah McShane and the Eastern Oil Company, which permits my clients access to her land in return for a sum of thirty thousand dollars. The contract, as you can see, is dated July 10, 1976." I turned back to the witness. "Miss McShane, this signature is yours, is it not?"

She stared at it this time, that telling bottom line, as though it were the subtitle to an exasperatingly obtuse foreign film. Finally, in a movement that seemed to originate in her knees, she made a shrug. I waited for her to say something, but she was a patient woman. The shrug was all she'd give me.

"Miss McShane, can you tell the court exactly how you came to sign this contract to give away development rights on your, as you put it, 'holy land'?"

Pause for translation. Another shrug.

"How many representatives of Eastern Oil, for instance, did you meet with at the time?"

Pause. Shrug. Whispering behind me, from the plaintiff's table. The judge shifting in his chair. "The witness will answer the questions, as directed," he said.

The translator cleared her throat. "Miss McShane does not understand."

"Does not understand what?" asked the judge.

Lucy Johnson was on her feet. "Your Honor, we would like to move for a recess."

The judge, however, had already determined that life was too short for the kind of unorthodoxies being displayed before him. He pushed up his glasses with a long, severe finger, so they rested snugly on the bridge of his tanned nose, and then hardened his eyes behind them. "Denied. Witness will answer the questions put to her."

"Miss McShane," I began again, "when the representatives of the Eastern Oil Company came to see you, did you or did you not understand the terms of the contract that they offered you?"

Upon hearing the question repeated to her in slow translation, Sarah McShane maintained her regal posture, but something twisted in the lower half of her face, a fissure opened and began to swell. She said something in her low mumble, and there was an edge to it. "Miss McShane does not understand," the translator informed us, in that same maddeningly even voice.

"Does not understand *what*?" the judge repeated, on his way to a bellow.

The witness was still talking, however, pushing the words out quickly; a dam had broken inside her, and the contents were spilling over. She was talking, and the translator was talking, and the judge was talking, and the stenographer, pounding away at her little noiseless machine, looked as if she was going to cry.

"The land is holy," intoned the translator. "It is holy, and it is ours, and there used to be much more—"

"Objection, Your Honor," I said.

"Sustained. Will somebody—"

"Your Honor," pleaded Lucy Johnson, rising to her feet, "may we approach?"

"No."

"—and it has been taken from us, where the dead are buried, and the spirits of the wind flow there, the dark cloud is at the door—"

227

"Miss McShane, when the representatives of Eastern Oil—"

"—the dark cloud, it is at the—"

"Your Honor, please, if we could only approach the ben—"

The judge, at this point, gave his desk a thumping with the gavel that made the entire courtroom vibrate. He craned his neck and opened his mouth to say something, something that would put us all in our respective places, but before he could begin I turned back to the witness and in a hushed, solemn voice repeated my question one final time: "Did you understand the terms of the contract you were offered, and which you subsequently signed on July 10, 1976?"

Sarah McShane's lower lip held firm, but a quaver was in her throat when she replied, without benefit of translation, "Enough."

After that it was simple. It could very easily have gone the other way, though. Had the judge kept on with his bellowing, or had my questioning been infected by any of the emotional shrillness that was already threatening to turn the whole affair into opera, the static would have become only more entrenched, and the judge might have dismissed the lot of us with instructions to play elsewhere. But I stepped in at the right moment, and then I kept my voice steady, steady and monotonous and inexorable, repeating the questions like a series of jabs. It was western reason versus native mysticism, and we were playing on my turf, and it was all but impossible for me to lose. Three times Lucy Johnson stood up to plead for a recess, and three times the judge denied her; she was already being threatened with contempt of court when I dismissed Sarah McShane from the stand.

The old woman had not answered a single question, and in a strange way both she and I were proud of that fact. Immediately upon leaving the witness chair, she regained her composure, nodding to us all with genuine beneficence as she followed the translator out the door to the corridor. The tension in the room went with her, as did most of the reservation people who had been observing the proceedings. By the time I introduced the remainder of my written evidence—attesting to the safety of *in situ* mining as determined by the Environmental Protection Agency experts who had inspected the grounds—the chamber felt hollow, emptied of all texture, the wake of a vortex. I had a pang of longing to be outdoors.

The judge thanked us all for our decorum and promised to render a decision within fifteen days. Then he took off his glasses and stepped down. He was barely six feet tall.

When I emerged from the building the sky was heavy with clouds and I was amazed to discover it was nearly five o'clock. The workmen had

228

knocked off across the street. The hotel framework, rickety and colorless, leaned against the grainy pink of the horizon. Past it stretched the Sangre de Cristos, slopes dotted with low pines, and beyond that, to the northwest, a reservation vehicle was threading its way along a bumpy road, transporting Sarah McShane home.

I went into the bar across the street and ordered a scotch. It was not very crowded, and the jukebox was between songs, so that I could hear the authority in my voice when I called to the bartender, though I did not really recognize it.

Someone else did. His name was Bruce Schultz. He was an associate with Sullivan and Peck, and he appeared to be several scotches ahead of me when he called me over to his booth. "I've seen you before," I said.

"Sure. At the office."

"No." He wore a gray suit and horn-rimmed glasses. His hair was short and black, streaked with gray, and he had small, dark, inexpressive eyes set far apart above a flat nose gone red from the sun and alcohol. Despite the gray, he looked young for his age, and lazy of manner, and when he raised his glass to toast me I was unsure what proportion of irony was intended, and toward whom it was directed. "No, I saw you at court this morning. You were in the back row."

"Guilty as charged."

"Someone send you to check up on me?"

He laughed. "Sorry. My own initiative. I take one, every once in a while. Another drink?"

I watched him head back to the bar. He chatted with a few of the lawyers standing there as he waited for his change. When he returned with the drinks, he showed few signs of intoxication other than a wetness in the eyes and a tendency toward declamation when he spoke, as though he were competing with loud music. But the jukebox, which I'd assumed was between songs, had merely been turned down; I could hear the sweet monotony of a country ballad rolling across the room.

"A lock," he said. "Without question. The Indian woman was crazy. Noble, but nuts. Did you see the look the judge gave her when she left the stand? Like she'd just taken a shit on his carpet."

"Really? I kind of thought he had a crush on her."

"Don't think so. Maybe the translator. Shapely young thing." He reached forward with his hand to punch me lightly on the forearm. "I tell you, that was a damn fine performance, all in all. You New York boys are something else. Thrust and counterthrust. Errol fucking Flynn."

"I hardly did anything," I said. "The law did it for me."

229

"God love the law," he said, and drained his glass. "Where'd you go to law school, by the way?"

"Cambridge," I said.

"In England?"

"No, no. Harvard."

"Well, don't be so bashful about it. Shit, most guys went to Harvard wear fucking maroon ties, just to show off. What's *your* problem?"

"It gives people the wrong idea sometimes."

"Oh? And what idea's that?"

"That it matters."

"You think it doesn't? You're wrong. That's exactly the kind of thing that greases the slide. You don't believe me, try throwing around the University of New Mexico—see how far it gets you."

"I meant to me."

"Oh. Well . . ." Uncertain how to answer, or whether such ideas were even worth answering, he looked into the decomposing shapes in his glass and frowned. "You were in control up there today, boy. I don't know where they teach you that, but it's no little thing."

To change the subject, I said, "Let's have some more drinks."

We drank to Harvard. We drank to the University of New Mexico. We drank to certain justices of the Supreme Court and to certain of our favorite verdicts. We drank to the First Circuit, then the Second, then the Third, and so on until we ran out of Circuits. I told Bruce Schultz some of the tricks to copyright law and he told me some about estate planning, and before we knew it, two more hours had passed and neither of us had made a single reference to the great, spinning world of things outside of our profession. It was an utterly typical barroom conversation between lawyers, the kind I had back on Nassau Street all the time, and it made me almost happy to be a member of a club that traveled so well.

"I'm getting married on Sunday," he said, and we drank to that.

"Mazel tov."

"Patsy's a nurse. Wonderful girl. She works in intensive care, in the nursery, with the premature kids. They weigh like a pound, these kids. Look like pink sausages. Patsy hooks them up to respirators and tries to get them through that first motherfucker week. It's life and death, man. She's got parents come in there and hand her hundreds of dollars so she'll give their kids special treatment. Most of the doctors speak in funny accents. God knows where they went to school. Nobody trusts them. I hate doctors, don't you? They're worse than us."

"I suppose so."

"She's been doing this for five, six years now, Patsy. She never knows

230

which kids'll make it and which ones'll croak. Sometimes she tries to predict, but she's almost always wrong. She says this is what she loves about her work. She also says this is what she hates about her work. Depends when you talk to her." Frowning again, he rubbed a finger into the ring his glass had formed on the table. "Me, I'm an associate. In a couple of years they'll make me partner, and then the shit will really kick in."

"How do you know you'll make partner? Not everyone does, you know."

"I know. Peck likes me. Every time a client gives him cigars or chocolates he gives them to me. It's an acknowledged dynamic at the office. Look at my teeth," he said. "Rotting out from under me, thanks to Peck and his fucking presents. He likes to see me eat and smoke right in front of him. Vicarious pleasure, he says. That's what comes of working with a health freak. But listen, the point is, I've got a different attitude than Patsy. I couldn't operate with hers. She's got a tougher set of rules over there, but lots of times it's nobody's fault. With us, there's always blame thrown around. Always. Tired?"

"Not really," I said, though I felt washed out and numb from all the alcohol, and from not eating.

"Then let me buy this round. This is my town, and you're my guest."

He went over to the bar and brought back two more scotches on the rocks. When he sat down, his face had a different cast to it. He scrutinized me closely, as though the drinking had numbed him too, or as though he was trying to get a fix on me. "I've been sitting here trying to place you, Errol Flynn. You didn't happen to go to high school around here, did you?"

"Yes, as a matter of fact."

"Lincoln?"

"That's right. How did—"

"Hot damn! I *knew* it!" He pumped his fist in triumph. "I'm incredible with faces. Some of us are like that, you know. You, for instance, I recall to have been a couple years ahead of me. One of those sulky types who hung around in the parking lot with the beatniks, right?"

"More or less."

"How's that for a kick? But you don't remember me, huh?"

I shook my head. I didn't remember Bruce Schultz at all; had probably never met him in my life. I had a lot on my mind. And yet I could not pull myself away, either. It felt so large, the force that had brought me to that table at that moment, the force that had aligned me with a reference point so long outdistanced, or thought to be. Had I begun to run laps

231

around myself? Was I about to pass myself? I did not have it in me to fight it any longer. "My name was Friedmann," I said. "I changed it after graduation. My father, you see . . . well, my father worked at the Lab."

"So'd my old man. Metallurgy."

"Mine was all over. Theoretical, eventually."

He whistled, impressed. "Guess there are a lot of us out there. Talk about your baby boomers, huh?" He chuckled with an odd satisfaction. He seemed almost on the verge of belligerence. "Baby boomers. That's us. No reason to change your name, though."

"I was trying to make a statement. There was a lot of protest going on at the time. I wanted to make something clear."

"To who, Errol Flynn? Who gives a shit, anyway, what your name is?"

"I do."

"You think you're clean, is that it?" Half risen out of his chair, he caught himself and sat down slowly, pulling the pen from his breast pocket. "I got news for you, pal. It looks like this."

With the tip of the fountain pen, he drew a wide circle on the cocktail napkin between us.

"Our west against their east, right? First our great-grandparents steal this land from the Pueblos and Zuñis and Navajos, all the old Anasazi types. Now, where'd they come from? Asia. Then our old men come out here and build this thing in the forties. What for? To fry thousands of Japanese. Now it's thirty years later, and you and me help the oil companies snatch what's left out from under those assholes on the reservation, and for what? It's so perfect it's gotta be divinely ordained. *Uranium.* A closed circle. We'll use it to scorch the Russians and the Chinese, and pretty soon all the nonwhites will be starved or dead, and all roads lead to New Mexico, the Land of Enchantment. Believe it, Errol Flynn: We're right in the thick of history here. Today is tomorrow is yesterday. A closed circle. All of us sucking the uranium tit. The plutonium tit, too. Falsies, I guess you'd call that one."

"You're drunk," I said, when he was finished.

"Legally intoxicated. Reflexes impaired. I should wait an hour, minimum, before driving home. But the logic is sound. My mother—my real mother—was Hopi, I tell you that?"

It was time to leave, I thought.

"She worked as a maid up on the Hill. My old man was on her like a bee on honey. Married her, even. He was only twenty years old. She was sixteen. She died when she had me. I killed her. So did you."

"You don't know what you're saying," I said. "We should go. Patsy will be missing you."

But he remained where he was, and I did too, and our four arms on the table's polished wood surface surrounded the circle he'd drawn like the stripes of a flag. "I should show you the reservation sometime," he said. "Be an education for you to see where that McShane lady comes from. Bet you haven't seen it firsthand, have you?"

I shook my head again. What *had* I done? What *had* I seen?

"You've got millions of tons of radioactive waste lying around. You've got people living in houses that glow. I mean that literally. The cancer rate goes off the chart. Plus the air's all full of coal, so the folks in Vegas can go blind from the neon. Those tribal councils we're using for testimony, you know they're bullshit, don't you? Hardly anyone votes for them out there. We've bought them off, man. Don't tell me I don't know what I'm saying. I spent my life here. Where've you been? Harvard? New York? Shit. You don't know shit about this place. Excuse me—"

He pivoted in his seat so that he could reach onto the next table. "You mind?"

Puzzled, they turned, the two lawyers next to us, in time to watch Bruce Schultz carefully bring their full ashtray around to our booth and, without ceremony, dump its contents into my lap.

"Ashes to ashes, Errol Flynn. I'll see you you in New York sometime."

And then he was gone.

Too tired to brush myself off, I sat in the quiet gloom of the bar for quite a bit longer, drawing three-hooped circles on the cocktail napkin with the pen he'd left behind. The lines fuzzed and blurred, from the moisture left by his glass. Meanwhile, on the wall above my head, the black hands of the clock made some circles of their own.

Finally, much later, I got to my feet. I slapped my clothes, and that was all it took to make the butts and ashes fall off me in a cloud. Then I weaved past the courthouse regulars, intent on their liquor and their women, and went to the phone in the back to dial the hospital, so I could tell Charlie that everything had gone as he had promised it would.

Chapter 24

And after that, perhaps, the dream took over.

Before heading back to Albuquerque that night, I stopped by San Antonio de Padua with a box of chocolate hearts. The lobby was deserted. The receptionist was bent over a notepad on her desk; I could hear her rhythmic breathing as I waited for her to look up and discover me. It was the same pretty twenty-year-old girl with the bright smile I'd met on my first visit.

"So when are we going to Taos?" I asked.

She dimpled, and I felt my ribs buckle against my heart. "You mean the choir," she said.

"Yes, of course."

"That was last week. Everyone said it was a special event. A very special event."

"And how is my mother?"

"Your mother?" Her high brow furrowed. "Oh, Mrs. Orlinsky. She's about the same, I think. I'm not really sure." She checked her watch. "It's past visiting hours."

"I keep missing her. Always running late."

"Yes," she agreed abstractedly.

"Everything's been so hectic lately. I've had this big hearing, and one of my colleagues is in the hospital, and half the time I'm running around without an idea in the world of what's expected of me. . . ." I heard what I was saying and I willed myself to stop. It seemed beyond all probability, the portent of some inner collapse: I was asking for forgiveness. I fought for composure, inhaling deeply. But the air in my lungs was smoky. "Is something burning?"

She crinkled her nose and sniffed deeply. "I do smell something," she said. "I think it's coming from you, in fact."

234

"Oh. Right."

"Were you in a fire?"

"Yes. The woods, you see. The woods are burning." I made an idiotic attempt at a smile. "That's from *Death of a Salesman.*"

"Oh. We read that in high school."

"It must seem very callous to you, leaving a sick mother alone like that. Not coming to visit more often, I mean."

"Oh no," she said. "It happens all the time. Besides, one of your friends stopped by to visit the other night. That was a nice thing to do. Mrs. Epstein said he was very charming."

"One of *my* friends?"

"That's what he said."

"May I ask his name?"

She fidgeted, swaying back and forth on her short fullish legs, as one front tooth bit down meditatively on her lower lip. "I don't think I'm supposed to give out that kind of information."

I took a breath and reminded myself that I was a lawyer, that there were research methods and research methods, and I thought about what Charlie Goldwyn would do in this situation. "Fine," I said agreeably. "But could you do me a favor? Could you go buy yourself a cup of coffee? I'll watch the desk for you. Here." I took out a ten-dollar bill and creased it once. "Have a danish too."

"I don't eat sweets," she asserted primly. Then she marched off down the corridor, past the open door of Deborah Rosenthal's office, and I sneaked a look at the roster of visitors for the past week. One signature stood up and knocked me over the head. It was grand, artfully composed, a neat blend of the functional and the ornamental, with a vivid black trailing line coming off the last letter into the right margin as though waging an assault on the page itself.

Arthur T. Gordon

The receptionist came back, brandishing an apple, and deposited the change from the bill in my palm. "I have to get back to work now," she said without smiling, and moved into the position she had occupied when I came in. As I turned to go, I could already see her bending over the notepad. Her hands were hidden from view but her shoulders worked steadily, in a sort of circular dance. She might have been writing a letter or an essay for college, or drawing a picture. She might merely have been doodling, the way people do when they're bored. Suddenly I had a powerful, irrational curiosity about it, but I was already standing on the carpet that triggered the glass exit door to slide open, and when I looked back and waved to her, on my way out, the image that greeted me was not the Indian girl at her desk at all, but the benign to-and-fro of my own pale hand.

Back in my hotel room, I took off my clothes and sat on the edge of the bed. A late movie was on television, but the reception was bad—the screen showed nothing but snow, a rampage of electrical static. I left it on and looked over the three messages they'd given me at the desk. One was from Charlie—he'd been asleep when I'd called earlier—congratulating me on my triumph and urging me to see him off the next morning. One was from Arthur, explaining when and where I was to meet him when I got to California. The last was from Mexico City. All the message said was *No message.*

I took a shower, sat on the bed, and dialed Joanne in New York. A man answered. His voice was low and proprietary. After a few seconds, he asked whether anyone was on the line. Finally, he cursed softly and hung up.

I turned up the volume on the television and listened to the roar of the snow. The sound was ferocious, but it did not build to anything. It merely topped over itself, oceanic, irresistibly neutral, a blaze without heat. It was a lullaby, I thought, an electrical lullaby to coax the fitful nation to sleep. It was pleasant, in a way. Soothing. Complete.

And then it was very dark. I was still on top of the bed, and the television was still on, and my mouth was foggy with sleep. I tried to sit up, but something pushed me back against the covers, something benevolent and assured. It was my mother. My mother in a black dress. She was saying something. I could hear the tinkle of her jewelry. Or maybe ice in a glass. No, it was not my mother at all. It was Sarah McShane. Her eyes were luminous gems, turquoise, and she was speaking to me in her deep Navajo monotone, her weight pinned against me, her breath like damp sod, ruined and black and smoky. I did not understand what she was saying, but I smelled it, the dark cloud, her breath, and then all of my senses sprang to life—I smelled blintzes, heard them crackle in a pan, saw them puff out and brown at the edges. I was in the kitchen, my mother's kitchen, and the smoke rose up over the pan in a cloud, and the whole thing—the stove itself—caught fire and turned white. It made a funny sound as it burned, a heaving sigh, as though of relief. My mother was standing there in her black dress and I was next to her. Together we watched the entire process. I believe we were even humming.

236

*   *   *

In the morning I drove Charlie to the airport. We needed two redcaps to help us with the luggage and the wheelchair, and when the time came for a tip, Charlie handed them a dollar each. "I'm a poor sick man," he explained. "Otherwise there'd be a lot more."

The airport was compact and well tended. I wheeled Charlie to the gate across a gleaming floor. Outside the polished windows, jet airplanes taxied slowly over smooth concrete, and the walls rumbled pleasantly from their vibrations. Charlie sat erect in his chair, surveying the terminal like an emperor. Dressed in his best pinstripes, reeking of cologne, he had an air of rejuvenation about him that went deeper than his clothes, or the weight he'd lost in the hospital. He had touched bottom, and it seemed to agree with him. All of his boasting and recklessness struck me now, as I prepared to take my leave of him, as yet another poker bluff around yet another unseen card. Only this time he'd gotten lucky. He'd been called, and forced to take a look at exactly what he had in the hole, and he'd found it a somewhat better bet than he'd supposed, or feared. "Let's get a paper," he said.

I pushed the chair up to a machine that dispensed copies of the morning daily, but Charlie got a pinched look. "Not that rag," he said. "Run over to the newsstand and get a *Times*. I want something to read, not wipe my ass with. I'm tired to death of this Mickey Mouse city. Aren't you?"

"It's not so bad," I said.

"What about you? When does your plane leave for the Coast?"

"A couple of hours. I've got plenty of time. I'll see you off, then I'll go have breakfast."

He nodded, distracted, and brought his hand up to his chest. "Christ, what if the damn thing goes out on me again? I don't want to die on a plane, Heshie. Even in first class it's a distasteful thought."

"The doctor said you'll be fine. He thinks you're a bull."

"A bull," he grunted. "I like that doctor."

"Just try and take it easy, and leave things to your associates for a while."

"Associates?" He grunted again. "They're all like you, my associates. Promising, but inconsistent. Nobody's dedicated to the great campaign." He glanced over the headlines quickly, then folded the paper with a snap and tucked it under his left leg. "Well, we'll give Fitz a try. We've laid out all the groundwork; there's not much he can bungle even if he wants to."

"He'll be fine. He's a team player."

"Sure. I agree absolutely. Whose team, is the question. You know who's behind this, by the way? You know who's trying to push me out?"

"Charlie, don't get—"

"Webber."

"Webber?" I shook my head. "That's impossible."

"That fucking ignoramus. The man wears bow ties. You know where he vacations? Ohio. That's where he vacations. I should have known. You got to watch the grinners, Heshie. The mediocrities. They're out to pull things down. That's their business in life. It's sexual, see. They're limp, and they pull down the hard things. Don't let it happen to you, is what I'm saying. Stay alert."

"I think I hear them calling your flight," I said.

I wheeled him to the gate, where they had just begun to board. The passengers, as they filed into the padded metal corridor, were composing their features into the blank, wide-eyed, imperturbable expressions they would hold for the flight's duration, a look of latent penitence, as though they were entering a shrine. The steward came over to wheel Charlie to the front of the line, but the big man waved him off, as he apparently was not yet finished with me. "Lucy called last night to say good-bye," he said. "Sweet kid, eh?"

"I liked her," I said sincerely.

"She told me you were brilliant in court. Ice cold and a razor. No hard feelings, though. She knew the squaw's testimony wouldn't go. The whole team's outclassed, they're grasping. It's a sad thing to see."

"So what will happen, do you think?"

Immediately I regretted asking the question, as it was the kind that Charlie never answered, the kind that made me feel foolish and unprofessional even for venturing. But this time was different; he blinked, and his eyes softened, and his enormous features composed themselves into a thoughtful, bruised smile that hung on until he boarded the plane. "Christ," he said. "We're not going to know, are we?"

I didn't say anything.

Charlie cocked his head at me. He looked dreamy. "I think she really liked me, Heshie."

"I'm sure you're right," I said. I bent down in front of the chair and, for lack of anything better to do, straightened his already straight tie. "She seemed like a class act, Charlie."

He nodded twice, and what he did next took me by surprise—it might have been the product of either terrific fear or terrific confidence. Reaching out with his big, meaty hands, he cupped my head and brought my cheeks forward to his, clutching me with real fervor. "All the luck,

Heshie," he said into my ear, and then he kissed me hard on the forehead. "All the luck."

When I broke the embrace I could see he was crying and I was ready to forgive him everything. But the steward stepped over to take control of the wheelchair, and I had to move aside. He turned the chair around so Charlie's back was to the gate, and there was that smile again, at once flimsy and game, and Charlie made a swatting motion with his wrist to remind me of racquetball. "You get back soon," he called out, and the last word I heard from him, tossed away as lightly as lightly as breath itself before he disappeared backward into the throat of the folding tunnel, was "partner."

I went to the coffee shop and played with the crumbs of a danish. The sky had gone ripe with midday sun. A brown haze stretched like a soiled veil up to the foot of the Sangre de Cristos. It was 10 A.M. The terminal swelled with Muzak and the quiet labor of the ventilation system. The planes landed and took off; they loaded, they unloaded; they were vessels of transition. I watched them for a long time, vaguely contented. To sit in an airport is to entertain a flirtation with the possible. The wallet in my pocket contained credit cards that enabled me to go anywhere I chose, make new steps, retrace old ones, establish connections. My eyes skimmed over the place mat before me. What is a life, after all, but a game of connect-the-dots on the place mat at an airport coffee shop? There, spread beneath my plate, lay a map of particulate matter, quarks and squarks, selectrons and gravitons, gluons and zinos and winos—all the tiny particles that, taken together, make the atom, the world, such a blur. There was not really so much empty space in it as I'd imagined. It was all liquid, a teeming pond. Every act was a stone I'd thrown, a moment that rippled through space and time like a seiche, rippled outward to nudge something or someone that would itself nudge something or someone else, ad infinitum. And now, briefly, though I knew it was only an illusion, the pond seemed to me to be lying still, and I seemed myself to be at the very lip of the water, poised with my arsenal of stones.

Ultimately, we're all in motion, spinning. Stasis is an aberrant joke.

I stood and pushed back my chair. There.

It went quickly after that. There was the counter. There was the attendant. There were her fingers, quietly thumping over a keyboard. There went the numbers, marching across the square dark screen. There was the ticket. There was the gate. There was the great white vessel. It swallowed me and bore me up. And up. And up.

It felt more satisfying than I cared to admit, to be in the air again.

Chapter 25

We sat on the runway for close to an hour, waiting for clearance to take off. Few of the passengers seemed to notice. The majority of the plane's seats had been sold to a tour group of Chevrolet dealers from the Southwest, who were accompanied by wives and mistresses. The men, at least, were having a wild time of it, elbowing up and down the aisles, slapping backs, and roaring with laughter at off-color jokes. The women remained in their seats, leafing through magazines with the detached stoicism of a jury.

I had an aisle seat in coach. The two seats to my left were taken up by a couple dressed in matching plaid slacks and white short-sleeved shirts. On the husband's right lapel, only inches from my shoulder, was a tiny pin that it took me some time to recognize as an American flag. "Bound for Hawaii," he informed me. "VIP tour. This here's the top sales group west of the Mississippi. A regular machine."

Some time later, when the plane was leveling into its flight pattern, he looked out the window at the canyons and mesas below and nudged his wife, who was already fast asleep beside him. "Wave good-bye, honey." She stirred for a moment, patted her white coif, and closed her eyes.

He was about fifty, skinny and hawk-nosed, florid-faced. His arms were soft and hairless, puffy; they hung out of his sleeves like a little boy's arms, all elbows. He was exactly the kind of person I'd spent my life avoiding on planes and trains by doing work for the firm, but I had no work with me, and so without much animation I responded to some of his questions about my work and home life, and politely asked the same of him. I suppose there was some sympathy in it too. Amidst all the revelry of his fellow salesmen, he seemed curiously alone, subdued. Several times, at the sound of laughter from another part of the plane, he half rose, his narrow face stretching into a hopeful smile and his reddish arms clenching, as though preparing to take flight himself. But something was weighing him down. In the end, we settled for each other.

"It's a good life," he told me, "the car business. A lot of these guys here, they're sellers, don't much care about the product. Me, I go way back with cars. Used to work in a factory in Texas, GM factory. Sort of lost my taste for it when they brought in the computers."

"I hear they're doing wonderful things with them," I said.

"Oh, they're the future, no doubt. I seen them catch things no man on a line can catch, and they're faster than jackrabbits. Makes a better product, absolutely. But I like the people side a things, y'know? So I went into sales. Arlene"— he glanced over his shoulder, at his sleeping wife— "she always said I was a natural with folks. I guess it's true. I love the look a man gets when he's being sold something he's not sure he wants. The mouth goes funny, soft like, and the eyes open wide but sort of turn back into themselves, y'know? Fact is, they're not looking at the car at all."

"I know what you mean," I said. "When I buy something, I always wind up looking into my own head, trying to picture myself using it."

"Exactly right. You're looking, y'see, at two key parts of yourself—the fear and the desire. If the desire isn't there, you can still get by on the fear folks have of not doing something. Y'see, nobody, in my experience, is afraid to buy. What they're afraid of is *not* buying. My wife Arlene, for instance. She didn't want to come on this trip. She don't enjoy travel one bit. Maybe she's even got a sweetheart back home; I don't know. Point is, she's more afraid *not* to come than she is to come. Americans, they don't like to miss out on things. That's why I sell so many cars. I run an ad on the local news at ten o'clock, and the next morning folks come on down to the showroom. Bingo, I'm off to Hawaii. This is how the machine works. You've got these big secret patterns to little crappy events. Hell, I been studying this. Did you know the chart of economic variations in this century corresponds just about *exactly* to the fluctuation of the Nile River over there in Egypt?"

I had to ask him to repeat that one. He did, with relish.

"Car preference works the same way. You I figure for a BMW, something sporty, right?"

"Toyota," I said.

"Mileage?"

"Eight-five thousand. It's six years old." For some reason, I felt sorry for my car—which had also, I remembered now, taken shit from Walter Todd that evening he'd had me to dinner—and felt compelled to defend it. "It still runs pretty well, though."

He leaned back, sipped his ginger ale, and looked around worriedly at his kinsmen in the next aisle. "Don't let them hear you. Everybody's sore as hell at the Japs. Personally, I think they do a good job, but they don't have our labor situation. Next it'll be the Koreans. Practically slave labor over there. Things'll even out, though. We'll catch 'em with automation. Tell me, you Jewish?"

After a pause, I told him I was.

"You guys are shrewd cookies when it comes to business, I'll tell you that. That guy Levi Strauss, for instance. Quite an operator. They say that Christopher Columbus was Jewish, originally. That true?"

I had never heard anything of the sort, but the idea that America had been discovered by a wandering Jew, one who put on *tefillin*, who mulled over the Talmud below decks, looking for a new synthesis, a new world— it struck me as wonderful, and I very much wanted to believe it. So, it appeared, did the man next to me. So I said it was true.

He nodded, satisfied. Soon he fell into a lengthy narration of the century's great business deals, and I was able to relax my attention somewhat. I leaned back and listened to the flow of his words, and to the untroubled exhalations of his sleeping wife, thinking about how little I knew of this country from my high window on Nassau Street, and how little of what I knew I really liked, or felt part of, or knew how to respond to. The trip was not a long one; in a while, the plane was banking through the fog south of San Francisco, and the fasten-seat-belt warning made its cheerful chime.

I had an odd idea. I wanted to find out the name of the fellow next to me without giving him mine. I don't know why I felt that this was important, why getting a name for nothing, no exchange, struck me as a sort of coup. I was operating either on a logic hidden to me or on none at all; either way, I indulged the impulse. The dealer had fallen temporarily quiet, his lids were closed, but lightly. The top fold of his plane ticket peeked out from the pocket of his shirt. I swiveled around to read it, but the name wasn't visible. The magazine in his wife's handbag seemed to be a better bet. I reached across, past his knees, poking with my fingers as though I had dropped something on the floor. The magazine was *Time*. There was no name or address on the front cover—she had obviously bought it at a newsstand.

Inexplicably, I felt panicked. It had just been a lark, a silly inspiration, but now that it had been thwarted, my blood went hot and I couldn't concentrate on anything else for the fifteen minutes remaining until our descent.

When the plane had finished with us, I followed the couple all the way to the terminal. It barely registered that I was on the ground, that I had arrived at my destination, that I needed a shave, that I had to rent a car. The Nagra, which I carried on a shoulder strap, weighed me down considerably. At the baggage claim I felt frantic and realized I was sweating. I took a deep breath, and then another. It occurred to me that in recent days things had assumed the texture of a dream, and that, from my present vantage point, there was no way to determine the point in time when the dream might have started. When one is in a maze, there is no supra-maze knowledge.

The luggage came pouring out of the chute, tumbling onto the conveyor belt and traveling in an ellipse. Around me, people pressed close. There were grumbles, coughs, exclamations of greeting and surprise, coos of pleasure. *Welcome,* I heard again and again. *Welcome.*

Slowly the belt emptied and the area cleared. Outside, the fog bunched thick at the windows.

"Sonny. Yo, sonny."

I turned. I don't know what I expected to find. Certainly not the Chevy dealer in the plaid slacks. But there he was; tall, improbably lanky, face splashed with blotches of red. The neck of his shirt was open a little too far, revealing a red, hairless chest.

"What the matter? Me and Arlene've been watching you. You look like you skipped right off the planet."

"I'm fine," I said, but I was worried. I felt light-headed, full of air. My body was no longer trustworthy; it would go its own way, it seemed, and I'd have to do what I could to catch up.

"That yours?"

He pointed to the conveyor belt, where a lone suitcase—mine—made its quiet orbit.

"Better pick it up, son, before the redcaps get their mitts on it. I know how those guys operate. Ruthless." Stepping in front of me, he reached down to grab the bag's handle. "Here, let me get that for you. You've got that other thing already. Say, what is that thing, anyway?"

"It's a tape recorder," I said.

"Expensive?"

"Yes, I think so. I'm not entirely sure. It isn't mine."

He yanked the suitcase off the belt, and I watched the confusion on his face give way to the storm of an idea. "Say, listen. We're fogged in here for a while, looking at a four-, five-hour delay. The wife 'n' me are headed over to the Wharf for some shrimp. Love to have some company."

"Sorry," I said. "I'd love to, but—"

"Wait a minute." He slapped his forehead. "Okay, hey, forget the

243

shrimp. I forgot about you people and shellfish. We'll get anything you want. Say the word: Italian, Chinese, Continental . . ."

"It's not that."

"Anybody picking you up? Late for an appointment?"

"No, there isn't, but—"

"Name's Gillespie," he said, extending his free hand. "But hey, call me Poke. Now, I want you to know something, son, and I mean this. I like you. You've got what I call a listening presence. It's an appealing, rare thing. My boy Gene had one. We lost him in '72, over in Da Nang. You fight over there?"

I shook my head no.

He drew close, lowered his voice. "Okay, it happens, I figure. But I ain't seen Arlene laugh out loud in five years. Now, why'n't you come have some dinner? I figure you'd enjoy yourself, seeing the town with old Pokey. I've been here plenty. Whattaya say? Just nod your head a couple of times yes and I'll run for a taxicab."

Slowly, reminding myself that there are a variety of routes to any destination, I nodded my head a couple of times yes.

True to his word, Poke Gillespie ran off toward the sliding glass doors to hail a taxi, dragging my suitcase behind him and simultaneously calling for his wife to follow. She looked up from one of the plastic seats clustered by the window, her gaze absent and disinterested. Then, heavily, she got to her feet, slung her travel bag over her shoulder, and made her way to the exit with the slow, halting formality of a royal procession.

When all three of us had climbed into the cab, and Poke had finished registering his disgust with the car ("Goddamn mongrel Ford—be lucky if we get there alive"), he looked over from his corner seat and bade his wife shake my hand. "You remember the fella from the plane, hon. Son, this is Arlene."

She treated me to a very frosty "How do you do." Arlene Gillespie seemed to want no part of our expedition. Like her husband, she was lanky, nearly anorexic. The deep red of her lipstick, and her hair, puffed into a round white bun, combined to lend her a certain ghostly, bloodless quality that her conversation did little to offset. As we took the hills of the city in jerks and sways, she rocked stiffly beside me, staring straight ahead and biting her lip with disapproval of her husband, who spent the entire drive regaling me with stories of his adventures a generation before in the merchant marine. "Now, back then we'd hang out over there on Farrell, in this little seamen's bar. Had a pool table in back so stained up with beer and a coupla other things, you could hardly get any movement at all on the break. That damn table was only good for one thing." He gave off a little howl of nostalgia, and slapped the window with his palm. "Now, over there's Alcatraz. Son, I swear, once upon a time you could hear the boys who were locked up there calling to you when you went by on your ship. They saw everything coming and going on the bay. Must've drove them damn near crazy. Sounded like coyotes, those boys. We'll get off here, driver."

The taxi left us off on Embarcadero, about four blocks east of the Wharf. The temperature was only in the fifties. Arlene Gillespie trudged a few paces in front of us, clutching the arms of her sweater. I wondered why she'd bothered to come at all. Then I remembered what her husband had told me on the plane, about fear and its power over desire. I thought there might be something to it. She looked shaky, imperfectly armored, like a child who, though reluctant to go off exploring, is fearful of being left behind. The gulls swooped low, skimming the surface of the bay. A foghorn moaned. The fog clustered around the lighthouse on Alcatraz; just beyond, the upper reaches of Angel Island loomed above the gray like a mythical floating city. It was almost impossible to distinguish, at first glance, sea from land from air; all were the same cloudy gray-white, all swaying, surging, commingling. Every thirty seconds or so, the beacon from the lighthouse would slice the fog like a blade. Each time, it seemed to precipitate a rush of adrenaline in Poke Gillespie, another door flung open in the vine-swamped mansion of his memories. He hollered and waved, entreating us both to join him in his pleasures. The party, he made it clear, was all on him.

We went to a seafood restaurant on the Wharf. When we sat down, Poke positioned me between him and Arlene; then, pulling at his napkin, he circulated a beam around the table so exaggerated and buoyant in its willfulness that it was a shame to see it smothered by the sight of his wife looking at the outsized menu. "What's the matter, hon? Nothing you like?"

"I'll be fine," she said dully. "Don't worry about me."

"Look, we can go somewhere else. Who gives a shit where we eat, anyway?"

"I'm fine," she said again. "Let's just go ahead and have our meal."

"Shit, hon, this city's *full* of places. They got spots where you can get any—"

"*Please.*" There was an awful tone to it, a pleading mixed with combat, and pride, and self-hatred, and resentment, and it made me very, very sorry to be sitting there between them. The situation intensified a moment later when the waiter came over, regarding us with the generous efficiency of a tourist slave, and made a comment that had doubtless worked wonders for him before hundreds of tables like ours in the past.

"Well," he said expansively, "here's the happy family. Is everybody happy?"

There was a constricted, mirthless laugh. It came from Arlene Gillespie. Her husband stared into the cold geometry of the butter dish, his red face going a good deal redder.

I looked out the window at the gray water. It was patently clear what I was doing there, what I had been doing, in fact, for so long. My inertia suddenly seemed palpable to me, so solid and close I could touch it, measure it, contain it—one shrug of the shoulders and it would fall from me like a blanket. Charlie had shown me the fierce satisfaction of touching bottom, and I felt it now, the anticipation of ascent. Deliberately I raised my glass of wine, took a small sip, and cleared my throat. "My name is Herschel Freeman," I said. "I live in New York, where I work as an attorney for a large Wall Street firm."

Both of the Gillespies looked up from their plates with dismay.

"When I was nine, my father brought me to the restaurant next door for Thanksgiving dinner. My parents were separated; they'd agreed I could spend my Thanksgiving up here, with my father. He was just back from Eniwetok, in the Pacific, where they'd exploded a hydrogen bomb. He called it a 'device.' We had a room at the Claremont Hotel, over in the East Bay. I believe the Lab paid for it. Should I go on?"

Poke Gillespie nodded unhappily, sipping his wine. He looked discomfited, but he was a man of principle, determined to hear me out. "You go on ahead, son," he said. His eyes flickered over to his wife, but she had retreated into her private thoughts, and her face gave no clue as to their nature.

"Thank you. Now, this was in 1952. My father was in his mid thirties at the time, about the age I am now. I resemble him, I think. My complexion is darker, and I'm a couple of inches taller, but essentially we looked similar. He had grown a mustache, which, he was told, made him look like a cardsharp. I did not know what a cardsharp was, but I didn't say anything. My father kept fiddling with the breadsticks and looking around the restaurant, as though he didn't quite know what to do with me. I'm pretty sure he never asked me a single question I could answer. He'd ask me only abstract things, like what kind of person I wanted to be, or what did it feel like to be a boy who didn't see his father much, or if I understood why there was a war with Korea. It was very difficult. Oh, there *was* one easy question he did ask: He wanted to know if I ever played with the present he'd given me for my ninth birthday."

"What was it?" asked Poke, through narrowed lids.

"An Erector Set. I told him yes, but it was a lie. My mother had thrown it out after a week, when I'd left it lying around the living room floor. There was a lot of vindictiveness in my family. My father and I weren't close. We'd never been close. There's nothing very unusual about that, I know. But the sadness, it's real. It's real even though you don't feel it.

"Anyway, after a while, just to say something, he began to describe what it had been like in the Pacific. It was on his mind, after all. But his manner was strange. There was no air of instruction about it, or performance, or any of the ways you'd normally tell a story to a child. It was just a very simple, detached account, the facts without embellishment. Maybe he felt I shouldn't know such things. Maybe he was worried I'd have nightmares. I don't know. He depersonalized it, completely. Facts. He told me that the device wasn't really a bomb at all—it was too large. They just put it in this gigantic shed and detonated it by remote control. From a distance, he said, the shed bore a resemblance to the Kaaba, which houses the sacred stones of the Muslims at Mecca. Or did he say that? Maybe I read it somewhere. I do know that at some point he went into details about the explosion itself. Fact: The device created a fireball over three miles in diameter. Fact: Trees on islands two hundred miles away were scorched black. Fact: Millions of gallons of water were vaporized into a steam bubble. All of this made an impression on me, of course. But the last fact is what did it. He told me that the island of Elugelab, where they had set if off, did not survive. That was how he put it. The island did not survive the explosion. It disappeared. There had been an island in the Pacific Ocean at such and such a point, and now there wasn't an island there any longer. There was no pride in the way he said it, but there wasn't any regret, either. All in a day's work. Well, I was nine years old and nervous about seeing my father and being so far from home. Also I'd just had a big meal, and we'd taken the ferry that morning, and I might have still been shaky from that. In any case, I threw up."

"Hell," said Poke, "those ferries'll get you every time, till you get your sea legs."

Arlene gave him a withering look. At some point in my story, she had begun to pay attention to me; her gaze had softened somewhat, and she did not seem quite so closed into herself. I knew she was wondering about my mother.

Poke devoured a chunk of sourdough and signaled to the waiter for more wine. Now that I had shed my listening posture, he seemed to be in need of other stimuli.

"Do you want to hear more?" I asked.

"No," said Arlene Gillespie. "But I have a question. Why did she throw away the Erector Set?"

Poke answered for me. "She was jealous. Jealous of the old man's influence. That's why. She was making a power play, it's obvious."

She had not turned to look at her husband when he offered his explanation. Slowly, mechanically, as though she had not been interrupted, she repeated her question to me.

"I don't remember," I said. "I might have it wrong. Maybe I was the one who threw it out."

"Now, why in hell would you do a thing like that?" bellowed Poke. "What kind of son would do a thing like that?"

"Maybe the kind that had a father like mine."

Poke banged the table hard. "Okay now, listen. I been sitting here, polite as a faggot, and now I'm gonna tell you something useful, and you're gonna listen. For a long time, y'see, I sold Pontiacs. I was young, just starting out in sales, learning the business. All day I sold Pontiacs, then I drove home in a Pontiac, then at night I'd dream about Pontiacs. To me, for that time, Pontiacs *were* cars. It was like a total identification. Then a little later I moved over to Chrysler, where I went through the exact same thing. Now I'm with Chevrolet. But no more of that. I've learned my lesson, y'see: Total identification gets you into trouble. It's too damn rigid. There are a coupla hundred good things and a coupla hundred bad things to say about any car, or person. Now, this is where moral choice comes in, I figure. You've got a choice about what you focus on. Me, I try to accentuate the positive. That's how I grew up, that's how I trained my boy, that's how I train my salesmen, and that's how I manage to get a trip once a year to some cozy beach place where they serve tall rum concoctions I can't pronounce. But people like you"—and he pointed a bony knuckle at the space between his wife and me—"you clutch onto the dark side and you don't let go. When one of my salesmen spends the whole afternoon test-driving a customer, and the guy says he has to go home and think about it, does my salesman get angry? No sir. He says sayonara, and moves on to the next. This is how an organization needs to function. You fix onto the larger pattern and you don't get hung up on the idiosyncrasies. You can't grind to a stop because somebody resents somebody else. That's the way you live your life, y'see. If a man's your father, you accept him for what he is and you go ahead with your life until you're a father too. Then you appreciate what's involved. Listen, sonny, nobody's got it over anybody else. Nobody's better and nobody's worse. It's all in the disguise. Somebody up there's charting *us*, and laughing his goddamn head off."

"Some people are better," said his wife, in a very small voice. "The dead are better."

"You've got to excuse Arlene," Poke said to me. "She's got her good points, of course. But sometimes she's sentimental, and it makes her sound stupid."

The sun, which had not as yet been visible, emerged for about a minute at the crease of the horizon. Then the new fog rolled in. I watched it stream past the bridge, wiping it clean of its orange paint, and overtake the lighthouse, then snuff out the lights of Marin as it headed east across the bay. It kept moving in and moving in. Suddenly I couldn't eat; I felt hot, crowded; my knees began to fan compulsively and my scalp began to itch. "I have to go," I said. "I've got to drive up the coast tonight."

"Hold your horses," said Poke. "We'll drop you at a car rental on our way back to the airport. Right, hon?"

"Oh, let him go," she muttered, with such weariness and suppressed loathing that even her husband, a Quixote of the positive, could not maintain his smile. "He's an adult. He knows what he wants."

Poke's splotched cheeks puffed out twice, drew in, and locked tight. Instantly I felt sorry for him, sorry and somehow responsible for the way our expedition had gone. It seemed to be a place where moral choice might come in. So, shaking his hand with both of mine, I said, "I'm driving up to meet my father. He's in Mendocino, I think."

"You *think*? Hey, whattaya mean, you *think*?"

But I was already halfway to the exit. Just as I reached the door, I had the sensation of having left something important behind. When I returned to the table, Poke had already taken the Nagra and my suitcase, which had been lodged between his chair and the wall, and placed them on the seat I had just vacated.

"Traveling light?" he quipped.

I waited for them to finish their meal, then he paid the bill and we went out together to find a taxi. The fog was so heavy, by that point in the evening, it was practically rain.

Chapter 26

"I want to make it clear," said Arthur Gordon, "that I will not ask you about Abby. Not that it's none of my business. Not that I don't have my idle curiosities. But it's out of my control at the moment, and I don't choose to make it my primary emphasis. For now, let's just get on with the film. Agreed?"

"Agreed."

"Good. Then sit down and have a drink. You look like hell."

In the dim light of the hotel bar, Arthur himself looked poised, hale, at the top of his form. He was wearing a lime-colored sport jacket and a denim shirt. Behind the tinted glasses his eyes were clear and alert, registering my appearance in a quick take and then dropping to the notes stacked before him as though checking a script for his lines. Our table, like all the tables at the bar, was surrounded by clusters of ferns; that concession to modernity aside, the place had an elegant, Victorian air about it, the kind of bar where one might sip good cognac, smoke good cigars, and easily enjoy some of the good life that in humbler surroundings seemed so elusive.

"And how was the drive? Some view, eh?"

"It was dark. I couldn't tell."

"Too bad. It's a sweet road, Highway One. Be interesting to look into its construction. Quite an enterprise, I imagine."

"I'm sure it would make a great movie," I said.

He shrugged. "And how are the Torborgs? Still picking lint from the navel of Mexico?"

"They seem happy."

"You say that as though it's some sort of achievement."

"I'm coming to believe it is," I said.

He made no answer to that, merely a curl of the lip, a suggestion that he could make allowances for the follies of another. After a moment, he uncrossed his legs and faced me square. "I saw you, you know."

"What are you talking about?"

"On Route Eighty-five. I saw you pass me. I was at a gas station, cleaning the windshield, and I saw your reflection go right by. Don't be coy. I even saw you look back at me after you accelerated."

"Did I?"

"Abby, she looked straight ahead, of course. A real trouper. It was her idea to take off, wasn't it?"

"This is not asking me about Abby?"

Immediately he lifted his arms high, in mock apology. "Forget it. I meant what I said before. Let's be peaceful."

"Fine."

"You missed some great footage, though. All that sagebrush and white sand. Howling wind through the canyons. John Ford stuff. For some reason, I connected to Stonehenge, I don't know why. Stonehenge and solar eclipse. It's the cycles, I think, the light and shadow. That's how we measure time, after all—a cycle of light. Maybe, maybe it's just the end of one particular day, you know? Consider the Biblical days of creation. They might last centuries. I mean, maybe we're just at the end of day number eight, you know? Food for thought. Speaking of which, while I was filming, an empty bag of potato chips flew across my field of vision and landed near Point Zero. Someone had used the spot for a picnic lunch. Can you imagine?"

"I've never been there," I said.

"Right. You said that. Bring back the Nagra with you?"

"It's up in my room. I've been using it some, Arthur. Just taping odd things on it. I hope you don't mind."

He leaned toward me hopefully. "What kinds of things? Things we can use?"

"I don't think so." I considered the raw material that had found its way onto that tape, drawn by the indiscriminate magnetism of its ear, and it was difficult, just then, to imagine a movie that would be sufficiently bizarre to go along with it. "I should have erased it, in fact. I'll do it tonight, before I go to sleep."

"Don't worry about it," he said. "I've got plenty of blank tape. The stores are full of it. The Japanese send us their immaculate technology, and we fill it with sound."

"Boom."

He tilted his head inquiringly and eyed me over the bridge of his glasses. "Are you all right, Hesh?"

"Where is he, Arthur?"

"Relax," he said. "There's plenty of time. Have another drink. Or maybe you want to go outside and smoke a doobie?"

"You said you found him." I leaned forward, took hold of his forearm, and locked my eyes onto his. "You told me you found him, you son of a bitch."

"Let go of me." He said it casually but with subtle force, and waited until I relaxed my grip before he slowly withdrew his arm. "Let's get something straight, shall we? I didn't lie to you, I didn't bring you into anything against your will, and I didn't run off with your wife. It's not your place to threaten me. I won't have it." He looked pointedly at his watch. "I think we should both go to bed, in fact. Tomorrow we'll take a walk, and I'll tell you the story. It's a pretty town; you'll like it. Oh, which reminds me . . ." Standing, he reached into the inner pocket of his lime jacket and removed an envelope with an unfamiliar stamp, which he tossed onto the table. "This came for you today. It's from Abby."

I looked at the letter as though mail itself was an invention alien to me, part of the conspiracy that was crowding me, moving in and in.

"I got one too," he added, offhandedly.

We said good night and I watched him leave. It struck me as incredible, the thought of how much had arisen between this strange little man and myself in the seven weeks of our acquaintance. I had used him and he had used me and we had both used and been used by his wife; it was as blurry and indeterminate and yet strangely symmetrical as the diagram that Bruce Schultz had sketched for me on that cocktail napkin, a few nights before.

There was a baseball game on the television over the bar. Giants and Pirates. It must have been extra innings, because when they flashed the graphic between innings there were rows and rows of numbers, most of them zeros, and they seemed to be coming out even. But it would not hold that way forever. In baseball you keep playing until somebody wins. And that's just about right, I thought. It had been a long, seesawing game, but I felt that I was coming to an end of sorts myself—the end of the continent, the end of the flashback, the end of beginnings. Through an open window I could hear the ocean, feel the salt-sweet moisture of its breath. Despite the surroundings, for once in my life I did not feel adrift or at random; for once in my life I did not feel homesick. Because I'd come home.

Azcapotzalco, Mexico
June 23

Hesh—

It's nearly noon and I'm writing this in bed, where I seem to be spending most of my time lately. I've been having such exotic dreams. Want to hear one?

I was hiking in a mountain valley. Everything was lush and dazzling. There were no people at all, which was a little ominous, but I managed to get along by myself quite well until I stumbled and fell into a small cave. Now here comes the strange part. In the cave were several—I'd say four or five—antique televisions. They were very ornate, with beautiful wood cabinets and elaborate antennas. I remember gasping at how lovely they were. But when I tried to turn them on, none of them worked. And then the floor of the cave seemed to slide, or melt, and I saw a man. I wasn't certain who it was, but he was lying very still on what seemed to be a sheet of ice, and his body was imbedded slightly, so that he seemed to be lying on his back, as though floating on a raft in a swimming pool (though, like I said, the water was frozen). At first I thought he must be dead, but then he looked up at me and smiled. He didn't try to get up, or else he couldn't. I had the feeling that he just didn't *want* to. In fact, he seemed to want me to join him down there. Finally, I turned around and ran up the mountain, and when I was very far away, I looked down and saw that he was still lying there in that same position, looking at me. That's how the dream ended: the two of us looking at each other from our respective altitudes, neither one of us moving closer.

The man, I suspect, was you.

It's funny, writing letters again. In the States I always use the phone. It reminds me of the diary I used to keep in high school (okay—and college too). How tired I'd get after a while of the first person, that ubiquitous I (Private Eye?). Sometimes I'd want to just break free, kill this Abby person who spent so much time whining and buzzing about like a gnat. I always felt like a butterfly waiting to happen. Oh, well.

Listen to me, even now. How tiresome you must find me, Hesh. Or, how did you put it? A crazed bitch. Very apt, that one. That last night here we really tore into it, didn't we? It was like taking a hammer to a wobbly, fledgling flying machine: Because it wasn't flying well enough or high enough, we were going to ground it forever. Well. At least it was passionate. And who knows? Things could always change. I do believe in change, it so happens. Valéry says that when we're born we are a whole crowd of people whom life reduces to a single individual, someone who eats and works and loves. But sometimes one of our other selves pops out of nowhere, when we don't expect it or when our guard is down, and if the circumstances are right we can actually *change*, become somebody else—the way Arthur has done, for instance, about half a dozen times since I've known him. I know how he does it, too. He's able to ignore his inner crowd and choose: be one self at a time. It's sort of naive, but it seems to work. And it's very attractive, in its way.

But so is the other way attractive. Refusing to choose, seeing the absurdity of such choices, detaching yourself from the mess of choice. It's your way, Hesh, and it's always been my way too, and it doesn't *work*—you keep everything open because you're afraid to get stuck, and you end up getting stuck anyway, and meanwhile you still haven't *done* anything. Look at *us*—even when we went for it, we didn't really go for it, as the kids say. Some pair.

Okay. I am now out of bed. I am in the garden, which is, as you know, somewhat overgrown with weeds. I have a cup of coffee on the table beside me, and the sun is hot on my shoulders, and the flowers are full of bees. Shy and Malla are still in Oaxaca (I didn't go; that, at least, should be good for a smile), performing some sort of holographic ceremony on Monte Albán in observance of the summer solstice. Good for them.

Oh, Hesh, I feel hopeful today. I may be all alone, but I feel smart and capable (and tan), and I have intentions of growth. I am also, I think, slightly pregnant.

Are you still with me?

I say I think because I haven't been to a doctor yet and obviously I have nothing to compare this to. But I *feel* something. And I never miss a period.

Here come the old gossips on their way back from the *zócalo*. I love the sound of Spanish on a hot, dull morning (oops—afternoon). Do you remember any Spanish, lover? Let me teach you something new, something I heard the other day from a neighbor. *Morir soñando.* It means "to die dreaming"—it's the name of a drink down south of here. You like it? It's exactly the way I've been feeling lately. Because things are taking shape inside me, and I've begun to come through, and this great barren nightmare might be nearly over. It's so strange, being a woman, trying to keep up with the caprices of your hormones. In a way, it tells you what you never really wanted to believe: that everything is rooted in the physical, in the body, and the rest is just commentary. It's so confining that it's almost liberating. Finally I feel a part of things. I don't feel inferior any more to every fat housewife with a kid in tow. I feel part of something larger.

But I'm boring you with my gushing, of course. Why write a letter full of "I" when all the person on the other end really wants to read is the stuff about "you"?

Very well. If you've been skimming so far, Hesh, then here's where you'll want to pay attention. I do not think I love you, Hesh. Not that you aren't lovable, and not that I am incapable of loving you at some point, but when I am honest with myself I don't think it's there yet. Maybe you feel the same way (I'm pretty sure you do). What I'm trying to say, I guess, is that, if you'll excuse the Garbo, I think I prefer to be alone just now. The Torborgs might go to Brazil—if so, I might sublet their villa, or I might spend the summer and fall in New Hampshire and pal around with my mother, whom I never see anymore. You don't have to visit, you don't have to call, you don't have to write. All I ask is that you do what you want to do. It may be too much to ask of you, or it may not be enough, but it is, I feel sure, the only way to proceed.

One last thing. I'm telling Arthur the baby's his. There's no way to be sure, ultimately (old Heisenberg gets the last laugh, after all), so it doesn't feel like any kind of a lie. Anyway, for now it hardly matters. Besides, maybe you two can still help each other with your respective pursuits. I hope so. I'd like to think this summer will be good for all of us.

Now I'm getting drowsy again. Even the lizards on the rocks are asleep. I feel warm and fat and sluggish. I can hardly move the pen, but I don't want to let go of it, either. I'm not all that brave a person. But you know that, don't you?

Abby

P.S. We were in Mendocino once. It's sort of like Nantucket, isn't it? We went out to watch the whales migrate offshore. You should do it if you get the chance.

P.P.S. I just read this over. Forgive me, Hesh, for sounding so glib. Forgive me, in general. Oh, God, the sun feels so strong today. . . .

Chapter 27

I finished the letter, folded it along its original creases, and put it back in the envelope on the bed table. Outside was a flood of blackness; even the stars were dim. It was four-twenty in the morning. I hadn't had more than five consecutive hours of sleep in weeks. My father, I remembered, had been an insomniac, and now I was getting a taste of what it felt like. You came to the point, after a couple of weeks, where you stopped fighting, where you gave yourself up to it, that swelling restless itch inside you, that feeble kicking. It was almost a sort of pregnancy, I thought. But the word had been in my mind already, from Abby's letter, and so I didn't find much to cheer me in the comparison.

I went over to the closet in my bare feet and brought out the Nagra. It felt light in my hands. I lifted it easily onto the foot of the bed, rewound the reel, and set it to Play, with the volume turned low.

Dr. Cyril Stone's waspy voice ghosted into the room. ". . . it reminded me of a conductor's bow at the end of a performance. . . ."

I took off my clothes and turned out the light. I lay with my hands folded over my chest, my feet crossed at the ankles, and let the darkness and the sounds of the tape wash over me. They eddied and pooled, as though driven by vagrant winds. Occasionally the voices grew indistinct, or faded, or mingled with the background noise—the rush of an engine, the wail of a distant siren, the clanking of mule bells, the slam of a cantina's screen door. Because it was late, and I felt light-headed, and perhaps because I was not wholly in command of my inner troops, I heard things that I couldn't possibly have recorded. How had I gotten Charlie Goldwyn on tape? Lucy Johnson? Had the tape been running when I sat with the Gillespies? With Bruce Schultz? And what about the choir from San Antonio de Padua? Twice I thought I heard Abby's low sex moan. And then, at erratic intervals, I heard what must have been my own voice, though each time I initially failed to recognize it. The pitch sounded off, nasal and lugubrious, with some of the petulant breathiness of a boy. I sounded, it dulled me to discover, exactly like my son Solly. And, taken together, the audio record of the past weeks sounded like nothing so much as a call-in show one might hear in the middle of an aimless night. I tried to listen honestly, without growing bored and without shutting my eyes, even during the painful moments. But it wasn't easy. The painful moments were all there were.

When the tape was over, I slid down to the foot of the bed and erased it. The dim gray light filtered through the curtains. I watched the room gather definition from it as I put in a call to New York.

"Well," said Joanne. "You're not dead. Or are you? You sound funny."

"Funny ha-ha or funny strange?"

"Most definitely the latter."

"It's the connection."

"Oh," she said.

"How about you, Jo? You don't sound so great yourself."

"Oh, I'm fine. Too fine for words." I heard the rip of a match against flint, the indrawn breath, and then the long, melancholy sigh she made when she exhaled. "Actually, I'm terrible. I handed Alan his walking papers last night. Or maybe it was the other way around. I can hardly remember, to tell you the truth. Oh boy. You know, sometimes I think we're just not cut out to live in pairs."

"We as in you and me, or we as in everybody?"

"That's a good question. I'll have to think about that one," she said. "Where are you, anyway?"

"Northern California. Mendocino."

"What on earth for? A girl?"

To the west the sky was clearing, the white haze thinning to blue. The sea looked rested, tranquil. "It's a hell of a spot for whale watching."

"Don't be cryptic," she said. "It's too early in the morning. How goes the Navajo case?"

"All done, for now. As is, I think, my tenure with Pinsker & Lem."

"Well, hooray for that."

"Check."

"So what *are* you doing, then?"

"It's a long story," I said. "But I think I found my old man."

There was a silence. At first I was certain she'd dropped the phone, left the room—simply walked away, the way she used to when I'd irritate or hurt her. But finally, in a subdued voice, she said, "So what now?"

"I go see him."

258

"And then?"

"Then I break loose."

"Oh Hesh," she said. "You're already loose. You've been loose your whole life. Don't you even know that much?"

I wanted to tell her that she did not understand, but I thought that perhaps she understood all too well. "Let me talk to Solly, Jo."

"He's at day camp. Why don't you call back around four, our time? He thinks you've gone off and left him for good." She paused. "Have you?"

"No."

"Good. So call back and tell him."

"I'll try. But in case I don't get to a phone, I want you to tell him I'll be back east in a few days, and we'll go to a ball game. Will you tell him that?"

"Whatever you say," she said.

"I mean it."

"Then tell him yourself. Make it a regular fathers-and-sons week." She inhaled again, and held it for two beats. "Oh, do whatever you want, sweetie. It's not up to me anymore to keep you fixed."

It seemed to be the natural end of the conversation, of all our conversations. But I wasn't finished yet. "Just one last thing, Jo. First, I want you to know that I trust you, and that this is sort of a delicate time for me. Second, I want to ask you a question."

"I'm all ears."

"Do you think I'm good?"

She laughed heartily. "A little passive, especially in the morning. But I always enjoyed myself."

"No, I mean good, in general. A good person. A good man."

"Have you had much sleep, Hesh? You sound groggy."

"Just answer the question."

"Well, I'd say about half and half, like most people. Disappointed?"

"Go on."

"You're capable of being a lot better than you are. What I said about the sex, in fact, applies. On the other hand, you don't seem to act out of malice anywhere near as much as a lot of people. But it's a dumb question to ask me. I'm not qualified to judge. And I don't like what it implies about your state of mind. Why all this mirror gazing? Just get on with what you have to do already."

"I will," I said. "Thanks."

"And come for dinner next week. I'll make Italian, and we can crack jokes at Alan's expense. Okay?"

"I'd like that. Thanks, Jo. I'll bring you back a whale."

"Stop thanking me, please," she said. "And just bring yourself, and maybe a Bordeaux. Now get some sleep, hon. You sound done in."

I *was* done in. The scrubbing I gave myself in the shower only roughed up and annoyed the numbness that had set in over my head and limbs; now that numbness moved through me stealthily, seeking out my soft spots, pushing at my joints, throwing wet sand over my movements. I thought about going back to bed. I thought about going down to the coffee shop. I thought about calling someone else, like Shelley Lubin. I liked the sound of the female voice over the phone, the privileged intimacy, the counterpoint. I would call Shelley and we would talk, and I'd feel better when I hung up. But knowing that that was how it would go, for some reason, sapped me of the desire to set it in motion.

Because I could no longer tolerate deliberation, I fell to the carpeted floor and went into a set of push-ups, intending not to stop until I hit fifty. Maybe Abby was right; maybe the whole thing came down to hormones, to the flops and swings of the body's chemicals. I'd do fifty push-ups and I'd get myself primed for the day's combat. Fifty's no big deal, requires no great strength. Only, at thirty-one, my upper arms turned to rubber and my chest caught fire. So I flipped onto my back. Sit-ups. I did them at a furious pace. They came easily, a joyride. I heard the slap of my back against the carpet, the whoosh of my breath. Forty-one. Forty-two.

I stopped at fifty. Rather, I paused at fifty, then pushed back onto my shoulders and began to bicycle in the air. My feet pushed at phantom pedals, pumping the slow invisible wheels of gravity. The body is happy when it imitates a machine. I counted backward from five hundred, listening to the rough wheeze of my breath, the valves doing their work in my chest. This I could do forever. I could go on for hours, days. I could kill time. That's what exercise is all about: ritual murder, an assault on infinity. That's what music is for, what books are for, what movies are for. Killing time. Really beating the shit out of it.

Only it didn't work. At one hundred fifty I bumped against an invisible boundary, and however hard I pushed against it, I could not cross. I bicycled for exactly seven minutes and then I had to stop. I had barely worked up a sweat.

At seven-thirty Arthur was already down in the coffee shop, hunched over a blueberry muffin and looking uncharacteristically dolorous. At first I assumed that his letter from Abby had unnerved him—framed against the window, he seemed forlorn and vulnerable and innocent, a small boy who had momentarily lost his way. When I sat down he didn't acknowledge my presence; he merely pushed the crumbs on his plate into a circle with his spoon and said, flatly, "They canceled my funding."

"Who did? When?"

"The Endowment. They denied my request for production expenses before I even got the chance to submit a reel. Said they'd overbudgeted, and I should try again next year. With a new project, of course."

"What about your other sources? Can't they raise it?"

He shook his head disconsolately. "All gone fishing, as they used to say."

"Arthur, we'll sue. It's a flagrant breach of contract. The whole thing's so transparently political it'll never even get to court."

For an instant, he seemed to perk up. "That's right, isn't it? We'd win. I mean, you're a lawyer; you should know."

"Right," I said. "I should know."

"But—but how *long* will it take?"

"Well, I don't know. Several months, anyway."

The air sailed out of him again. "It's no good. Even if I win, I'll make enemies who could finish me in the domestic market. I'm not going to do this whole fucking film just to have it wind up on French TV." He took a breath and turned to the window, his mouth an uneven line. "Well, it's over, then. On to something new."

"No."

He kept talking. "I've got those profiles in the works. That piece on Ezra Pound has promise. May be able to get George C. Scott for the voice, if I play my cards right. They'll eat that up. . . ."

"Arthur," I said, "it's not over. We'll fight and we'll win. Let's see it through."

"Well, well. A new Hesh." He cocked his head, raised one eyebrow; behind his glasses his eyes showed, of all things, amusement. "And just what do you propose we do?"

"We finish shooting the preliminary footage. When you've got what you need, you go to the editing room and I get busy writing letters on my Pinsker & Lem stationery. It'll be the first work I've done in years that I might actually believe in. My last hurrah."

He nodded cautiously, pushing his crumbs around. "That obnoxious fellow Goldwyn you told me about: Can he help? I had the feeling he's something of a bulldozer."

"Yes, he'll help. He owes me a favor. And he's very well connected." Presuming, of course, he didn't die of a heart attack first.

Arthur Gordon was not the sort of person to spend a great deal of time mulling things over, and he did not disappoint me now. A single penetrating look, to see if I was as serious as I sounded, a little rubbing of his chin, and half a cup of coffee later, he pushed back his chair. "Let's walk," he said, "and I'll tell you how I found him."

The village of Mendocino stands poised between a dense pine forest to the east and, to the west, the rugged Pacific shoreline. In the summer, the weather differs markedly on either side, as the fogline extends to a point only a mile or so east of the water and then no farther. This leaves the town in a state of confused temperature, erratic visibility, and profuse fertility, as sorrel and dune willow and bog rush and sagewort all compete along the sides of the path for their share of the sun. We were walking north and west along the cliffs, which snaked jaggedly over the water. The sea was pale, algae-clumped; it heaved in the channels like an enormous stomach. Gulls and cormorants circled overhead, their sounds shrill with mockery. We made slow progress. We were having trouble negotiating the path, with the Aaton and the Nagra weighing us down. This didn't stop Arthur from talking the entire time, however—filling me in on the Urizen project, which sounded ludicrous—but it was difficult to hear him over the waves, as they broke against the black rocks like the repeated slamming of a heavy car door.

"Christ, Arthur. What are you trying to sell me now?"

"Hesh, I know it sounds fantastic. I resist the idea completely, even now. But it's all in my notes. The material isn't even classified anymore, some of it. These guys were going to send a ship the size of a sixteen-story *building,* for God's sake, soaring through space! At a hundred thousand miles per hour! Carrying laboratories and factories and kitchens and hundreds of people! Fantasy, right? But consider—a couple dozen top physicists, working under maximum security conditions for five years, playing around with serial fission, and pusher plates, and shielding, with a list of advisers as long as your arm . . . I mean, if this was a fantasy, *what* a fantasy, eh?"

"Even if it's true, what do you need my father for? You've got Lytell."

"No I don't," he said. "First off, he's not willing to go on film. He's quite firm about this. He says he has a tacit agreement with the Princeton people, and he also has this disarmament thing he's pushing, and he doesn't want to confuse the two. Personally, I think he's just vain about his pockmarks, but that's neither here nor there. Then there's the fact that Nugent and Harnick are dead, which pretty much exhausts the progenitors. Besides, the whole thing, I maintain, fits right into the film we're already doing. It's more of the same. Man the maker, out looking for new worlds, right?"

"I have no idea."

"Trust me."

I smiled. The frustration rose in my chest. Finally, I couldn't stop myself from blurting, "Who *are* these guys, anyway?"

"Pioneers," said Arthur patiently.

"They sound like a pack of fools."

"Look, maybe it's guilt," he said. "They're guilty. They need to find an escape hatch. They lit this awful fuse, see, and now they're looking for a way out. It's a moral imperative."

"That," I said, "is a load of shit."

"Not necessarily. Sometimes, you know, we look in the wrong place for answers. Sometimes motivation is the last thing to look at."

"And what's the first?"

"Why, the deed," he said. "The deed itself." He stopped in his tracks. "Hey, let's take a rest."

We came to rest on a large, flat-topped rock at the land's edge and set down the equipment. Back the way we'd come, I had a view of the wood-shingled roofs of the town, clustered tightly, as if for safety, from the Pacific's chilly gales. The day—now that the fog had begun to lift—was turning out to be fine and dry, and we were winded and sweaty from the walk. Arthur wiped his glasses with the tail of his denim shirt. I looked out at the ocean, at the glints of light off the peaks and swells, the crests of heady foam. I thought about what Abby had written in her letter, about circumstances favoring a change in our characters, and it struck me as more than possible that she and Arthur had it right. Breaks in continuity did not have to equal breaks in character. It could all be the same story, the same film; all could be made whole in the editing room. In the memory. You had only to will it so.

"So where," I asked, "is this Buck Rogers land exactly?"

He blinked. "Why, right here, of course. About three miles northeast of town."

"But this was all fifteen years ago. What makes you think he's still here?"

"Oh, a little bird told me. A Myra bird, in fact."

For an instant I was baffled, but then it came together into its pattern. "The divorce. You traced the papers."

He nodded, pleased. "To a little law office in downtown Mendocino. Naturally, there's no Friedmann in the town directory, so it took me a few days to find it. It's very well concealed, I might add. But AG Productions is a tireless outfit."

"So you found the abandoned Urizen site?"

"Yes. Only it wasn't abandoned."

"How do you know?"

"I saw it, I tell you. I could see lights and hear machine noises from the road. It looks like quite an operation. A regular nuclear Shangri-la."

"And that's where we're headed now."

"That's where we're headed now. We walk along the rim until we hit the north gate, then we bend east. But I wanted to take a breather first. It's a dramatic spot. I think we should savor it, don't you?"

He rose, spread his legs so that they straddled the rock, and pissed luxuriously over the side. By the time he had finished, his mood had swung again. He must have been on something. He paced nervously on the promontory, his fists clenching, his tendons forming knots. He was either on something or a manic-depressive or both; I'd suspected as much for some time. I decided to wait him out. He moved around for another minute or so, clearly agitated. Finally, unable to contain himself any longer, he turned to me a face on which defiance and embarrassment each had their place, and said, "Guess what? I'm going to be a father."

I didn't hesitate. "That sounds just fine, Arthur," I said. "Congratulations."

"The synthesizing moment, Hesh. Minkowski's space-time continuum made flesh. You find your father and I find my son. A convergence of inarticulate forces. Almost makes you believe in the occult, yes?"

"Whatever you say, Arthur."

He reddened enormously. "What? I'm full of shit again, is that it? Is that what you think?"

"It's just that I don't know what the hell you're talking about. Who's Minkowski?"

"Oh, *nobody*," he whined sarcastically. "Just a humble teacher of math. You might have heard of one of his students, though. Sloppy little fellow named Einstein. Ring any bells?"

"I don't see what this has to do with you and me," I said evenly.

"You don't see much of anything, do you? You have a failed imagination. No wonder you move so slowly. No wonder Abby tired of you." He stepped toward me, nearly tripping in the process. "I should take a swing at you. That's what I feel like doing, and a man should do what he feels like doing, right Hesh?"

"Absolutely. Positively. Right on."

He paused midstep, his lips curling into a tight smile. "Right you are," he said. "Tell you what. Let's say we're friends."

"We're friends."

"Good boy. That's the stuff. In fact, you just gave me an idea."

He fumbled open the Aaton's case and withdrew the camera, fitting it with an Angenieux zoom lens. Then he moved over to the Nagra, turned on the power, checked the controls, and fitted a clip-on mike to the lapel of his jacket. When that was finished, he came and fitted me with a mike too. "What the hell is this?" I asked.

"Time to get you on film, that's what." He sat down some three yards away, his rear flat on the ground, framing me in the lens. The Nagra's headphones were around his neck. He pulled them up to his ears.

"Now?"

"Absolutely. This is the time. Your energy's up. Ripe for confession. You've got that lean, purposeful look about you. Who knows when we'll see it again. It'll play, believe me."

I threw up my hands and half turned, so that I could look at the ocean.

"Good," he crooned. "Pensive profile. Thoughtful. Brando on the roof. Want a cigarette? We could go for something Belmondo here."

"I don't smoke."

"Pity," he said, checking the levels. "We're rolling, by the way. Say anything that comes to mind. Don't worry about relevancy."

I said, after a moment of deliberation, "Fuck you."

"I like your intensity," he said. "Plus that great ocean behind you. You're a dream. Don't stop."

"I don't know what you want from me."

"Sure you do. I want you to cooperate. I want the inner man."

I looked down at the lines on the backs of my hands. They formed a series of webs so complex and neatly assigned that there must have been an intelligence behind them. "You'll have to get me started," I said.

"Again?" he quipped. "Okay, fine. Get you started. So tell me, please, Herschel Freeman, son of the absent physicist Dr. Eli Friedmann, tell me: How was my wife in bed?"

I laughed and turned away.

The camera stayed with me. "Stubborn lady, right? Likes to go her own way. Comes a little quickly, maybe, but some men prefer that. Right?"

"What's your problem, Arthur?"

"Can you give me that again? Wind's up. Please, into the mike."

"I said what's your problem."

"No problem. You're solving them for me, one by one. Of course, it's only fair. I give you your father, you give me—"

"You don't know what you're talking about."

"Stop mumbling. Please, into the mike. You're not coming through the headphones."

"You don't know what you're talking about. You're not half the director you think you are."

"No?" He sat on this for a moment, letting the camera trail up and down my body, lifting and lowering his shoulder. I could almost feel the impact—a sucking, a cool, insistent pull.

"Get that thing out of my face. I mean it."

"Don't panic. Just try to remember your lines. Even the best freeze up sometimes."

"I'm not an actor," I said. "You hear that?"

"I hear it," he said. "But you're wrong. You're an actor, all right. But a bad one. You don't know how to do it. You don't want to. You don't want to act and you don't want to write. You want to tag along and have some kicks while others do the work. You take direction, all right—you were born for direction. You're a shapeless mass, Hesh, and you're looking for contours. I've been feeding them to you but you're too fucking dumb to see it. You should thank me, you know. You should be on your knees to me." He moved in closer still. "I gave you a reason to come here. I gave you Abby. I gave you your father. I am the provider, Hesh. I am the creator. What does that make you?"

I stood up and surprised him with a lunge at the camera, wrestling it out of his hands. The lavaliere wires became hopelessly entangled around us; as we thrashed on the ground, they seemed to be pulling us closer together. Gordon was four inches shorter than I and at least thirty pounds lighter—it didn't take long to get him on his back. I gathered my weight forward and dug my knees into his biceps to keep his upper body still. Perched above him, I indulged a sadistic impulse: I drew the Aaton to my shoulder and shot him through the lens. He looked close, furious, his glasses atilt. Taking them off as he writhed below me, I folded them and stuck them in my pocket.

"And just what is this supposed to be? *Saturday Night Wrestling?*"

"Shut up."

He strained against me, fuming, cursing me steadily under his breath. I held the camera on him.

"You've got to adjust the focus. The lighting will be off. You have no idea what you're doing, do you? You're just wasting film."

I dug my knees harder into the flesh of his arms. He squinted at me in fury.

"I won't stand for this. You're crushing my lavalieres. You're hurt—"

"Just shut up," I said. I could feel his bones with my knees. So smooth and light. And the flesh like a bit of wrapping paper. There's so little that keeps us separate, really. Cross these tiny boundaries and we're one thing, oozing, bubbly, slick, and dark. I saw the foam accumulate at the corners of Arthur's mouth and realized there was foam in my mouth too. "Let us come to an understanding, okay? I don't know what role you may have played in pushing Abby and me together—"

"Damn straight you don't."

"At some point, I stopped caring about the—what did you call it?—the motivation. I stopped caring about that. So did she, I hope. Anyway, so much for the immediate past. As for the future, that'll be up to her. But right now we've got something going here that requires our cooperation. What I'm saying is we're partners now. We're codirecting this. Understand?"

"That's a joke. A regular comedian, you are."

"This camera," I said, turning it over in my hands. "How much did you say it goes for? Like, for instance, if I happen to throw it over my shoulder and it happens to fall into the ocean, how much would you be out, exactly?"

"You're a schoolboy," he muttered. "I won't have this."

"So here's the arrangement. I'm going to give you my complete cooperation on all matters relating to the film, and I won't throw this nice expensive piece of equipment into the water."

"And you get what? My wife?"

"No. I get . . ." It took me a few seconds to find the word. "I get a say."

Despite himself, Arthur giggled. "A say. A say. A say in *what*, may I ask?"

"The film."

He frowned. "Let me up, already."

I eased off him and laid down the camera in its case. Untangling ourselves from the mike wires, we brushed ourselves off. I handed Arthur back his glasses. They weren't dirty, but he took his time cleaning them, anyway. Finally, he said, "I won't give up creative control. I don't work that way."

"I don't expect you to," I said.

"All you want is a say."

"Right."

"I don't get it," he said. "You elude me again. But I don't see why I shouldn't agree. No, I don't see why at all."

"Let's get on with it, then," I said, and we moved off our suspended perch and made our way north.

After an hour we came to an aluminum fence that turned us east. With the ocean at our backs we moved faster, cutting our own path through the cypresses and pines. The sun was high; its warmth was tempered by the wind, which dried the sweat on our faces until the skin went stiff. Beside us marched our shadows, stubby and dark. A couple of paces ahead of me, Arthur's desert boots clawed footholds in the soft earth. The length of his legs notwithstanding, he was a solid hiker. And so, I discovered, was I.

Chapter 28

Spring 1964: Recital at Rouen Cathedral

It begins with a hush, a suspension. On his lap, the *Duino Elegies* and an open notebook. The music is coming.

Fingering his pencil, drawing in his breath, he looks at the ceiling. It requires him to lean his head back against the hard wood of the pew, rubbed smooth by half a millennium's worth of fingers. He breathes deeply of the cathedral's cold, musty air as he takes in the ceiling's intricacies. For weeks he has been visiting the great halls of Europe, and it is still all he can do to comprehend the immensities of scale, the feats of engineering that made such works possible.

How, exactly, for instance, did they align the support network of arches and buttresses so that the thrusts balanced so neatly? And under what conditions did they achieve the detail, the precision, of that gray sculpted stone? And then the gauged particularity of the stained-glass windows, the spreading petals of the rose, which seem to revolve in the diffracted light of afternoon. It's a marvel, all right. The eloquent unity in multiplicity; the delicate equilibrium of matter balanced by matter. The whole structure sweeping into the sky, restrained and yet, beneath the restraint, wild with aspiration. It makes him, for a moment anyway, want to cry out. Because he can see the shadows too. There is the triumph of this place, but there is the degradation of the Inquisition. The light and the darkness. And yes, he knows them both. How he knows them both.

And now here it comes, the Chaconne, that huge D-minor chord like a warning, like a dragon's breath, and then the clarity of the melody, like a beam of light, pointing at the harmonic structure beyond. Bach! Marvelous, sublime Bach!

Oh, it's clear, it's clear. No accident at all. He has been traveling in this direction for a long time. His work has led him here. His life too. His life in work, his work in life. All lines arrive at this quadrant, this thick spaciousness that surrounds him, encloses him. This is what has been left behind. A compensation. According to Eddington, the galaxies are running away from us, as though from a plague spot. This, he thinks, is what has been afforded us in their wake.

Number and music. Heisenberg, Schrödinger, Einstein, Kepler—it goes all the way back to Pythagoras. Number and music are one. Abstraction and harmony. Objective and subjective. Each pair twisting like a gyre. *Moving form.*

Will you listen to him play that thing!

On his notepad, he makes sketches. Some are rough attempts to capture the symmetries of the cathedral. Some are designs that seem to come to him almost automatically as he sits there, listening. He feels it. He feels the music rising in him, right up his spine, flowing upstream, into his head, where it pulses and explodes. It is good. Full. So good and full. It is a lover. It is making love to him. Something is being generated within. He is aware, intensely aware, of the organs within. They are swelling, rising, blooming. He is . . . he is giving birth. Ruthie, he thinks, is this how it feels? Is this me? Is this our children? Is this the Music of the Spheres?

Rilke: *Du musst dein Leben ändern.*

Eli Friedmann, beneath his notepad, has a whopping, almost painful, erection.

Oh God, will you listen to that man *play!*

Chapter 29

You could tell it had once been an impressive place. The lawn sloped gracefully to the south and to the east, its plane dotted with stands of eucalyptus, redwood, and cypress. The arrangement was so artful that it had to have been engineered; the landscape hugged the terrain like an expensive suit, its rough material smoothed out, restrained, even, in a way, elegant. There was some evidence of neglect, however. The cedars to the north showed signs of rot. The tennis court was overgrown, its rusted chain-link fence sagging with age. There was a small, ragged pond in the middle of the grounds, and even from a distance we could see it was choked by toadstools, the water too green and slick with an oily film. On either side of this pond stood two squat domed buildings, some thirty yards apart, made of wood and glass. They appeared at the crest of the lawn, slightly elevated—seen from below, they resembled immense golden mushrooms. But as we drew closer we could see where the wood had been cut away in spots to accommodate work spaces or materials that the designers of the buildings perhaps hadn't anticipated, and these modifications in the outer walls had been performed in a patchwork, hasty fashion. In a few places the insulation showed through in smoke-gray streaks. The closer we came to the buildings, the more irregularities appeared. Even the darkened window glass looked heavily scarred; it neither reflected the sunlight nor absorbed it, but seemed instead to smother it entirely.

Two hawks circled solemnly overhead. I was sweating heavily, and my mouth was dry.

"Check out the parking lot," said Arthur. "I count ten, eleven cars."

"I don't see any security."

"True. Hard to figure. Possibly hidden cameras. With these people, you'd have to figure state of the art. Which reminds me . . ." He took the

Aaton out of its carrying case and fitted it with a wide-angle lens. "Establishing shot. The light here's unreal. Why don't you get a level on the Nagra?"

I did as he suggested. "What am I trying for, exactly?"

"Oh, just wild sound. Ambient noise. It'll give us more options in the editing. Just let the thing run for a while."

I listened through the earphones. The whisper of the breeze in the cypresses. The caw of an occasional crow. A faraway whirring, like a drill. I closed my eyes to concentrate. For a moment I had the illusion of dreaming, of imminence. There was a steady rasping sound coming through the earphones that I thought at first was electrical, a humming discharge of power. But it was only another illusion. I was holding the boom too close; the sound was my own breath.

After a couple of minutes Arthur said, "That's it," and we turned off the equipment and headed closer in. As we moved forward it became an easier matter to distinguish the signs of human presence in the building to the left. A voice, a radio, a cough, the occasional clatter of tools. There was no noise coming from the building to the right. I guessed it to be a storehouse of some sort.

A row of slate tiles formed a straight walking path between the side doors, linking the two domes at the waist. Above each door hung a wooden plaque with etched golden script. They read simply: *Urizen*.

Arthur went in for a tight shot on the sign. "What do we tell them?" I asked.

"The truth. That we're scouting locations for a film. I'll show them my union card. We'll have no idea, of course, what's going on inside. Just admired the architecture, wanted to have a look-see. And then, hopefully, you'll spot your old man, and everything after that will be a piece of cake."

For the present, I was willing to believe this was true. In fact, I needed to believe it. I was as much a sucker for a happy ending, I thought, as anybody else.

At the door Arthur paused to tamp down his hair, smooth the folds of his jacket, and wipe his glasses. When he was finished, he turned to me. "So what do you think?"

I took a breath. "I'm ready."

"I meant, how do I look?" he said. "Like an up-and-coming young *auteur*, or just a tramp with an inspiration?"

"Fine," I said. "You look fine."

"Then let's do it."

I reached for the doorknob, expecting to find it locked, or at the very least expecting to hear an alarm go off when I pushed it open. Nothing.

The door swung heavily on its hinges; there was a rush of cool air; and, beside me, I could hear Arthur make an audible gasp.

The room was huge and cold and seemed to slope endlessly around itself. The circular ceiling was high and smooth; because of its skylights and gray hue, it gave the impression of receding from the eye, a slow fade toward the heavens. Worktables were scattered like islands across the concrete slab that was the floor. The walls were lined with shelves full of tools. From a back room, which was partitioned from the rest with cinder blocks, there came the relentless humming of a power saw. A radio dangled from a picture hook; a faucet dripped noisily into an aluminum sink. The room smelled of sawdust and coffee and human perspiration. It was unlike any place I had ever been.

Neither of us moved from the doorway—we seemed to be waiting for instruction. We might have been on one side of a two-way mirror, watching a control group perform in a unique experiment. Only I had the sense that we had somehow landed on the wrong side of the glass.

"Look," said Arthur.

He pointed along the left wall, where what appeared to be mechanical drawings draped loosely over each other and spilled across the margins of a worktable's surface. A young man left his lathe to check something on one of the blueprints. He was tall, stoop-shouldered, slight of build; his brown hair was pulled back to hang behind his neck in a lank ponytail. Against one hip a tool belt flopped. Then, and only then, did I notice the others. There must have been a dozen in all, men and women ranging from late teens to around sixty, bent over the scattered tables, dressed in jeans and flannel shirts, their movements timed to the rhythms of their respective work spaces. I did not know who they were or what they were building, but they did not appear to be nuclear physicists. "Something's screwy," muttered Arthur, clutching the Aaton. "This is not what I expected."

We left the doorway and moved warily along the wall. No one had spotted us. No one had even looked up. Suddenly I felt slight, ridiculous, inconsequential. It was how I'd felt when I'd first entered the nursing home and been told my mother wasn't there.

I could hear the ticking of my own watch. Wild sound.

And then I caught sight of something in the shadow of a lathe, and my breath caught short. It was merely a wooden box, a large rectangular open-topped contraption with an uncomplicated mechanism, and yet the sight of it sliced deep into my memory like a dredge, and when it reared forward to consciousness I nearly laughed out loud from the strange congruity of the recognition. Because I knew. I knew what it was they

were building in that domed room. I knew what it looked like and I knew
how it worked. I knew a thousand things I had forgotten I knew, and now
I knew them again. And I felt the circle closing.

And then I sort of stopped breathing for a while.

It happened all at once, an unexpected reflex, as though someone had
punched me in the stomach. At first it was easy and slow, like being
underwater. But then I began to require air in a new way. My mouth
opened, only it was not working properly—it was taking in nothing,
letting out nothing. My temples swelled with blood. I was trying to
breathe and talk, but I couldn't get my breath and I couldn't find any
words. Arthur looked worried, baffled. I waved my arms at him and tried
to call out, but I had no wind. I flailed and pummeled the air with my
fists, a shadow boxer in the fog, until the dome floated down from the
ceiling and yawned as though to swallow me whole. . . .

And then for a while there was something cold and solid at the back of
my head, and I was watching small rubbery shapes float around the
gray-blue ceiling like angels. I was aware that I was on the ground, that
I had somehow fallen from a great height. The young man with the
ponytail touched a damp cloth to my brow. He had a soft, moony face;
behind his little round glasses, his eyes were a limpid blue. In the
background I could hear Arthur talking, explaining who we were. He had
his wallet out and was extracting the union card from its plastic sheath,
which required him to put the Aaton down. It tilted on its handle only a
foot or two away. Without moving my head, I could see my supine figure
made small in the lens. I looked like a dead man.

"I think he's fainted."

"Let's bring him into the back office."

Dimly, I was aware of being lifted to my feet. My body seemed heavy
and soft, insensitive to the details of its afflictions. Under one shoulder
was the fellow with the ponytail; under the other, a padded giant with
orangy skin. Arthur hovered nervously, directing traffic. "Steady now,"
he was saying. "He's all worn out. Been edgy for weeks."

They laid me on a threadbare plaid sofa in the windowless office. After
a minute I began to recover my bearings. It was a small and cheaply
appointed room, paneled in imitation wood. File cabinets were piled six
feet high along one wall. The other walls were spotted with framed
certificates and blueprints. An oversized calendar, depicting arctic landscapes, hung over the desk. Arthur eyed it thoughtfully. He seemed to be
calculating the odds of getting into the editing room by Labor Day.

The giant brought me a paper cup full of cold water. While I drank it,
he watched me carefully. "Good?" he asked, when I was finished.

I nodded yes.

"Then I'm gonna get back to work." He looked up at the man with the ponytail. "Okay by you, John?"

The man called John nodded. "Thanks, Tiny. I'll be in soon." His eyes followed the big man out the door, then turned in time to watch me attempt to rise to my feet. "Maybe you should stay where you are," he suggested. "In fact, maybe all three of us should sit down, and you can tell me what this is all about."

Arthur remained where he was. "Actually, we were hoping to speak to the person in charge. Is he around?"

The man smiled apologetically. "Well, you see, we don't really have anyone in charge."

"No one in charge," repeated Arthur.

"But I do a lot of the administration around here," he said. "Name's John Shaw. Maybe I can help you. You say you're doing a film?"

"A documentary, actually," Arthur corrected. "For public television. Possibly even feature release. It depends on a number of factors. I won't bore you by going into them. The point is, we're scouting locations."

"Well, that must be very exciting." John Shaw's eyes trailed uncertainly from Arthur to me. "Are you all right? Dizzy? You're awfully pale."

I nodded that I was fine. "Actually," said Arthur carefully, "we were hoping to speak to Eli Friedmann."

Behind his granny glasses, John Shaw's gaze was blank, even sleepy. "Who?"

Something snapped in Arthur's face. He had done everything right, and he had come up empty again. I knew how he felt.

"Feldman, you say?"

"*Friedmann!*" Arthur wailed. "Eli *Friedmann!*"

Slightly flustered in the wake of this outburst, John Shaw directed his guileless stare at me. "Are you guys sure you've got the right place?"

"We're not very sure of anything, Mr. Shaw," I said.

"This *is* Urizen, isn't it?" demanded Arthur.

"Yes," Shaw said mildly. "It is."

There followed a pause, during which the three of us tried to collect our respective wits. I felt myself sinking deeper into the sofa. I was about done.

"Maybe you'd like a tour of the shop?" asked Shaw, trying to be helpful.

"Shop?" chirped Arthur. "What shop?"

"I can show you around the assembly—the pipe room, the mill room, where we put together the trackers—"

Arthur broke in. "What are you *talking* about?"

275

"These trackers," I said. "Are they three-manuals or four?"

"Hesh . . . ?"

John Shaw lit up. "Well, right now we've got a commission for a couple of four-manuals. One's for Dallas, for the City Center. I'll be happy to show you the plans, if you like."

"Hesh?" Arthur had stepped forward with a look of such open befuddlement, such stormy incomprehension, that I might almost have been moved to laughter had I not felt so logy. "Hesh, please tell me what the fuck is going on. Otherwise I promise to explode."

"Sit down, Arthur." He did, but reluctantly, his hands knitting into themselves over the camera that lay cradled in his lap. "This is an organ factory," I said. "They make organs."

"But—"

"Let me finish. I think you may have been right, though. He must be here. There's a slider chest on the table out there. I've seen it before. It's like a model he built years ago, when we were all living together. It's his; I know it's his."

In fact, I thought, it's mine.

"You never said anything about organs. You never said one fucking thing about organs."

"Who knows what'll turn out to be important, when you look at a man's life?" I turned back to Shaw, who was following our conversation closely, one hand tracing the edge of the screwdriver in his belt. "The design," I said. "Whose is it?"

"Well, a lot of people contributed. It's a collaborative effort."

Arthur's knuckles whitened. "Would you listen to this bullshit? Can't we ever get a straight answer from this guy?"

"Shut up," I said. Then, to John Shaw, "Was there an original design? Something you built upon?"

"Of course. Edward Baker founded the place. This is his shop."

"Tall man. Brown hair. Slender. Is that right?"

"Yes," he said, and leaned forward excitedly. "Yes, that's him. Did you know Edward? Are you a friend of his?"

Before I could answer, Arthur jumped in. "That's right. From New Mexico."

"Oh? He used to live in New Mexico?"

Arthur's eyes went narrow behind his tinted glasses. "You didn't know that?"

"He was from New York. That's all I knew. We never talked very much about his background."

"You keep talking about him," I said, "in the past tense."

276

"That's because he's no longer here."

It took a half minute for this to register. Then Arthur threw his hands over his eyes and crouched forward. "Oh shit," he moaned. "Oh holy fucking hell. He's dead, and it's Goodnight Irene."

John Shaw directed at him a gaze of mild irritation mixed with sufferance. I began to recognize something in him that was deliberate, almost pious, a controlled air of practiced spirituality. In his soft, smooth voice, he said, "He's playing at being dead, yes," and then looked down at the blade of his screwdriver, and none of us said anything else for the moment.

No longer here. Beyond guilt and beyond punishment and beyond reconciliation. Beyond, perhaps, all else but acceptance. I had my head down, and when I heard a sniffle I wondered if I was in fact crying. But then I looked up and saw the trails that lined John Shaw's cheeks as he fingered the screwdriver, his eyes averted. "I'm sorry," I said. "We shouldn't keep you from your work any longer."

"It doesn't matter," he said. "There's all the time in the world. I had great feeling for the man, you see. He was practically my father."

Arthur nudged me, but I said nothing.

"I'd dropped out of school young. This was '68, '69. I hitched up the coast, met a girl, got pretty heavy into hallucinogens. I was a wreck. Used to scrape by on some carpentry work I got through a friend. He fixed me up with Edward. He was working on the town hall tracker back then. He'd built it himself. When I met him he was installing it, tinkering with the voicing, but he needed some work on the facade. So I joined up. Working here straightened me out. The pay was terrible—still is. And the work itself is pretty dull. Took me a while to adjust to it, to stay with a piece from design to installation, put up with the boredom. You guys coming here—especially you passing out like that—well, that's about as much excitement as we've had in months around here. Tiny was practically jumping up and down."

"Who's Tiny?"

"The Samoan. He's a pipemaker."

"Are you trying to tell us," demanded Arthur, "that you don't know what this place used to be used for?"

Shaw shrugged, either oblivious to, or deliberately ignoring, the hostility in the question. "Some kind of scientific research, I think. I'm not real sure. It was pretty run down when I got here. We've fixed it up some."

"Tell us more about Edward," I said.

277

"Will this help you with your movie?"

"Yes," I said. "It will help the movie a lot. You see, we're using a character very much like him in one of the major roles. Only he's been hard to get a clear picture of. He seems to have moved around a lot."

"Sure," said Shaw, "on that motorcycle of his."

"A motorcycle?" asked Arthur in wonder. "No shit."

"Really he liked the look of it more than anything else. He wasn't any Easy Rider speed freak. I remember he wanted to use the chain links for a pivot, to make the organ joints more flexible. Just because he liked the design. He was always playing around, trying to improvise. Like once I was riding with him in my old Dodge, and the thing kept stalling out on us. I thought sure it needed major transmission work. But Edward just opened up the hood and did something I'll never forget."

"What's that?"

"He just turned the filter around. Just a simple, elegant solution. Car ran fine after that. It was funny. You got the feeling that as time went on he got more and more old-fashioned, more into the old technologies. Tiny and some of the others are into rock music. They tried to get Edward interested in designing synthesizers, but he didn't bite. He was into the old masters, guys like Silbermann. Moving backward, I guess. And he was pretty forgetful, as people go. Used to walk into the shop on election days and ask me who he should vote for. The funny part of it was, I didn't follow those things any more than he did."

"Nixon's gone," commented Arthur, with some sarcasm.

"Yeah, I heard about that one. I know about Carter too. They say he's pretty smart. Used to be a nuclear scientist, they say."

"Who says?"

"This magazine used to come in here. Edward would leave it lying around. Don't recall the name, but it had a little clock on the cover."

Arthur knelt down and took up the Aaton, fitting it to his eye. "Did you know he used to be a physicist himself?"

John Shaw smiled generously for the camera. "It doesn't surprise me."

"And would it surprise you to know he worked on the Manhattan Project?"

"What's that?"

"They built the atomic bomb," I said.

"Oh."

"Hiroshima," said Arthur, over the lens. "Nagasaki. You know what we're talking about."

"I know what you're talking about," Shaw said patiently.

"Can you picture it? Your boss, Edward, working on this thing that killed a hundred thousand people?"

John Shaw smiled and shrugged. If the camera was bothering him, he didn't let on. It wasn't running, anyway, but I doubted if he knew that.

"It doesn't sound to you," Arthur went on, "as though they must be two different people? Your Edward and this man we're talking about?"

John Shaw turned to me. "Is that the way it sounds to you?"

"I don't know what it sounds like to me," I said. I gestured down at the Nagra, which sat, idle, by the foot of the worn sofa. "I'm still gathering information."

"For the movie."

I nodded. "For the movie."

Shaw ran a hand through his fine long brown hair. "There's this expression we use over at the Zen Center. *Ji-ji-mu-ge*. No separation between things."

"And what's that supposed to mean?" Arthur asked. It was interesting to see him, for once, in the position of seeking, rather than supplying, the explanation to an aphorism.

"I don't know if I can explain it. I suppose it means that while it's true that somebody's past can cause their future, it's also true that a future can cause a past. What I mean is, a lot of things going on on all sides can determine what happens at any single point."

"A lot of people in Japan didn't have a future," said Arthur, "thanks to what happened in the past."

John Shaw made his sad patient smile and reached for his wallet. When he had it open, he brought out a small black-and-white photograph, the kind you can have made cheaply in the five-and-ten, and came around the desk to show it to the two of us. Arthur put down the camera and slid over to see better.

The woman in the photo had a wide face, small features, and long black hair combed straight down over her cheeks. If there was a single grain of frivolity in her nature, the image before us kept it well hidden: She stared reluctantly at the camera, opaque and serene and mildly put out, as though tolerating the antics of an impulsive, tactless child. She had the look of a woman who had traveled halfway across the globe in pursuit of a quiet space, a gentle man.

"My wife, Suki, was born in Tokyo," explained John Shaw. "I met her at the Center three years ago. She's helped me see that everything is mutually arising. People in Japan, by and large, don't resent Americans for what they did during the war. They understand that enemies are two parts of one thing. There's no separation. All things are from the whole."

"Was Edward Baker into this Zen stuff?" asked Arthur, not trying overly hard to conceal his contempt.

"No, I don't think so. But he might just as well have been. You heard me say before he was playing at being dead."

"Yes," I said. "I wondered about that."

"It comes from a language used in Japan, *Asobase Kotoba*. When I say he was playing, I mean he was a man who had such control of his own powers that for him life was like a game. There was a lightness to what he did in the world. Look at his organs—they practically sing before you even touch a key. He played at designing them. He played with clothes and food. He played with his bike. Eventually, I guess, he played with death."

"*Amor fati*," muttered Arthur, and turned away.

"Some games are sicker than others," I said.

John Shaw's gaze lingered over the photograph of his unsmiling wife. "All games," he said, "are one."

Out in the main room, where Tiny and the others were still at work, a buzz saw whined its way through wood.

Chapter 30

In the fall of 1947, I attended my first funeral. It was for one of my father's colleagues—I don't remember his name—who had died in a Lab accident involving radiation. As I was only four years old at the time, the funeral itself made only a pale impression. But there was a piece of music my father had played on the Los Alamos chapel organ, a piece he wrote himself, and that music, and the peculiar isolation I felt in the first row of the chapel as my mother leaned back against her seat and my father played from his invisible, elevated perch, must have imprinted itself upon me. For now it was some thirty years later, and I was lying in the middle of the floor in the second Urizen building in the last hour of the afternoon, and I was hearing it again.

The room had the exact same dimensions as its twin to the west, only it was almost entirely bare, used for neither work nor, as I'd thought, storage. Illumined by a single row of fluorescent lights, an immense wooden frame, fit for a cathedral organ, hung over a large portion of the perimeter. It extended at the sides and flowed along the sloped walls, obscuring much of the window glass, seizing possession of the room with muscular, outspread arms. At one end loomed the pipe assembly, grand and silvery, its component parts calibrated to ascend and descend in perfect symmetry. The frame itself was painted a fiery crimson. The whole construct looked powerful enough to blow the roof off.

"This was the last one," John Shaw had said, flicking on the lights. "This room used to be lined with computers. You can see where the wall paint is faded. Later we used it for storage, until Edward took it over for the Super."

Arthur snorted. "Super?"

"He was aiming to compress the wind delivery, make it real small, but at the same time jack up the volume yield. Wouldn't let anybody help him with it, either. Not with the construction and not with the voicing. This was toward the end. He'd hardly ever show his face in the shop. Some people resented it. We were supposed to be a collective. But he was always in here, trying to get it right. Then one day, after about two years of work, he just gave up."

It would have been the right time, I thought, to ask exactly how and when he'd died. But I was not so eager to know as all that. There was something else I wanted to know first. "Does it work?"

Shaw hesitated a moment, then made an ambiguous nod.

"Which is it, yes or no?"

He let out a breath. "See, the thing about a tracker is, you hear *everything*. It shows all your faults. It's not like your electropneumatic instruments. You can't get away with anything."

Arthur had run out of patience. "Hey pal, all he asked was, does it work?"

"I suppose," said Shaw, "you'll have to decide that for yourself."

He strode over to the wooden staircase along the western wall and disappeared from view. We could hear him climbing into the framework above our heads. He fumbled with a latch, made some adjustments, and then it was quiet. Arthur and I looked at each other over the cases of equipment as the organ let off a few preparatory notes.

"Hey," Arthur said.

"What?"

"I was talking to that Samoan before. Something about a fire. Clogged flue, they think. You want to hear this?"

I thought about it. "I don't know."

"Listen, they never found the body." He moved toward me, reaching for my shoulder. "You think it's possible?"

"Man," I said, "what isn't?"

John Shaw cleared his throat noisily above us. "You might want to lie on the floor," he called down. "That's the best way to listen to these things."

We traded another look, then went into the middle of the room and lay down on our backs on the cold floor, the second time for me that afternoon. Arthur had some trouble finding a comfortable position. The waning sunlight was still on the ceiling, in long streaks, but they were trailing west.

"Hesh," Arthur hissed, "this floor's like fucking *ice*."

"Shh. He's about to start."

At first I was ready to dismiss what I heard, to reject it as raw, unfiltered noise. It did not, in truth, sound like music at all. It was wild and grainy and discordant, an atonal symphony of water and earth, wheezing along erratically through deep basso rumblings and high alto chirps and whistles. After a time I began to recognize a bit of a melody. It was something like Bach, but there were strains of other things in it too—even, I thought, the *Kol Nidre*—and as it unraveled I was able to recall that it was this same approximate blend, these same hopelessly mingled tones, that I had heard him play at his colleague's funeral. My father was not so forgetful a person, in the end, as all that. He had captured something essential in the music, in the organ itself. Perhaps it was the voice that had rumbled in off the desert that July morning in 1945, the one that followed the light—a sort of roaring infant's sound, a thunderous gurgle, thirsty with need and rapture, straining to feed itself with all it knows of nature. It was so thoroughly human a sound, so much a part of things, that it must, I thought, have always been with us— summoned, but not invented, at Trinity. *Creation*, it seemed to roar, *is the act of discovery.* . . .

The organ played on. For the most part, the melody was lost in the process of its delivery, the form of its entrapment. You could hear the inner workings of the instrument howling and scraping, a stung demon rattling the bars of its cage. The voicing was rough, blurry, and unfinished; it left trails, and tripped into holes; it echoed and boomed, trying for grandeur but failing at all else but ambition and suggestion. And the acoustics of the domed room were terrible. Every note was thrust back into itself, pushed into its own artificial subtext. The music seemed to pull itself apart at its very center. Nonetheless, John Shaw played the piece dutifully, as if in homage. It had no beginning, no middle, no end; it was excruciating. And yet I felt certain that what I was hearing was in fact what I had been intended to hear—that the organ, the room itself, had been designed to achieve precisely this effect, this wash of sound that enveloped you and dissolved you simultaneously, that made you feel intolerably small and then picked you back up and put you at the center of its wheezing vacuum, made you the organizing agent, the master listener, the artist. It was extraordinary and also at the same time very ordinary. It was as wayward and unfinished as my life. And I was in no hurry for it to end.

"*Hey!*" yelled Arthur. "*You hear this?*"

I didn't say anything.

"*Christ, let's get the equipment out. We've got the sound track right here!*"

I didn't move.

"*Hesh,*" he shouted, "*it's perfect! Like someone stuck a mike into hell itself. Let's use it!*"

I turned to him. His jaw was opening and closing like a pantomime, and his face was streaky with tears. He hadn't moved, either.

"*We can't!*" I yelled. "*It's too—*"

"*What?*"

"*We can't!*"

But in the roar of the organ the words were tossed up, like feathers in a vortex, and Arthur, though he nodded agreement, did not seem to understand me. We remained where we were, two boys before a wanton fire, looking for a serviceable heat.

Chapter 31

Dear Abby—

Every night I commit these two words to paper and then pause. There's never been much love between my country and me, but somehow, when I see those words on the page in my hasty lawyer's script, I feel the tug of that garish despair I remember from call-in shows: The American Voice. Well, we each come out of exile in our own way, and I suppose this salutation is mine. Dear Abby. Let me tell you my story. . . .

I have spent most of this past week sanding a piece of mahogany into a spiral about six inches high. Originally, it was meant to serve as the cornerpiece for a section of an organ chassis. But somewhere along the line it got twisted up, so that it now resembles, I'm sorry to say, an ineptly served ice cream cone. Tonight I put it on a shelf above my narrow bed, where I keep other fallen, useless things, like my unfinished letters to you, and my key to the Pinsker & Lem gym. That's one difference between my father and me, I suppose. Most likely he'd throw the piece out, or leave town, or just try to forget he ever made such an imperfectible thing. I, on the other hand, tend to hang on and on, even to the disasters—maybe especially to the disasters— even when the poor twisted thing is beyond salvation. For better or worse, hanging on seems to be my salvation.

Hence this letter. And the fact that I have stuck around here for a while. I've found that I sort of like working with my hands, though I'm pretty bad at it. Most of us are bad at most things, but it doesn't seem to stop us, does it? We're bad at living. We're failing at it all the time. We can't possibly win this living game, not with the clock ticking, not with all these countdowns. It's insane even to try. And yet look at us.

Speaking of insanity, I do miss Charlie Goldwyn. My former secretary tells me that he's down in Boca Raton, screaming at the fish and challenging people to fights. Early retirement can't be easy on him. Especially the way he was squeezed out, with those allegations of misconduct in the Eastern case. Of course, most of the allegations were true. But not all, I don't think. It's funny—it turns out that the big moose was right all the time: He did have enemies at the firm who were out to get him. But they'd never have pulled it off without the inside man, that double agent he carried in his chest.

Oh, and I suppose I miss Arthur too. I'm certain he's been in touch with you, so you know he's staying at my apartment indefinitely. When he left for the East Coast, he still thought he had a chance of pulling the production money together somehow, once he got out of the editing room. I can see him now—hunched over some rented Steenbeck, chattering away as he tries to cull the footage into something with a semblance of coherence. I wish him luck. But I have the feeling that even if the money doesn't come through, he'll be fine. He has at least two or three other projects he's been making notes on. For a few days he got a lot of use out of a sensory deprivation tank we found here. It's an old, rusty thing, about the size of a bathtub—the scientists used to monkey around with it back when this place was used for research. Now it's a toy for some of the kids who work here. The idea is it frees up your theta waves, or your right-brain functions, or something. Anyway, Arthur claims to have had vivid hallucinations. Every time he came out of the tank he had a new idea for a film.

I tried it too, but only one time. What happens, Abby, is you float in a saline solution in total darkness. The only sounds you hear are your own pulse and your own breath. After Arthur's boasting, I'm afraid I had pretty high expectations of what would happen to me when the lid was closed. Some primal shock, some finding my own center. But the fact is, very little happened. I lay there for an hour and my neck went stiff from the unfamiliar position of my head, and toward the end my bladder began to ache. Arthur claims that, like meditation, it takes practice. This may be true, but no thank you. What I found, I think, was more valuable. I found that when I reduced my environment to almost nothing—when I let myself float, freely, unproductively, purposelessly—I found that somewhere deep within, where I expected to find stillness, there remained these jabs of restlessness and yearning. The heart, the bladder, the mind. They will not keep still. And why should they have to?

It must be eight, eight-thirty by now. Outside, the sun is traveling its downward arc. The ocean thrashes and sprays, riddled with its swimmers and its floaters, its living, its dead, its inanimate. There are whales, as you said, traveling the invisible currents, headed for the Arctic from Mexico. I have not gone looking for them yet.

Now, after work, alone in my room, I try to write. Oddly enough, I find myself writing about Los Alamos. Most of what I put down is just conjecture, of course, bearing no greater relation to the truth than a series of dreams, fitfully imagined. But Abby, a remarkable thing is happening to me. I find that when I remove myself from the sketch entirely, I am able for perhaps the first time to feel a measure of empathy for my father. Okay, maybe it's not so remarkable, but it's a beginning. That's all I've been looking for, really—a way in, a starting point for a project of my own. Maybe it's coming from working in his shop, experiencing what he must have experienced—the daily push-pull of indifferent materials, the seduction of a design and the betrayal of its execution, the hunger for new combinations. He isn't here, and yet he isn't entirely absent, either. He has not made good his escape any better than I have. We can't. What's the use trying to flee the planet, the solar system, when you carry what you run from inside you?

Things seem very restful, Abby, but soon I'll have to figure out the next move. My money is running out, for one thing, and in America that's a peculiarly intense form of dissipation. Even here I seem to be losing ground. But maybe that doesn't have to be the case. You, for instance, are going in the opposite direction, your belly swelling with the raw stuff, the blood and the bone. I see you before me now, growing bigger, pushing into unknown territory, gaining, gaining—and I know that Mexico was not a mistake. It was foolish, yes, even cowardly, but it was other things too, a stab at something we may someday be equal to. We're working at it right now. We're making something. It takes patience and craft and flexibility. There's art in it, Abby. At least we've got to believe there is.

And now I had better go out to the lobby and phone my son. He's expecting to hear from me tonight, and I'd like to stop disappointing him for a change. I worry about him. He's nearsighted and inward and clumsy on his feet, and he doesn't always look around when he should. I don't want him stumbling along some edge he thinks is solid and have it crumble on him. There'll be time enough for that, in any event, later on.

I put down the pen and stretched. There was some change on the dresser, and I walked over to get a dime for the phone. It felt cool in my fingers. For a while I stood there, jiggling it in my palm, and watched the sun dip toward the crease of the horizon. Soon there was only one sliver left. It hovered over the blackening waves, the shadows so long they seemed to stretch backward forever, into deepest, inmost space.